D0442186

THREE FACES *of an* ANGEL

THREE FACES
of an
ANGEL

a novel by
JIŘÍ PEHE

translated from the Czech by
GERALD TURNER

JANTAR PUBLISHING 2014

First published in Great Britain in 2014 by
Jantar Publishing Ltd
www.jantarpublishing.com

First published in the Czech Republic in 2009 as
Tři tváře anděla

Jiří Pehe
Three Faces of an Angel
All rights reserved

Original text © 2009 Jiří Pehe
Translation copyright © 2014 Gerald Turner
Book design © 2014 Jack Coling

Printed and bound by CPI Group (UK) Ltd, Croydon, CR0 4YY

ISBN 978-0-9568890-4-1

CONTENTS

Foreword   iii

THREE FACES OF AN ANGEL

  I   Round the Globe in Search of Happiness   1

 II The Way Up is Down   119

III Fall from a Tower   231

FOREWORD

IT IS RARE, that a political commentator and philosopher, who has written several books, hundreds of weekly commentaries for newspapers and journals, been adviser to a president of his country (Václav Havel) and has written a biography of another president (Václav Klaus), who is Director of the Prague branch of an American university (NYU), blogs on the current cultural and political situation in his own country, on the nature of democracy and on the problems of globalisation, is also a novelist.

After studying law and philosophy at Charles University in Prague, Jiří Pehe left his native Czechoslovakia in 1981, and settled in New York. It may be regarded with a measure of irony that he worked there among other jobs, as a night receptionist, a position held by various of his older countrymen: banned writers and dissidents under the communist regime. His situation was, of course, quite different and he moved on to the School of International Affairs at Columbia University while Czech writers had to wait until 1989 and the collapse of Communism to regain their places in Czech literature. After 1988 and work at Radio Free Europe as well as heading Central European Research in Munich, Jiří Pehe returned to his home country. Unlikely though it may sound, he has also written three novels that have been published in the last eight years.

His first novel, *Na okraji zmizelého* [On the Periphery of a Lost One] (2006) and his third *Mimořádná událost* [An Unexpected

Incident] (2013) explore what happens when the houses of cards we build in order to achieve 'success' to shelter us from the vast unanswered questions about the sense of life, turn instead, to frame a dead end street. *Three Faces of an Angel* which appeared in Czech in 2009 and has now been translated into English in this volume, could be considered the centrepiece of the trilogy. Admittedly, angels are not customary inhabitants of our century, nor of the last – described as 'my crazy century' by Ivan Klíma', who experienced the two extremities of political power that had shaken the new Czech Republic at the centre of Europe. (The country's name had changed half a dozen times in the course of that crazy century). The characters of Jiří Pehe's novel, hovering between fiction and reality, also experience these extremities: they are moulded, carried, and ultimately destroyed by the contradictory forces of this century. The novel uncovers this turbulent period with its linguistic, national, and racial complexities; its brutality occasionally tempered by humour; and, ultimately, its absurdity.

Three Faces of an Angel is formed of three parts, an elastic frame that extends back and forth through the characters' contrasting memories, as they recall or try to forget events. Part One, called 'Round the Globe in Search of Happiness' is a long letter written by Joseph Brehme to the mother who had abandoned him as a six year old child because he was born 'illegitimately,' as the language and outlook of the period stamped it, and she was ostracised by her family. Shades of reproach darken the letter covering the events of forty years but are lightened by the happiness the letter writer seems to have found as he concludes. Much happens during those years of Joseph's life. He becomes a virtuoso violinist, supported and enhanced by friendly teachers and their families, and his own indisputable talent. Musical themes move in and out of this part of the novel, illuminating only in passing the tumultuous events happening in the background.

The whole text of Part One throbs with Central European culture. The reader encounters Austrian writer Robert Musil, whose *Man*

---

* *Moje šílené století,* first published in 2009 and then in English as *My Crazy Century* in 2013, translated by Craig Cravens

Without Qualities was considered one of the most influential novels of the time; Karl Kraus, the flamboyant Viennese journalist; and Egon Schiele, the Austrian painter whose startling paintings are displayed today in the Czech town Český Krumlov (Boemisch Krumau under Austria/Hungary's rule – now a European heritage treasure). There is Sigmund Freud, born in Freiberg, Moravia (today Příbor) not far from the Bohemian village Kalischt (Kaliště today [Literally: "Boar's Hollow"]) where Gustav Mahler was born.

The novel's characters are embedded credibly into this complex central European cultural landscape. A flash of irony reveals the incident cutting short Joseph's promising career and sends him off to war in September 1914. Joseph is enlisted to go East and is thrust into the horrors of the 'Great War' with its shifting borders, horrendous trenches, changing relationships between Czech and German soldiers (rarely touched upon in fiction), and Czech soldiers absconding to the Russians. As the martial waves recede and the *Czech Brigades* become established behind Russian lines, an officer suggests establishing a Czech string quartet.

The reader may recall with a smile the adage: where there are Czechs, there will be music but the text is driven forward with the intensity of life itself. Throughout the rapid movement of Part One, the reader watches figures being tossed about helplessly by the vicissitudes of the early 20th century. Jiří Pehe reveals the twisted, ambiguous fates in the turbulence of Central Europe with increasing sympathy.

—

Part Two entitled 'The way up is down' is told in the voice of Joseph's daughter Hanna, whose language is less formal than that of her father: the turbulent times have changed again. Orphaned at the age of seven, Hanna wakes up from one of her dark dreams: it is 1968. Outside the walls of the psychiatric hospital where she is kept, there are the noises of the exciting and hopeful year of the Prague Spring but Hanna dwells in the disarray of her memory about the past with her Jewish grandparents. No matter how they had tried to protect her, under the

Nazi occupation she became a 'Mischling' (the official designation for a person of 'mixed blood') and was forced into hiding. The trauma of three years in a 'black hole' with the sustained anxiety of being discovered, the darkness, cold and hunger pursue her until the end of her days. Yet during this time the author lets the reader experience her gradual initiation into sex and literature. Life, as the novel shows again and again, is never simple. In 1945, the family is discovered. By a most unlikely accident – perhaps not so unlikely if we consider the general conundrum of the times – the Gestapo officer who is in charge of 'solving the case' is Karl, Joseph's long lost half brother from the German branch of the family. The novel travels along a precarious border between fiction and reality. 'Unlikely' scenes such as this fictional one, as we know from memoirs and reports, could actually happen – and did happen. Fiction echoes reality and vice versa.

With Hanna, we move through the ups and downs of her life and the frantic search for her identity. She becomes "an Aryan" temporarily; she ruminates about God and reasons for punishment; suffering without being guilty, being deprived of education, the choice that human beings are given or not given (a theme that reverberates strongly at the end of the novel); and bears witness to the emaciated figures of Germans fleeing Eastern Prussia and Poland. Finally her origin that had pushed her into the 'dark hole,' is now being used to get her Gestapo uncle off the hook: she becomes again Hanna Brehmova, the Jewish girl, whom he had saved from certain death. When she finally goes back to Czechoslovakia with her Czech name on her passport, times have changed again. Czechs who had grown up in the west and returned home with the Allied Army are frequently labelled as 'capitalist spies' and sent to Soviet labour camps. The whole generation is crushed by the power struggles of ideologies that create false images and act on these.

—

Part Three is called 'Fall from a Tower.' The millennium has passed and the atmosphere in central Europe has changed once again. The language becomes that of a contemporary intellectual and academic. Little Sasha, who had played chess with his mother Hanna and tried to help her overcome despair, is now fifty three years old. He is the internationally famous philosopher Alex Brehme, who has published many books, teaches at Columbia University, gives lectures on television and (the reader will enjoy the twinkle in the author's eye), does not need to chase women because they fall for him easily. On 7 September, 2001 (the date is bound to cause the reader's apprehension), we find him sitting at his desk in New York, trying to begin writing a diary that might help him find out what has really happened to him in the 'successful' life that now overwhelms him with doubts about the sense of it all.

The viewpoint of the main character has changed again. While Parts One and Two describe the action in sometimes graphic detail, Part Three considers the psychology of the storyteller in greater depth. Guided by the mysterious figure of a woman, Alex begins to talk about himself. He gives up his vanity and role of famous professor and confides, analyses and doubts his own motivations and actions. As he searches through his past, his reader re-experiences events from a different point of view.

—

Thereafter, the focus changes once again. As the coat of ice around Alex's psyche begins to melt, the text moves into an academic scene of which Alex is an outstanding member. Amidst cliché-laden discussions about the end of history and the contemporary Zeitgeist, Pehe lets Alex turn his critical gaze on his colleagues: their limitless egos, their need to be constantly reassured about their exceptional qualities, as they throw phrases current in academia around the narrative. The reader might wonder about this unexpected attack on academic mediocrity but is bound to recognise the freedom Alex achieved when he shed his pretences, his false certainties.

Reminiscent of a coda in a musical composition, the deepest questions touched upon lightly earlier in the text, emerge fully on the last pages of the novel. Do we have a choice in our lives? Did the family who were crushed have a choice? What is the nature of choice in human life?

~

Certain themes in this novel emerge gradually. An important one is the very act of writing. Embedded in the flow of events, the characters make the decision to start writing, be it a letter or a diary. The reasons seem to differ in each case but the motivations turn out to be similar: by giving their confusing experiences written shape, the characters try to create or retrieve some kind of order in their ragged, unpredictable, even seemingly circular lives. At the age of forty (it is 1934 when Europe is reeling on the verge of great disasters), Joseph has the need to tell his dying mother that now "there is at last a certain meaning and order." During the Prague Spring, thirty-three years later, when his daughter Hanna wakes up in the psychiatric hospital after suffocating dreams, she asks for pencil and paper because she urgently needs to give her jumbled story "some sort of time sequence." Her son Sasha, looking toward the future at this crucial time of 1968 might want to know some day "what the past was like." It is 2001 when that same Sasha, now a middle aged man, decides to start a keeping a diary, for he feels that "if I can capture my fears and thoughts on paper...perhaps I'll understand what's happening to me." The author wants to stress the importance of writing as creating order, as bearing witness to the various forms of human life.

Another theme, pulling the characters in opposite directions, is the struggle with language. Joseph grew up "in two linguistic worlds." His daughter Hanna is even more drastically and uneasily suspended between German and Czech. The Czech "-ová" ending of her name is removed when she stays with a German family but is rapidly reinstalled for political reasons when times and ideologies have changed. Speaking several languages, usually thought of as a positive quality, becomes painful and dangerous when these languages are tied to ideological thinking.

Then, there is the theme of the tragic Jewish population of Central Europe, which features most strongly in Hanna's story. The most tragic subplot dwells on Hanna's grandparents, the Kleins, who converted to Christianity in order to be assimilated, who later started to accuse each other of betraying their faith and returned to Judaism in 1935, inadvertently sealing the fate of their grandchildren.

Ariel, the angel, who gives the novel its title, appears many times throughout the text. Encouraged by Ariel, Joseph writes to his mother and draws solace from this translucent figure without really knowing whether it was real or a figment of his imagination. Ariel seems to appear to the characters at crucial moments, changing his appearance, becoming someone they have known or would come to know, even predicting the future. At one point, his appearance gives rise to a discussion about angels as messengers of God, *Malakhim*, as they were known in Hebrew. They were, as Hanna learns, a reminder that there existed another order higher than that of humans. It is in Part Three that Ariel becomes both paradoxically more concrete and more mysterious, presenting Alex with the final choice of his life.

It is obvious that these comments merely attempt to pry open a door that would permit the reader to catch a glimpse of the teeming scenes of this novel. For the reader who walks through this door, a world displaying the rich colours of human life is waiting to be explored.

Dr Marketa Goetz-Stankiewicz, FRSC
Vancouver, February 2014

Angels, (they say) are often unable to tell whether they move among the living or the dead. The eternal torrent whirls all the ages through either realm for ever, and sounds above their voices in both.

RAINER MARIA RILKE,
The First Duino Elegy*

*Translated by J.B. Leishman and Stephen Spender

I

ROUND THE GLOBE
IN SEARCH OF
HAPPINESS

$\mathcal{D}$ear Mother,

The news has reached me that the intensive radiotherapy you have been undergoing at the Jedlička hospital has not been successful and that your health continues to worsen. Apparently you are to be transferred to the newly opened Hospice in Brno. However, that is not the only reason why I have decided to write a letter at the outset of this year of our Lord nineteen-hundred-and-thirty-five, in which, as maybe even you remember, I shall celebrate my fortieth birthday.

After almost three decades, during which time you never answered any of my letters, I am also writing to you because I have been instructed to do so by Ariel, an angel. I shall not write more about him now because without proper explanation of all the circumstances you would rightly deduce that I had lost my mind.

I am writing this letter in Czech because it is your mother tongue. Although I use Czech for everyday communication and for writing official reports, German is the language I express myself in most easily. Therefore, I shall apologise in advance for any awkward turn of phrase.

I must confess that before I penned these first lines I pondered at length about how to address you. You gave me life, so according to natural and human laws, you are my mother. However, you abandoned me, when I was just six years old, and in spite of my many entreaties you never laid claim to me again.

Although I remember more about my first years of life than children whose fate has been happier than mine, and therefore have not had to look back again and again to their early childhood as a place of refuge, I cannot recall how I addressed you during my first years of life, when we were still living together. Thus, in the course of years you became a stranger to me and so I shall use the formal mode of address.

Just in case you lay this letter aside before you reach the end, as you most likely did with my earlier letters, I will divulge at the very outset that there is at last a certain meaning and order in my life, which I have obtained thanks, above all, to the fact that, ten years ago, I was fortunate enough to meet a woman whom I adore. As a result the last few years of my life have been filled with a happiness I had never known before.

After the dreadful events of the war and the many blows that fate dealt me, I now have a family. I am firmly settled. And I am not loath to say that I have now found meaning in my life, although that meaning is something other than I first imagined it.

Very shortly, God willing, my family will grow by two more children, because, according to our doctor, my wife will give birth to twins. What more could I wish for?

As I have already indicated, one of the reasons I am writing this letter is because the angel Ariel ordered me to tell you my life story. And yet I sense that it was not his intention to make me describe in detail my various adventures and tragedies, although I cannot stay silent, of course, about the dramatic events that befell me. The underlying message of my letter is, I hope, that it is possible to achieve happiness in a life full of suffering so long as we believe that everything in store for us has a hidden purpose and we meekly accept it.

I hardly need to stress, Mother, how little I hoped at certain moments of my life that I would ever attain such a blessing. As you are well aware, I never knew my Father. The only information that I have about him I read in my birth certificate. I therefore know that my father was a certain Joachim Brehme. However, I know nothing of any import about him, because you never spoke about him. I gathered from various hints that he was a musician who belonged to some orchestra from Germany, and that he was briefly in Prague.

I long regarded your silence on this as a great injustice. It was hard for me to reconcile myself to the fact that I bore the surname of a man whom I was not permitted to know and whose existence will always remain a mystery to me. I have no idea why my father never visited me even though he paid for my education until I was nineteen years old.

The record in the registry states that Joachim Brehme, of German nationality, was born in Hamburg in 1855. So he was already forty when he fathered me, Josef Brehme. You were twenty years younger than he. Was he living abroad at the time? Was he so taken up with his work that he never again found occasion to visit Bohemia?

How did he meet you? How did you get to know each other? I know absolutely nothing about it. All I know is that you loved music and that you attended concerts from a very early age. I remember that when I was very small you used to play the flute. Did you meet my father during a concert tour to Prague?

Should you find the strength to reply to this letter, perhaps you could disclose more than the little that I learnt during my first years of life or from the record in the public registry.

I admit that my early childhood was almost as happy as these past few years with my family but you were never happy. I know that your family turned utterly against you after I was born because you had "spawned a bastard". You used that very phrase on one occasion, I remember, when you were talking to your female companion, who lived with us in a small apartment in the Old Town of Prague. What did you do for money, in fact? Did you live off some money sent by Joachim Brehme to support you?

I often saw you cry and just as often you would engage in long conversations with your companion that were difficult for me to follow as a child. I simply sensed something oppressive about those exchanges and the potential threat that everything might take a turn for the worse one day. Your behaviour and what you said often betrayed a helplessness that filled me with apprehension.

Klára was your companion's name. Since you renounced the right to be my mother, you will not be offended if I admit to you that as a child I loved Klára much more than I loved you. I can still picture her: tall and bony, and quite a bit older than you. She could have been my grandmother, and she treated me as if she were. She had a long face with sharply chiseled features and blonde hair usually worn in a bun that made her expression even stricter. There was also something severe in her austere manner of dress. Despite this, she was very kind, especially to me.

Unlike you, who in between bouts of despair and depression, often shouted at me, Klára was always full of understanding and would make a fuss of me.

Sometimes I would hear you scolding her for spoiling me when I had wheedled something out of her. However, I soon realised that you were dependent on her. The apartment where we spent those first years was hers, and it seemed that Klára was your anchor.

I still don't know whether you really loved me. If you did, then that love was hidden beneath layers of guilt, bitterness, pangs of conscience and despair. Maybe at that time you were still hoping that Joachim Brehme would come back to you. Or wasn't it him you were talking about on the occasions I overheard you trying to convince Klára that "he" would take care of you and me?

I recall that Klára was very skeptical about him but consoled you, nevertheless. She would remind you that neither you nor I were particularly badly off. You did not share her opinion, however.

But what makes me write that it was a happy period of my life? It is not only that I was still living with you in those days and you did occasionally find a moment to play with me, or tell me stories and even cuddle me, in spite of your despair. It is not just because Klára treated me with care and affection and spoiled me a little. I also regard that period as happy because the world seemed to be a serene and friendly place in spite of the gloomy atmosphere of our apartment and your odd behaviour.

I recall how I would often go to the river with Klára and you to feed the gulls. I can still clearly see the route we took. Our house stood a short distance from St Giles' church, which we had to pass on the way to the river. Then, most often, we would head for Charles Street and make our way from there to Charles Bridge. Sometimes we would walk along the embankment as far as the National Theatre and then on to one of the islands. I can still smell the scent of the water as it slowly flowed by and recall the peculiar sense of melancholy that emanated, particularly in autumn, from the figures of the fishermen dotted about the surface of the river.

Klára was kind but also very anxious. She was afraid I would get lost or fall in the river, or that I would be cold. On the occasions you went with us you tended to remain silent and looked very sad. Or at least that is how I remember you.

As I now realise, you were brooding over the fact that your family had disowned you and thus had been banished from a lot of things that you understood, while I had the impression that the world was fine. I didn't particularly miss my father in those days, because there was nothing with which to compare my situation. I was almost entirely in the company of two adult women. Only on the odd occasion by the river did I make friends with other children. Some of them were accompanied by their fathers and only then did I wonder where my father was. However, I never plucked up courage to ask because "he" was swathed in some sort of strange mystery, and on top of that he was one of the causes of your constant despair.

You're bound to remember that there were several families with children living in our building, but most of the children were older than me and they did not take much notice of me. The Gebauers who lived across the hall had a boy and a girl that were near to me in age, and I would have liked to be friends with them, but they avoided me and scarcely replied to my greetings.

On one occasion I overheard Mrs Gebauer arguing about something I did not understand. Only later, in a conversation between you and Klára did I finally realise what it was about. The Gebauers, devout Catholics, had forbidden their children to play with "the bastard". They regarded you as a "woman without morals". What they thought about Klára and her relationship with you, I do not know. One thing is certain – that I cannot remember the names of those two children. I never made their acquaintance.

I do not have many specific memories of that period; only impressions. The nineteenth century was drawing to a close and you and Klára would often discuss what the next century might bring. Klára read a great deal. In her room there were piles of books of every kind, which, as she informed me mysteriously, dealt with "things to come". She maintained that the nineteenth century, during which no European wars had occurred since Napoleon, had ushered in peace and prosperity for all time.

In the coming century, Klára declared with certainty, the world would be transformed into one great prosperous factory, in which everything would be driven by steam and electricity, and even some children's toys would be driven by little motors. She believed that industrial production would ensure all necessities, so that no one would endure hardship. She said the Austro-Hungarian monarchy would be transformed into a democratic federation in which all the nations would be equal and it might even ally itself with other European monarchies; and in the knowledge that the time of wars was finished for good, they would create some kind of all-European confederation.

Of course I am reporting Klára's theory as it is recorded in the memory of a man who is now forty years old. No doubt I have embellished it somewhat during the intervening years. I do remember, however, that you were skeptical about Klára's theories and on occasion, you would vehemently dispute them, though mostly without success. Klára was firmly convinced that she was right. With a passion that contrasted with the kindness she showed me, she would rarely let you finish what you were saying before zealously supporting her own arguments.

Sometimes you would also talk about politics. I'm fairly sure I'm not wrong in thinking that you were a staunch supporter of the Czech national revival and the Czech nation's independent political ambitions, while Klára firmly believed in the Austrian monarchy.

By now I've forgotten most of your political disputes. But there was no way of escaping them, as the apartment was small and the kitchen was where everything important happened.

I remember with particular clarity one impassioned argument that seemed to go on for ever. It concerned the Jew Hilsner and the death sentence he received for the alleged ritual murder of a Czech girl. You were firmly convinced of his guilt, while Klára despised the Czech politicians and journalists who kept the affair alive with their anti-Semitic statements. I was only four years old in 1899 but I can vividly recall the affair still.

That was when I first heard the name of Tomáš Masaryk. Klára regarded the man who had defended Hilsner with great admiration. Maybe it was also because at that time Masaryk, like herself, was still in favour of preserving the Austrian monarchy. Had Klára lived to see it, she would have undoubtedly been surprised that, twenty years later, it was he who negotiated the destruction of the monarchy and the creation of an independent Czechoslovakia.

I expect I shall never now discover the tie that bound you and Klára together. Could she have been a distant relative of yours or of my father? Had he placed you and me into her care? Or were you just friends? If you were, it was a very strange and unequal friendship. After all, Klára was not only older than you, she was much better educated. And unlike you, she was financially independent.

It now strikes me that Klára was actually taking care of you but the relationship was not particularly affectionate and you quarrelled quite often.

In spite of that atmosphere, the last years of the nineteenth century were a period of happy tranquility for me. I can remember the portraits of the Emperor, with his long mutton-chop whiskers and his uniform. I found him likeable; there was something calming about him. I must have seen him as reassuring. Klára too had a high opinion of Franz Joseph, and sometimes she would tell me anecdotes about his life instead of a bedtime story.

At that period Prague was a prosperous and thriving city, with new houses being built everywhere. I recall how sometimes I would make

Klára or you stand and gaze with me at the many building sites. Klára used to say they were building "in the Parisian style". It was only later, when I visited Paris, that I realised that Prague's *Jugendstil* [Young style] had little in common with Parisian architecture.

There is another important thing I should mention from that period, and that is music. You played the flute, though not particularly well. But Klára had a piano in her room, which she played with a certain virtuosity, or so it seemed to me at the time. I know that she attended a music school in her youth and she would often talk about her musical education. She played the piano regularly, every day, and she also taught me the rudiments of music. It was she who started to teach me German, in which we would subsequently converse during our walks. Besides she spoke German more often than Czech.

She apparently knew quite a lot about my father, because more than once she commented on my progress, saying that I had inherited my father's musical talent, as well as his ability to understand and feel music. Thanks to Klára I was able to read music much earlier than I could read or write words or numbers. She still taught me to read and write when I was only five. Maybe the fact she taught me in German explains why I have always felt that I understood German better than Czech.

Late afternoons at Klára's piano were among my happiest moments. Sometimes you would join us, but more often than not you simply sat passively in an armchair and watched us from a corner of the room.

I can recall how every day I would look forward impatiently to the moment when Klára got home from work. I've no idea where exactly she worked. It was most likely some official department, because she would leave for work well attired at 7am and regularly return around four in the afternoon. You could not wait for her to get home too, because it freed you from your parental duties. In my opinion you were unable to cope as, quite often, you would go out as soon as Klára arrived and return late in the evening.

I must admit that most of the time I did not miss you. Whereas the days spent with you were full of apprehension and rebukes, my late afternoons and Sundays with Klára were filled with calm, as if with her arrival and your departure the mood in the apartment changed. I am not able to describe it well now, it is simply a feeling that no doubt reflects the subsequent unhappy events.

Yes, unhappy, because that harmonious world which, in spite of your never-ending outbursts of despair, I would idealise so many times afterward, ended in a two-fold catastrophe. Firstly, just a few days after the twentieth century was ushered in, Klára died, and her death deeply affected you. She had come down with a severe chill before Christmas, as I am sure you remember clearly, and was forced to take to her bed the day before Christmas Eve.

One reason I remember it so clearly is because Christmas was generally a happy time. During that period even you would try to forget your wretchedness and for a few days I became the focus of your attention. In that fateful year, however, Klára had a hacking cough and I was only allowed a brief daily visit to her room. Although she was running a high fever, she always urged me to play at least one of our pieces.

Then they took Klára off to hospital, where I was not allowed to visit. On the third of January, at the very start of the century she had dreamed so much about, Klára died. The word "pneumonia" that you gave as the reason of her death will always remain for me a death sentence and a nightmare. Later, many of my comrades-in-arms would die in Russia of pneumonia. In fact everything that happened after Klára's death was sinister.

We went on living in Klára's apartment, but I sensed that we would not remain there long. I knew that you could not afford the rent. You would often go away during that period, leaving me on my own in that gloomy apartment, with Klára's shadow everywhere. I used to sit alone in her room at the piano and fantasize that if I played one of the compositions she had taught me and then turned round, she would be sitting on the edge of her bed again, where she always listened to me. I would spend days playing driven by that foolish hope, but the apartment remained empty.

A few weeks later you announced that we needed to have a serious talk. You might prefer me not to describe our conversation, but I must, for the sake of completeness. I remember that you adopted a gloomy tone that did not please me in the least. We sat at the table in the kitchen where Klára's ghost still hovered but she could no longer protect me from what was to come. You had received an offer of marriage, you said. Then for a long time you said nothing.

I had no inkling of what you were driving at. At first I thought my father had returned. I did not find the thought at all disagreeable; on the contrary I was glad. Then it occurred to me that your future husband might be someone else, and even that did not strike me as in any way ominous. I could not understand why you wore such a serious expression and were choking back the tears that prevented you from speaking. I wanted to know whether we would be moving, but it was evidently the wrong thing to ask, because then you started weeping uncontrollably.

For several minutes you were incapable of speaking. Only then did you explain to me what was going to happen. Although you spoke haltingly and burst into tears again and again, my future emerged clearly and unavoidably from your words.

The man you were intending to marry, you said, was a close friend of your family. Yes, you used the word "your" and you were right. It was not my family. They had never accepted me. Your suitor, a very conservative man and quite a lot older than you, would marry you and provide for you, and partly for me, on condition, however, that you give me up.

I did not understand straight away what you meant by "give me up". It hung over me like a sword. Something menacing alarmed me, I did not cry, but simply started to sob. You handed me a handkerchief and went on with your somewhat confused explanation.

You would be incapable of providing for me, you said. You did not want to remain single for the rest of your life; you were still young, after all. Naturally you would prefer us all to live together, but it was impossible.

You repeated it over and over again and an unbearable tension started to build up inside me.

"There needs to be order in our lives," you pointed out illogically. And yet I remember those words as if I heard them yesterday.

You repeated it several times: "There needs to be order in our lives."

And then you said: "I thought I was capable of rebellion, but I can't cope. I can't live like this, utterly disinherited…".

That precise expression "utterly disinherited" stuck in my memory. I would later recall it during fits of pique against you and your family. And I would endow it with a certain mocking undertone, because in fact you had decided to exchange your "disinheritedness" for mine. As if I, a little child, were stronger than you! Or as if I deserved it for some reason! I was the one to pay for your mistake, because you had not been responsible enough to pay for it yourself.

And so it came about, Mother, as you well know! At the age of just six years, I was dispatched to a boarding school in a small town not far from Prague, whose name I am still unable to utter because it is associated with that dreadful experience.

The period I was separated from you was so traumatic for me that I am unable to recall many of the events. As Prague intellectuals were later wont to say, under the influence of Freud: I had "displaced" them.

However, I clearly remember my first impressions of boarding school. It was no orphanage, the pupils mostly came from well-to-do families and the language of instruction was German, in other words, the language of the upper classes. The fees for tuition, board and guardianship must have been high. In view of that fact alone, it is a mystery to me why my father did not visit me at least, seeing that he made a financial contribution to my education, as you mentioned without any further explanation in a letter you sent me at that time. And I also fail to understand why, instead of school fees, he was unwilling to send you money for rent and keep, which could have kept us together. Was the use of his money perhaps contingent on conditions related solely to my education? Can you answer that question for me?

Although I never met him, my father was omnipresent, not only because of the money that enabled you to send me to boarding school.

He would also constantly confront me because my fellow pupils and teachers would ask me about him.

I would reply unthinkingly with words I had learnt: "My father's name is Joachim Brehme, but I have never met him."

The teachers reacted either with mute astonishment, no doubt thinking I was a poor waif, or would hasten to reassure me that my father was bound to come and visit me one day. Some of my fellow pupils were crueler, at least until I got to know them better. My "non-existent" father was a welcome source of jokes at my expense.

As you know, the school itself was situated just outside a small town and our dormitories stood close by. I have no wish to go into any great detail about the few years that I spent there, because they were essentially uneventful and timeless. Consequently I have almost nothing to latch onto in order to describe my life in those days at any length.

Apparently the old buildings of the school and the residence were once a military barracks. I still have a fairly clear picture of them. The entire interior was austere and characterless; only the school grounds were pleasant: a long avenue of old linden trees that were fragrant in the summer. Behind the dormitories was the "spielplatz," as we called the place, although it was mostly used for morning assembly and drill. Football and other sports were played a bit further away on a large riverside meadow.

Six boys shared each dormitory, but that applied only to the school year. During the vacation, when there remained just the few boarders who had nowhere to go, we all lived together in a single dormitory, while the other dormitories remained empty.

The daily routine was paramilitary, because the school's main function, of which you were perhaps unaware, was preparation for subsequent military service. At precisely six in the morning a loud bell would wake us, and this was followed immediately by compulsory drill. Our communal breakfast took place in a vast dark room with a large crucifix on the front wall and lasted precisely thirty minutes. Lessons started at eight and the time between breakfast and our departure for the school was occupied with cleaning. Every day the wardens would check with military thoroughness whether our beds were properly made and our cupboards and personal things tidy.

There was also little variety in the content of our lessons. It was a school in the old Austrian style in which the emphasis was on discipline.

In spite of all the misfortunes that befell me in my childhood, I was very lucky. You see the teacher of music at that dank and austere school was a certain Josef Steiner, a man who had a major influence on my subsequent life. Although he looked more like a gymnastics teacher, being tall and well built, he was nonetheless a sensitive musician, who had been drawn there because of the lack of opportunities in Prague.

In that atmosphere of omnipresent drill and mindless rote learning, his lessons were a welcome oasis. Steiner not only recognised early on that I had musical talent, he also rightly guessed that if I were to play the violin I would make greater use of my talent than if I stuck solely to the piano. I will never forget the day he brought a child-sized violin from the music department for me to try.

I had never before held a violin in my hands. With you and Klára, I learnt to play only the piano and the flute. Both of those instruments interested me, but neither of them entranced me like that little bit of wood. It concealed a mystical voice that spoke to me and moved me to tears.

The first notes coaxed from that violin must have been dreadful, even though to me they sounded beautiful. Nevertheless, in the military surroundings of that boarding school, Josef Steiner must have recognised a kindred spirit because he asked me whether I would like to take lessons with him. I accepted with enthusiasm.

Thereafter, in a school I detested with all my heart and where I was constantly miserable, I found a refuge that helped me to survive that period. Steiner gave me lessons three times a week at the end of the school day. I do not know whether he talked or corresponded with you about it, or whether he received any payment. There was never any mention of it between us. I believe he did it for the same reason as mine: those lessons were a release for both of us. Should you reply to my letter, you might divulge to me what the situation was with

Steiner that time. I never had the courage to ask him.

That violin was a refuge for yet another reason. Although in time I made friends with a few of my fellow pupils, I tended to feel uncomfortable in the company of the other boys. I was different, and not just because I was so alone. What made me even odder in their eyes was that although I had both parents, it was as if I had none. They regarded me as a lone wolf. At first it rankled with them but in time they learned to respect me.

I could only recover gradually from the shock caused by your decision. I could not understand your betrayal, and in fact I have never stopped inveighing against you inwardly. Even now as I write these lines I can feel my heart race and I have an overwhelming sense of grievance. In those days I was constantly engaged in an internal dialogue with you, which was sometimes full of fury and hatred.

After my arrival at boarding school, in a corner of my soul, I hoped that what had happened to me had happened by mistake and everything would sort itself out somehow. I did not understand why I could not live together with you and your husband. You would surely realise one day that I was not bad, that I had done nothing wrong!

In those days I used to write you letters to which you never replied – not counting that very first letter, in which, with the help of the few words that I knew how to write, I endeavoured to explain to you that some awful misunderstanding must have occurred and that I wanted to live with you. I even blamed myself for not having always behaved as you wished and promised that I would certainly do better. Yes, I used to tell myself that it was most likely punishment for some failing of mine that you did not wish to divulge to me.

The letter I received in reply floored me. You wrote that we had to accustom ourselves to "the new situation"; after all, I wasn't so badly off, many children in the world lived in much more miserable conditions. You told me that the school I was attending could offer me far more than you could. I was to understand that you wanted to lead a normal life and that your husband and your entire family insisted that institutional care was the most suitable thing for an "illegitimate child".

There is no way I can describe how utterly devastated I was by your letter. I must have read it through a thousand times over, most probably because you had failed to respond to any of my subsequent letters. In time I stopped writing to you and started to harbour toward you an antipathy verging on hatred. Only occasionally, when I was really anguished, such as during the first vacation, when almost all my fellow-pupils left along with Josef Steiner, did my animosity abate, and I would be willing to forgive you. But the opportunity never presented itself as you never came to visit.

Perhaps at this point I should mention how I was affected by having grown up in two linguistic worlds. Neither of those languages was neutral for me. Even now I am split in two. German, which, thanks to Klára, is associated with the nice things I experienced in her company in my earliest years, was also the language of my father, who, however, never made any effort to find me. And it was also the official language of my school, the school that I initially detested and later bore with difficulty.

Czech was your language, but you had abjectly betrayed me. I wrote my letters to you in German. In your one and only letter you replied to me in Czech. Nonetheless I have always felt more Czech than German. After all, even Klára considered herself first and foremost a Czech. Czech was also the mother tongue of Josef Steiner.

Maybe it was also because of my ambivalence toward spoken and written languages that I adopted with such ardor the universal language of music. The violin became everything for me, as did my lessons with Steiner and the time I spent practicing.

My second refuge was books. Although the school had a good library most of the pupils seldom used it.

Steiner was not only an enthusiastic musician; he was also a poetry lover. It was he who introduced me to Mácha, Vrchlický and Neruda, among others.

In spite of his German-sounding name, Steiner regarded himself as a Czech first and foremost. In school lessons he addressed his pupils in German, during my private tuition he spoke to me in Czech. He would often give me Czech national songs to play, from his own hand-made songbooks. In fact, it was thanks only to him that I did not forget my Czech in that overwhelmingly German-speaking environment.

There was another highlight, Mother. He was Hugo Beňáček, a boy with fair hair and freckles all over his face. He helped me endure the seven years of exile. We were drawn to each other by our love of literature – Hugo had no musical talent. On the other hand, he was much more adept at all kinds of sports than me.

Hugo was a year older than me and was therefore in a higher grade. And that was an unusual feature of our friendship, because it was an unwritten rule that the older pupils did not befriend their juniors.

And how did the two of us become friends?

It happened in third grade, when I was almost nine. Apart from Steiner I had had no real friends until then. Admittedly, I had become better acquainted with the boys in my dormitory, but most of them never made any effort to befriend me. And I made no particular effort either. During that period I was a pensive, taciturn boy, and moreover my interests seemed eccentric to most of the other boys. After all, their goal was to become officers in the Austro-Hungarian army.

I got to know Hugo better thanks to the book *Paradise Lost* by the English poet John Milton. Although it was scarcely explicable in that German-speaking school, the school library's copy of that rare volume was the Czech translation by Josef Jungmann. Steiner drew my attention to it.

I do not know who told Hugo that I had the book on loan, but for some reason he wanted to read it as soon as possible at all costs. And so he stopped me on the school corridor during recess and asked me if my name was Josef Brehme and whether I had *Paradise Lost*. All the while scrutinising me carefully.

I nodded.

He told me he was interested in reading *Paradise Lost*.

I did not know how to react, because it was not clear whether it was a friendly request for me to let him have the book when I had read it, or whether, as an older and stronger pupil he was ordering me to bring him the book straight away.

He noticed my confusion and assured me that he would happily wait. He simply did not want anyone else to get it first.

That made me smile. It struck me as funny that Hugo could possibly imagine that there could be any interest in Milton's *Paradise Lost* in our school, and told him as much.

He acknowledged that I was right and laughed.

But a certain Josef Brehme did a lot of reading, he commented. The name appeared on the library cards of almost all the books he had borrowed from the library.

In any event he knew more about me than I did about him. Perhaps he had been following me for some time. I think now that *Paradise Lost* might well have been a pretext to make contact with me.

Hugo spoke to me in Czech. That was also important, as I realised later. In fact he was taking a bit of a risk, because the teachers did not like to see pupils conversing in Czech during classes, and not even during breaks.

Eventually he introduced himself and offered me his hand in a friendly fashion. He added that if ever I felt like discussing books, I had only to say.

That was more or less how our first conversation went. Hugo and I frequently discussed various books after that, and occasionally he would bring one himself. He knew I was taking violin lessons and that I spent a lot of time practicing, but he did manage to persuade me to play football with him at least from time to time – it was his favourite game.

Because I was very ungainly in those days, the other boarders used to poke fun at me at first, but Hugo, who for some inexplicable reason had taken a strong liking to me, would act as my protector. Once he even got into a fight with a boy two years older than himself, whom he overheard uttering some rude comment about me.

Thanks to the violin, I would occasionally perform at school events and later won a certain respect among my fellow pupils. Steiner was enthusiastic about my performances and placed great hopes in me.

Around the time I made Hugo's acquaintance, Steiner announced to me that I would most likely be needing another teacher, otherwise, he said, my exceptional talent would "atrophy". I can still picture us sitting in his dim study in the music department and Steiner telling me that in view of my progress he would try to persuade the school management to allow me to travel to Prague once or twice a week to take lessons with his brother Karel Steiner, who ran his own school of music there.

I must admit that what immediately caught my imagination was chiefly the thought of travelling to Prague, a city that was connected with all my most cherished memories. After all, I had not set foot there since you, Mother, packed me off to boarding school! Even you did not live in Prague any more, because you had moved to your family's home in České Budějovice. For me, Prague was Klára, and the happy first six years of my childhood. Paradise lost.

Only later did I fully realise what Steiner was offering me.

He said that he would request you, Mother, to arrange for my family to help pay for my lessons in Prague. Since I had no idea how my education had been paid for hitherto I thought it better to say nothing. Steiner slapped me on the shoulder.

There was nothing for me to fear, he assured me. His brother would be willing to teach someone who had my talent, even gratis. If I continued to progress as rapidly as I had so far, I would one day become a virtuoso. He would speak to his brother.

I have no idea what agreement Josef and Karel Steiner came to in the end; we did not speak of it again.

Perhaps you could clear up that little mystery for me. What is certain is that money was never mentioned and that my teacher succeeded in obtaining from the school management what he had promised, and from the beginning of my fourth year I was able to travel to Prague twice a week. I also recall that soon after the conversation that changed my life, I saw my first opera.

I vividly remember taking the train to the centre of Prague. I recall how surprised I was that the journey was so short. I was happy and excited. After all I was leaving the school and the residence for the first time in three years! At the same time, however, I felt sad and disconsolate because I was returning to the city where the first period of my childhood had come to such a sudden and cruel end. I no longer knew anyone there. My entire world had shifted inside the walls of the boarding school.

Two intense experiences awaited me in Prague. The first was my meeting with Karel Steiner, to whom it sufficed that I play a couple of short compositions by Otakar Ševčík, Dvořák's *Humoresque* and finally one piece by Bach.

"You're right, Josef," he said, turning to his brother, who had been more nervous than me the whole time. "It would be a sin to let talent like that go to waste."

He regarded me attentively. And then he asked if I had ever been to the opera.

I had to admit truthfully that not only had I never been to the opera, I had not been to any musical concert either.

With a smile, he announced that today the premiere of Dvořák's *Armida* was in store for me. He said he had four tickets. One was for his wife, Eliška, of course, but he was happy to let us have the remaining two if we wished.

Josef Steiner was delighted; my reaction was more one of anticipation. I did not exactly know what to expect.

I will never forget that experience. Not only did I see Antonín Dvořák with my own eyes (for the first and last time), but that opera, which was in fact almost a fairy tale, beguiled my childish mind. *Armida* is seldom performed these days, but nevertheless I hope I will take my children to see it one day. According to the yellowing programme, which I still keep, the premiere took place on March 25, 1904. But it is a date I would remember anyway.

The libretto was written by Jaroslav Vrchlický based on the epic poem *Jerusalem Delivered* by Torquato Tasso, whose poetry I would spend my evenings reading. It is the story of the love of Armida, the daughter of King Hidraot of Damascus, for the Frankish knight Rinald, whose troops are to conquer Jerusalem. When, at the very end, Rinald kills Armida, who was dressed as a knight, the tears poured down my cheeks.

Many distinguished people were assembled in the National Theatre that evening, at least so I was assured by Josef Steiner, who seemed to know the faces of all the politicians present. I found it hard to concentrate fully, however, on account of Eliška Steinerová. Perhaps it was due to the fact that I had spent almost three years solely in the company of men and boys, but I found her ethereal, beautiful and attractive. On the way to the theatre she had already questioned me about my affinity for music, and she was interested to know where and when I had started to learn the piano and later the violin.

I think I spoke rather incoherently, because I felt extremely nervous in the company of that kindly woman, besides which I was distressed at the thought that I would be bound to mention Klára in relation to music. I felt utterly wretched and by chance we happened, at that moment, to be passing the house where I had spent the first years of my life. That was maybe another reason why my voice quavered when I told Eliška Steinerová about my first music lessons, and explained how and why I had ended up in boarding school.

I had not had a very easy life so far, she commented sympathetically.

She stroked my hair in a motherly fashion and took me by the hand. She held it the rest of the way and all of a sudden it was like old times on my walks with you and Klára.

I could not sleep that night. My mind was on Eliška Steinerová, how she had clasped my hand and treated me with maternal kindness. My thoughts were also full of the beautiful scenes of the fabled Orient, along with snatches of the tragic story of Armida, and Dvořák's exquisite music. I determined that I would never allow the sweetheart whom I must surely meet one day to come to a tragic end like Armida.

The following day I travelled back to school with Josef Steiner and my life returned to its customary routine. But now there was the promise that after the vacation it would undergo a major change, as I would be travelling to Prague twice a week. When I pondered on it,

I found it impossible to decide what I was looking forward to more: the lessons with Karel Steiner, or the possibility of seeing his wife Eliška on occasions.

In the end, however, even my vacation was transformed, and in a fairly surprising fashion, for the first time, in fact, since I had entered the school. Previously vacations had been a time of dreadful loneliness for me, when I would secretly yearn for you to appear at the gates of the residence.

It was Hugo who wrought the change. One day he asked me whether I might not like to spend the vacation with him in Poděbrady. He had no siblings and his parents would be only too pleased if he brought a friend home with him. The idea greatly appealed to me, but I told him I was not sure you would give me permission to leave the residence. Hugo told me that he would see to it.

And he did. His father, a spa entrepreneur, as he described his profession, wrote to you and obtained your consent. It gratified me but also caused my rancour toward you to mount. Whereas you refused to reply to my letters, you continued to decide my fate behind my back in correspondence with people you did not even know!

Another thing that happened before that wonderful vacation in Poděbrady has remained in my memory. It was May second, I still recall. Although I had no violin lesson that day, I went to the music department to ask Josef Steiner about something. He was sitting quietly by the window and there were tears in his eyes. At first I thought that something tragic had happened to him or his family, and it suddenly struck me that it somehow concerned my future. But Steiner told me that Antonín Dvořák, who was a family friend and whom he all but idolised, had died the previous day.

Even I felt a sadness. It was not personal sorrow, but I found it hard to come to terms with the fact that the man who had written that marvellous opera that was so full of life and whom I had seen up close only a few weeks earlier, was no longer among the living.

My first vacation spent away from the boarding school was splendid, my dear Mother. So splendid that I shall never forget it. I do not intend to narrate here all the boyish adventures I enjoyed with Hugo, but I certainly ought to point out that his family treated me with great kindness. Perhaps because deep down they were sorry for me, and maybe also because it was obvious how fond Hugo was of me.

But there was something else exceptional for me about that vacation. Although the Beňáčeks were of Jewish faith, they were not religiously organised. However, Hugo's mother Sára often talked about God. But she spoke about him quite differently than did our teachers at school in divinity lessons or the school chaplain when we attended compulsory church services. Hugo shared my lukewarm attitude to those divinity lessons, but unlike me he would often indulge in ironic comments about the Catholic Church.

For a long time I was unable to understand those taunts, but then one day he confided in me that he attended those divinity classes and church services only because they were compulsory – his parents, and therefore he also, were Jews.

He told me it with his typical grimace, which I can picture even now. From various books I had already gained some idea of what Judaism was, but nonetheless I invited Hugo to explain me more about it.

His explanation was fairly confused; in fact, all it actually amounted to was that Jews had a different faith from that of Christians and certain special customs, but otherwise they were not very different from "us".

I wanted to know why his parents had sent him to our boarding school.

He shrugged and thought for a moment. Then he explained that his father had decided he would be a soldier. Jews had no boarding schools that prepared boys for military service, he added ironically.

It struck me as odd and I preferred not to ask how Hugo's parents accepted the Catholic practices in our school. But I was more curious about something else.

I recalled the passionate arguments you used to have with Klára, Mother, on the subject of Hilsner. Fears began to whirl through my mind that you might know that the family with whom I would be spending my vacation were Jews. After all, your quarrels with Klára were the result of your strong anti-Semitic views. I could not resist asking Hugo about Hilsner.

He eyed me quizzically for a moment.

His parents naturally said that the entire indictment had been trumped up. And if I was asking whether there was any truth in the myth about Jewish ritual murders, with which Hilsner was charged, then he, Hugo, knew of none.

I assured him that that was not at all the purpose of my question. And then I told him about the arguments Klára had with you, and how Klára had passionately defended Masaryk.

"Your mother is a singular person," he commented, when I had finished my account.

One reason I am noting it here, my dear Mother, is because that is how you were assessed by an eleven-year-old boy.

Hugo immediately revealed to me that the Emperor had commuted Hilsner's death sentence to life imprisonment. I was glad that Hilsner had not been executed. It would have greatly pleased Klára had she still been alive.

That summer in Poděbrady was also important for my future because Sára Beňáčková set me on the path to God. Until then I did not actually believe in Him. Neither you nor Klára brought me up to believe in God, although I had been baptised. And at school religion was simply a subject that dealt with a whole lot of dogmas that I found hard to believe. Moreover, our teachers and the school chaplain were very boring. It was as if teaching at a boarding school for budding military officers blunted any passion that God might ever have awakened in their hearts.

As far as I understood, God was a much more abstract being for Hugo's mother, than was the case in Christianity, where He took human form. Moreover, Sára had had a philosophical education. She often enjoyed reminding us that she was one of the very few women to have studied the subject at university.

God is the cause of everything, she would say during our conversations on the terrace of their house. Yes, God is the cause of everything but it is not easy to find Him, because in our world He manifests himself only in the form of relations and passions.

I wanted to know what she meant by saying that God was passions or relationships.

She replied that we encounter God only in love for another or in powerful relationships with others. Only then can we truly transcend our innermost being, only then can we escape the prison of our self.

Her words profoundly gripped me, even though at that moment I did not entirely understand what she meant by them.

God is present in every genuine conversation, in every dialogical relationship, Sára added. "You play the violin beautifully, for example. That's a form of dialogue too – a conversation with something higher."

I am sure you can appreciate, Mother, that I am interpreting my conversation with Sára very freely, using concepts that I acquired much later. But the essence remains. What particularly stuck in my memory was Sára's reference to my violin playing, because I knew what she was talking about. It had always been clear to me that when I was playing, I was in conversation with something higher than myself, and that it was a conversation via beauty. I was pleased that someone had put into words something that I had always felt.

That was the beginning of my incessant dialogue with God, which gradually displaced my internal monologues targeted at you. Belief in God also helped me to survive the dramatic events that occurred later. Without faith in God and my conversation with Him, and without the vision of Ariel, I would certainly have not survived all those atrocious events.

My idea of God was always very personal and I came closest to Him through music. I felt that music, out of all forms of art, was closest to God, since it was the most abstract form of beauty. Although I realised subconsciously even then that some kind of spontaneous evolution of matter, however it combined over billions of years, could, in unique circumstances, engender an organic molecule, nonetheless it could never give rise to the sort of perfection in which beauty is manifested, such as in Beethoven's Ninth Symphony, for instance.

There exist forms of human expression through which we find

ourselves in harmony with God, and for a moment we speak to Him in a common language. For me the entire universe is written in musical notation. It is precisely through music that I touch the very essence of everything. Except that God's score is infinitely more complex than anything we are capable of fully grasping.

I don't know whether God also manifests Himself in our world through proscriptions and prescriptions, or through morality and the law, if you like. I always believed that we have been given a certain freedom in this respect and that what is more important for God is the constant process of creation, in which human beings are the most important instrument. I do not maintain, however, that God is indifferent to how we behave, or to whether we act morally or immorally. In the long run every truly deep relationship and every profound dialogue has ethical implications. I hope this is so, partly because I very much wish for you to be obliged one day to explain how you treated me before God's judgment seat.

How odd, that while in that summer of 1904 I was finding God, Europe was starting to plunge ever more rapidly into the crisis caused by the "death of God," about which various philosophers and scholars had previously spoken. They, of course, were talking only about the death of God in the human mind, that is more in the sense of a kind of collective psychological process than about the actual death of a metaphysical God. Through the emancipation of reason and the technical discoveries that followed, man had come to the conclusion that he no longer needed God, that he could understand his world even without Him. How naive!

Perhaps I have digressed slightly, dear Mother. I am sure I did not think along those lines at the age of ten. At that time I found God above all because I needed a companion in my solitude. The explanation I received from Sára Beňáčková, corresponded with something fundamental in my soul.

On my return from vacation I felt appreciably better at boarding school. Not only did I now have a real friend, I had also gained a substitute family, one might say. It would be very hard to describe to you what it meant to me. In Poděbrady I had become very strongly attached to Sára Beňáčková in particular. Of course she was somewhat eccentric for her time, but from my very first days at the Beňáčeks' it was obvious that Sára felt a need to take motherly care of me and show me favour. Even more than to her son in fact! Maybe it was due to my situation, and maybe because I was much more emotional, and must have appeared to Sára more vulnerable than Hugo.

Hugo was not at all put out by her obvious sympathy for me. He modelled himself on his father Otto. He always maintained that one day he would like to be a businessman like him, even though he enjoyed reading and was more sensitive than the majority of our fellow pupils. That must have been the reason why, on several occasions during the vacation, he was bold enough to contradict his father's view that a boarding school with a military regime was the best place for his education.

I think that even Otto Beňáček was beginning to realise that his son was rather too independently minded for a future soldier. He had a rich imagination, which, unlike mine, was focused on business and travel. Hugo owned, for example, a book with pictures of hotels at the Hungarian spas, and was constantly browsing through it. Thanks to him I still have inscribed in my memory such exotic names as Sárvár, Eger, Zalakaros, Bükkfürdö or Bogács.

He would often compel me to listen to his disquisitions on ways of extending the range of services offered at some spa facility or other. Understandably, his excursions into the world of business were very naive and impractical. Nevertheless it was obvious that Hugo's father had been wrong to place his son in our school. He had failed to see that Hugo was his natural successor.

Hugo's mother was much more of a paragon for me. Sára Beňáčková used to say that I did not fully appreciate what a great gift I had. Everything would be easier for me in life, she said, because even when times were bad I would have a spiritual home. I promised myself that if in future I proved incapable of earning a living by playing the violin, I would study philosophy like she had. I wanted to be like Sára – a free, impractical spirit for whom the entire world is the subject of reflection.

During the vacation Hugo grew taller and stronger. His hair started to darken and within a few years he would no longer resemble the freckle-faced fair-haired boy from the period when we first met. At that time I almost looked a weakling alongside Hugo, and slightly rickety, even though I was not much smaller than him.

After the vacation my weekly routine changed. For one thing, I started to travel back and forth to Professor Steiner's and for another, Hugo's parents, who often paid us visits, would take us at weekends on trips in the environs or even to Prague.

That year, for the first time, I also spent the Christmas season away from boarding school. Although they were Jews, the Beňáčeks celebrated Christmas, albeit in tandem with Jewish Hanukkah: each day for eight days they would light another candle on the candlestick that stood in the living room. On each of my visits Sára Beňáčková had to explain to me again and again the meaning of the various Jewish holidays, because there are so many of them and each of them has a complicated origin.

The Beňáčeks were truly very good to me. When they received the news that I would be taking lessons in Prague, it was they who bought me my first violin. Previously I had played a violin that Steiner loaned me from the school's music department, which was not practical because I had to return it after every practice. Not only that, it was not very suitable because the thoughtless treatment of several generations of pupils had inevitably left its mark on it.

All of a sudden it was as if I had two families. During my trips to Prague, on which Josef Steiner at first selflessly accompanied me, I became friendlier with his brother's family than would normally be appropriate for a pupil. This was largely due to Eliška, who was clearly touched by my story, and after my lesson invariably invited me to their apartment on the floor above, where she usually prepared various sweetmeats for me. When she later discovered that I enjoyed reading, she would also put aside some books for me.

I loved Eliška Steinerová from the depths of my heart. Had you not abandoned me, dear Mother, maybe I could have loved you in the same way despite your unfortunate nature. But because you never gave me the opportunity to do so, she became my substitute mother. On each occasion I looked forward eagerly to seeing her again and would count the hours remaining until my next visit to Prague. Eliška was also the reason why I made the progress on the violin that her husband expected of me. The thought that one day he might announce that he would no longer teach me, maybe terrified me more because it would mean losing contact with Eliška than because of the loss of a brilliant teacher.

Karel Steiner was a kindly teacher, but also strict. He could not abide slovenliness or lack of preparation. I recall how he once lost his temper when I had failed to improve my performance of a piece by Bach since the previous lesson.

"You can't have done enough practice," he snapped at me, and the blood froze in my veins. I tried to convince him that I had worked diligently to eliminate the shortcomings in my playing, but he simply commented ironically that I was too gifted to repeat elementary mistakes. And he demonstrated the proper fingering at a slow tempo.

He was right. I really had neglected my practice that time on account of problems I was having with one of the wardens. His name was Hans Oberfalzer and he was the scourge of the entire school. He was not keen on my privileges and only respected them because Josef Steiner had succeeded in convincing the school's management that if I became a celebrated violinist one day it would be good for the school's reputation.

"Hanzi," as we nicknamed Oberfalzer, was of a different opinion, however, and left me alone only because he was instructed to do so by "the powers that be". But whenever the opportunity arose he would cause me minor inconveniences or injustices, such as preventing me from being able to practice enough.

Like all boarders, I had to do duty in the evening as gatekeeper from time to time, recording arrivals and keeping an eye out in case of anything untoward happening on the corridors. I tended to volunteer for weekend duties because I had nowhere to go anyway, unless Hugo's parents came and took Hugo and me on some excursion. But Hanzi started to insist that I do weekday duties as well, on the pretext that he had no one to replace me. It was a lie, of course, but I bowed to his pressure for fear that he might exact even worse revenge.

It was only when Karel Steiner rebuked me that I complained to his brother on our way back from Prague. He was extremely annoyed that Hanzi was preventing me from practicing after lessons and said a number of rude things about him, whose vehemence took me aback. I was afraid he might do something rash that would set Hanzi against me altogether.

I don't know how Josef Steiner eventually managed to induce Hanzi to leave me alone, at least to the extent that he stopped forcing me to do mid-week duties. However the warden would occasionally order me to rearrange the things in my closet or re-make a perfectly made bed. Luckily he remained at our school for one more year only and in 1905, another warden replaced him after the vacation.

At that time I was up to my ears in work. Apart from having to prepare for my violin lessons and practice, Professor Steiner insisted that I should tackle the theory of music. He therefore set me chapters of various books – mostly German – to study. I have to admit that I had to struggle hard before I managed to understand some of them. Nevertheless I did my best to satisfy all his requirements, and this contributed to my general education.

Only with hindsight did I realise how revolutionary the beginning of the twentieth century had been in all areas of human activity. In Czech music the era of Dvořák and Fibich was coming to an end and Leoš Janáček was becoming known. Otakar Ševčík was active at the Prague Conservatory and the violin virtuoso Jan Kubelík was at the height of his success, along with the singer Emmy Destinn.

I followed all those events only from afar, of course, and I only learnt about most of those outstanding performances and new creative achievements indirectly from the Steiners. Eliška enjoyed recounting to me the plots of operas she had seen with her husband at the National Theatre or describing her experiences at concerts. From time to time the Steiners would take me with them to a concert. Thus it was that in 1905 I first saw Kubelík perform with my own eyes, and Steiner even introduced me to him after the concert!

I was subsequently fated to meet Kubelík quite often, but I will never forget that first meeting. He played Brahms' violin concerto with such virtuosity and commitment, that it came as a slight shock. I was convinced that even if I were to study the violin for another hundred years I would never be even half as good as he.

I confided my feelings to Eliška.

"Kubelík is a genius and you are still very young," she smiled. "But you will definitely be very good one day."

Her words pleased me even though her answer could be interpreted to mean that there existed geniuses and then there were the "very good", of whom I was one.

For that matter Europe was teeming with geniuses. Gustav Mahler was composing in Vienna, where Arnold Schönberg was just becoming famous. In Finland, Sibelius was composing beautiful gloomy music, while in Russia, Igor Stravinsky, whose music I admire unreservedly, was just reaching maturity. The beginning of the century was simply a time of ferment, particularly in the Austro-Hungarian monarchy. It was as if the decline of the monarchy provoked artists and intellectuals to great creative feats...

Sometimes I would steel myself to write you a letter to which I already assumed I would not receive an answer. I wanted you to know, nonetheless, that I was making progress and that maybe you had made a mistake in sacrificing me to your marriage. Apart from those moments I thought about you less and less, which was just as well. My days were fully occupied and playing the violin was a release.

I have little recollection of the political events of those days. All that sticks in my mind is the news about the workers' revolt in Brno and the revolution in Russia, maybe because I happened to be study-ing a violin piece by Tchaikovsky. Reports of Russia's lack of success in its war against Japan started arriving in 1904, and then in autumn 1905 discontent in Russia gave rise to a revolutionary movement that demanded democratization and a genuine constitutional monarchy. Our teachers followed news of the Russian revolution with close attention and in their lessons they would discuss the situation in that country with us, albeit with vastly differing motives. Some Czech patriots welcomed the Russian revolution chiefly because they perceived the future of the Czech lands as part of some pan-Slavonic empire, and they found a democratic Russia more attractive than outdated czarist absolutism. On the other hand, orthodox proponents of the Austrian monarchy and rule with a strong hand feared that the revolution in Russia might lead to further democratization of the Austro-Hungarian monarchy.

Tension reigned among the teaching staff of our school as it did throughout the monarchy. It was clear that some of the teachers were Czech patriots and supporters of a pan-Slavonic empire even though they spoke to us in German; others, who were overtly Czech, were dyed-in-the-wool supporters of the monarchy. This was also confirmed for me by Josef Steiner.

My own political views at that time were very vague. Only occasionally would I get to hear the names of Czech politicians and political parties. Almost no one talked about politics with me, so I did not even know what was going on in the Czech lands. All I remember is that universal suffrage was introduced in 1907.

When it came to the future of Austria-Hungary I was still under Klára's influence. Maybe that is why it never occurred to me that the Austro-Hungarian empire would ever disintegrate. I knew from various discussions with my classmates or occasional reading of the newspapers that the main quarrels between Czech politicians were over the role that the Czech political leadership should play in the Imperial Diet in Vienna and who should be representing the Czech lands there.

But by and large I had no time for anything else but work. After all, violin practice alone took as much as several hours every day. The only moments of rest were my trips to the Beňáčeks during vacations. Moreover, I took part in sports twice a week, Hugo having convinced me that it was good for my health, and so, under his guidance, I learnt to play football fairly well.

Sometime in the spring of 1908, after a successful public recital, the Steiners invited me to a café.

I sensed that they had something important to tell me. But when, as we sat there in those great leather armchairs, Karel Steiner followed his words of praise with the recommendation that I should study music at the Conservatory, I started to tremble all over.

I was stunned by that vision. I could wish for nothing more, but immediately my mind was full of all the possible obstacles that might present themselves. I had been secretly dreaming of studying at the Conservatory for several years, but each time I banished the thought and preferred not even to mention it to the Steiners. After all, its fulfilment depended on so many things that were beyond my control!

For one thing, it would be necessary to obtain your consent, dear Mother. And where would I live? Who would take care of me?

I immediately spelt this out to Professor Steiner. He gazed at me for a moment and then said something that took my breath away.

He told me that he had already been in correspondence with my mother. He had explained to her that I was exceptionally talented. He said I could live with them – Eliška had expressed her willingness to take care of me, and besides, she had long regarded me as her own. And, as I knew full well, they had no children of their own.

This was too much for me – at that moment tears started to roll down my cheeks. Could happiness really have smiled on me and granted in one go my two dearest wishes – to study at the Conservatory and to be in close proximity to that affectionate woman?

Eliška handed me a handkerchief and I noticed that she too had tears in her eyes.

Steiner grinned. "But now I've got to convince the Conservatory to take you," he said.

As far as my violin playing was concerned, he said, he had no concerns. Josef Brehme was the most talented violinist he had ever had the honour to teach. The main thing was that I should be able to cope with the music theory and learning a second instrument.

And so I spent the next few weeks in strenuous study of music theory and piano practice. Although I had been playing the piano for years in the music department and on occasions had even practiced duets with Josef Steiner, there was no comparison with my violin playing. In the end, however, it proved sufficient, dear mother, because I was accepted by the Conservatory, as you know! No doubt Professor Steiner's recommendation helped, although whenever I asked him he would always reply modestly that I had owed my place solely to my talent and diligence.

Of course I yearned to go to Prague, and to the Steiners furthermore, but it was not entirely easy to leave the boarding school nonetheless. Over the years I had become accustomed to the daily routine and had got to like several of the teachers. What grieved me most of all, of course, was that I had to take leave of Hugo! He was leaving too and was entering a commercial academy in September, but not in Prague, unfortunately.

Our leave-taking was sad, even though we promised that we would pay each other regular visits. Hugo insisted that I should visit them during the following vacation, seeing that I would not be able to come to them that summer on account of my having to stay in Prague and prepare for my studies. But things were to turn out differently, as often happens. Hugo and I did meet again, but many years later and in incredible circumstances, as I shall subsequently relate, dear Mother.

Some time in July of that year I wrote a letter to God.

Dear God,
   I don't know how to thank You for everything You have done for me. I am writing to You because I do not believe that You dwell only in churches. You were always with me when I was playing for You.
   Dear God, I want You to know that I realise what enormous good fortune I have in all the misfortune that has happened to

*me. Whatever plans You have for me, I will always humbly abide
by them.*

Yours, Josef Brehme

That was more or less the text of the letter. Perhaps what I wrote was
presumptuous, because I certainly had no notion of what plans God
had for me. The idea that I had was simple. I would complete my
studies at the Conservatory and become a distinguished violinist.
And should any problems arise they would be only minor obstacles
on the path to that bright future.

God left me in that dream world for a few more years, for which I
am grateful to Him. They were happy years, even though almost every
day questions came to my mind that I would have loved to have asked
you and my father. There was scarcely an evening when I would not
fall asleep longing for one or both of you to appear so that I could
show off to you everything I had achieved. I would tell myself that
that would redeem me and then everything would be fine. Only I was
never to see either of you.

Otherwise my life was eventful and interesting. Suddenly I was
free. I was no longer obliged to rise straight after reveille and then
do compulsory drill. Quite simply, study at the Conservatory was in
no manner reminiscent of a military regime. And also I did not have
to be in bed after lights out, which was how each day at boarding
school ended.

That is not to say, of course, that I had no duties. Eliška was kind
but had two fairly strict requirements: that I keep my room tidy and
that I ask her permission if I wanted to stay out later in the evening.
Eliška's husband, for his part, would often remind me that should I fail
at my studies it would be his failure too, because he was my guarantor
to a certain extent. Maybe that was also why I studied harder than if
the Steiners had been my parents.

That year Josef Steiner returned to Prague too. He had been ap-
pointed music teacher at a high school in the Old Town, and as he
lived not far away I saw him often.

The Prague Conservatory, which was then housed in the Rudolfinum and where I studied for the next six years, was associated with names that had previously been legendary for me: Josef Suk, Jan Kubelík, Otakar Ševčík, Rudolf Friml, Oskar Nedbal, Jaroslav Kocian. And Antonín Dvořák had been Director of the Conservatory until 1904.

Dear Mother, rather than describing in detail my studies, about whose progress you were apparently regularly informed in letters from Karel Steiner, I would rather recall the intellectual ferment to which I was witness in those years. Prague was crammed with artists, writers and intellectuals, or at least so it seemed to me.

Suddenly I had the opportunity to associate with a vast number of interesting people, as well as read magazines and newspapers, and even go to film shows from time to time. Some films I even saw five times, because cinema, which was then a totally new art, captivated my imagination.

Prague was then home to some remarkable people. At the time I arrived in Prague Jaroslav Hašek was editing the journal *Woman's Outlook* and shortly afterward he became editor of *Animal World*. Max Brod, who was subsequently responsible for publicizing the works of Leoš Janáček, lived here, and it was possible to bump into Czech poets such as Stanislav Kostka Neumann, František Gellner and Otokar Březina.

There were painters and sculptors. If I recall rightly Antonín Slavíček died two years after I arrived here, but that was also the year of Alfons Mucha's return to Prague!

It was impossible to take in all those stimuli. The world seemed to be hurtling forward in an explosion of creative hypertension and was looking for new forms of expression. It was the era of Robert Musil, Karl Kraus, Sigmund Freud, Thomas Mann, Gustav Klimt, Egon Schiele, Oskar Kokoschka, Rainer Maria Rilke, Alexander von Zemlinsky and Wassily Kandinsky.

And I could go on and on. The only reason for recalling those particular names is to let you know that I suddenly seemed to be tossed into the current of a torrent and was obliged to contend with it. At the boarding school I had been isolated from most of those influences. I encountered poets and writers only indirectly through the books in the school library, which anyway lacked their latest works of course, whereas in Prague I was suddenly surrounded by fellow pupils and by teachers who talked about the latest trends in art, and about interesting books, revolutionary articles and other exploits – as it all happened. Moreover, many of them were actively engaged in the arts and played a significant role – in music at least.

Something was about to snap in Europe. Even then it was obvious that we were standing on the frontier of two epochs, that the old world was ending and a new one was beginning. I don't want this to sound too personal, but it strikes me that the first year I spent in Prague in its entirety was the final turning point. After all, even here they were already discussing the special theory of relativity of Albert Einstein, which has significantly changed the way we think about the world, Schönberg was composing his *Gurrelieder* and Kandinsky was getting ready to found the arts association *Der blaue Reiter* in Munich. The form of expression had changed. The fixed order had disappeared and art form now shifted to abstraction and experiment.

It was also the time of discussions about the nature of the future. Schools of philosophy and utopias appeared, inspired by the writings of Marx and Engels. It also found expression in art. Young rebellious poets in particular were burying the old world and trying to build a new world on the basis of theories created by Marx. It was still too early for me to suspect how strongly my future life would be affected by the Russified version of Marx's doctrines.

There was indeed much more that I could not suspect. Such as that my future journey to Russia would start the day I met Sabina Groffová at the age of fifteen.

Sabina was my age and was studying piano and voice. Fate brought us together through the good offices of no less a person than Kubelík, who recommended her to my professor as someone who might accompany me on the piano at my public performances. He thought that she did not have sufficient talent to become a solo singer or concert pianist, but recognised that she had an exceptional ability to accompany solo performers.

Professor Steiner agreed to this. What he valued most was her great sensitivity and adaptability. He considered Sabina a brilliant idea of Kubelík's and further evidence of his genius.

Steiner insisted that it was already necessary for me to find someone who was not over-ambitious and would be willing to learn to understand my style of playing. Someone who would be capable of communicating with me by exchanging glances if possible.

I was a bit worried that Sabina might take umbrage if I suggested to her that she specialise henceforth in accompanying a still unknown violinist and renounce a career of her own. But she must have been prepared by her teachers for our first conversation, and so without any great reflection she assured me that it would be a great honour for her to be allowed to accompany me. She told me she had no ambitions as a soloist.

I contemplated her with interest. In the café not far from the Rudolfinum where we were seated, the sunlight shone through the window onto her face. A firm chin, nicely shaped lips, a small nose and blue eyes, all framed by long brown hair. Her face radiated an odd mixture of indecisiveness and fear, but from time to time she would laugh out loud and say something self-deprecating.

It was above all her mother's dream that she should be a professional musician, she told me with a grimace.

It was not that she did not love music. Indeed she had a certain talent, otherwise the Conservatory wouldn't have accepted her. But her own wish had always been to do something practical.

Sabina's very frank declaration took me aback. I was unable to imagine any other profession for myself. From the first moment that Josef Steiner had handed me a violin, my sole ambition had been to become a violinist.

I asked her what she meant when she said she wanted to do something practical.

She confessed that she wanted to be a journalist, for instance, or the director of a theatre.

I pointed out that these were very different professions

Sabina gave an almost guilty smile, something she did quite frequently. In fact, she did not know what she wanted to be. All she knew was that she would definitely not become the concert artiste her mother had in mind.

But she did not mind accompanying someone else?

Not at all, she replied. That was what she was best at. She had already played with Professor Kocian and with Professor Málek. And she had even accompanied Machatý.

I expressed astonishment. Did she mean that cellist in his final year, for whom everyone predicted a splendid future? She must be good. Had they ever played Dvořák's Cello Concerto together?

She nodded.

I told her that it was odd I had not heard of her before.

She shrugged. She had heard about me, though. From Kubelík himself! He thought I had great talent.

That gratified me but I didn't show it. I realised that it was the first time I had had a conversation with a girl! All the women in my life had been much older and had tended to treat me in a motherly fashion. Sitting opposite me now was a good-looking girl who was gazing at me with a mixture of admiration, uncertainty and self-deprecation. Never before had I been in a situation where a woman had gazed at me.

I have decided, dear Mother, that in this letter I will be frank not only with you but also with myself, and so I will admit that it did me good in my immaturity, and so I started to swagger a little. I reeled off all the things I had ever played on the violin and all the places where I had performed. I talked about the great composers as if they were my friends. But when Sabina asked me about my previous life I was suddenly lost for words. I found it hard to talk about you above all. And there was nothing at all to say about my boarding school.

And that was the moment when Sabina's advantage over me became evident. Whereas I had wanted to dazzle her with my knowledge and my successes, she, in an entirely artless – one might say "feminine" – fashion induced me through her questions to relate to her my friendship with Hugo, my admiration for his mother Sára and my love for Eliška.

I did not notice in the least that I was revealing far more about myself than I intended. I only realised it when in response to my story about how I had always looked forward to my lessons with Professor Steiner and how happy I had been that they had invited me to live with them, Sabina declared:

"Eliška is a sort of a second mother to you, isn't she?"

In my effort to mask my discomfiture I replied somewhat sullenly that Eliška wasn't my second mother since I had no first mother. She did not give me the opportunity to have one.

Sabina fell silent. I realised that I had been doing all the talking and I had asked her nothing. But when I did it became apparent that she also was loath to speak about her family.

Her father had died when she was still small, she said. Then she swept her fingers through her hair as if forcing herself to go on. Her mother was a very unusual person, she continued. "Do you know what I mean?"

I shook my head to indicate that I did not.

There was always someone different living with them. First it was Alfred, who was a musician. Then it was Gottfried, sergeant major in the army. At present it was some František, a poet...

I commented that it need not be so bad having a poet at home.

Sabina's response was skeptical. He might be a poet but he was also crazy. Like her mother. Maybe it was better to have no mother than to have one like hers.

I reflected on this. I was not convinced about what she had just said. If only she knew how much time I had spent explaining to you in my head what a mistake you had made by getting rid of me. What would I have given in those days simply to live with you, however eccentric you might have been? I did not conceal from Sabina that you too were absolutely ordinary, which was why you had succumbed to the pressure of your bourgeois family.

She told me that her mother was very beautiful – and still young.

Her mother had been nineteen when she gave birth to her.

Sabina, as I understood, nourished no hope at all of her situation improving in the near future. Others might have found the idea of having a beautiful mother appealing, particularly one who was young and bohemian, but for Sabina it was a misfortune.

She immediately confirmed this.

The real reason that she didn't want to become a concert artiste was because her mother wished it. She didn't want to be like her mother. She wanted to lead a normal life.

I didn't know whether to sympathise with her or pity her. At that moment her greatest ambition in life seemed to be ordinary. It was odd, because as it soon turned out, Sabina was not at all ordinary.

At our very first rehearsal together she convinced me of her extra-ordinary ability to let herself be led, while at the same time, when necessary, herself leading the soloist she was accompanying. She had the most amazing memory. Whereas I had to play a piece many times over in order to memorise it, Sabina simply read the score through a few times. During concerts she almost never needed anyone to turn the pages for her.

We became a well-coordinated duo. Sabina maintained that it did her undoubted good to cooperate with me. She was an inspiration to me in spite of her declared adulation of normality and ordinariness. Maybe she really did want to lead a thoroughly ordinary life as a kind of rebellion against her mother's extravagances, but she herself was a perfectionist and admired perfection. Indeed as it later turned out, she was far from despising her mother. On the contrary, her main problem was her admiration for her mother, coupled with the conviction that she would never attain her level of perfection.

But apart from that, my relationship with Sabina was thoroughly complicated. I was attracted to her, that I cannot deny. But at the same time she repelled me. You see she reminded me of you, Mother. At least, in respect of what she used to say about herself. Whenever I saw her sitting quietly and impassively in some corner and silently bemoaning her fate, I would suddenly see you during our walks with Klára. I think

I had an unconscious fear that behind the facade of indifference and resentment there might stalk a betrayal like the one you had inflicted on me. Naturally that had an unfortunate influence on my attitude to Sabina.

At first, our moments together were more or less confined to musical activity, and if we ever spent time together outside school hours, Sabina's behaviour toward me was neutral. Whenever we entered a café together, for instance, and I would introduce her to students or people from Prague bohemian circles as my friend or "artistic companion," she mostly simply smiled timidly and would always take a seat at the side of the table where she anticipated the discussion would be least intense. She rarely said anything herself.

I once asked her why she never joined in the conversation.

She shrugged and said that she did not know what she would talk about.

I protested that she had interesting opinions about lots of things.

She raised her eyebrows in astonishment. Did I really think so? She did not regard her ideas as interesting. Besides most of those people were interested in me. It was said of me that I would one day be like Kubelík, so people liked being near me. They would admire me even if I talked nonsense.

It was hard to get through to Sabina. She never showed what she felt for me, apart from occasional comments about my musical achievements. Maybe that was why I was so surprised by what happened on our first trip beyond the borders of the monarchy.

I know precisely when it was, and not just because it was my first opportunity to play in a prestigious concert hall in London, which was then regarded as something like the capital city of the world. I also remember it because we made the trip just at the moment when the "unsinkable" Titanic was making its maiden trans-Atlantic sailing. It was the month of April 1912.

Looked at with hindsight, the sinking of the Titanic on April 14, was a portent of the era that was to come. For several years spectres had been slowly coming to life in Europe that no one had under control.

Politics were archaic and were incapable of keeping pace with scientific and economic developments.

The old order had collapsed, as was obvious in all fields of human activity, and meanwhile the monster of romantic nationalism was growing stronger and stronger. The new inventions, discoveries, artistic works and unprecedented intellectual achievements were totally devoid of that humility toward God that used to be an innate feature of Europe. Until the end of the nineteenth century, rationalism, the official ideology of the modern age since the eighteenth century, had been grounded in an ethical code that was actually Christian.

People gradually came to the conclusion that they did not need God and even in the sphere of morality that they could manage on their own. Suddenly the existence of God was simply a cosmological question, and what is more, even in cosmology God simply became a hypothesis and ceased to be a lived reality that awakens in each of us humility in the face of our own inadequacies.

The Titanic was one of the most important symbols of that newly-acquired human arrogance. The very assertion that it was unsinkable filled me with dread. Whenever I read those blasphemous declarations, I recall saying to myself that the ship was bound to sink.

With Sabina as my accompanist, I was fated to play in London for some of the people who would die in the Titanic four or five days later. I know for certain that some of the passengers were there because after one of the concerts one young American told me that my playing had captivated him. He was also a musician apparently and what he called a "music promoter". He said he would immediately start to arrange performances for me in New York, adding that his voyage to America would be very rapid this time because he was taking the fastest ship in the world. I could also count on sailing to America on a ship like the Titanic, he laughed.

Professor Steiner, who accompanied Sabina and me to London, was delighted with his offer. He considered a trip to America to be the next logical step in my career.

Sabina reacted in her own distinctive fashion that she would most likely be afraid of the transatlantic voyage. The trip across the English Channel was quite enough for her.

As Steiner was due to dine that evening with a friend who was professor at the Royal Academy of Music, I remained alone with Sabina. I had received a very respectable fee for the concert, and so after a few interviews with journalists and the inevitable photographs, I invited her to a restaurant.

Probably encouraged by our success, Sabina was more chatty than usual and spoke to me about her plans. She told me she would like to establish a private music school where she would teach small children. She said she was very fond of children and, moreover, that she would have the feeling of doing something useful. I agreed with her. I told her about Klára. Without her I would most likely never had become a musician.

We talked for at least two hours. Toward the end of the evening, Sabina gazed at me for a long time before asking me, quite surprisingly, what I really thought of her.

I did not understand exactly what she meant and told her so.

What she meant was what did I feel for her, she said after a moment's hesitation.

I was taken aback. Sabina was clearly expecting a spontaneous answer and did not want me to reflect. She blushed slightly and placed her hands under her chin – a sure sign of her dissatisfaction.

I told her truthfully that I held her in esteem as my best friend...

This did not satisfy her. She wanted to know if that was all.

Only then did I realise what answer she was expecting of me, and it was my turn to blush. However Sabina did not suspect that I was blushing out of confusion and saw it as a sign that I was too scared or shy to admit my deeper feelings for her. So she did something that was quite unusual for her: she took the matter into her own hands.

"You love me," she sighed. "And I know it."

She was now gazing at me in a way she had never done before, which unsettled me even more.

I was panic stricken. If there was one thing I was sure of, it was that I did not love Sabina. As I said earlier, she reminded me too much of you, Mother, and in fact I was frightened of her. I surmised, however, that I must not offend her by rebuffing her out of hand, because she could easily turn into my worst enemy.

I answered noncommittally. I said something intended to convey that I liked her too, of course. I assumed that Sabina would interpret my words correctly as meaning that although I did not love her she mattered to me and I wanted us to remain friends. But she took them to mean something else.

She laid her hand on mine and almost in a whisper confessed how much my words had gladdened her. She had been afraid I would rebuff her. She had been planning to tell me for so long. It was clear to her that I myself would be incapable of it. I was such a shy person, wasn't I?

I was too much of a coward to admit to Sabina that I had no interest in a deeper relationship with her. On the way back to the hotel she took me by the hand and I made a great effort not to slacken my pace because I feared she might want to kiss me. But it happened anyway. In the hotel corridor, outside our rooms, Sabina leaned toward me and kissed me on the lips.

I mumbled in confusion that I had to think it over, and fortunately – perhaps unfortunately – she nodded understandingly. Although the evening had not turned out as she had imagined, she probably told herself that it was best not to rush things with someone as shy as I was. So we said good night and I fled into my room.

Oh, my God, I said to myself in panic. What am I to do?

The situation seemed hopeless, because I had no wish to wound Sabina or to lose her as a friend. With a touch of expediency, I was already wondering what I would do if she stopped accompanying me at concerts.

But Sabina clearly thought she had heard from me the answer she had hoped for, and the next day, unlike me, she behaved pleasantly and naturally. It was our last day in London, so we went for a walk in that wonderful city in the company of Professor Steiner. Whereas I was taciturn and preoccupied as I struggled to find a solution, Sabina was unusually talkative and she would touch my hand conspiratorially whenever Steiner was not looking.

I don't even know how we spent that long journey back to Prague. I must have feigned tiredness most of the time and slept. We parted company at the station and I firmly hoped that everything would sort itself out somehow.

But it didn't. About two days later Sabina announced to me at the conservatory that I was invited to their home for dinner, and that she had spoken to her mother about me.

What had she said?

"That we love each other," she answered calmly.

I struggled with a surge of indignation. It was clear that I was losing control of the situation. Red in the face, I was about to tell her the truth when Sabina butted in.

I was not to regard it as an engagement party, she said. Her mother quite simply wanted to make my acquaintance.

Her words made me realise how odd it was that I still did not know Sabina's mother. If she had ever attended any of our concerts she had never come to introduce herself. My annoyance suddenly gave way to curiosity and so I eventually consented to Sabina's plan. It was one of the biggest mistakes of my life.

Something happened, you see, that I had not anticipated in the least, and which I will find hard to relate to you in particular, Mother. From the moment I first exchanged a few words with Sabina's mother, Johana Groffová, I fell hopelessly in love with her. She was a truly gorgeous woman. She instantly noticed how unsure I was in her presence and she also knew why. While Sabina attributed my stammering and blushing to my nervousness in the presence of a mother for whose daughter I had certain feelings, it did not escape Johana's notice that I scarcely looked at Sabina, and, moreover, that I was actually irritated by her attentions, whereas I could not keep my eyes off her mother.

I cannot recall what we talked about that evening, but I remember perfectly how delighted I was when Johana told me privately that she would like to get to know me better. What if she were to invite me to a café some time?

I agreed instantly, even though I was not sure whether she was inviting me alone or with Sabina. I expect she noticed what was on my mind, because she immediately added that it would only be the two of us, of course. She said we needed to have a proper talk.

I had to wait several weeks for the assignation, which caused me mental torment. On the one hand I looked forward to our meeting with a mixture of impatience and trepidation, while on the other I was burdened by the fact that I could not be frank with Sabina. Were I to tell her now that I had no interest in a full-blown relationship with her, it would jeopardise my meeting with her mother, or so I imagined.

And so every time I went somewhere with Sabina I had to put up with her holding me by the hand. Sometimes I even had to kiss her, although I would often clearly indicate by my gestures and behaviour that I resented her importunity.

Then she would say that I was charming, and she would muse over whether I was naturally shy or whether it was because of the lack of women in my life.

I would suffer in silence as soon as she started to enlarge on those reflections. Most of the time I would try to steer the conversation toward music, but on that subject there was a certain tension between us. Whereas I was still fascinated with modernism, which at that time was represented – for me at least – by Schönberg or Janáček, Sabina preferred the nineteenth-century masters, and she liked most of all Mozart and Bach. We would even quarrel over our musical tastes from time to time.

Sometime in 1912, the two of us performed a series of concerts in Munich and Vienna. During our stay in Munich we visited an exhibition of pictures by Kandinsky, who also had a great affinity for Schönberg. I was enraptured by Kandinsky's paintings, regarding them as the emergence of an entirely new vision of the world that was related to what was happening in science, for example, but Sabina did not find them particularly interesting. The same thing happened in Vienna, where we had the opportunity to view Egon Schiele's pictures.

On that trip, the contrast between our views of the world became all the more apparent, and on top of that I was obliged to ward off

Sabina's overtures by all manners of pretexts. Although she was fairly conventional, she had no firm religious grounding and so was not of the view that certain things should wait until marriage. She even spoke about it openly, which unnerved me to such a degree that I resorted to a defensive lie to extricate myself. I told her that I was very religiously minded, as Sabina well knew, even though I did not attend any church, and I was not sure whether physical love before marriage was not a sin.

This was no lie as regards my faith. But it was a lie to say that my faith implied attachment to any divinely ordained ethical canon. Naturally, Sabina interpreted my lie just as it suited her, in other words, as a further sign of my "charm," as she put it. And moreover she took what I had said about marriage to mean that I wanted to marry her one day.

I have to admit that I am in no way proud of my expedient behaviour. After all, I was giving Sabina certain grounds for hope chiefly because I was afraid of losing such an excellent accompanist and was looking forward to meeting her mother again.

It was some time at the end of 1912 that I finally received a note from Johana. She announced to me that she would call for me at the Conservatory and we would go somewhere where we could "talk together calmly". That expression alarmed me at first, because it struck me that Johana might be wanting to have a heart-to-heart talk with me about my relationship with her daughter or some other misdemeanour. I was wrong, as it turned out.

In the café, Johana talked only about music and art. I was overjoyed to discover that she and I admired the same composers and painters. I still don't know whether this was a ruse on her part or whether she really did like them. She must have known about my tastes from Sabina.

At that meeting she surprised me in other ways too.

First of all she decided that she would call me "her Paganini". I was not sure whether she meant it ironically or out of admiration, but whatever the case, it was the name she stuck to

Then she had a brief conversation with me about Sabina.

She knew that I did not feel for Sabina what her daughter felt for me, she said at the outset. However, if it was no trouble to me I was not to spurn her. She said that Sabina was utterly dependent on me.

I assured Johana that I had no intention of "spurning" her as she put it, and I also confirmed that I truly did not have the same feelings toward Sabina as she had toward me.

Johana suddenly said something that shocked me.

Yes, that was obvious, wasn't it, otherwise why would I reject a girl who was not at all unattractive and was literally offering herself to me?

So Sabina had confided in her my rejection of her attempts at physical love!

As if unaware of my discomfort, Johana struck at a further sensitive spot. She was interested to know if I really had such strong religious convictions as I made out to Sabina.

I did not want to lie to her, so I admitted that I had fabricated that slightly.

And then came the fateful question: So you wouldn't say no to every woman, my Paganini?

As she said these words, fixing me with an inquisitive but by no means mocking gaze, I was overwhelmed with excitement and trepidation.

I blushed a deep scarlet and blurted out: No, definitely not!

Johana smiled and changed the subject. When she had taken leave of me, saying she would soon be in touch, I was left in an overwhelming state of mental confusion.

I will not beat about the bush, dear Mother. I cannot leave this episode out of my story if it is to make any sense.

Yes, a few weeks later I became the lover of Johana Groffová.

When Sabina left Prague for a week with a choir, Johana invited me home. There is no need for me to go into detail, but I would like to say that it did not happen on my initiative. Maybe I simply played willingly into Johana's hands when she started to talk about her age and sighed that she was already thirty-seven years old. She wished she could be eighteen again like Sabina and I.

I protested that I had never met a girl of my age who was as beautiful or interesting as she was at thirty-seven.

That was enough for her. She took my hand and said, "You really are sweet, my Paganini." And then she kissed me.

The next few weeks I lived in a complete trance. I even neglected my violin playing somewhat. I had an agreement with Hugo that I would visit him that summer in Poděbrady, but in the end I wrote to him that I could not come because of "urgent matters".

By "urgent matters" I meant my constant waiting for the next signal for when I could see Johana again. It was not difficult to arrange our trysts because it soon emerged that Johana had a key to the apartment of a certain Colonel Helmut Ganz. She told me he was an old family friend who was then stationed with his company in Graz. So we got together whenever Johana felt like it.

I am sure you're saying to yourself that it is strange that I was enraptured by a woman much older than me, and, equally, that she was interested in such a young man. I cannot speak for Johana. She was eccentric and, as it turned out, depraved. But at that time I truly loved her, even though I knew our relationship could not last. No doubt Freud would have explained it as a form of search for my lost mother, as a kind of fixation. But I was not seeking maternal love or understanding with Johana, her attraction for me was above all physical.

And why do I say that Johana was somewhat depraved?

No, I do not have in mind sexual practices, I am referring to the fact that she enjoyed cheating on her daughter, even though she sincerely loved her!

"What if Sabina were to see us?" she would sometimes observe, for example when we were dining in bed. She would say it with a conspiratorial look on her face; she was not at all ashamed of her behaviour.

I, on the other hand, felt guilty toward Sabina. I had been well and truly trapped. If I were to bring my platonic relationship with Sabina to an end it would have definitely angered her mother. And at the same time I was afraid that if my relationship with Johana were to continue, Sabina might start to investigate why I had broken up with her.

It was a very odd situation. I must admit that on several occasions, purely out of a sense of guilt, it crossed my mind that I should start also sleeping with Sabina, but I immediately realised that she would probably tell her mother. What would be her reaction?

On the other hand I was not entirely sure that I was the only one who had a relationship with Johana. I wanted to believe it, but sometimes I would not see her for an entire week, and when I asked what she had been doing or whom she had seen in the meantime, she would give an evasive answer. Or she would tell me she had been at a concert or dining with a "family friend".

However, it didn't look as if she brought anyone else but me to the colonel's apartment. Eaten up with jealousy I would lay little traps for her, such as deliberately leaving a book on the bedside table. But the next time we met everything would be just as it had been on the previous occasion.

Once Sabina mentioned to me that her mother had not been home the night before. My throat went dry and I could think of nothing else. I knew that Sabina still had a singing lesson so I immediately set off to Johana's.

When she came to the door it was clear that it was an unpleasant surprise for her.

What was I doing here? Was I crazy? Did I want Sabina to surprise us?

I told her that Sabina was still at the Conservatory and that I had just been speaking to her.

Johana invited me in, smiling.

"So, what's up, my Paganini?"

In a voice faltering with agitation, I told her what I had learnt from Sabina. She reacted in her typical fashion.

"My Paganini is jealous. Isn't that lovely? Eighteen years old and jealous of me!"

I wanted to know where she had been.

She assured me she had been at a woman friend's. She went to a concert with her and then went home with her. The friend lived out in Nusle. They had chatted and she had then spent the night there.

She stroked my hair tenderly.

Then her eyes flashed and she said: "Well, get on with it, seeing that you're here. We don't have much time."

Johana was like that. Much later I found out that she had several lovers. She had been at her friend's, though – she also had female lovers. I was simply something to diversify her range.

But I was finding it increasingly difficult to be torn between Sabina and her mother. A few months after Johana became my mistress I renewed my dialogue with God, but this time chiefly about morality. Although I had a sense of tremendous moral failure, I was incapable of ending my relationship with Johana. Several times I tried to indicate to her that we were behaving immorally, but she only laughed.

"Immorally? But I enjoy it!"

For her, something was moral if it gave her enjoyment, however degenerate it might be. And yet her arguments always disarmed me because I enjoyed my relationship with her so much that I couldn't be without her for very long. So I begged God to forgive me, at least.

The Steiners, with whom I still lodged, were very indulgent and even respected the fact that sometimes I didn't come home at all.

One evening Eliška could not contain herself and asked me outright whether I had a girlfriend. I was about to say something vague, but she went on without waiting for my reply.

It was all right, she said. I used to be such a recluse! But I ought to take care. Did I know what she meant?

I knew very well what she meant. She had no idea how low I had sunk!

She warned me not to ruin my career because of some rash act. I was still young.

I could not help smiling to myself. There was no danger of what she feared. I would not father any child with Johana, of that I was sure. In fact the risk I faced was something quite different. And as often happens I had no inkling of what it would be.

My love affair with Johana Groffová lasted about two years. For two whole years I systematically lied to Sabina. I did not have the courage to stop deceiving her. She was not entirely naive, however and started to suspect that I was not telling the whole truth.

After all, it wasn't particularly hard to be suspicious because I would disappear several times a week, and I would reply evasively to Sabina's questions. I expect she noticed that I tended to be unavailable when her mother happened to be out. But maybe the connection did not immediately occur to her, as her mother was often not at home.

Sabina must have discovered the truth when she discovered a scrap of violin manuscript with a few words on the back in my handwriting. I had sent the note to Johana by messenger. It was to inform her that I could not come to the colonel's because I would be standing in for a sick colleague at a recital that evening.

Why had Johana kept that letter in particular? After all, it was at least a year old when Sabina stumbled across it. I don't know. Unfortunately that short text betrayed not only our relationship but also our trysting place.

Amazingly enough, Sabina did not succumb to her emotions and decided to proceed very methodically. It was her methodical approach and thoroughness that had devastating results.

It was 1914 by then and I had just completed my studies at the Conservatory. My professors all agreed that after graduation I should continue my studies at the Vienna Academy of Music. They managed to obtain funds for the stipend from various Czech associations and so it seemed certain that I would be departing for Vienna after the summer vacation.

I was pleased about it, as my personal situation would be elegantly solved thereby. Sabina decided to remain in Prague, where she had managed to find a position at a music school. However, she regarded my departure for Vienna as simply temporary. She even went as far as to hint that my return would be the moment for us to talk about marriage.

But as you know, dear Mother, events took a quite different turn. First of all Archduke Ferdinand was assassinated in Sarajevo and Austria declared war on Serbia. The European powers seemed to lose their senses, and before long two parts of Europe were at war with each other. My contemporaries were conscripted into the army en masse. It seemed that I was safe for the time being as I was a graduate of a prestigious music school and was shortly to enter another. Moreover, I was already well-known then.

Regrettably Sabina did not have the strength to confront me and her mother outright. So she decided to make use of Colonel Helmut Ganz. He too had been a lover of Johana Groffová's for many years, as I was later to discover. She had been unfaithful to him as she had to the others. She even told me she would marry him when he moved back to Prague. And perhaps she would have. After all, a well-heeled colonel would not be a bad catch.

I knew that Colonel Ganz made regular visits to Prague, because while he was there Johana and I had nowhere to meet. I did not suspect, however, that Johana was having an affair with her "old family friend" and promising him a happy future with her.

Why did Sabina never tell me anything about their relationship? I expect she too knew nothing of it and only found out about the colonel's existence when she discovered my letter.

It was most likely then that she started to investigate who the colonel was, and when she figured out that her mother was having an affair with him. Perhaps that is when she hit upon her planned revenge.

What is certain is that Sabina not only discovered the location of Colonel Ganz's Prague apartment (by following me or her mother?), she also traced his address in Graz and sent him a letter in which she divulged everything to him.

Ganz acted with forethought too. Whereas in the past he had always alerted Johana in advance about his trips to Prague and how long he would be staying, he now arrived in secret and met first with Sabina.

That day Johana and I arranged to meet at the colonel's apartment as usual. Coincidentally it was supposed to be one of our last encounters, although naturally I promised Johana that we would see each other regularly on my visits to Prague.

The colonel's arrival was perfectly timed. Johana was so sure that her husband-to-be was preoccupied with his troops on account of the incipient war, that she did not even leave the key in the lock. So the colonel was able to unlock the door with his own key and caught us very nearly in the most delicate of situations.

He was a tall, fairly good-looking man. Although he appeared severe and almost threatening in his uniform, he made no scene. In fact, he seemed to be enjoying himself in a slightly sadistic fashion. He spoke quietly, facing toward Johana, who, to my astonishment did not seem put out at first. She sat bolt upright in bed, the coverlet up to her chin, and fixed a cold and even contemptuous gaze on the colonel.

I'm unable to describe exactly what was said, as I was the one most terrified. I was incapable of taking in the conversation between the two of them and I cowardly reassured myself that the matter mostly concerned the colonel and Johana. Even though I had slightly suspected it, it nevertheless came as a shock when I heard the colonel talking about their marriage and how pleased he was that he had uncovered Johana's perfidiousness in time to avoid making a "fatal mistake".

Johana reacted to his words with scorn. She demanded that the colonel should let us get dressed, as it was undignified to discuss in this fashion.

It was chiefly Johana's behaviour that was undignified, the colonel opined. Not only was she a strumpet, she was an odd example of a strumpet. Making love to a lad who could be her son, and who also had a relationship with her own daughter.

It was immediately apparent to Johana, as it was to me, that the colonel had been talking to Sabina. Besides he confirmed the fact. He also mentioned the letter I had sent her.

Johana observed him angrily. Never before had I seen her so agitated.

It was her business whom she made love to. She did what she liked! And then she added something, which I believe, changed my life irrevocably.

"Josef's a far better lover," she said. "And I much prefer him to you."

Up to that moment the colonel's gaze had been fixed on Johana. Now, however, he turned and scrutinised me with an ironic sneer.

I heard him muttering as if to himself. "Right, I see. That's the way it is, is it?"

Maybe Johana realised that she had gone too far because a look of alarm appeared on her face.

The colonel continued gazing at me.

Eventually he said: "You're young and fit, and what's more, you're a man of action, so I hear. We're going to need you in our sorely tested army. We shall meet again, young man."

He clicked his heels, did an about-face, and left.

Johana tried in vain to stop him, almost screaming at him that I was not to blame. Let him take revenge on her, but leave me alone.

But it was too late. The colonel marched off and Johana was instantly seized with hysterics.

She started to wail: "I've ruined you, my Paganini. He'll wreak vengeance, vengeance – I know it."

I said nothing, because I still had not realised the implications of everything that had just happened.

Johana even started to sob, something else she had never before done in my presence, and between her sobs she spoke her daughter's name.

Only now did my thoughts return to Sabina. Irrespective of the fact that I had wounded her terribly, the catastrophe had yet another dimension. In the space of a few minutes I had discovered that Johana had someone else apart from me, and moreover my future was very uncertain if the colonel intended to fulfil his promise.

Without a word I slowly dressed. In fact I didn't know what to say. Johana was now crying her heart out, but I had no desire to console her. I stopped in the doorway and waved goodbye to her. She looked up and gazed into my eyes. She suddenly appeared defenceless. Even then she was beautiful and on many occasions afterward I would strive to recapture the way she looked at that moment. I never met her again.

It was also many years before I saw Sabina. I received only a letter from her. She wrote of the torment she had suffered when she discovered my note to Johana. She also related in great detail the results of her further investigations. Thus I found out that Johana had had several lovers, including women. There was no reason for me not to believe it.

Despite the efforts of the Steiners and the professors at the Conservatory who interceded in my favour, asking for my "lapse" to be pardoned as a youthful misdemeanour and for account to be taken of my outstanding talent, Colonel Ganz took his revenge on me precisely as he had said. He undoubtedly had contacts in the highest places. Not even an intercession by the Viennese academy had any effect. Even some Czech and Austrian politicians tried to prevent me being called up into the army – with equal lack of success.

And so, in September 1914, instead of Vienna, I headed for the barracks, where I was enlisted into the army. After a short period of training I left Prague for the Carpathian front somewhere on the borders of Galicia and eastern Slovakia, along with the other soldiers of the 28th regiment to which I had been assigned.

I needn't describe, dear Mother, all the snubs and taunts I came in for from the Austrian officers and even some of the Czechs, on account of being "an artist". The word soon got around why I had been enlisted and some of the Austrians in particular went out of their way to take revenge for their colleague's sullied honour. Fortunately the 28th regiment consisted largely of Czechs and many of them, as I soon discovered, had no great longing to fight for Austria-Hungary. Hence they regarded my immoral behaviour as almost an act of anti-Austrian resistance.

It was an absolutely absurd situation. After all I was one of the Czechs who believed in Austria-Hungary and had no wish for it to disintegrate! Moreover, as both you and Klára had indicated to me long before, my father was a German. Nevertheless the vengeance of an Austrian officer, who was possibly justified in punishing me, turned me into little short of a Czech hero.

In reality, my only objective was to survive and not injure my hands. I knew that if I managed to survive and return in time to my music studies, it would be possible to make up for lost time. And even if I was unable to play for a long time, no one could take from me what I was already capable of. I would be sure to find some way to continue my career.

I'm sure you remember, dear Mother, that while I was still in Prague I wrote you a letter in which I informed you that I had been enlisted, although I did not go into the details of how it had happened. To my great amazement you reacted to my letter within about two weeks – the first time since the memorable letter that you sent in reply to me at the boarding school when I was six years old!

I was expecting you to be sorry for me, because I might soon fall in battle, after all, but instead you launched into a tirade against me! You had been informed of my "degenerate behaviour," as you put it, and you reproached me for letting you down after you had placed such hopes in me. All you could do now, you said, was to trust that my imprudence would not cost me my life!

I read your letter over and over again, unable to credit the degree of your effrontery. I wanted to sit right down and write to you, and in fact I started to do so. But then I discovered that I lacked the words. I would have had to describe you my entire life, from the moment you sent me to the boarding school – all those unending days full of angst and vain hopes, my despair. How could I have managed it? Words were simply inadequate.

I wanted to ask you why I should render a moral account to you of all people, and where you found the audacity to judge me. But then I decided to say nothing. What would be the point? If you had not understood anything by that moment, then you would never understand.

I was all alone once more, just as in my early childhood. It looked as if by offending good morals I had gravely disappointed the Steiners too. I had hoped that they would at least come to say goodbye, but they did not show up when our regiment departed for the front. It looked as if the waters had suddenly closed over my past.

Naturally there was no way of me knowing that Professor Steiner and his brother had worked feverishly up to the last moment to save me and get permission to see me. But by then, the military machine had me in its power and refused to admit them within the walls of the barracks. Moreover I very soon set off for eastern Slovakia where, at the beginning of 1915, the 28th Infantry Regiment took up positions on the Carpathian front. Of course it would have helped me a lot in the subsequent years if I had known that the Steiners had a letter with the signatures of several dozen of my colleagues, in which they expressed solidarity with me in spite of the danger involved.

From the outset the Carpathian front was to play an important role in my life on several occasions. The first time was shortly after our arrival. As I was slowly dragging my enormous kitbag to the tent I shared with the soldiers of my platoon I caught sight of a familiar face. My heart almost stopped beating. Marching toward me in the uniform of an Austrian soldier was Hugo Beňáček! He was at least a head taller than me but his face had not markedly changed since the last time we saw each other.

He instantly recognised me. We stood face-to-face, unsure of how to react and then we fell into each other's arms.

Whereas Hugo was seemingly so surprised that it took him a long time to utter a single word, there suddenly welled up within me all the despondency that had gripped my soul in the previous month, and I broke into unmanly tears in front of Hugo.

This unwanted scene did not escape the attention of other soldiers. But I could not care less about their curious stares. My joy at coming upon the best friend I had ever had, in this of all places, overrode everything else.

Hugo turned out to have been serving in the God-forsaken place for several weeks already and had only recently been assigned to the 28th regiment. He had been obliged to join up almost immediately after the war broke out.

Later he would comment ironically that his father's dream had at last come true.

As I was to discover, Otto Beňáček had every reason to be proud of him. Not only had Hugo finished the commercial academy, he had also started to manage his father's sanatoria very successfully. At first he spoke rather evasively about his mother, which I put down to the fact that he had already been critical of her years before. It later turned out that Sára Beňáčková had left her husband for another man a few years previously and moved to Salzburg.

That explained why Sára had never looked me up in Prague. I had often pondered the reason. After all she was as much a music-lover as I, and would certainly have not missed the opportunity to attend one of my concerts.

We had plenty of time to chat because little happened in the first few weeks. Now and then fighting would break out with the Russians on the other side, but it was not particularly fierce, although it naturally caused casualties and loss of life. Some of the Czechs, who were already closely enough acquainted to trust each other, hinted that they would attempt to desert at the first opportunity. They simply balked at fighting their Slav brothers. They maintained that we had to contribute to the fall of Austria-Hungary, because if the Germans and Austrians were victorious, Germany would devour us all.

From time to time scouts from the other side would infiltrate our positions. They were members of the so-called Czech Battalion that had been set up in Russia by resident Czechs and deserters. We learned from them that there existed the nucleus of a Czechoslovak army whose aim was to assist the establishment of a Czech kingdom as part of the Russian Empire.

At that time I was no patriot, so talk of that kind seemed preposterous to me. I thought to myself: The Germans are an educated and cultured nation. Why couldn't we be part of Germany? It would afford us more opportunities to fulfil ourselves.

I did not speak about this openly, however, as it was not clear which of the Czechs was of like mind.

Although rumours of desertions were rife among the soldiers of our regiment, it took me a long time to make up my mind what to do. On the one hand, I hoped that the situation in Prague would be resolved somehow and I would be recalled, and on the other, I realised that I would be locking the door behind me if I deserted. I assumed that there would be no means of return should Austria-Hungary win the war. At the same time, I was afraid of receiving a wound that would prevent me from playing the violin. I told myself that if I did not soon receive a pardon from Vienna that would enable me to return to Prague, the likelihood that I would be wounded in combat would be considerable.

Almost nothing now tied me to the Czech lands apart from music and people associated with them. I had lost all my friends and had no family, because, dear Mother, I had long ceased to regard you or my father as my parents. I was sure that with my prowess as a violinist I could find my feet in Russia or anywhere else, such as America, for instance. I was thus full of doubts and was in two minds how to act.

Sometimes when we were in the trenches guarding the entanglements for hours on end, Hugo would try to persuade me that the best solution was to desert to the other side at the earliest opportunity. He had his own motives for this. He had been transferred to the 28th from another regiment on account of some anti-Semitic incident. Maybe his superiors hoped he would be better off in a regiment that was predominantly Czech. Except that anti-Jewish comments about Hugo could be heard even here.

So Hugo started to delude himself that things would be better for him on the Russian side. He didn't think that the Russians would be more tolerant toward the Jews, because after all, we had heard various things about the pogroms in Russia. But he was convinced that a lot of the harassment he had to put up with was connected with the army. I tried to prove him wrong, reminding him of our boarding school, where, apart from that one exception, he had never suffered from anti-Jewish prejudice. But Hugo would not be dissuaded.

Ever since it arrived, our regiment was regarded as a risk because it was composed primarily of Czechs. And indeed anti-Austrian sentiments were rife in it. An order was issued banning the singing of Czech songs – I had sometimes accompanied my comrades on a damaged violin that someone brought me. However, I think that the main reason for the soldiers' defiance was not so much Czech nationalism, as the Austrian commanders supposed, but poor supplies and the diseases that spread among the troops.

A rumour circulated for a long time, dear Mother, that during the Russian offensive of April 3, 1915 almost all of our regiment deserted to the other side. But later I was to meet many more who were captured by the Russians than those who had deserted. Many of the Czechs were quite simply so decimated by hunger and disease that they were incapable of withstanding the Russian attack. Many soldiers from the 28th Regiment later joined the legions, but it was not a majority.

How did I come to find myself on the other side of the lines? It was slightly against my will, actually. When the Russian offensive started on April 3, it didn't look as if the majority of Czech and Slovak soldiers were intending to fight tenaciously. I was crouching in a trench alongside Hugo while Russian bullets whistled overhead and an artillery shell burst from time to time. We had no intention of returning their fire.

Then we saw some of the soldiers to our left conferring about something. Some of them were leaving the trench and crawling forward between the entanglements and the wires. Hugo squeezed my elbow and whispered to me to stay where I was. He himself moved along the trench to the place where the soldiers had started to crawl out. He was about a hundred metres from me, but even at that distance I could see that he was engaged in a lively discussion with the soldiers. A moment later he returned and said we had to make up our minds right away. Apparently a route to the Russians had opened up to our left and the spies from the Czech Battalion maintained that the Russian troops would not fire on us.

I was paralysed with indecision, even though it was clear there was no time to lose. Hugo impatiently waved at me to come. Then there was a burst of activity to our right and it looked as if soldiers were fleeing from the trench there too. Suddenly one of the Austrian officers, Lieutenant Waldherr, emerged from the linking trench, and when he spotted what was happening, he aimed his weapon at Hugo. who was crawling out of the trench.

Hugo stood facing him, his hands above his head, while a short distance from him, as far as I could make out from my emplacement, other soldiers were crawling in the direction of the Russians. Hugo looked at me in terror. It was obvious that if the lieutenant arrested him he would be court-martialled, because no doubt, his intention was to desert. I had no choice. Although I risked being hit by enemy fire I dashed as fast as I could to the two of them. Hugo realised the danger I faced, and so when the lieutenant ordered him to lay down his weapon he threw his rifle at his feet.

When Waldherr bent down to pick it up I smashed the butt of my rifle into the nape of his neck. He fell to the ground and groaned and for a moment I was tempted to help him. I stood over him indecisively for several moments, but as soon as the officer slowly started to raise himself from the ground, Hugo yanked me toward him with full force. He was holding his own rifle and the lieutenant's. We ran a few metres to the spot where the other soldiers had disappeared, and leapt out of the trench. We crouched and fled between the entanglements, out of range of the lieutenant, out of Austria-Hungary.

I have no idea how long it took. Every now and then we would crawl, then we would run again until we eventually reached a small birch thicket. Suddenly a hulking fellow in a Russian uniform reared up from behind a tree and blocked our path. I shouted something in Czech to Hugo – I think I was asking him what we would do now, but the man in the Russian uniform displayed no sign of enmity.

He welcomed us in the purest Czech.

And while Hugo hugged his compatriot, who looked just like a Russian muzhik who had not washed for a month, I sat down in the grass and the tears streamed from my eyes.

So it's final, I said to myself. I can't go back now. I'm a deserter.

The Russian side of the front was in a state of total confusion and hardship. The most important thing for me was that I had managed to stay with Hugo, my only support.

First of all, we were interrogated at the camp by Russian officers, assisted by Czech interpreters. They chiefly wanted to find out whether we had deserted to their side with the intention of fighting against Austria-Hungary, or whether we had been taken prisoner against our will.

There were some who had no intention of fighting on any side. They were sent after a while to prisoner-of-war camps somewhere in Asia. I must admit I was tempted to declare myself a prisoner of war, because fighting on the Russian side meant not only risking injury or death for a cause whose meaningfulness I somewhat doubted, but also confirming for good my status as a deserter.

I finally decided to enrol with those who had decided to fight on the Russian side. My reasons were threefold. The first was Lieutenant

Waldherr, who, as Hugo informed me, would certainly report to his superiors that I had knocked him out. The second reason was the hope that as a soldier fighting with other Czechs for the Russians I would enjoy more freedom than as a prisoner of war. Hugo and I had noticed that the members of the Czech Battalion, which consisted partly of old Czech settlers – predominantly from the Volyn province – and partly of earlier deserters, enjoyed a fairly free regime. The third reason was Hugo himself. I wanted to stay with him at all costs. I expect you're saying to yourself, dear Mother, that my motives were base and not those of a patriot. Yes, I admit that was indeed the case in those days. I was not at all prepared for such a situation. After all, I had spent six years in intensive study of music alone, convinced that one day I would became a famous violinist. But we also had had love and reverence of the Hapsburg monarchy drummed into us at boarding school. And when it comes down to it not even the Steiners were patriots to speak of. Like me they were proud of Czech musicians, but they lived in cosmopolitan surroundings, since music is a universal medium.

Admittedly the Conservatory was mostly a Czech milieu, but the music world in Prague was very much influenced by the German population. Moreover, many of the books and other teaching materials were written in German. In addition, I admired German culture. After all, many of the greatest composers and musicians were Germans or Austrians.

So I'm sure you'll appreciate that I was not naturally disposed to patriotic emotions. I was not brought up a patriot in my childhood. So I became a Czech patriot only gradually, even after I deserted.

I was greatly influenced by the national fervour of the soldiers, who were proud of their nation and would not have hesitated to lay down their lives in the struggle against the Habsburgs. What had an even greater effect on me later was the news that Professor Masaryk was organizing the establishment of a Czech state. I would often think of Klára in those days. What would her inclination have been?

The period between Hugo's and my desertion and the battle at Zborov, which was another watershed in my life, was connected with a story that was much more important than my growing patriotism. It centred on a girl named Ester. I got to know her at the beginning of 1916.

At that time we were encamped just outside Borispol, which was not far from Kiev, the Ukrainian capital. I say encamped, but you must not imagine that there was a barracks. The troops lived in huts located here and there in the surrounding villages and assisted the local peasants with their farms or lived in a temporary camp. A Czechoslovak Brigade was soon to be officially established and some of the Czechs were feverishly working to bring it into existence.

Hugo and I made the acquaintance of Lieutenant Čeček, who was to become our commander. He was interested in music, so he knew a bit about my case, although he never suspected that he would find me among the deserters. So he asked me about the circumstances that had caused me to end up here. Finally he asked me whether I was interested in setting up a military band. I disappointed him somewhat when I explained that it would not be the sort of setting in which a violinist might exercise his skills, besides which I did not have the requisite education or experience to be a conductor.

A few days later, however, the lieutenant came with a new idea that caught my imagination. He suggested that I should become a member of a string quartet based in Kiev, which performed for front-line troops in particular. So once more fate smiled on me in an odd fashion. Just as I had once received a helping hand from Josef Steiner, so now again I was aided by someone who believed I deserved it on account of my musical talent. Although it took some while for Čeček to obtain the necessary permission from the Russians for me to move around freely and travel to Kiev for rehearsals, he eventually achieved it in February of 1916. The other members of the quartet received me in a gloomy building on the outskirts of the city, which I reached after riding for two hours on a horse-drawn cart belonging to one of the army supply units. The eldest of the three was Viktor Fedotyenko, the first violin, who made no impression on me at first. At his side was a slim man with a blond mop of hair and a piercing gaze – the cellist Vasily Lapityev. And behind them stood Ester Kaminska, a beautiful girl about twenty years old, whose pale face was framed by black curly hair. She was holding a viola.

At that very moment I knew I would fall in love with Ester. She remained silent during my conversation with the two men as if not wanting to interrupt them out of respect. However, I was soon obliged to call on her assistance, as my knowledge of Ukrainian and Russian was then still meagre. And Viktor and Vasily did not understand my Czech.

They also had difficulty with German, but fortunately Ester spoke Yiddish, which is archaic German. I was delighted she became our interpreter, because from the outset I had taken a liking to her rich alto voice.

They told me that the second violinist had recently died of tuberculosis, and when Viktor had started looking for a replacement, the news reached him that Josef Brehme was among the Czech troops. He said he had heard about my talent before the war from a colleague who had lived in Prague. I was flattered, of course, but warned Viktor that I had no experience of playing in a quartet, since I had been preparing for a solo career.

When we started rehearsing it became obvious that playing in the quartet would be no great problem for me, and after two rehearsals it seemed as if I had always been a member of the quartet. I was extremely gratified that they lent me a better violin on which to practice when I wasn't with the quartet, and thus I was able to rehearse more demanding pieces from the solo repertoire. That helped buoy up my faint hope that I would be able to return to my career as a solo violinist after the war. It was important to me that I could once more make music, and above all I was happy that I would be seeing Ester on a regular basis.

My regime was fairly relaxed. Admittedly, I had to report regularly, either in our encampment beyond Borispol or at the local Russian army headquarters in Kiev, but otherwise no one restricted my movement. When we set off for our first concert, which took place not far from Zhitomir, the Russian military headquarters issued me with some kind of pass that entitled me to leave Kiev.

The quartet's repertoire was not particularly demanding. After all, we were playing for soldiers who were unfamiliar with classical music, but after the rehearsals we would sometimes play more challenging pieces for our own benefit. Viktor and Vasily were both competent musicians, although they had clearly not received the best musical education. Notwithstanding, I made no attempt to take over from Viktor as first violin, because the quartet was above all his creation. Anyway, he knew very well that Ester was a better musician than he. She had studied viola at the Kiev Conservatory and was one of the first women to graduate.

Many times I tried to get to know her better, but she would always resist my suggestions that we go for a walk after a rehearsal or concert. She usually told me she needed to be home early. Later, when she realised I was hopelessly in love with her, she would sit with me for a while after the rehearsal, but she permitted me only to hold her hand.

Viktor and Vasily both noticed that I was courting Ester but they decided to ignore it. And then one day toward the end of 1916, Viktor took me to one side and informed me in Ukrainian, which I had learnt to understand more or less in the meantime, that Ester came from a very conservative family, and he explained that her father, a well-known rabbi, would never allow his daughter to enter into a relationship with a "goy".

In the end I confided in Hugo my unsuccessful attempts to get closer to Ester.

He urged me to take into account that everything here was different. In order to survive at all in these villages, the Jews were obliged to adhere to their customs and live as if in a ghetto. It was their defence. Hugo had read somewhere that there had been dozens and even hundreds of pogroms here.

At the first opportunity I asked Ester if that really was the only reason she rebuffed me, and I opened my heart to her. I confessed that she had bewitched me from the very first moment, that I loved her voice, the way she expressed herself, her playing. And that I found her exceedingly beautiful.

I was surprised at myself, because while I had been in Prague I tended to be shy in the company of girls. After all, the affair with

Johana had been orchestrated by her.

Ester said nothing. And then at last she told me that she was touched by my profession of love but said she would have to reflect on it all. When I asked her what her family would say about our relationship, she gave no reply.

I started to toy with the idea of leaving the quartet should Ester reject me. I suffered unbearable torment. Except that, as usual, dear Mother, events took a totally unexpected turn.

The turning point came when Hugo also obtained travel privileges after Viktor and I had interceded on his behalf. Ever since hearing my stories about it, he had had an enormous longing to visit Kiev, at least, from time to time. And since he had a diploma from the commercial academy and had even acquired practical experience under his father's guidance, our superiors entrusted him to help the quartet with organizational matters.

What happened next, however, I had not anticipated in the least. When I introduced Hugo to Ester, he looked her over with a certain wariness, as if checking whether I had given him a truthful description, whereas from the outset Ester treated him much more cordially than she had me. I put it down to the fact that she felt more at ease chatting to a young Jew, and this thought put my mind at rest for a few days.

Soon, though, I discovered that she had a real interest in Hugo. And worse still, Hugo started to court her openly. He was obviously captivated and even fascinated by her. It didn't surprise me; after all I too found her exceptional, but when, a few days later, he informed me that that Ester had asked him to see her home and he requested me to wait for him in the building where our quartet rehearsed before going back to the encampment, I was seized by an uncontrollable spite.

I did wait for Hugo, but when he returned I tore into him with fury. It was the first time we had ever quarrelled and I was overwhelmed with sorrow as a result. Hugo did not react aggressively, but simply explained that he too had fallen in love with Ester, and he even asked my forgiveness.

But I was in a belligerent mood. I could not bear the thought that

Ester, that brilliant musician, should prefer a businessman to me. I accused Hugo of planning it all and of craftily worming his way into her affections.

He took offence and said nothing to me the whole way to Borispol. Later he came to see me and announced that he would try to behave with more restraint toward Ester in the interest of our friendship.

If you think, dear Mother, as you read these lines, that I behaved foolishly, you are right. I ought to have known that Ester would have the final word that she was the one to say which of us she wanted, not to mention that it was quite obvious by then that her heart belonged to Hugo. And that was confirmed during our next trip to Kiev. The two of them disappeared immediately after the rehearsal without a word of explanation, and Hugo did not return to camp until the next morning.

He looked very happy, in spite of my reproaches. When I asked where he had been, he retorted that he had seen Ester home. But when I insisted, he told me the whole – for me painful – truth. They had spent the night in the room where our quartet rehearsed. They had apparently returned after the rest of us had left and hidden from the night watchman, who made the rounds of the building before locking up.

I preferred not to enquire further. It was obvious that out of love for Hugo Ester had violated all the restrictions that her faith and her family imposed on her, or she was not as conservative as she had told me. In either case I felt deceived.

For several weeks, I was incapable of communicating with Hugo. The tension between Ester and me was even greater. I reproached her for her behaviour, even though she had never given me any grounds for hope. She also stopped talking to me, which was naturally detrimental to the atmosphere in the quartet.

I confided in Viktor, hoping that he would be on my side, but surprisingly he tended to exonerate Hugo. In fact he told me what I didn't want to hear – that the heart rules the head.

The year 1917 arrived and there was tension in the air. Russia was radicalised and one increasingly came across Bolshevik agitators in the Ukraine too. They would explain to the soldiers and civilians that there was a need for radical transformation of social conditions and the establishment of total equality for all. They maintained that the best solution for Russia was ending the state of war and concentrating on its own problems.

Hugo and I were back on speaking terms, but our conversation never went beyond what was absolutely necessary. He was very dejected at that time, no doubt mainly because the military commanders had banned him from travelling to Kiev on account of his day's absence without leave. So it came as an enormous surprise when one day I caught sight of Ester not far from our camp and shortly afterward, Hugo in her embrace!

I was seized by bitter resentment but there was nothing I could do. Thereafter, they met regularly during the spring of 1917.

Meanwhile Kerensky's government had taken power in Russia. And because it was more favourable toward Czech demands for the creation of a Czech army in Russia, a Czechoslovak Brigade was soon established, with two regiments in battle readiness. Hugo and I were assigned to the First Battalion of the First Regiment under the command of our own Lieutenant Čeček. The brigade command and other leading posts were held by Russian officers for the time being.

As our regiment was preparing for battle, it was harder to make regular trips to Kiev, but we continued to give our concerts as usual in spite of the difficulties. After one of them, Ester once more left with Hugo. As on the previous occasion, Hugo did not get back by evening and was missing for several days, which earned him an official reprimand.

Around that time the Czechoslovak Brigade received orders to relocate to the town of Sarny. The Czech volunteers, hitherto in scattered groups, had been redeployed there from various parts of the Ukraine. A few days later the troops started to advance toward the small town of Jezerna, and then took up position on a section of the front line near Zborov. I might have been able to avoid that advance and stay in Kiev, but I could not put up with it all any more. I didn't tell Viktor the truth, however. I explained to him that I had to leave for the front and told him that I would of course return to the quartet, if it were possible.

When I was taking my uneasy leave of Ester, she suddenly fell into my arms and kissed me on the cheek. I was not to be angry with her, she said. It couldn't be helped.

And then, in a voice full of anxiety, she begged me to keep any eye on Hugo. Maybe I wasn't aware of it, but Hugo loved me as a brother. Perhaps I didn't even realise how distressed he was about what had happened between us.

I must admit that I returned to the regiment with a sense of overwhelming sadness. After all, I had known deep down from the outset that Hugo was in the right, not I, that I had never had any justified claim on Ester. And that I had been behaving stupidly over the previous months. I therefore determined to apologise to Hugo – except that he was not at camp when I arrived. He had been dispatched with the pioneers to Zborov to prepare the way for us.

I didn't even meet him when we arrived in Zborov. The commanders must have realised that his physical prowess fitted him for operations with the pioneers close to enemy lines. After our deployment to Zborov, I set to work with the rest building an intricate network of trenches and entanglements. We were often obliged to flee from bombardments by the Austro-Hungarian army and a good number of our soldiers died as a result, even before the battle itself.

The battle commenced early in the morning on July 2. As the Russian artillery cannonades roared over our heads, we waited in the trenches for the order to attack, while our machine guns and artillery fired salvo after salvo. About four hours later, around nine, the order finally came. Everywhere there was acrid smoke and a deafening racket and I resigned myself to my likely death.

When the order to attack was given I joined one of the many small groups into which the soldiers were divided. That tactic, which differed from the usual military practice, allowed us great mobility, to which the Austrians were unable to react even though they were better armed. In less than an hour, during which we saw many of our friends and enemy soldiers die in indescribable agony, we captured the first enemy line. We were helped by the fact that on the other side Czech soldiers were deserting en masse. In the hours that followed we captured three more enemy lines and achieved that famous victory. Amazingly I didn't suffer even a scratch.

I was then given the task, along with another soldier from my platoon, to return with a group of Czech prisoners and collect the wounded on the way. Having laboured my way with them through the tangled mass of smashed defences and barbed wire and the craters left by exploded shells, I caught sight of Hugo! He was sitting with his back against a wooden stake, the top of which had been torn off by an explosion. His face wore a strange glazed expression, but he was still alive. What had happened, for God's sake?

I shouted out his name while I was still a good way from him and started running toward him. I could see he was pleased that I was there.

I knelt down by him to see where he was wounded. He was gripping his stomach with both arms and the bottom of his uniform was blood-soaked.

It was a grenade, he said oddly, as if trying hard to smile. Goodness knows where it came from – it exploded over there. He pointed in the direction of the crater.

I suddenly realised how afraid I was for his life. I couldn't keep back my tears, but even so, I tried to comfort him. Two of the deserters who were crouching nearby helped me carry him to the field hospital. I explained to them in a rambling way that Hugo was my best friend, the only one I'd ever had, in fact. I could see sadness in their eyes but I don't know whether they were sad on account of Hugo. After all, they too might have just lost their best friends on the other side of the lines.

The surgeon at the hospital ripped open Hugo's uniform and tried to staunch the blood, while I sat by Hugo, holding his hand. I knew I had to tell him everything that I would not be able to say again. He was obviously dying. This was evident from the behaviour of the field surgeon, who would dash over now and then to the soldiers groaning alongside whom possibly still had a chance of survival.

I told Hugo that I had met Ester before I left. She was thinking of him. I was to give him her heartfelt regards.

His expression brightened slightly although he must have been in great suffering; blood trickled constantly from the exposed wound.

I wanted to beg his forgiveness for my foolish behaviour but I was choked up with anguish and sorrow.

But then I felt Hugo squeeze my hand. I looked into his eyes. He seemed to be trying to draw me nearer to confide something in me. I placed my ear close to his lips.

Did I recall, he whispered in a hoarse voice, how he and Ester had disappeared?

I nodded.

He was in her village. They were engaged and would be married. I was his closest friend: I'd be his best man wouldn't I?

I tried to hold back my tears. I didn't want to alarm Hugo with the obvious reality of which he was yet unaware.

He smiled and went on squeezing my hand. That faint smile was still on his lips when, within barely a minute of asking me the question, he departed this life.

That is my memory of the glorious victory at Zborov, Mother. They say that our heroic deeds laid the foundations of Czechoslovak statehood, and that it was there that the glory and authority of the legions were born. But for me, Zborov will remain the most dreadful place I know. There they buried my friend, who had helped me survive the unbearable childhood that your selfishness and weakness had prepared for me.

The next day, there occurred what is probably the oddest thing I have ever experienced. I spent the night that followed Hugo's death in a dreadful mental state. I was haunted by terrifying dreams. I was tempted to put an end to everything. I reproached myself for having treated him unjustly, and I also pitied myself. I was now cut off from everyone and everything I had known before I was enlisted.

I could not rid myself of the sight of the dying Hugo, nor of the soldiers whose corpses littered the battlefield at Zborov. Memories of our first acquaintance, of his friendship at the time of my greatest hardship, and of our vacations together came back to me. I reproached myself for not finding the time to seek him out after leaving for the Conservatory. And I also agonised over how I was to break the news of Hugo's death to Ester.

Early next morning, before daybreak, I left the trenches where many of the soldiers had spent the night after the victorious battle, and set off to find the temporary morgue, thinking that I would find Hugo's body there. I am not really sure why I wanted to, all I know is that in the gloom I lost my way among the trenches and entanglements and wandered away from the line of battle. Deep in thought, I stopped by some trees surrounding a large rock in the middle of a field. I suddenly had a sense of something strange.

It is impossible to describe precisely. It was apprehension mingled with a strange, almost joyful excitement. On the rock I caught sight of some kind of translucent figure, whose face, if it had one, was hidden within a mane of hair. I have no idea why I thought the figure was that of a woman.

I assumed that it was simply another of my nocturnal hallucinations and nightmares, though I knew I was not asleep. Although the figure had no mouth it started to speak to me. I could hear no voice and yet I understood its words. And for some reason I knew its name: Ariel.

I fell to my knees in fear. My whole body shook.

The angel, for I believe it was an angel standing on that rock, told me he had some news for me:

I would endure much suffering and also meet with great adventures. A new era was coming that would be more terrible than anything I could ever imagine. But in the end I would find happiness, but happiness quite different from the one I had dreamt of.

I would meet the angel once more in my life but he would not address me again. After Ariel appeared for the second time I was to sit down and write a testimony to my life. He could not tell me in whom I would confide, but I would be able to tell when I saw him again.

The apparition remained standing a few more moments on top of the rock, but it said nothing more. I was so awestruck that I could not even open my mouth to ask about Hugo. I am not even sure what I wanted to hear: after all, Hugo was dead.

The figure started to dissolve, and before it disappeared seemed to wave to me in response to my unuttered query. A sense of peace, a strange kind of bliss, almost, overwhelmed me. As if the angel had told me that Hugo was all right.

I'm fully aware, Mother, that it will occur to you that I might have lost my reason as a result of Hugo's death. I never ruled it out – after all I truly was in a dreadful state of mind. Nevertheless the image of the angel remained with me throughout the years that followed and helped me survive. Without Ariel's promise that I would eventually find happiness, I would have died for sure.

A few days ago the angel appeared to me once more. And as he said that time at Zborov, he no longer spoke. But I saw him distinctly at the side of our marriage bed where my wife sleeps. He stood there and I was once more incapable of opening my mouth to ask who he was. He again dissolved like vapour and before he disappeared he motioned to me as he had then, and again I was overwhelmed with a strange feeling of peace.

This time I was not terrified. On the contrary I was pleased that the prophecy had been fulfilled, although I have no idea what it means. I cannot rule out that this time too it was just a dream. It could have been the effect of tension, because we are expecting my wife to give birth to twins. Nevertheless I consider that I should not conceal Ariel's revelation from you, even if it is only the fruit of my imagination.

For many years I have racked my brains over what Ariel meant when he said that I would know to whom I were to write the letter about my life. It never occurred to me, Mother, that in the end I would write it to you. I had long ago given you up for lost. However, by a strange coincidence I found out about your fatal illness just before

Ariel appeared to me the second time, and said to myself that this was maybe a sign.

It has often occurred to me that Ariel is a symbol of how little we people have any control over the course of our lives. Perhaps, whether he really exists or is just a figment of my imagination, he is trying to tell me that I am not to be proud: that happiness might be someone quite different from what I dreamt about in my pride.

Whatever is the truth about Ariel, his prophesy started to come true several months after the Battle of Zborov. In Russia the Bolsheviks, whose agitators had been active amongst us earlier, had now come to power, and that totally altered our situation. Although the Ukraine had already declared independence in June 1917, the events in Russia had an immediate impact on us. Whereas the expanding Czechoslovak brigades had fairly good relations with the Kerensky government, co-operation with the Reds was tricky. Moreover the Russians cancelled the Brest-Litovsk peace signed with the Quadruple Alliance bringing about the collapse of the Eastern Front, where so many of my comrades, including Hugo, had lost their lives.

Although more and more soldiers were joining us, allowing the establishment of the First and then the Second Czechoslovak Division, the Czechoslovak units were obliged to withdraw eastward. They were driven back by the advancing Germans and Austrians, whose armies conquered an extensive territory without any major battles.

Before those events, in the autumn of 1917 I had been given permission to visit Kiev, where I managed to find Viktor, who informed me that after my departure the quartet had disbanded and that he had had no news of Ester for several weeks. However, he told me the name of the village she was from and I immediately set off for it.

It was a smallish *shtetl*, as the Jewish settlements were known in Yiddish. It was not hard to find Ester, as everyone there knew Rabbi Kaminsky.

I don't intend to describe to you, Mother, the dreadful scene when I told Ester about Hugo's death. Suffice it to say that she fell to the ground like a stone, and when I eventually managed to raise her, we wept for long time in each other's arms.

Then we sat on the steps in front of their house, because she did not have the strength to walk up them. There, on those stairs, Ester confessed to me that she was pregnant. I was at first overwhelmed by the thought that Hugo would never learn this joyful news. But suddenly I felt a kind of satisfaction for the first time since his death. Something of him had remained after all!

When Ester calmed down slightly after a long afternoon, she seemed to be even slightly content in her misfortune to be bearing Hugo's offspring, however she burst into tears again and again. She was forlorn that her child would never know its father.

She introduced me to her father, who scrutinised me searchingly for a long time. I begged him not be angry with Hugo and Ester, because a love such as theirs was something rare. Perhaps it all had to turn out that way, I added.

The rabbi replied that everything in this world was to some purpose. No doubt the meaning of their union would be made clear one day.

I wanted to know what he meant by it, but he simply said nothing for a long time.

"Thanks to you they became acquainted," he said eventually, "and so it's possible that thanks to Ester something tremendous will happen to you."

Rabbi Kaminski was a mystic, as Ester had once told me. He exuded a strange power and I could not resist describing to him what I had experienced on the night after Hugo's death. I admitted to him, just as I did to you in this letter, Mother, that it could have been a mere figment of my sick mind.

But the rabbi saw something else in that vision. He grasped my head in his hands and kissed me on the forehead.

"To be chosen," he said at last, "can bring great happiness or great suffering, but usually both."

As I took my leave, I promised to visit Ester and her father again. I was able to keep my word when the Czechoslovak Corps, as our units were later called, retreated eastwards. But it seemed that there was to be no end to our disasters.

At that time independent Ukraine was headed by Symon Petliura, whose people were known, among other things, for their anti-Semitic sentiments. They declared that many of the leading Bolsheviks were being recruited straight from the Jewish settlements and ghettoes. They were right about that, of course, but they refused to see that the reasons for that situation were to be found in the dreadful poverty that reigned in most of the *shtetls*, which led to the radicalization of many young Jews. For the anti-Semites, who connected the strong representation of Jewish intellectuals and revolutionaries in the Bolshevik movement with the existence of Judaism per se, the solution was to organise pogroms.

I recall this because when I visited Ester's home village I found not a single living soul. All the cottages had been burnt down and the people from the neighbouring villages assured me that no one had survived.

I went on systematically searching for Ester and her father until our troops were finally forced to retreat beyond the Volga, but in vain. I blamed myself to a certain extent for their disappearance. I felt that I was somehow connected with some fatal misfortune that particularly afflicted those I loved.

I was seized with deep despair. Besides, the situation even looked hopeless for the Czechoslovak units. It is true that Masaryk was negotiating with the Bolshevik government about our gradual redeployment eastwards as far as Vladivostok, from whence we would be shipped back to Europe to join the legions on the western front, but in a Russia that was in the throes off chaos and civil war, the Czechoslovak Corps became a sought-after ally. Compared to the Russian army, we were better equipped and trained. By that time our units already numbered tens of thousands of men.

The plan for our redeployment seemed clear, but at that time we had no inkling of the obstacle we would have to overcome. The Reds were trying to prevent us from using the Trans-Siberian Railway, so our units were obliged to resort to force to do so. It was an almost superhuman task, because nobody who has not travelled through Russia can imagine how big and treacherous that country is.

For some time, our commanders hesitated between concentrating the efforts of the Czechoslovak Corps on making a withdrawal or, on the contrary, establishing new fronts along the Volga. It was only when it turned out that we would not be receiving the requisite support from the French, Americans or Japanese, whose advance across Russia from the east had been halted somewhere near Lake Baikal, that the decision was finally taken that all the Czechoslovak troops would withdraw.

I, my dear Mother, was supposed to take part with my unit in defending the railway near Chelyabinsk. We were sent east in the spring of 1918. It was immediately after the idea of redeploying the Czechoslovak Corps in Europe had carried the day. As a result of that decision, all the Russian commanders left us, so it was necessary to train a new command in which Czechs were in the majority. Nevertheless, even afterward a section of our troops fought for some time along the Volga, and near Kazan and Tsaritsyn.

News of those battles reached us with delay because our journey through that incredibly vast land caused us to be totally isolated. Unless you have been there, it is very hard to envisage the endless horizon, the emptiness of the plain, or the poverty and backwardness of the Russian villages. It was a totally different world from the one in which I had spent several years of my life in Prague. There was nothing there, just infinite emptiness! It was hard to maintain the hope that there was something else somewhere beyond it, that there was any possibility of escaping it!

I was racked at that time with thoughts of the utter futility of everything. After Hugo's death and Ester's disappearance there was a gaping emptiness in my soul that resembled the Russian horizon. I was utterly lost in a world where there seemed to be no end and which lacked any kind of order. I had seen so many people die during the battles and my journeying through Russia that I began to wonder about God's intentions. It seemed improbable to me that God could be so vain and profligate as to allow such a waste of human lives. After all, every human being, even the most primitive, was an extremely complex organism that was a manifestation of everything its parents and society had invested in it. Each of us was an abundant repository of emotions, ideas, hopes, passions, sorrow and humour. Could all this be so insignificant to God that He could look on while millions of human lives were destroyed in wars as senseless as the one I was fighting in?

I do not like to contemplate it but I am sure I have human lives on my conscience. I had to shoot in order to survive. I was never close enough to the soldiers on the other side to declare with certainty that it was my bullet that caused someone's death. But I fired. And not just into the air.

Many a time I asked myself whether I had the right to. After all, that too could be a test on God's part. Why did I have such an ob-stinate attachment to my mortal existence, which had so far brought me mostly torment? And why was I willing to kill others in order to survive? After all I cannot delude myself that I fired my weapon in the name of some higher idea.

When the war was over many talked about us as the heroes who had fought for Czechoslovakia. But I don't know what I was actually fighting for. Most of all, I expect, in order to return to my career of solo violinist. Perhaps I was also driven by an instinct of self-preservation. But what if overcoming that instinct at moments when we are deciding whether to kill someone else in order to survive is not the biggest test that God sets us? But I just cannot grasp, Mother, why God would want to set us such a test. Even at that time I could not grasp it.

Had I not been fortified by the miraculous encounter with Ariel, which prevented me from rejecting my faith in God, I don't know how I would have come out of it all. Another help was my old violin that I would play in the evening to my comrades in our temporary billets.

After a journey fraught with adversity, my unit met up with the other legionary battalions near Chelyabinsk. That was also where we had our first battle with the Red Guards, provoked by a group of Hungarian soldiers who had just been released and became caught up between them and us. The Bolsheviks endeavoured to disarm the Czechoslovak units, for one reason because of their assistance to the White Army and for another, because they wanted our weapons.

At first the battles were not as strenuous as later when the power of the Reds increased. Nevertheless several of my fellow combatants lost their lives, and during the "Chelyabinsk incident," which is now written about in the history books, I received a bullet wound in my side. Within a few days we had occupied the whole of Chelyabinsk.

Because I had taken part at the Battle of Zborov I was regarded as a hardened soldier, even though I was only twenty-three at the time. Consequently, at Chelyabinsk I was assigned to assist with setting up the Czechoslovak cavalry regiment named after Jan Jiskra of Brandýs, which was officially established almost exactly a year after Zborov.

There is probably little point, Mother, describing to you in detail all our displacements or our skirmishes with the Red Guards. But maybe it would interest you to know that in July 1918 some of my comrades-in-arms took part in the legions' expedition to Yekaterinburg, where the Bolsheviks held the Czar and his family captive. There has been frequent speculation since about why they failed to save them, and they have even been accused of being the possible cause of their deaths, because the Bolsheviks executed the Czar's family in the house of Ipatyeyov after hearing that the Czech legions were approaching.

I did not take part in that expedition, thank goodness. I would not have liked to witness what my comrades are said to have seen in the house of Ipatyeyov. However, I would have liked to have been in Yekaterinburg somewhat later, because the composer Rudolf Karel, who happened to have been on holiday there when the war broke out, later joined the legions, and at the beginning of 1919 he founded the Symphony Orchestra of the Czechoslovak Legions in Russia.

A number of orchestras had already been created in Russia, but I was never near enough to any of them and their standard was never high enough to make it worth my while to travel to see them.

However, I would have considered it a great honour to play under the baton of Rudolf Karel, except that in the summer of 1918 the newly created Central Command of the Czechoslovak Corps ordered me to Omsk which the legions had already taken in March.

In Omsk it was necessary to pave the way for the creation of the Czechoslovak Reserve Regiment, whose chief aim was to ensure the training of new members of the legions. Some of us then joined the guard detachments around the Trans-Siberian railroad. Not only were we supposed to protect it, we also had to ensure the eastward transit of the legions. Some of them lived in Omsk itself, in the buildings around the station, others were billeted in cars with stoves that we called *teplushky,* using the Russian expression.

I was dispatched a bit further east, to Kormilovka. I spent over a year with five other legionaries guarding the section of the railroad between Omsk and the small town of Kalachinsk, a territory about a hundred kilometres in length. We lived in a wooden building adjacent to the station, from which we could observe movements on the railroad. We used a locomotive drawing an armoured car to travel up and down the railroad. Sometimes we went as far as Omsk, where the high command had its headquarters, or we travelled east to Kalachinsk.

Kormilovka was a typical Siberian settlement, in which you would be hard pressed to find anything pretty. The houses were scattered here and there without any apparent plan. Some of them were hidden among trees, mostly birches. The countryside there tends to be nondescript. The major feature is the River Irtish, which flows through Omsk before joining up with the River Ob. Another river flowing past Kormilovka is the Om, which helped create the bogs in the surrounding steppes, which are the source of enormous swarms of mosquitoes. I expect the only reason we managed to endure the misery they caused, was the fact the summer was so brief. The Siberian winter started some time in October, and the temperature between December and February regularly dropped to as much as thirty degrees below freezing.

The steppes there bear poetical names: Barabinskaya, Vasyuganskaya, Kulundskaya. In those endless steppes the rivers turn into bogs in places, because there is no gradient. In the spring and fall the soil of the steppe is so waterlogged that it is impossible to travel along and the only accessible route is the Trans-Siberian railroad.

The little unit I was entrusted to command comprised the Czechs

Karel Frolík, Mojmír Šimáček and Václav Šťastný, and the Slovaks Miro Kuba and Ján Velko. Karel, a skilled blacksmith, came from České Budějovice, the city where you were living, Mother. Before the war he was an ironmonger, so we put him in charge of repairing weapons and railroad locomotive parts, as well as manufacturing various implements.

Mojmír and Václav, both big, strong fellows, were peasants from Jičín. Václav, who had been accustomed to getting plenty to eat before the war, was always hungry. He was outstandingly talented at acquiring food, from which we all greatly benefited. Miro and Janko had known each other before the war. They were both from Bánská Bystrica, where they had been forestry workers, and they had remained bosom friends in Siberia too.

Karel was the only one of them to have fought at Zborov on the Russian side like me, while Miro and Janko had let themselves be captured by Czechoslovak units and Mojmír and Václav had deserted to the Czechoslovak Corps only later.

It was my great good fortune, mother, not only to acquire five devoted friends in those five men, but also to come by a good violin once more. It was lent me along with a collection of scores, which I would voraciously play through in my free time, by the headmaster of the local school, Ivan Fedotov.

Our sojourn at Kormilovka was far from tranquil. On several occasions we were obliged to repel small bands of Reds who would attack our train, and we also fought with various bands who had no political affiliation. There was widespread hunger and so our units, which were well provisioned by Russian standards, were a frequent target for marauders.

As the Czechs possessed skills unknown in Russia, they established their own economy. Some units of the legions cultivated grain and raised domestic animals, while others worked as butchers. We even had our own workshops for repairing the trains and weapons, as well as a well-developed system of distribution.

Admiral Kolchak, the supreme commander of the White Army, who proclaimed himself sole ruler of Russia, had his headquarters in Omsk.

For a while we worked well with him, except that the White Army comprised all sorts of people, including storm troops who used the chaos to sow violence and needless bloodshed. We therefore had to be cautious at all times and constantly reassure ourselves that our superiors were not swindlers or common criminals.

It is hard to describe to anyone who was not in Russia in those days what dreadful chaos reigned there. Straight after the Battle of Zborov, when our units withdrew into the Russian hinterland, we were witnesses to unbelievable cruelty and mayhem. Then, after the Russian Revolution the Reds and the Whites confronted each other, and we often found ourselves in the midst of their skirmishes.

We were to witness similar pillage later as we advanced into the heart of Russia. During our redeployment to Chelyabinsk we frequently came across entirely plundered villages, irrespective of whether Communist agitators were operating there or whether they were under the control of the Whites. For most of the locals, Petrograd was too remote and they had no idea at all what the fighting in Russia was about.

Within several months the country's entire structure collapsed. It was obvious that power in Russia would be taken by anyone who filled that vacuum. The destitute people we encountered everywhere were waiting for a saviour. Perhaps that explains why every kind of religious sect promising salvation thrived in that omnipresent confusion.

Shortly after our arrival, Kormilovka was attacked by one of the wandering bands that proclaimed allegiance to Kolchak but in reality had nothing in common with the Whites. The band first terrorised the local population, but later their leaders started to hanker after our equipment and weapons, particularly the machine guns. Although we were better trained, we were few in number.

We managed to hold off their onslaught for several hours. I had stayed with Karel Frolík in our building by the station, while the two Slovaks were firing a machine gun from the armoured car at anyone who tried to come near. Mojmír and Václav had barricaded themselves in another building from whence they could snipe at the railroad embankment, behind which several bandits were crouched, but they did not have a good view in our direction, so they could not help us.

When it was beginning to look as if the attackers would withdraw empty-handed, a few of them finally did manage to make a dash and hide from the machine-gun fire behind our building. We knew they would not find it easy to break in, but then we smelled smoke.

Because we could not tell whether they were trying to drive us out with the smoke, or were trying to set fire to the building, Karel went down to see. I heard him go downstairs and then there was silence.

Suddenly I heard an enormous racket coming from the entrance to the building. Karel had apparently smashed open the door and started to shoot. Someone yelled something in Russian – most likely he had been hit by a bullet, and his comrades opened fire. Pandemonium broke out, because suddenly the machine gun started to rattle from our armoured railroad car.

A few minutes later, as if someone gave a command, all firing ceased. I took a look out of the window to try to find out what the situation was, but I could not see Karel or any of the attackers. The smoke was thicker and I started to be anxious about what lay in store for us. Then I heard Karel's voice calling for help.

I ran to him straight away. His right foot was bleeding. He could not crawl to safety because he was jammed in the banisters of the steps leading down to the front door. He must have fallen so awkwardly after he was hit that he broke the leg that had not been wounded.

There seemed to be no one outside the building. To my right I caught sight of two attackers dragging their wounded comrade away. So I went out warily, gripped Karel under the armpits, and pulled him upstairs with every ounce of strength I had.

But then I made some bad mistakes. I went out to reassure myself that all the members of the band had left. All too late I noticed that one of them was hidden behind the corner of the building. I managed to fire at him, but he was faster. Something hit me, I felt an enormous pain in my leg, and I collapsed to the ground as if I'd been felled.

When I managed to get to my feet I found myself staring into the face of a grimy individual with an unkempt beard, who was pointing his rifle at me and shouting at me to raise my hands above my head. I had no option but to obey.

He gestured with the rifle for me to head for his comrades, who were shielding themselves from the machine-gun fire behind our building. When I got there I discovered that the smoke we had smelled upstairs was coming from a bonfire by the wall. Fortunately there were no flames as the wood was damp.

The Russians were arguing about something. Although they were speaking rapidly and in the local dialect I understood that I was to act as a shield to protect them from our machine-gun fire.

They pushed me out into the open, and at that moment I hoped that Miro and Janko would recognise me before opening fire. The machine-gun really did remain silent and the bandits slowly moved to safety with me in front of them. When our odd group finally reached a safe spot, I expected that the Russians would shoot me without mercy. They had other plans for me, however.

While a handful of our enemies, hiding behind the railroad embankment, managed to keep my comrades in check, I was brought before a bearded man who was obviously the leader of the band.

He wanted to know if I was the commander and I nodded. There was no point in denying it.

In return he shook his head. There were always problems with the Czechs, he mumbled to himself.

I shrugged and tried to explain to him in my less than perfect Russian that neither he nor the Bolsheviks were our enemies. We were withdrawing eastwards. All we wanted was to leave Russia.

He said nothing but simply gave a sign to the others, and they started to push me in the direction of a nearby grove, beyond which the bogs began.

My leg caused me unbearable pain and I was limping badly. But I could walk and so I followed them along the path between the bogs. They knew there was no need to hurry as my fellow combatants would not dare follow them here. They would be going to certain death.

We continued our trek for about another hour before we emerged from those swamps. In a small clearing in the middle of a wood a dozen bandits were seated around a fire, and a short distance away there stood some horses fastened to trees.

They allowed me to take a seat by the fire too. Soon their leader arrived and sat opposite me.

My name is Andrei, he said, and he eyed me searchingly.

I introduced myself also and he beckoned for them to bring me tea.

He pointed at my leg and asked how serious my wound was.

I answered truthfully that I did not know. I told him the wound was bleeding and that I had probably lost much blood.

He said nothing for a moment. Then he told me that they were not intending to kill me. We were not their enemies. They had attacked us because we had arms and ammunition. They were fighting the Reds, not the Czechs. They had taken me hostage in case my fellow combatants pursued them.

I was relieved and at the same time I was tempted to ask him why they terrorised ordinary people who had done nothing wrong.

He must have guessed what was on my mind.

The times were complicated, he informed me. In order to be able to fight they sometimes needed to take what they needed by force. Even from those who were not consorting with the Bolsheviks.

I thought it better to remain silent. His words did not explain why they killed them, as we had seen. After his band's previous raid we had found several people shot in their plundered homes.

I asked Andrei what he was intending to do with me. Did he want to leave me here? He must realise that I would have great difficulty finding my way back

He pondered again for a moment.

I was right, he then agreed. People could easily get lost in the marshes. But he could not spare any of his men to accompany me. He would leave me at Semyon's and let him decide.

I was naturally interested to know who Semyon was.

He replied that Semyon was a magician, a shaman. He worked miracles. He would cure me.

The idea did not appeal to me at all, but what was I to do? After all, Mother, just consider that I had been dragged off into swamps in the middle of Siberia. It would have been easy to drown in them. I noticed how cautiously Andrei's people trod and how they were constantly making sure they were on the right path.

I wanted to know where Semyon was to be found.

Further in the marshland, I learnt. Apparently he had been dwelling there with his people for several years already.

Then Andrei ordered two of his comrades to guide me to Semyon's.

Fear could be seen on both their faces. They started to argue with Andrei about something. They spoke excitedly and rapidly. I guessed that they were trying to persuade him to relieve them of the task.

But Andrei insisted.

So I got up laboriously from the ground and set off in the direction the two were indicating. My leg was now noticeably more painful and my head swam. I was not sure how long I would manage to walk.

The bandits ahead of me said nothing. From the clearing we went back to the marshland. It was early evening already when we cautiously set off for the edge of the swamp. After walking for about an hour we caught sight of a light somewhere in the marshes.

One of my companions told me to wait there. This was where they apparently left supplies and gifts on occasions for Semyon and his people, lest he set evil spirits on them. Noticing my astonishment, he explained that Semyon was capable of turning me into a wolf or a frog. He had miraculous powers.

It was rather comical, dear Mother, to see that scoundrel who had goodness knows how many murders on his conscience, in childish fear of some kind of spells, and, along with his crony, crossing himself again and again.

Then the two of them dragged some brushwood to the spot where I had sat down and set fire to it. As they hastily departed they fired two rounds into the air. No doubt this was a signal for Semyon.

Darkness fell quickly. The wood in the fire crackled softly and from time to time I goaded myself to get up and bring more brushwood. But movement became increasingly difficult and I had no strength left.

How strange, I thought to myself. I have travelled from Prague all the way to here, to a spot that might be most aptly described as "nowhere." I tried to get clear in my mind what had preceded my fall into "nowhere." I started to lose faith. Despite the fact that Ariel had promised me happiness, on the edge of that godforsaken Siberian swamp it seemed certain that I would die.

Strange images and memories ran through my head. I would recall with absolute clarity fragments of conversations with Klára that I had long forgotten. I was back again at the boarding school, and then with Hugo during our vacation time in Poděbrady. I recalled word for word one of my debates with Sabina. Nor was I spared, as if it were happening for the second time, the scene where I was sitting with the dying Hugo. And worst of all I could once more hear your words as you were telling me that we must separate.

And I also started to dream oddly sensual dreams, in which I experienced with intensity my amorous antics with Johana. But this time I had no pangs of conscience such as when I recalled them in my waking hours. If that was the first phase of dying, then God would seem to have been endorsing Johana's assertion that nothing that gave pleasure was bad.

I do not know whether I eventually managed to fall fast asleep or whether I lost consciousness. I came round in a hut littered with animal hides. It was already morning and daylight was streaming in.

Above me stood a man of some fifty years with a long beard and a piercing gaze. When he saw me open my eyes he held a cup to my lips and ordered me to drink its contents. The fever that shook me as I awoke, began to abate.

He waited for me to drink all the bitter liquid and then introduced himself. It was Semyon himself.

He examined my leg. The bullet had gone clean through the muscle. A mild infection, nothing serious.

From his speech it was clear that he was not uneducated and indeed he seemed to know something about medicine. I wanted to ask him about it but he pre-empted my question.

He had once been a medical student, but he had come to realise that everything physical was in reality merely an expression of the spirit. And conversely, much of what is spiritual is expressed through the body.

I admitted that I had heard from Andrei that he was a shaman.

Semyon grinned. A shaman he certainly was, but only for the likes of muzhiks and bandits such as Andrei. They were superstitious people who feared shamans. Why contradict them?

When I asked what he was doing there in the middle of marshland, he replied with a serious expression: "We have intercourse with God. There are several of us."

I was interested to know why the Orthodox Church was not good enough for them.

"Church?" Semyon asked with irony. "But that's the biggest problem of all! They totally failed to understand Jesus's teachings. God would have to be crazy to visit all of those churches and priests of theirs, who make a business out of Him. Jesus preached equality and poverty. In his teachings the spirit and the body are one. The Church has turned the body into a subject of shame, particularly the female body. It has humiliated women and sanctified all the inequalities that Jesus preached against."

It did not sound at all outlandish to me, Mother. I fully realised that one can have a profound relationship with God without being a member of a church. And yet it was still not clear to me why Semyon needed to live in total isolation if he needed to be in contact with God.

He said that he and the others not only conversed with God here, but they had genuine intercourse with Him, as I would see for myself. He instructed me that the Christian world had lost its way immediately after the apostles had distorted Jesus's message. In his view the catastrophe became inevitable when Western Europe passed through first the Renaissance and then the Enlightenment. He believed that the Bolshevik revolution was simply another emanation of the Enlightenment, which had now reached as far as Russia. It would inevitably end in disaster, because Russia was incapable of accepting any great idea other than as a religious message. And then it would distort it.

I was extremely weak, so I was not fit to argue, even when Semyon explained to me that if Russian Bolshevism were to triumph, it would be merely a worse version of the belief in scientific and technical progress, to which western civilization had fallen prey. They both led down blind alleys and would end in disaster, because they were both based on the dualism of spirit and body, he declared as the final words of his monologue. I asked him no further questions, even though it was not clear to me how, on that island in the middle of marshes, the unity of body and spirit was to be achieved.

My own body was in great pain, and however much I had tried, my spirit had proved incapable of alleviating the agony. The potion that Semyon had given me, on the other hand, proved effective. The fever disappeared entirely and I could feel sleep overcoming me. This was no longer the semi-consciousness that I had fallen into the previous evening, but some kind of pleasant exhaustion.

A few moments later I really did fall asleep. When I once more opened my eyes, the oddest spectacle presented itself to my gaze. Although I was still lying in my bed, I found myself in a room whose high ceilings and spaciousness gave me the impression of an empty barn. The walls were hung with all kinds of objects and pictures that seemed to have some religious purpose. Standing around my bed in a semi-circle were some twenty people – men at the rear, women in front with Semyon. Some of them were scarcely more than girls. Others were older than me. They observed me intently.

"Our brother has woken up," I heard Semyon utter in some kind of semi-chant, at which moment he started to sway his hips rhythmically from side to side while singing a song whose words I did not manage to understand. He went on singing that simple little song over and over again, while the assembled women imitated his swaying movements and repeated the words of the song after him. Gradually they entered a trance and started to stagger drunkenly, uttering wild shrieks as they danced.

I was at a loss as to what I was to make of that spectacle. It was clearly some kind of religious ceremony, but its meaning escaped me. No prayers were said and the dance was not accompanied by any comprehensible words. And even the song turned into a sort of murmur.

In the end, the women shed their clothes and gathered round my bed in such a tight circle that I was aware not only of their swaying hips and breasts but also of their body odour. Semyon was also naked, and I noticed that his male organ was fully erect. It occurred to me that the dance had excited him and he would be embarrassed when he realised it, but he came over to one of the women and copulated with her in front of my eyes. He had intercourse with some other women, as did the rest of the men afterward.

The spectacle disgusted me, but at the same time it excited me almost against my will. Suddenly several of the women started to touch my head and my arm. One of them removed my blanket and touched me also below, until in the end she was grasping me there. And all the while all those women continued to emit that strange melody unremittingly.

I wanted to extricate myself somehow from that encirclement of human bodies, but I did not have the strength to. And so I was unable to resist my increasing excitement, as I was being caressed by the hand of a woman whom I could not at first see through the rampart of bodies. I felt her sit on me and I was a bit afraid that she might touch my leg wound, but she was very careful. The moment I entered her the women around me stepped back and I was able to see a girl about eighteen years old, as if in a trance, and still crooning the melody that Semyon had started shortly before, moving faster and faster to bring her and me to a climax.

At that moment, Semyon was not having intercourse with the other women. He stood close by and uttered words resembling a prayer. Surprisingly I felt no shame. When it was all over my body and mind were filled with a curious peace.

Semyon approached me and declared: "Now everything bad in your body and spirit has been sucked out of you. Think of God."

He handed me a cup with some sort of drink. It clearly contained a different stimulant, because after drinking it I felt light and liberated from my body. Sleep once more overcame me.

When I awoke I found myself back again in the hut with the animal-skin hangings. Semyon was sat at the table, reading from a book.

Suddenly I could not be at all sure that what I had experienced had been real. I would have liked to asked Semyon, but I could not summon the courage. So I asked him at least for some water because I was very thirsty. He motioned toward somewhere in the corner of the room, where a girl emerged from the gloom with a jug. It was the same girl who had had intercourse with me a few hours before.

I now felt embarrassed for the first time. She smiled and stroked my hair. Then she poured me some water.

Semyon stood up and slowly came toward me.

He told me I was too bound by convention. All of us who came from there had petrified souls. Apparently I was not among the worst affected. Perhaps I was an artist. Was he right?

I nodded.

"Your great anxiety is due to the fact that they made a soldier out of you," he said. "You need God, but you are capable of talking to Him only through your art, and that has been taken from you."

I protested that I did play on occasions. I had a violin and no one had taken it from me so far.

Semyon was undoubtedly correct in asserting that I was inseparably bound to the civilization from which I had come. I still find it easier to feel I am speaking with God in the beauty of the complex musical compositions of the present day than in rituals that are supposed to enable me to merge with nature, such as those Semyon let me experience there in Siberia.

Then Semyon pulled my bandages aside slightly and examined my wounds.

It was improving, he assured me. His assumption has proved right. I needed to rid myself of tension. I had been full of it. And also full of sorrow.

I remained four more days in Semyon's commune. Every day the same ritual as the first day was repeated, but on each occasion it was a different woman who assumed the role of priestess in an effort to suck the bad out of me.

Semyon would also speak to me every day and I would try to fathom the essence of his belief. Maybe he had a genuine concern to rediscover some kind of absolute unity and therefore mixed pagan ceremonies with belief in Christ. Perhaps the unbridled sexual congress in which he involved me meant to him what music meant to me. Nevertheless my wounds healed much quicker than they would have in a military hospital. Whether that was due to those pagan rituals or thanks to the arcane potions that Semyon gave me to drink, I cannot tell.

On the fifth day, Semyon announced to me that he would hand me over to a group of Reds who had started to forage in the area and they would take me to Kormilovka. When I asked if it was safe, he replied with irony that they all feared him, Semyon. Nobody would do me any harm, neither the people from Andrei's band, who were encumbered with superstition and the baggage of Orthodoxy, nor the Reds, who believed in unstoppable progress and science.

I thanked him with a certain bashfulness for his unusual therapy and hospitality, and then one of his men brought me to a group headed by a disagreeable, dour man, who introduced himself as Yefim Karaganov. Little did I know that I would have the doubtful honour of meeting him again, in circumstances to which I shall return in my story. There they released me.

It goes without saying that my comrades were happy to see me again. They had every reason to assume that I was no longer among the living. For my part I was glad to hear that Karel was still alive. They told me that they had taken him to the military hospital in Omsk.

I preferred not to give anyone any details about my meeting with Semyon. And I have reflected at length, dear Mother, about whether to mention it at all to you, except that Ariel had instructed me at Zborov to write the story of my life, so I suppose I must not remain silent about anything of importance.

Life at Kormilovka returned to the usual routine. Occasionally we would receive an inspection visit from some of the legions' top commanders and we would have to ensure their safety, but mostly the trains did not stop. And sometimes an armoured train would arrive there, heading with soldiers for the eastern section of the railroad around Lake Baikal, where many treacherous tunnels hampered the fighting, so that it was necessary to send reinforcements from Omsk.

While I was stationed in Kormilovka, in Europe the war was gradually coming to an end. When we learnt one day that Austria-Hungary had fallen and an independent Czechoslovakia had been proclaimed, we wept like small children. We celebrated the event until the early hours and yet at the same time we were sad because we could not be sure of ever seeing our country again.

As you might imagine, Mother, I used almost every spare moment for violin playing. Although four years had already elapsed since the moment my promising musical career had been forcibly interrupted, when I did my evening practice on Fedotov's violin I felt I had forgotten almost nothing, possibly also because of my performances with the Kiev quartet. But even if that had not been the case, I was capable, in that God-forsaken Siberian wilderness, of resigning myself to the thought of performing only as a member of an orchestra if I was unable to resume my solo career.

At this juncture, dear Mother, I must confide in you another important occurrence from that period that also concerns you.

Ivan Fedotov, about whom I have already told you, had a nineteen-year-old daughter, Tanya. She too had formerly studied piano, although she was a rather mediocre pianist. Sadly she had not received real professional training, because the only piano in the wide vicinity was in the school where we would meet to make music together. Nevertheless, I was pleased to be able to play with her, and she was also the first woman in a long while whose company I could enjoy on a regular basis.

I cannot say that I fell wildly in love with her as in the case of Ester, but I found her attractive. She was a sturdy girl with Slav features, blonde hair and a nice figure. Although I held back in view of my lack of success with Ester, Tanya was clearly beguiled by me. I do not know whether it was my violin playing or my exotic origins. From there in Siberia, the Czech lands seemed almost like paradise, particularly in the light of everything I had told Tanya about them.

One way or another, not long after we were acquainted she told me she had been waiting a long time for someone like me. I was surprised how quickly Tanya's feelings had matured, but I replied that I like her very much too. Yet I was rather taken aback by her frankness. She truly had few inhibitions and just two days after making her feelings known to me, she came to my bedroom and stayed there the whole night. She reacted to my fears about what her father might say by explaining that she did what she liked. She declared airily that unlike her conservative father who used to support the Czar, she was a freethinker. She told me that she sometimes stayed overnight at a girlfriend's in Omsk and her father did not miss her at all.

I preferred not to ask anything further as her lack of convention suited me. However she spent almost too much time with me so her father could not fail to notice where she went. I was rather alarmed when one day he called me in for a chat, but he was his usual urbane and mild-mannered self. He simply begged me not to abuse Tanya's libertinism. He added that he was glad she had chosen me in partic-ular, a man of education and talent, but he would prefer us to respect conventions. But by then it was too late.

What made that interview particularly vexing for me was the fact that I had no idea how my relationship with Tanya would evolve and what I should promise Fedotov. So I restricted myself to platitudes. I told him I was not passionately in love with Tanya, but I liked her, even though some of her opinions, particularly about the political situation in Russia, I found repugnant.

On one occasion, for example, she declared that after the victory of the Reds everything would change for the better. I asked her what she meant by "better."

"We will all be equal," she opined. I tried to explain to her that in my view a much better solution for Russia would be what Kerensky had in mind – democracy, in other words – and then a gradual, resolute effort to improve conditions in the country. But she saw things differently.

Democracy was not appropriate for Russia, she maintained. Her argument was that there was too much poverty and inequality in the country. If the Russians introduced democracy, those who now held the reins of power and possessed the wealth would remain powerful in the future. They would simply govern differently.

I argued that this might not matter if the rest would benefit from it. But she did not give an inch of ground. According to her, Russia needed radical modernization amounting to a revolution in thinking.

In response I said that even if that were true, the terror, which the Reds were using to achieve their objective, would prevail in the new society also, and in that I was not mistaken, as I now know.

But Tanya was obdurate. She tarred with the same brush customs and institutions that had proved their worth elsewhere and customs that were typical for Russia. She failed to understand, for instance, that working for someone who was propertied was not a form of serfdom, from which Russia had only recently extricated itself. In her opinion there was no room for property in the new society.

Even marriage was a thing of the past, she told me. I could see that she might be attracted by the Bolshevik ideology's idea of complete equality between men and women, but Tanya raved about some sort of communitarian life in which all the women would belong to all the men and vice versa. And everyone would bring up the children jointly. She told me that Russia was only the vanguard of a world revolution that would introduce similar advantages everywhere.

I said nothing about the fact that I had experienced communitarian life recently not far from Kormilovka, and that it was a far cry from the modernity that she enthusiastically advocated. It struck me more like a return to prehistoric times.

At the end of 1918, Tanya informed me that she was pregnant. I was shocked, as I am sure you can imagine, Mother. After all, at that time I had no future in front of me. It was obvious that if everything went according to plan, I would leave with the legions and never return again. And the high command of the Czechoslovak corps would certainly not permit me to take Tanya and the child with me to the military transport.

I had no wish to remain in Russia, and definitely not in Siberia. Although we had managed to maintain an armistice with the Red Guards and Kolchak did not control this part of Siberia yet, it looked likely, nevertheless, that the Reds would eventually be victorious. And at that point I would not even be able to stay in this country, because a Czech legionary would probably have little hope of surviving among them.

It soon transpired that Tanya's libertinism was no more than a pose. The pregnancy wrought a change in her and she started to talk about practical matters. Above all she wanted to know if I were willing to take her as my wife. And whereas only a few weeks earlier she had extolled free love, she now spoke about nothing but the family.

I did not refuse to marry her – I naturally felt responsible for the unborn child.

I therefore made the trip to the high command in Omsk. My superiors had no objection to my marriage, and in fact they offered to organise a marriage according to our traditions. They warned me that Tanya would not be allowed to travel eastwards with the legions. Perhaps she could come and join me when I had got back to Prague.

Understandably, Tanya was not enthused by the thought of my departure. She feared that we would never see each other again, but we had no choice. We therefore agreed that as soon as the war with Russia was over or that circumstances permitted, she would leave for Prague with the child. And were it not possible immediately she would try to sort out the necessary formalities for the journey at the Czechoslovak Consulate, which would undoubtedly be established in Russia. And so, dear Mother, in March 1919 I was married in Russia at a ceremony conducted by an officer of the legions.

I don't know whether is was a coincidence or something premeditated to do with Ariel, who had appeared to me at Zborov, but Alexey, my son, was born on the night of July 2, 1919, precisely two years to the day after Hugo's death. As far as you are concerned, Mother, that event, about which you previously had not the slightest inkling, simply means that a grandson of yours is possibly living somewhere in Russia. But, as you will realise from the next part of the story, not even I know where.

I was pleased about Alexey's birth but there was little time for rejoicing, as more and more Czechoslovak detachments were streaming eastward, and on top of that, not only had we to repel repeated attacks, both minor and large-scale, by Reds, but also, on occasions, to do battle with the uniformed rabble that claimed allegiance to the other side.

For the time being, Tanya was living at her father's. Sadly she no longer had a mother. Most of the time, she had to cope with Alexey alone, even though I spent as much as time as possible with them. I longed to teach my son Czech and I would constantly make naive attempts to ascertain whether he had any aptitude for music, which was naturally impossible at his age.

What made our situation even more difficult was the return of Yefim Karaganov to Kormilovka at the time when Tanya's pregnancy was already evident. Ever since he had brought me back from Semyon's, I had known he was a Bolshevik supporter, but I had not suspected he was Tanya's former suitor, as only now she admitted to me. He had no idea about our relationship because he had been obliged to flee Kormilovka in the spring of 1918 when Kolchak's White Guards combed the city.

After his return he first provoked a bitter row with Tanya, and when she came to me to hide, Yefim inveighed against me, saying I had cunningly seduced her. I could not explain it to him, because my wife's honour was at stake: it was she, rather, infected by his Bolshevik libertine theories, who seduced me.

I told him that I would not allow my wife to be endangered.

He cried out like a madman that he would take revenge on her for her betrayal, and that we two would meet again. Tanya would no doubt inform me who he was.

Had I suspected that not only was Yefim Karaganov one of the Red Guards, but that he had a reputation as a criminal before the revolution, as Tanya informed me when, after our meeting, he once more disappeared, I would have handed him over to Kolchak's men. But she did not explain why she had got mixed up with such a dangerous individual.

Alas, Yefim intended to carry out his threats. And so our unit now came more frequently under malicious fire and nothing came of our repeated requests to Kolchak's men to deal with the Red partisans. There was no question of our pursuing them – after all we were unfamiliar with terrain in the swamps and the steppes, and we also lacked the manpower. We even had to ask for reinforcements, because on one occasion we were almost surrounded.

Being in a state of constant alert exhausted us. Since it was obvious that Yefim's motive for the attacks was the fact of his being jilted, it was necessary to find a solution somehow. It crossed my mind that it might help if I were posted elsewhere, but that would mean leaving Tanya in Kormilovka.

To begin with, she lived in my quarters most of the time, but then increasing numbers of higher ranking legionary officers were billeted on us. The amount of space was being reduced all the time, and on top of that, many in the unit did not think it right that Tanya should live at the unit's headquarters, and so she returned to her father's. She was convinced that Yefim would not dare set foot in town, because everyone there knew him and had a good memory of how his detachment had openly attacked our position near the station. He risked being denounced by one of the locals, most of whom continued to support Kolchak. In that case, the legion would either try him in the field or hand him over to the White Guards.

In the summer of 1919 there was a lull in attacks by the Reds, apart from occasional skirmishes with various groups. We subsequently learned that they were preparing to drive Kolchak out of Omsk. So the first two months after Alexey's birth were peaceful in comparison with the previous period.

But one day Yefim and his comrades returned and out of the blue we found ourselves under fire from the swamp beyond the railroad tracks. Whereas Mojmír and Václav managed to get into the armoured railroad car, where Karel was on sentry duty, the two Slovaks and I returned the fire from the station building. We discovered that the attackers were Yefim's men only when they dashed to fresh positions.

I shall never cease to blame myself for not being more alert and seeing through their ruse. As it turned out, the attack was simply intended to distract our attention. When the firing ceased and I set off in search of Tanya, I found the door of her father's house smashed open. Ivan Fedotov lay on the floor. He had been shot in the head. Of Tanya and Alexey there was no trace.

There were no attacks by Yefim's men in the days that followed, so I concluded that they had managed to abduct Tanya and my son beyond our reach. The only solution was to launch an immediate search but at that time our detachments were being moved to Irkutsk and Vladivostok and the Supreme Command were unable to place any troops at my disposal.

I was in a state of mental torment. I seemed to be jinxed although I could not tell why. I asked Ariel mentally what he had meant by the happiness that would one day befall me, because so far each happiness had been only temporary, and followed by some further adversity. There was nothing for it but to hope that Tanya and Alexey were both alive, even though there was no trace of them.

Tanya managed to escape when Yefim's unit once more advanced on Kormilovka. She returned in a dreadful state. Her face and body were covered in wounds and she was running a high fever. She tried to relate to me what had happened to her, but the fever caused her to hallucinate and then become unconscious. Nevertheless I managed to grasp that Yefim had wreaked a truly inhuman revenge – he had let every member of his unit satisfy their lust with her. He had taken Alexey to some unknown destination saying that he would bring him up to be a man fit for life in the new society.

Tanya assured me that there was no point in pursuing Yefim's unit, because it had withdrawn after her escape, besides which, it had a perfect knowledge of the area.

I placed my comrades on guard at the station and Karel and I drove Tanya to our field hospital in Omsk. Throughout the journey she was delirious. At one moment she would be declaring that she was with me in Prague, and then she would be awake again and wanting to know her father's whereabouts. I lied to her as I was unwilling to tell her about his dreadful end. Before we reached Omsk she sank into unconsciousness. Nothing more could be done for her and she died a few hours later in the hospital.

We buried Tanya in Kormilovka, in the grave where her parents lay. Every day until our departure I would visit her grave. I still blame myself for not having found Alexey. One day I will travel to that godforsaken country and look for him. He would be sixteen by now.

But not even Tanya's death and Alexey's disappearance brought our ordeal to an end. Yefim must have had his own people among the local inhabitants and he was well informed about happenings in Kormilovka. He attacked us once more during the preparations for our departure to the east, as if he wanted to make use of this final opportunity to kill me. His unit was now much bigger and better trained than a few months previously, so a fierce battle ensued.

We were extremely lucky however, that there were about sixty other soldiers waiting with us in Kormilovka for the next train – otherwise none of us would have survived. Although the soldiers repelled the Red Guard's initial attack, some of Yefim's managed to reach the building I was living in unnoticed and opened fire on the windows of my bedroom.

That man hated me to such an incredible extent. There was no other reason to attack us. Wherever possible the legions had reached a truce with the Reds. Our main task now was to get away from there as fast as possible. It must have also been clear to Yefim Karaganov that Kolchak would not hold out very long after our departure.

Besides, we were starting to have problems with Kolchak too. Over the previous months he had unleashed a reign of terror in Siberia. His units were setting villages on fire and killing people en masse on the slightest suspicion of collaboration with the Reds. As a result he was losing not only our support, but also the support of those who had originally feared the Reds.

I survived Yefim's last attack without a scratch, but Karel who was firing from the window with me, received a bullet wound in the chest. I had to keep on firing and was unable to take care of him. I heard, rather than saw, Karel dying behind me. The Reds suddenly withdrew when our soldiers at the station opened fire and killed three of the assailants.

So on the day before our departure I senselessly lost a friend who had stood loyally at my side at Kormilovka. The memory of his mournful fate weighs on my mind still. We buried him in the Siberian earth and raised a monument, which the Bolsheviks most likely destroyed.

The journey to Vladivostok was not an easy one either, dear Mother. The White Army quickly lost its positions and the further we moved eastward, the greater the anarchy that reigned. Bands under the leadership of Semyonov and Ungern von Sternberg terrorised the local population and heeded no rules. Entire villages fell victim to their unimaginable ravages. Dreadful hunger was rife and even cannibalism was widespread among the Russian units on both sides.

We might never have reached Vladivostok had not Russian gold bullion fallen into the hands of the Czechoslovak legions some time earlier. The Soviets wanted it back at all costs so they were willing to sign an armistice with the legions and deliver coal for our locomotives. I happened to be present at the signature of that agreement on February 7, 1920 at Kuytun station on the Trans-Siberian Railroad. One clause of that agreement was the surrender to the Soviets of Admiral Kolchak, who had been taken prisoner by the legions. He was almost immediately executed without trial in Irkutsk.

On the first day of March that year the gold bullion was handed over to the Soviets at the station in Irkutsk. According to the soldiers who witnessed the event, there were several thousand chests of gold, coins and other valuables, which were loaded onto eighteen railroad cars.

I reached Vladivostok, dear Mother, at the beginning of March along with the other soldiers. After all those hardships I could at last live in hopes of returning home, although I had no clear idea of how we would get there, or by what route. Nonetheless it looked as if my trials, which had started six years before when Sabina and Colonel Ganz had decided on their revenge, were drawing to an end.

In spite of the many battles, I was in good health, and, as I have already told you, during my wanderings through Russia I even had the opportunity to practice the violin. I had not forgotten my art, but I had forgotten that, according to Ariel's prophecy at Zborov, fate had other plans for me.

A few days before I was due to embark with the other members of the Jan Žižka of Trocnov Rifle Regiment aboard the ship Mount Vernon, I was called on to perform guard duty at the docks in Vladivostok, where thousands of legionaries were waiting to be shipped out. Two of them got into an argument and came to blows. We pulled them apart without any great difficulty and marched them off to headquarters for questioning. I slung a kitbag belonging to one of them over my shoulder and hung it up in the waiting room at headquarters alongside a burning stove, unaware that the bag contained ammunition. Shortly afterward there was an explosion, and I felt a sharp pain in my left hand. The explosion had blown off half of my index and middle fingers.

The soldiers who dashed to my aid comforted me by saying that the outcome could have been worse, and that was indeed true, but on the way to the field hospital I knew this was a tragedy for me. I think that at that moment I would have preferred death. It was obvious that I would never again be able to play the violin. Maybe the only reason I did not kill myself was that I was curious what form the happiness Ariel had promised me would take after all that.

Those missing finger joints made a hole, which mercilessly swallowed my hopes. Whereas the other soldiers rejoiced after we set sail at the thought of nearing home, I was filled with hopelessness. I had no idea what I was going to do. Moreover, by my reckoning no one was waiting for me. After all I had spent the entire period believing that the Steiners had disowned me too.

Our ship was at sea for a long time. From Vladivostok it set course for San Francisco, and then from there to Panama, then along the American coast to the town of Norfolk, and finally straight to Europe, to the port of Trieste, where we disembarked. I reached Prague on August 16, 1920, after six years of incredible adventures and trials, richer by a son who was still perhaps living somewhere in Russia, and poorer by the loss of my best friend and the two women I had fallen in love with during those years.

When the train entered the Prague outskirts I wept like all the rest. Many soldiers had leapt out of the train at the first stops in Czechoslovakia and kissed their native soil. A few years earlier not many of them had believed they would ever return.

Since I anticipated, dear Mother, that no one would be there to meet me, I let my comrades who had families waiting for them alight first in Prague, for the news of the legions' arrival had spread. But when I came down the steps of the railroad car I could see Josef and Eliška Steiner waiting on the platform! They welcomed me like a lost son and they too burst into tears.

Later we spent many hours relating what had happened to us. Thus I came to know about all the things they had undertaken in vain to rescue me. And I also learnt that Karel Steiner was no longer alive. He had died of Spanish influenza in 1919.

I won't relate to you, Mother, everything that happened next, as you are no doubt familiar with it from the press and from others' accounts. We legionaries were now celebrities thanks to our "anabasis," as our march through Russia was called. Politicians maintained that without us, an independent Czechoslovakia would have never come into being. They said that it was only on account of our heroism that Masaryk had enough political leverage to put pressure on the governments of the Entente powers.

And most important of all, apparently, was the Battle of Zborov, and I still draw some comfort from the thought that Hugo's life was perhaps not entirely wasted.

There followed reunions that were more painful for me than the one with the Steiners. They included a meeting with the Beňáčeks, to whom I had to relate what I knew about Hugo's death, as well as a trip to České Budějovice to visit the parents of Karel Frolík, who had died at my side at Kormilovka.

The Beňáčeks had received the news of their son's death several years ago and had had time enough to reconcile themselves partly to the dreadful fact. But they were dismayed to learn from me that Ester, the love of Hugo's life, about whom they had first learnt from me, had died along with her child – their grandchild.

In return, I learnt that after the war Sára had returned from Salzburg to Prague, and although she no longer lived with Hugo's father, they often saw each other, possibly out of a need to talk about their son.

When I visited the Frolíks at České Budějovice, I discovered that they were acquainted with your family, Mother. Although I had been unable to contact you, it just so happened that you used to shop at their hardware store. They were astonished to learn that I was your son. I also found out from them that no children had been born to the marriage for which I had been packed off to boarding school.

I expect you will be surprised, Mother, to learn that, like many other legionaries, I accepted the offer to serve as a gendarme, because it was clear that I would not be able to earn my living from teaching music theory. Apart from the substantial salary that the job offers, I also enjoy various other advantages, which the state awarded us out of gratitude for our services. And apart from that, I occasionally supplement my earnings by coaching music pupils.

In order to play the violin again, at least for my own benefit, I taught myself to play the violin left-handed, although it was very hard. I use my left hand to hold the bow, for which the thumb and the two undamaged fingers suffice. The standard of my performance has declined, naturally, but the opportunity to play my favourite pieces gives me pleasure and a sense of fulfilment that is lacking in the work of a gendarme for someone with artistic talent.

My first posting was in Prague. Although I had no real affection for my new profession I received successive promotions, so that I was not at all badly off after my return from the war. I rented a small apartment in Holešovice, the first dwelling I had chosen for myself.

It was also my good fortune that Eliška and Josef Steiner remained friends with me. Sometimes we attended concerts together and Eliška and I liked going to cafés and restaurants together, where we would occasionally take part in discussions with people from the arts. There was once more a flourishing cultural life in Prague. Many of the writers and poets that now shine in the Czech intellectual firmament I had got to know when they were budding authors. I am grateful to Eliška that I was able to meet some of them.

One day when we were out together I happened to catch sight of Sabina in a café in the centre of Prague. I was in two minds whether to address her, but in the end I asked Eliška to excuse me for a moment and I went over to the table where Sabina was dining.

It was an odd encounter. In spite of everything that had happened over those many years since we last saw each other, our initial embarrassment almost immediately gave way to that feeling of intimacy that we had long shared. We did not have much time for conversation as Eliška was waiting for me, but we agreed to meet again the next day.

When we met, Sabina confessed to me how she had reproached herself terribly all those years for what she had done. Yes, she had wanted to revenge herself on me, but had she known what would be the consequences of her action, she would never have done it.

I told her sincerely that I did not feel any resentment against her, and that I possibly deserved such a punishment. I then related to her everything I had gone through in Russia. She burst into tears and when I had finished she stroked the stumps of the two fingers on my mutilated hand.

I discovered from her that she was married. She had been alone in the café the previous day because the school where she taught music finished late in the afternoon and her husband, also a musician, was out of town.

I plucked up courage and asked about Johana. Sabina looked at me in the same way she had at the age of fifteen when speaking about her bohemian mother.

"My mother is living in Paris," she said. "She married a French diplomat immediately after the war."

I thought to myself that Johana and Paris were well suited to each other.

Ariel's prophesy started to come true, dear Mother, in 1925. That year I was posted for several weeks to Ushgorod to help train local policemen in Transcarpathian Ruthenia. My stay there was drawing to an end when one of them came to me with a request. He told me he knew a woman in Uzhhorod who would be travelling to Prague with her son in the same train as myself. Could I accompany them and guide them to their relatives in Prague if I had the time?

I consented. I was pleased to have something to pass the time on the long journey.

Prior to my train's departure I paid little attention to my surroundings, as I was unable to take my mind of Hugo, who was buried not far from there. Only later did I catch sight of my Ukrainian colleague and behind him a woman with a boy about eight years old.

That woman was Ester!

Already from a distance I could see that she had changed little. Beautiful black hair, a pale complexion and deep-set eyes.

It is impossible to describe to you, Mother, our surprise and emotion. After all, for all those years we had thought that the other was dead. I had good reason to be convinced of Ester's death, and for her part she told me that she had believed it unlikely that I would survive the journey across Russia. After the war she had searched for my name in concert programmes from Prague and elsewhere, which she asked friends to bring back for her. But she had never come upon my name.

We spent the journey to Prague telling our stories to each other. It turned out that Ester had survived that dreadful pogrom only thanks to the fact that she had left for Kiev to take up an offer to play in the local orchestra. When she heard about the pogrom she rushed home, but in the place of her home she found just a burnt-out ruin with the incinerated corpse of her father.

She went back to Kiev and weathered the war with the help of friends. That was where her son Daniel was born. She had not named him after his father, because the name Hugo sounded foreign to Ukrainian ears, apart from which it was unpronounceable for many people whose native tongue was Russian.

After the war she had managed to leave Kiev while the Soviet Union was coming into being, and stayed with her relatives in Uzhhorod. I learnt from her that some relatives of her father were living in Prague, having managed to leave the Ukraine for Austria-Hungary before the outbreak of war.

While she was relating her story I observed Daniel. He was a quiet lad, who gave the impression of being a bit sad, but he had Hugo's athletic build and he was tall for his age. I could see Hugo's features in his face. He really did resemble him very much, which filled me with a strange melancholy. After all, he was only a few years younger than Hugo at the time we became friends.

I told Ester about my meeting with the Beňáčeks and she promised to visit them and me as soon as she had settled down a bit in Prague – and the visit indeed took place.

About a week after my return to Prague, we all met together with Otto Beňáček in Sára's apartment. Ester immediately won the hearts of them both, and not only because she had been Hugo's love. I understood them better than they could ever possibly imagine, although I naturally made no mention of my frustrated love for Ester.

What touched me most, however, was their instant affection for Daniel. After all, they had suddenly acquired a grandson, even though we had all been convinced that he had never been born! Daniel fell in love with his grandmother and grandfather straight away and spent lots of time with them, although at first he found it difficult to understand their Czech or German.

Ester turned out to be my path to happiness as Ariel had prophesied. She took me to see her relatives, the Kaminskys just at the moment when their friends, a couple called Klein, were staying with them.

We chatted for about an hour and I was slowly getting ready to leave. However, Ester urged me to stay a little longer so that she could introduce me to their daughter, who would arrive shortly. She said the daughter would like to see me as Ester had told her about my adventures. Moreover, she would be interested in my erstwhile music career, as she taught music at one of the Prague gymnasiums. Eventually there was a knock at the door and Mrs. Kaminsky went to the entrance hall to receive the visitor.

And then the door of the room opened, dear Mother, and there she stood, Karina Kleinová. I am utterly incapable of describing the feeling that overwhelmed me. At that moment I knew that she was the luck that Ariel had spoken about to me! I knew that I would love her unreservedly – indeed I already loved her – and that she would be my wife. She, for her part, fell in love with me at almost the same moment, as she later told me.

It was the oddest welcome. I am sure that both the Kleins and Ester were surprised, because Karina and I stood facing each other for quite some moments before we were capable of taking a single step. There was absolutely no need to introduce us. I felt that I had always known her. I had carried her in my heart my entire life. I was even assailed by an odd sense of gratitude toward Hugo. After all, if Ester had decided in favour of me instead of him, I might never have met Karina, let alone court her.

When we recovered from our first shock – there is no other word to describe our state of mind – we started to talk, and I was immediately captivated by her voice as I once had been by Ester's on our first meeting. I am sure it is not simply my own predilection when I say that Karina is amazingly beautiful. I knew already that she was Jewish, so did not really expect her to be a blonde. I rather thought she would resemble Ester.

Then my attention shifted to her almond-coloured eyes. They were deep-set and beautifully formed, and there was a certain gravity in them, though it was not sadness. She too was observing me with interest. Her gaze came to rest on my hands and her face displayed a look of compassion.

Her first words were that she already knew a lot about me from Ester, but would like to hear more.

I would be very pleased to tell her everything I knew about myself, I replied.

She laughed.

That laughter penetrated deep into my heart and I still find her full-throated rippling laughter intoxicating.

Our second meeting took place only two days later at one of the cafés I used to frequent with Johana before the war. It was an extremely curious but useful coincidence, because it allowed me to realise how different my feelings for Johana had been. And so it struck me with a certain irony that I would be unable to keep the promise I had jokingly given Karina immediately we were acquainted, namely that I would tell her everything I knew about myself. Well, not straight away, at least. How would I seem to her if I told her about that strange affair with Johanna, a woman twice my age?

I was the one who did most of the talking, because Karina asked me many questions. From time to time I had to interrupt my narrative because of my emotions, particularly when speaking about Hugo's death. And some things I concealed from Karina, including my encounter with Ariel and his prophecy. I did not want her to think me insane, and also I was afraid that she might think I was only interested in her on account of a prediction. I also concealed from her that I might have a son somewhere in Russia, or even that I was briefly married. I will have occasion to disclose that to her when we know each other better, I told myself.

Then it was her turn to tell her story. Before she started to teach at the gymnasium, she had studied at a music school and later at a teacher training college. So far her friends were mostly former fellow-pupils. She was also friends, she said, with some of the teachers at the school where she now taught. I concluded that she was six years younger than I, and was only twenty-four years old.

I assumed that Karina was Jewish by religion and asked her if she had some friends in the Jewish community. To my surprise she told me that her parents had converted to Christianity before she was born. Her father had privately returned to Judaism and apparently was studying some sort of books and most likely practiced his religion in secret, but she had never been properly initiated into Judaism. Nevertheless everyone assumed she was Jewish, if only in view of her name. In reality, though, she did not have many Jewish friends. And she had met Ester only thanks to her father, who was acquainted with the Kaminskys.

To tell the truth, I was somewhat relieved because for two whole days before our meeting I had lived in fear that her parents might not approve of our eventual relationship simply because I was not a Jew. When I discovered that Karina had been baptised and that she even attended Mass once a week, whereas I never went to church even though I was baptised as a child, it was a weight off my mind.

Notwithstanding, her parents, and particularly her father Albert, did turn out to have certain misgivings about my origins. The problem was that they were fairly confused about what they actually were. On the one hand they had converted to Christianity and behaved as converts wherever they went, but on the other they regarded me as a "goy."

Karina revealed this to me with a touch of bitterness as soon as we started talking about marriage, and she immediately told me that it was pointless for her parents to resist, as she had made up her mind to marry me the moment she met me at the Kaminskys' apartment.

We married in 1927, as I expect you know, dear Mother, because I notified you of my marriage at the time, although I did not invite you. We had postponed our wedding partly because I had been promoted to brigade commander, which meant a possible transfer. And at the end of 1926 I was indeed transferred from Prague to Úvaly, a small town just outside Prague. As it was clear I would be staying there for some time, and that I would be better paid, I officially asked for Karina's hand in marriage.

However, during those two years we saw each other very often, almost every day, because we could not bear to be apart. We would go to concerts or to the theatre and Karina also started to associate with my friends, although Ester remained her closest friend.

I was pleased when Ester was able to join a Prague orchestra less than a year after her arrival in the capital, thanks to my contacts in the musical world. At first she stayed at the Kaminskys', but then she rented a small apartment close by, which was convenient because they took care of Daniel when she was on tour with the orchestra.

The same year I married Karina, Ester introduced to us a colleague from her orchestra whom she had decided to marry. Although I had always imagined that she would remain single because of her memories of Hugo, I was now pleased at the news. She was still young, as you know from my story, and no one could begrudge her for not refusing this offer of marriage.

Before our wedding I naturally had to divulge to Karina the secrets of my life that I had concealed from her for almost two years since our first meeting. First of all I told her about Johana and her daughter and I admitted that I was now ashamed of my behaviour at that time. Karina was surprised by the story but afterward she reassured me that I need not be ashamed of my relationship with Johana. After all, I had been young and she had been beautiful. As for my dishonourable treatment of Sabina, I had been punished more than enough.

She showed greater interest in my marriage to Tanya. Again and again she would mention the possibility that I had a son somewhere in Russia, who would be eight years old by now. Naturally she did not reproach me my marriage to Tanya, instead she shared my grief over Tanya's fate.

My legionary comrades, many of whom I had not seen for several years, attended our wedding. Mojmír and Václav came, both of them now married, together with a number of commanders I had been in touch with at Kormilov, as well as my present and former gendarme-station colleagues. And naturally my present and former friends from the world of music also came.

Karina was intent on a church service and I agreed, but on just one condition: I wanted our wedding to take place on July 2, the tenth anniversary of Hugo's death. Initially, the Beňáčeks, Karina and her parents found the idea rather morbid. It was as if I wanted our marriage to commemorate my friend's death. But I persisted. I explained that it was my gift to Hugo. After all, before his death he had begged me to be his best man at his wedding with Ester.

I never told anyone about Ariel. Only Ester knew about him, because she had been present at my conversation with her father, Rabbi Kaminsky. But she kept it to herself, realising that it was my secret.

That wedding was also my act of thanksgiving to Ariel. When the wedding feast was over and Karina and I had left for Úvaly, where

I had bought a small house with some financial assistance from the Kleins, I went out into the garden toward dawn and thanked Ariel. You see I do not believe he was simply a messenger predicting my destiny, but that he had also helped shape my destiny – as my guardian angel. I wanted to tell him, precisely on the tenth anniversary of our encounter, that I was thankful to him, because not only had his prophesy of disasters come true, but also his prophesy of a happiness that I had been incapable of imagining at that moment.

In Karina I had found everything that I had been looking for, Mother. Perhaps I am a little sad sometimes that I am unable to give concert performances, but my love for her is so great that I would not be able to give concert tours and lead a migrant life without her.

I am also happy that my country was spared the Bolshevist plague that I had encountered in Russia. And although originally I was not particularly in favour of an independent republic, I feel great satisfaction that I can be justly proud of the Czechoslovakia that I live in and serve. There is, it is true, a sabre-rattling lunatic in Germany, who could possibly prove a threat even to us, but the Germans are a sensible nation. They are bound to get rid of him in the end.

The crowning point of my happiness has been the birth our two children, Hana and Arno. I also informed you of their births at the time. They are now aged seven and five. And as I mentioned earlier, very soon, maybe tomorrow, twins will be born to us. We will truly be a large family and I will achieve what you denied me. What more can I ask for?

I visited Klára's grave and told her all about it. She would surely be surprised to learn what her little Josef endured and where his wanderings ended up. And I'm sure that in the end she would have liked this state, because we can be proud of it. And I know that she would not have begrudged me the love I have found.

Of course I regret sometimes that I could not share it all with you; that I had to struggle through life on my own. I would like to know whether you found a little happiness at least, whether that great sacrifice that you made under pressure from your family fulfilled at least something of what you yearned for. The greatest thing that one can encounter in life is true love. Did you encounter it in the end?

I wish you no ill, Mother. Maybe if we were able to talk together some time I might be able to understand your motives better as a grown man, than when I was a child. I am sorry that you are suffering from a disease that is apparently incurable. Should Ariel appear to me again I shall ask him to help you get better. In fact this letter is a way of asking it of him, since I am writing it at his request.

As I told you, I saw Ariel once more yesterday. I am sure it means something, and hopefully, only good things.

I will finish this letter when the twins are born, perhaps as soon as tomorrow, because I think my story so far would not be complete if I did not give you news of two more grandchildren.

Both Hana and Arno ask about you from time to time. Should you be interested in getting to know them I'm sure it would mean a lot to them, because they don't understand why they have never met their other grandmother.

Yesterday I built them a swing in the garden. I was unbelievably happy in my work, because I realised that I have been able to give my children something I never knew as a child. As I write this letter, I hear from time to time through the open window Hana and Arno shouting with excitement as they swing back and forth... It's a windy day and sometimes the swing moves on its own in the wind when the children are not there. Then comes silence, a total silence that fills me with anxiety for some unknown reason.

I will go take a look at them...

II

THE WAY UP
IS DOWN

Last night I had one of those dreams that put me into a state of depression. I was again in a dark underground hole, like many times before. I was looking for a chink that might let in some light and fresh air, but there wasn't any. When I told my grandparents to open the door they whispered to me in alarm that we mustn't. But I was suffocating and I couldn't stand it. When I woke up I was soaked with sweat as usual and my hands were shaking, so Sister Alžběta immediately ran off for some of the blue pills. Then I sat for quite a long time on the bed absolutely tense and wondered for the umpteenth time how to stop myself having such dreams again. I didn't think I'd come up with anything, because I'd not come up with anything yet but the idea came to my head that I might write it all down. All of sudden it was crystal clear. I have to write it down and rid myself of it.

When the doctor came on his rounds I told him I needed paper and a pencil. He asked what I wanted to write and I told him it was about the story that was hounding me. If I write it down I might find some relief maybe. He shrugged – he had his doubts. But as soon as the director came in the door he went over to consult him. The director looked in turn at the doctor and at me, and then remarked to me "We'll give it a try with you." As he was leaving I overheard him say under his breath that they had no idea what my problem was anyway, so why not give me pencil and paper. So I was given a pencil and a notepad with squared paper that I now write on.

It took me some time to know where to start. I was in a state of anxiety and as I pondered on it all I realised that it wasn't enough just to describe it – just to say that it happened – because I already know that. What I must do also is to think about why it all happened and most of all to try to explain it. And I have to give my story some kind of time sequence because everything is so jumbled up in my head that sometimes I don't know what happened earlier and what happened later. I didn't know whether I'd manage it but I started to write anyway.

It's 1968. Apparently there are great things going on outside the walls of the hospital. My son Sasha was here a few days ago and he told me how they had set up a student organization at his school. He said that if things continue as they are, Communism has had its day. Maybe he was partly the reason I decided to start writing this. He's full of hope now and looking to the future, but maybe one day he'll also want to know what the past was like.

I'll start with this scene. It's a spring day in 1935 and my brother and I are playing in the yard of our house at Úvaly. Arno is sitting on the swing that Father built for us and from time to time I give him a push which fills him with wild delight but at the same time I'm keeping an eye out for what is happening inside the house. I know that the twins are due to be born today. For weeks now Father has been talking about how we are expanding into a really big family. I expect a really big family means a lot to him because on a couple of occasions I've noticed he's had tears in his eyes when he has been talking about a really big family.

Grandma Kleinová – our Mummy's mother – is staying with us. We call her Grandma Hela. They're all very nervous. I can feel it but I don't know exactly why because Grandma has reassured us goodness knows how many times that birth is something absolutely simple in modern times. So simple in fact that there was no need for Mummy to go to hospital. In the end she had her way even though Father was against it. She said that in our days a midwife has all possible disinfectants and modern equipment at her disposal so she is just as good as the doctors at the hospital. And she's cheaper too.

Except that I then hear through the door and windows Mummy's cries growing louder and I want to cry and I would cry if I didn't know that Arno will start to scream uncontrollably if I show any weakness. Instead I push Arno on the swing and listen with bated breath to the fragments of Mummy's voice distorted by some awful pain. It went on for ages, I don't recall exactly how long – after all I was only seven at the time. I only remember that at the end of it all Grandma Hela comes out and tells us that twins have been born – two little girls, but we mustn't go inside yet because Mummy's not feeling too good, and they have to help Mummy first.

Grandma is all shaken up and suddenly she calls to Grandpa to telephone the hospital to come quickly because things look bad with Mummy. And then that terrible thing happens that changes the lives of Arno and me forever. A few minutes later our father staggers out of the house dreadfully pale and his trousers are all covered in blood. He gazes at us in a way I've never seen before as if he was somewhere else entirely. In another world.

"Your mother has died" he says in a strange voice that terrifies me almost more than what he has just said. Then he turns round and goes back inside. Arno and I stand there. The swing that Arno has just jumped off of sways on its own in the breeze. All of a sudden there is a dreadful silence – a dreadful endless silence. I strive in vain to catch the sound of Mummy's voice, which would mean that Father was mistaken.

And then I hear the shot... Arno gives me a searching look because at the age of five he can't make any sense of what is happening. But I know straight away. I know everything. And I start to fall. This is when I first start to fall into that black hole, even before Grandma Hela stumbles out of the house and falls to the ground like a puppet with its strings cut.

So that was the end of my father's dream of happiness that he wrote to his mother about in a long letter that came into our hands only several years later. And it was also the end of our happiness, because everything that happened afterward, except for a few things, was like a weird dream. And that's what I'm going to write about now. But before I start I have to say that quite often an image comes into my head that I didn't experience myself because it was created a good while afterward when Grandma was relating it as we sat in that hole underground.

That's when she told me what had happened. Our father had staggered indoors and gone into the bedroom where Mummy's lifeless body was lying in the bed. He stood looking at her with that empty gaze. Grandma, who was half out of her wits, ran into the next room where the midwife was washing the twins. Father took several steps over to the bed and lay down alongside Mummy, and as if he was getting ready to sleep he leaned toward her and kissed her. He took her hand in his and with his other hand he reached for his service revolver lying on the bedside table. When Grandma returned it was obvious to her what he was intending to do but by then she couldn't prevent it. Take care of the children, Father said and then shot himself through the head.

I don't know whether Father's actions were responsible or irresponsible. The reason I write that is because Grandma sometimes said that it was irresponsible. How could he have done it she'd say seeing that he had lived almost like an orphan the whole of his life and suffered so much on account of it. But I truly don't know how Father was supposed to have behaved. I've wished a thousand times of course that he hadn't shot himself because our lives would have been totally different. But who am I to judge? Maybe he just didn't have the strength any more. Maybe he plunged into the abyss after Mummy just because he was so firmly tied to her.

I wrote that yesterday at the beginning. I find it slow work because my sight is bad on account of the hole that I'll write about later. The director stopped by and watched me for a little while. It must have been comical to look at me writing with my nose almost touching the paper. But I felt good about myself afterward. I didn't dream at night or if I did it didn't wake me up. Perhaps I'll get relief when I'll have gotten this nightmare out of myself and onto paper.

So what came next? Everything was thrown into disarray but for some reason I don't remember everything. I expect I displaced it as one psychiatrist said many years later. But one thing I didn't displace was Father's funeral.

I can recall quite precisely sitting with Grandma and Grandpa at the cemetery chapel holding hands with Arno who keeps blubbering and because he doesn't understand what has happened is asking me when Mummy and Daddy are coming. There must have been half of the gendarmerie from the entire Republic and definitely everyone who fought as legionaries in Russia with my father. For that reason it went on for an awful long time. There were so many speeches that Arno eventually fell asleep on my shoulder. And I also remember that my parents' joint funeral was also curious in that most of the talk was about my father, as if my Mummy wasn't right there alongside him in that coffin. It was odd because a lot of what happened to us during the war occurred chiefly because of Mummy, or rather because of the fact that she was Jewish like Grandpa and Grandma Klein. And it made no difference at all that long before she married my father the Kleins had converted to Christianity. But I'll come to that.

On that occasion she just lay in the coffin and it didn't occur to anyone that the fact she was Jewish was significant in any way. Even though I now know that not far away across the frontier in Germany it was significant. I also didn't make much sense of what was said by a famous violinist. He played beautifully and then said that the majority of the people in the chapel most likely thought of it as the death of a gendarme and legionary on account of so many uniforms. But in fact, that man declared, here lay one of the most talented violinists the country ever had. And if things hadn't gone awry he would have been one of the most famous people in the republic. Actually I only recalled the words of his oration when I was reading my father's letter in the hole. Only then did I understand what that violinist had meant when he said that things had gone awry.

Things went awry for us too. After the burial I lived with Arno at my grandparents the Kleins. Although they were converts and used to go to church before my mother's death sometimes they would let something slip out to the effect that their daughter's tragedy might have been slightly predestined by the fact she fell in love with a goy. Which only goes to show how dreadfully ambivalent Grandpa and Grandma must have been.

They had converted to Christianity at a young age at the time of the Hilsner Affair. There was only one God after all. The same in both the Old and New Testaments Grandpa used to say. In fact he and Grandma used to attend some special Sunday School to get a proper Christian education but at the same time they never lost interest in Judaism. Apparently Grandpa's family had lots of books at home because one of their forebears had been a rabbi and Grandpa used to study those books in secret and then tell Hela about them.

It strikes me now that it must have been hard for them. On the one hand they wanted to conform but on the other they tried to lose the faith they had given up out of fear. These days they would be said to have identity problems. When their daughter Karina married my father they were admittedly pleased that their grandchildren would be more assimilated than Karina but at the same time they feared the union with a goy. Even though they both came to have great affection for my father.

When my mother died they started to accuse each other of betraying their faith. That dreadful misadventure had happened to them, they said, because they had betrayed their origins out of cowardice. God had punished them. And so in 1935 they both started attending the synagogue once more and to steer Arno and me toward the Jewish religion. In so doing, they unwittingly sealed our fate because according to an ordinance issued in July 1939 by the Protectorate government on the basis of the Nuremberg Laws, not only was anyone who had at least three Jewish grandparents considered a Jew but also those who had only two Jewish grandparents but had joined the Jewish religious community after September 16, 1935.

We talked about those things much later. Mostly when we were hiding in that hole. At that time after our parents' death we all moved to a small village just outside Kolín, which the Kleins travelled to each day because they owned a store there. They sold my parents' house at Úvaly and they deposited the proceeds from the sale in an account in our names so if there hadn't been a war followed by Communism I expect I'd be a rich woman.

In those days though I was more worried about school than money because I had had to transfer to a new elementary school in Kolín, where the Klein's store was. I would drive there every morning with Grandpa and Grandma in the black Škoda automobile. They took Arno with them as well because he used to spend the day with them at the store until he started attending school. Arno had quite a good time. They had a tendency to spoil him so he quickly forgot about his parents.

I was worse off. I used to have bad dreams and sometimes I would burst into tears in the middle of a lesson. I just couldn't help it. Of course the teachers knew I was an orphan and what had happened so I enjoyed certain privileges such as being allowed to get up without asking permission and go out into the passage to cry.

In time memories of my parents started to pale because they were never mentioned in the Klein household. This was deliberate on their part in order to protect us – to let us forget, as they told us a few years later in that hole where we used to talk about everything possible. They would have succeeded had it not been for those dreams in which my parents used to appear from time to time. Or those moments before I went to sleep when I'd remember Mummy holding me in her arms at bedtime for instance and telling me a story and how she had smelled so lovely. All of a sudden I would have a precise memory of her scent and I would bury my head in my pillow and weep. And sometimes I would imagine that nothing had happened and that scent really was coming from Mummy and she was sitting on the side of my bed and I mustn't open my eyes in case it turns out not to be true.

And quite often I would remember my father playing the violin. Although he was missing two fingers that he lost in the war he managed to flip the violin over somehow and play beautifully even without those fingers. I would usually sit hidden under the piano listening to him without him knowing. Sometimes he'd even play with Mummy. She would accompany father on the piano and never took her eyes off him. And he didn't take his eyes off her for that matter.

Or during those years in Kolín I would often picture our father hugging Arno and me to himself and then seating us on either knee and telling us stories that he had made up. Some of them were set somewhere in Siberia where there was always lots of snow and dreadful frost. Now I know why.

Before I forget I must mention the twins. Grandpa and Grandma thought about keeping them and yet they sensed that they were too old to cope with bringing up four children especially since they still needed a nurse. But again they didn't tell us the main reason until the war came and we were in that hole. It was mainly because the two little girls who had come into the world out of my mother were too strongly associated in Hela's mind with her daughter's death. She said it would have been hard for her to bring them up with love, even though she knew of course that they were not to blame and that she herself was partly to blame for her daughter's death by insisting on the midwife. So immediately after the event the two little girls were offered for adoption. In fact I don't even know their names and have no idea who adopted them. That was intended to remain an official secret. The appalling thing is that we never heard of them again. On the other hand that adoption must have spared them a lot of pain. That is unless by sheer chance they were adopted by some Jewish family.

As I said, under the laws that came later, Arno and I were fully-fledged Jews – *Volljuden* was the German expression – mainly on account of my grandparents' decision to rejoin the Jewish community and take us along with them. Except that they'd have regarded us anyway as First Grade Mixed-Breeds or *Mischlingen des ersten Grades* as the expression goes in that precious language. At first the *Mischlingen* were not treated the same way as *Volljuden*, but later even they were at risk.

My parents died in 1935 at a period when things were still normal in Czechoslovakia. But two years later some of our fellow pupils were starting to jeer at us because we were Jews. Even though we had inherited the German surname Brehme from our father and in fact we were, when all is said and done, a quarter German and therefore also at least slightly Aryans, as the Germans considered themselves. Everyone at the school knew we belonged to the Kleins that owned the store on the square. And everyone knew that they were Jews. Converts maybe but Jews all the same.

In any case conversion would not have helped Grandpa and Grandma because according to subsequent laws they were simply racially Jewish and the difference between Jewish converts and non-converts was inconsequential if you had at least three Jewish grandparents. And they had eight.

One way or another, in the eyes of the Czech fascists who had been emboldened by the events in Germany, a Jew was anyone who had a Jewish name or features. On one occasion I retorted that my father didn't have Jewish forebears and one classmate who used to brag about his Aryan origins explained to me that maybe Arno and I weren't Jews according to Protectorate law, we were just *Mischlingen des ersten Grades*. However, according to Jewish law, we were Jewish because our mother was Jewish so we'd just better stop pretending we weren't. Anyway there was nothing we could do about it. Everyone knew we were and were keeping tabs on us. And that was that.

When I told it to Grandpa he got really mad and wanted to go to the school because, as he said, Czechoslovakia was no Nazi country where they could get away with something like that. But by then Hela was already afraid. "Just don't stir things up Bertie," she begged him, "and besides what would you hope to do with a nine-year-old boy?" And I expect she was right – what would we have done with him?

In those days we still comforted ourselves with the thought that Hitler might not rule over us because if he tried anything the Czechoslovak army would repel him. And as for those Jewish laws that are called *halacha*, as Grandpa explained to me, it's true we were Jewish because Mummy was Jewish but we were a totally assimilated family! We were simply Czechs.

Except that things went awry as I wrote before so our conviction that we were Czechs was no help to us later, even though at that time there were still people who took us for Czechs. In the village we had a number of friends who couldn't care less about our origin.

Grandpa had lots of friends. There was one in particular who had a small farm and a workshop and was capable of repairing things better than any engineer and he would often frequent the local tavern to play cards. Grandma didn't like it because Grandpa would sometimes stay quite a long time in the tavern and the next day he'd be tired in the store and sleep it off in the store-room. But it was the sort of life he liked. He enjoyed beer, cards and his pals. And they liked him because he was great at telling all sorts of stories, particularly jokes. Everyone called him Bertie, like Grandma. Nobody called him Albert.

Grandpa tried to be as Czech as possible and not just so that nobody should suspect he was something else. But the fact is that when he was home and not at the tavern or at the counter in the store he would be studying his books, and through them, taught himself fairly good Hebrew. However he used to say that Czechoslovakia was the Promised Land. He loved this country if only because it had had Masaryk as President for so long. His portrait hung above Grandpa's writing desk.

Those four pre-war years were happy ones when I compare them with what happened after. I had pals at school and above all I was a good pupil unlike Arno. Maybe I idealise that period a bit but I do know that if I had been able to attend school normally who knows where I'd have been today and I wouldn't have such shortfalls in my education or speak Czech so badly.

My favourite memories are of our maths teacher, Mr. Piták. He said that I was the best in the class. This was quite unusual because girls aren't generally good at maths. Piták would often hold me up as an example to the others but above all he was a kind man and never raised his voice. When I had to leave his class he stroked my hand and wished me all the best with tears in his eyes.

It all happened really fast. First, Beneš who Grandpa didn't like at all, replaced Masaryk. "Beneš is a bureaucrat not a politician", he used to say. "If the Germans invade he'll chicken out because he's chicken-hearted". Later in that hole, he used to speculate about what would have happened if Masaryk had still been alive at the time of Munich. Masaryk died in 1937 and that was a real blow for Grandpa. After that, everything went downhill. Munich, mobilization, demobilization, occupation...

Then things grew worse for us. I was eleven in 1939, so I already had some understanding of events. I saw how lots of people suddenly changed. Some were even afraid to speak to us. After the Jewish Property Ordinance in 1939, Grandpa and Grandma had to close their store. There was apparently some way of getting an exemption but Grandpa decided that our store would only be a red rag to the Nazis. If he hadn't had some money saved, goodness knows what would have happened to us.

Around that time they also issued the decree I mentioned already about who was or wasn't a Jew. At first it didn't affect us directly but in 1940 an ordinance was issued that banned Jewish children from going to school. Grandpa spent a long time trying to convince officials that Arno and I had been converted to Judaism from Catholicism as non-responsible minors. He emphasised that we had both been properly christened and in view of the fact that only two of our grandparents were Jewish we were *Mischlingen des ersten Grades*. But the officials were scared because our status was unclear. Maybe my description of what happened is not entirely reliable because it was Grandpa who spoke to the officials and all I know is what I heard from him. What is certain is that they banned Arno and me going to school.

And on top of everything else that year, the Germans defeated France, on which Grandpa had placed his last hopes. Well, after that, there was no helping us.

For a while Arno and I attended an educational club that the Jews organised instead of school. It wasn't too bad because we found new friends there and learned interesting things that they didn't teach in normal schools. But then came October 1, 1941 and the Jews had to start wearing yellow stars. And when Grandpa made a fresh attempt to persuade the authorities that Arno and I weren't actually Jews according to law he almost got himself shot. He came home with his face smashed and told us that some Nazi that he'd shouted at in desperation had thrown him to the ground. Grandpa was lucky that they didn't execute him on the spot.

We went around with those stars on for about half a year and had to put up with all sorts of injustices but then came the worst blow of all and the reason I'm here and what "drove me round the bend." We received a summons to join a transport.

Grandpa read it through and then his face went pale and he rushed off somewhere. He quite simply disappeared. He returned that evening and said we weren't going to join any transport because it would be the end of us. He had his sources of information. And because he and Grandma had been Catholics for many years he also had friends and they would hide us.

He said he had been preparing for this eventuality for some time already. One of the friends he played cards with, a certain Alois Kalivoda, had a small homestead in the neighbouring village where there was space for us to hide. Grandma asked him suspiciously whether Kalivoda was doing this for free just out of the goodness of his heart, even though he must know that they could shoot him out of hand for something like that, but Grandpa brushed her question aside. It was only later in that hole that he admitted that he had given Alois all his savings and some jewellery.

We fled from our house at night. We went on foot. Grandpa went in front and kept an eye out in case we were seen. For that reason we made our way to Kalivoda's homestead across the fields and then skirted a wood. It stood alone about a kilometre away from the neighbouring village.

Kalivoda was waiting for us, a tall good-looking fellow about forty years old. He was very nervous and the fear screwed his features up into tearful grimaces that made him look a bit like a little boy. His whole body was trembling. He told us that under the disused stable currently used to store timber, there was a cellar that he used mostly for storing potatoes and some meat that the Germans would requisition from him if they knew about it. They would probably shoot him on the spot too so it didn't make any difference whether they shot him on account of some smoked meat or because of the family of his old pal. There was a concealed entrance into the cellar from the barn.

We were able to see for ourselves how difficult it was to find the entrance, because the wall between the barn and the stable consisted of planks nailed together. But if one knew about the entrance, all that was required was to move a couple planks aside to reveal the steps leading down into the secret cellar. And when the planks were replaced and fixed at the back with a hook, nothing was visible from the barn.

Kalivoda mumbled that we will just have to hope – it would be over soon. He later admitted that Grandpa had led him to believe that we needed to use his hiding place just for a while because we also had other options. Grandpa could easily have led him to believe anything he liked because Alois was none too bright.

During those first months Grandpa tried to convince us too that we would only be in the hole for a short while because the English would arrive at any moment and the main thing was to avoid the transport. He was right about that because after the war I discovered what had happened to most of the people who had obediently joined the transport.

It's no easy task to conceal and feed four people Grandpa used to argue from time to time. Perhaps it would be better if Alois only hid the children. Except as he used to say too if they failed to bring Arno and me with them to the transport now that the authorities had decided that we were Jews and had to wear yellow stars then they would shoot him and Grandma on the spot because it would be obvious that they were hiding us somewhere. And so to my relief the four of us went on hiding. If I hadn't had Grandpa and Grandma with me in that hiding place and was left alone with Arno in the hands of a total stranger I'd have already gone mad back then.

It was never clear to me why Alois Kalivoda helped us. As it later turned out he was far from courageous and the mental state we observed on our arrival was nothing out of the ordinary for him. He always seemed to be on the edge of a nervous breakdown. Maybe he really did hide us on account of his long-term friendship with Grandpa – the members of those gambling fraternities had firm ties as Grandpa maintained – but I expect the main thing was the money and the jewellery that Grandpa gave him. In any case that very first evening he begged us earnestly never to leave the cellar on our own unless he gave us a signal. And we must speak quietly because sometimes noises from the cellar could be heard in the stable. Of course we did as we were told. We didn't want them to kill us or him.

There were two small fairly dry rooms in the cellar, which had vaulted ceilings. In the room at the rear there was a pile of potatoes in one corner and an old cupboard in the other, which was locked with a big rusty padlock. That was where Alois Kalivoda hid his smoked meat as we discovered a few days later. In the first room a lamp with a dim bulb swung from the ceiling above an old table. The table-top had clearly been put to every possible use probably for pig-slaughtering and suchlike as it was cut and scored all over. Four rickety chairs were arranged around the table. Kalivoda had prepared make-do mattresses for us in that room made out of straw-filled sacks and he had brought us old blankets. There was nothing else there.

I realise that in the situation we found ourselves, there was nothing for it but to be thankful – but in those early days when we still had the memory of home comforts fresh in our minds, it came as a shock. And on top of that, the cold in the cellar penetrated our very bones and there was no way of escaping it apart from lying under the blankets fully dressed.

We could only wash from time to time when Alois felt that the coast was clear enough and allowed us to creep out into the barn where he brought a few washtubs of water. On those occasions we'd also wash our things and dry them somewhere in the loft because they would never have dried in the cellar. Sometime later he took Grandma's clothes and mine and burnt them and gave us men's. It made sense because if there was a raid it would stick out like a sore thumb that he was drying women's clothes when everybody in the neighbourhood knew he lived alone. Going to the toilet was the most complicated thing of all. Alois had put an old bucket with a lid in the room we didn't sleep in and he would take it out every few days.

A lot depended on his mood. Sometimes he was so terrified by our presence that he would be overcome with a fit of rage and start to shoo us back into the cellar from the barn and scarcely let us come out. At other times, he would bring us milk and food that he had managed to find and he'd chat with us in a friendly manner.

We spent our time in the cellar mostly chatting. We had an old chess set and I would play Grandpa and Arno at chess several times a day. That's why I'm such a good player. Nobody has beaten me even here in the loony bin.

Grandpa had also brought a few books in his case by Dostoevsky and Mann as well as some of Masaryk's writings. I didn't read all of them because it was too hard for me. Grandpa obviously didn't have us in mind when he took those books.

On the other hand I read over and over again with great attention father's enormously long letter to his mother, in other words my other grandmother. Grandpa and Grandma Hela said they had found it written out on father's desk. They said they had intended to send it to his mother but about three weeks after father's death they learnt that she had died.

Grandpa originally thought I should read the letter when I'd be a bit older but then he decided that after all the things I had been through I was already mature enough.

And so at the age of fourteen my father's entire unhappy life story unrolled before me. Grandpa and Grandma would glance at me as I sat reading it in the light of that feeble bulb and sobbing often but they didn't say anything.

In a strange way, the time I spent in that hole became etched into my soul. Even now, I still gasp for breath for no reason and open all the windows because in those days I'd often have the feeling I couldn't breathe.

But the main mark in my soul was the feeling of total alienation from the world. And the ever-present fear that one day the Germans would find us and then kill us even though we hadn't done anything wrong. I also felt responsibility for Arno. I would tell him various stories about our parents and I'd even make things up a bit because I was afraid he'd forget about them altogether. Even Grandpa and Grandma often talked about them now unlike before. Most of all, they would recall my mother Karina when she was a little girl. They had loved her a great deal. She had meant the world to them. Often those memories would leave them in tears.

Grandpa in particular would brood over what might have been... For instance, if France had been better prepared for the war and defeated Hitler. Or if Czechoslovakia had defended itself. Or if that little squirt Hitler had been shot in the First World War.

According to Grandpa, the Czechoslovak Republic had been a noble undertaking. It hadn't always been up to scratch politically but it was a democracy. Grandpa would also go on and on about various politicians and he had a particular opinion about all of them the same way he had about the political parties. I had never paid much attention to that before the war but thanks to Grandpa I almost became an expert on the First Czechoslovak Republic while I was in that hole.

I can say the same about pre-war literature. Grandpa had an excellent memory and so he would recite long poems by Nezval, Halas or Březina. And not only that. He'd also narrate entire novels by Jirásek, Poláček, Olbracht, and Hašek, who was his great favourite. And in the same way that he loved some authors, there were writers that he hated such as Viktor Dyk. He had great talent but Grandpa maintained that he became a fascist.

Most of all, as I mentioned before, he loved Masaryk and like-minded people such as the Čapek brothers or Ferdinand Peroutka. I could still pass an exam on Masaryk's writings because Grandpa knew them all and he would mull over them all in great detail.

His other favourite topic was football. He was a great fan of Slavia. He could spend hours describing their various crosstown matches with Sparta or talking about the individual players. Even though I've never seen a single football match in my life, I still have the pre-war football league stats at my fingertips.

We had plenty of time for fantasizing. Apart from spending endless hours in the dim light conversing, playing chess or reading, we would spend hours and hours in silence. At such moments Arno would come and sit by me and I would put my arm round his shoulders. For Arno's benefit, Grandpa would recount the novels of Jules Verne that were so enthralling they could have been films.

Arno learned to draw splendid pictures in the cellar. Alois had given him some paper and a few coloured pencils, and because he only had memories of the outside world he started to draw it. And his drawings got better and better until they were almost more beautiful than the real world. He also drew various scenes from the Jules Verne stories. We hung them up around the walls and it gave a bit of a human touch to our two dreary rooms.

When I could bear it no longer in the cellar I would creep out at night without Alois knowing. I would sit in the garden or lie down in the grass and observe the stars. I could only sense the trees, bushes and fields around me beyond the fence but sometimes when the moon was out the outlines of things loomed out of the darkness. Sometimes a dog could be heard barking in the distance or a rustle in the grass betrayed the presence of animals.

I recall that at those moments I was filled with amazement and a strange defiance. Amazement that I existed and defiance because again and again I would puzzle about why I'd been denied the right to a normal life, why I didn't have parents, why I had to hide in a cellar – and why I had no friends... Because of the constant danger of death I had a really intense awareness of my existence. My life was filled with wonder and at the same time, it seemed like a really cruel joke. Like a weird dream that would be forgotten later.

Grandpa and Grandma were scared of my excursions to the garden. They warned me not to tempt fate. What if someone caught me napping? But I was livid at fate. If all that fate could offer me was living in a cellar, then it was directly inciting me to tempt it. If I'd been the only one that mattered, I almost wouldn't have cared if they did catch me out. At least something would happen I'd say to myself. Any thing other than that stifling anxiety down below. If I hadn't been aware that I'd have been putting Arno and my grandparents at risk, I might have stopped hiding.

I spend a lot of time remembering my parents. I could see them in front of me, going together on a walk to the woods that started just outside Úvaly and stretched all the way to Klánovice. Or taking the train to Prague like when we went to the fair and Arno and I would be screaming happily on the swings and roundabouts while our parents held hands like lovers.

In my life before, everything had had some kind of order and meaning that were connected whereas life in that cellar was order with no meaning. Because mere survival has no meaning. It's simply a matter of instincts and fear of death.

We had been down there several months when my periods started. Grandma asked Alois to bring some linen cloth or cotton wool. I thought he was a really kind man but afterward I noticed him spying from a distance when Grandma and I were washing ourselves in the barn. It was immediately obvious to me why – I already had quite big breasts and I'd grown a lot so by then I was taller than Grandma.

Alois came to see me one evening when we were taking the air at the back, behind the barn where no one could see us because there were woods on that side of the garden and anyway the whole of Alois' land was surrounded by a high fence. Alois asked me to come to his place to help with the housework. I don't know why I didn't refuse straight away – maybe I was enticed by the thought of seeing the interior of a normal house again. Only Arno was nearby so I told him to tell Grandpa and Grandma that I was going to help Alois and I'd be back in a little while.

First of all Alois went to the fence to make sure that the coast was clear and then he waved to me to run across the yard. It had been several months since I'd been inside a real house where it was warm and even cozy compared with our cellar.

That time Alois didn't try anything with me. He gave me some sweet pastries he had in the kitchen and asked me whether I would scrub the floor. He said it was too much for him that he had to take care of the animals and other things to do with the farm. And he also had us to worry about. But he didn't go to the animals. He sat at the table and watched me working until I finished the job. He didn't say much. He was mostly silent. And eventually he took me back to the cellar.

Grandpa and Grandma were horrified when they discovered that Alois had taken me away but they hadn't dared go after him in case they were seen. They quizzed me about what he had wanted and they pondered on it for quite a long time. Of course you can help him they said. After all he's helped us a lot too. But be careful – he lives on his own and you're already a big girl.

After that first excursion to Alois' I started to get bigheaded. I told myself that he probably needed company too and if all he wanted was for me to wash the floor or tidy up then the trip was worth it. So I went to help him a second time. And again nothing happened. He only asked whether I could cook, and when I said I could, he asked me to cook him a few potatoes and fry him some sausage that he pulled out from somewhere.

He let me take a little of the cooked food with me when I went back. For Grandpa and Grandma it was a real feast. After all for weeks we'd only eaten half-cooked potatoes that Alois brought us once a day. Maybe he's just lonely Grandpa suggested and admitted that he'd enjoy a game of cards with Alois but Alois only invited me to his place.

He also showed me an escape route. If someone turned up unexpectedly and started to bang on the door I was to run into the back room and climb out of the window into the garden then run round the barn, open the gate and carefully close it behind me and then return quickly to the cellar.

Alois guessed that Grandpa was probably wondering why he never invited him too. He knew Grandpa would have liked to play cards with him. So Alois explained that he could only take risks with someone who was young and agile and not with someone who was almost sixty years old.

I visited Alois almost every day for about two weeks and each time the same thing happened. He would ask me to cook him something or tidy up and would sit in the kitchen watching me and making the occasional remark. Whenever I cooked he would always give me a little for the other three in the cellar. It didn't even seem too risky because nobody ever called on Alois at home. He himself would go to the tavern on occasions, but he had little inclination to go there now, he said. He told me that in that wartime atmosphere even his old pals were scared of saying something untoward while they were playing cards, and God knows what would happen then. You wouldn't credit how many informers had crawled out of the woodwork he added.

He also divulged to me that the Germans were looking for us of course and some people were speculating about where we had disappeared. But he, Alois, used to maliciously confuse them with his own speculations. He would tell people for instance that we had lots of friends among the legionaries thanks to our father and that the legionaries had spirited us off to Russia where they still had contacts.

I was starting to think that things would go on like that with Alois forever, and I even started to take a bit of a liking to him because apart from peeking at me he behaved decently. But one day I was surprised to find him washed, shaved and dressed in a clean shirt and trousers. I asked him if he was going somewhere but he just mumbled something. I tidied up a bit in the kitchen and when I was washing the dishes Alois offered to let me take a bath. I was already convinced that he was no threat to me and the thought of a hot bath mesmerised me and that was a mistake.

I took off my clothes in the bathroom and immersed myself in the water that Alois had heated up for me in to large cooking pots and poured into the tin bath. I closed my eyes and luxuriated. Because I'd not known such bliss for several months it took me a while before I realised he'd come in. I quickly sat up and pulled my knees up to my chin and wrapped my arms round them.

"What are you doing here?" I asked him as calmly as I could although I wanted to scream. He told me with an odd expression that he simply wanted to help me wash.

I protested that I didn't need any help but Alois bent over me, took some water in his cupped hands and poured it over my back before starting to stroke my neck and shoulders.

"It won't do you any harm," he kept repeating, as if in a trance. He was panting aloud and was obviously extremely aroused.

I went on sitting there with my knees up to my chin hoping for him to stop but he stooped toward me and tried to kiss me on my temple. I was about to tell him that I would complain about him but I immediately realised that I had no one to complain to apart from Grandpa and Grandma and they were prisoners like me.

"Look" said Alois as if he was reading my thoughts "you can't give me away because it would be the end of you. And it would be the end of me too, because they sentence you to death for harbouring Jews. So there are lots of people you answer for."

Although I was scared out of my wits and wanted to cry I remember finding his logic surprising. What can I do I asked myself. I was trapped so I gave in.

I was simply ready to do anything to get out of that cellar at least from time to time. After all as soon as I started going to help Alois I knew I was treading on thin ice. But at that time I justified my acquiescence on the grounds that I had no choice. I was going crazy down there. I had been suffering from claustrophobia from the moment we arrived, and in addition that constant sitting in the semi-darkness was causing problems to my eyes and I still have them even now.

I have to admit that Alois did not treat me violently. He helped me out of the bath brought a towel and dried me and caressed me all over. Then he took me to his bedroom and laid me on the bed. While I quickly crept under the duvet he turned out the light. When I felt his hands on my body I decided that he wouldn't get even a peep out of me. I'd punish him by being as cold as stone even if I enjoyed it. He touched me gently and whispered that I was beautiful. He pushed away my hands that I was covering myself with and he kissed me in those places.

Maybe because I had already lived so long in extreme conditions it didn't seem so terrible to me. Of course it was horrible that he of all people, someone so much older, should force me to do his bidding as I was convinced at that moment. I had imagined my first night with a man quite differently and yet I felt I was yielding to him against my will. He wasn't at all brutal even when he penetrated me. On the contrary he tried to show me tenderness and he respected the fact I was doing it for the first time. And when it was all over he actually sobbed quietly.

"I'm sorry it happened that way" he said. "I couldn't help myself. I find you so attractive." I said nothing, but went to the bathroom and gathered up my clothes. I put them on and then climbed out of the window into the garden. I could see him standing nonplussed in the middle of the room.

Back in the cellar I lied to Grandpa and Grandma that I hadn't brought any food this time because I hadn't cooked for Alois just tidied up for him. Although neither of them asked me anything I felt with some sixth sense that Grandma had an inkling of what had happened. I lay down on my paillasse and buried my head in it. A rush of tears came to my eyes. I couldn't believe what I had done and over and over again I tried to convince myself that I probably had no choice that I couldn't be sure that Alois wouldn't take revenge and give us away even though he would be giving himself away too.

I was burdened with guilt all the same. I couldn't hide the fact that I had quite enjoyed it. I despised myself and at the same time I replayed in my head everything that had happened a short while before and could feel once more Alois penetrating me. As if the bliss that had made me sigh out loud and dig my fingers into his back had been caused against my will.

I felt dishonoured but I also felt new in some strange way. I almost didn't sleep at all that night wondering about what my poor parents would have said about it.

After that Alois left me alone for a few days. I was glad because I couldn't imagine how I was supposed to behave toward him now.

For several evenings in succession, he brought us food and exchanged a few words with Grandpa who each time would ask if there was any news from the front and that was all.

One morning when I crept out into the barn before dawn I saw a German automobile pull up in front of the gate. I rushed back into the cellar fastening the planks behind me and putting the catch on the door before rushing in panic to announce the news to my grandparents and Arno.

I ran through the false wooden partition with Grandpa and tried to guess what was happening. Words in German that sounded like orders were followed by stamping feet and Alois' terrified voice. The Germans wanted something from him but it didn't seem as if they had come to search the place. Then we could hear their footsteps not very far from us and the smell of cigarette smoke reached us through the chinks in the planks. Two of the Germans had obviously decided to take a look in the barn.

Those moments seemed interminable to us. I could speak German fairly well, because the Kleins' first language was German and they would often switch to German although as Czech patriots they tried to speak Czech at home. And my mother and father would also speak together in German.

That meant that I could understand what the two in the barn were talking about. They were definitely not looking for anything. One of them spoke about some girl he was planning to visit when he'd go home to Augsburg. Then someone called them and all of a sudden we could hear the German vehicle driving off.

Alois came about an hour later white as a sheet. He told us that the Germans had come there for water but even so his nerves were totally frayed. He even took my grandfather to task. "Bertie" he almost shouted at him "we originally agreed that you'd only be here for a little while."

Grandpa looked guilty.

"I know, I know, Alois" he said "but things turned out differently and we have nowhere to go."

Alois brushed his answer aside. He must have realised long ago that the people who were supposed to hide us were a figment of Grandpa's imagination. Then he turned to me and asked if I'd like to come and cook something.

I nodded. I didn't know what to do. On the one hand I dreaded the moment when I'd be alone with Alois again but on the other I was sorry for him because those Germans had scared the wits out of him. And I also suddenly felt grateful to him. After all he had actually been generous to Grandpa by just shrugging off his admission about the true position we were in.

In the end it was much easier with Alois than I had anticipated. I had imagined that embarrassed silence would ensue or a complicated explanation about what happened last time. But when I came to him he stroked my hair and there were tears in his eyes. His hand on my head gave me an odd thrill like on that first occasion and I let him put his arms around me and kiss me on the neck and breasts. Alois then took me in his arms and carried me to the bed. For the first time this was real lovemaking because I threw off all inhibitions and determined to satisfy him. When we finished I rested my head on his shoulder. We lay there like that in silence. Then we made love again.

I went back to the cellar that evening with food and in a much better mood than the last time. Grandma said nothing but most likely she knew that if the thing she suspected had happened it would have been hard for us to talk about it.

In time I invented for myself a theory that I was actually doing it for our family. That I was putting Alois under an obligation in this way and controlling him to a certain extent. And that I was also improving our situation by all of this because otherwise it was unlikely that Alois would send hot food to our cellar almost every night.

But the truth was that I was becoming dependent on sex with Alois. He was a huge fellow with brawny arms but he would caress me when making love and he didn't hurry. Compared with the men I met afterwards, he undoubtedly had a gift for sex. But it left me conflicted – I didn't manage to convince myself that I only went to see him on account of the others in the cellar. I was taking an increasingly active part in our lovemaking.

Often, I was impatient for him to summon me and scarcely had I arrived than I would be undressing him and playing with him. I used to be so impatient in fact that I'd undo his trousers in the kitchen and straddle him, caressing him lengthily inside me.

"You won't stay with me, Hana, when it's all over" he used to say, and each time I'd just place a finger on his lips and urge him to let things take their course. But things went wrong yet again.

Some time toward the end of 1943 I discovered while making love to Alois that he was all hot and his breathing was noisy and laboured. The next day he stayed in bed and I crept into the house without his permission to find out what was the matter with him. He looked really bad. He had a dry cough and his lips were cracked from the fever and when I came again in the evening to see him he was delirious. He refused to go to the doctor fearing what would happen to us if they kept him in hospital. He made it through the night but by morning we had no choice.

I promised him that if he really had to stay in hospital we would be very careful about what we did. We had enough food – there was a pile of potatoes at the back of the cellar. That was fine, he gasped, but he'd have to ask his relatives to feed the animals at least once a day. He implored me to be doubly careful. I promised him that we would be twice as cautious.

Then I spent the whole day watching out in case he returned but the house remained empty. The next morning we caught the sound of someone walking in the barn and by the footsteps we guessed it was a woman. A little while later the steps could be heard from the stable beyond the barn. Then the cows' hungry mooing and goats' plaintive bleating stopped. It continued like that for about a week and we were becoming more and more nervous because it was impossible to imagine what would become of us if Alois never returned.

About five days after his departure a strange thing occurred. I can remember crawling into the house through the half-open window at the back near the barn in the same way I did with Alois, and then walking through the dark interior with an oddly tense feeling. Eventually I went into the bathroom and removed my blouse and while I was washing I inspected my face in the mirror. I could see my father's nose and my mother's eyes as well as her blonde hair. I also scrutinised my breasts and belly. I noted with satisfaction that I looked well in spite of all the hardship. And all the while my mind was on Alois and the thought that this all belonged to him now.

There is only a weak light bulb in the bathroom and I suddenly start to feel dizzy probably due to straining my eyes in dim light. I grab onto the wash-hand basin to stop myself from falling over and at that moment there seems to be more light in the bathroom. I look up and I almost cry out in amazement because instead of my face in the mirror there appears some sort of space. It strikes me that it is like looking out of an open window. Quite simply there is another room beyond the mirror. It is not like anything I've seen before and it is empty apart from a table in the middle of it. It is diffused with a weird milky-white radiance.

Then I notice a silhouette standing by the table. It was almost hidden somehow in that bright light so that it wasn't immediately visible. Now I do really yell out in fear particularly when it moves. Its back is turned to me and it is slowly turning. At first its features are out of focus but then I see the figure's face with absolute clarity. It reminds me of someone. I frantically strive to remember who, and then it suddenly strikes me that it is father's childhood pal. His photo hung above father's desk. He said he fell somewhere in Russia.

I realise I've read about him in father's letter. Is this Hugo who was killed at Zborov. How come I didn't immediately associate him with the photograph that Father had treasured for so many years? I say Hugo's name out loud but the figure doesn't react. Then because I've read Father's letter at least ten times in the cellar it occurs to me that I am in the presence of Ariel. Now when I say the name Ariel a sort of flicker of agreement appears in those vague features.

This angel's specialty seems most likely to be predicting the future. I can hear a voice. He is speaking to me without moving his lips and I know precisely what he is saying. You will become the exact opposite of what you are and then you'll become the opposite of that opposite it declares in a peculiarly deliberate manner. You will meet someone who will help rescue you from the depths but his fall will drag you back into the depths. You will rise again but the abyss will draw you to it ever after. You will find release at its bottom.

Then he disappeared. He didn't say he'd return like he did to my father. He simply disappeared and left me a message that was totally mysterious. I stole back to the cellar and was unable to get to sleep the whole night.

The next morning Alois returned. I was pleased to see him and I spent a long time stroking his hair but he wasn't capable of making love. He told me it was pneumonia and that he really ought to be lying in hospital still but he had persuaded them that he needed to go home on account of his farm. What he didn't tell me and couldn't tell me in fact, was that he had been delirious in hospital and kept on talking in his fevered condition about me, my grandparents and Arno. And one Czech do-gooder – one of the attendants – had gone and reported it to the Gestapo.

They arrived the next day. I caught sight of them in time and bolted by our tested escape route. I have nothing to reproach myself for. I made no mistake. They went straight there but they didn't know precisely where to find us. I could hear Alois trying to persuade them that it must be a mistake, but they assumed – quite rightly as it turned out – that if they searched for us they'd find us.

And they did. We endured two hours of sheer dread as they tramped here and there and screamed orders over our heads. In the end they started to pry open the planks above and then the way was open for them. I thought they'd shoot us right away – we had already said our goodbyes – but instead they led us upstairs and loaded us into cars along with Alois. We had no idea where they were taking us. For most of the journey I was convinced that they were taking us to some execution ground but our journey ended in front of the Gestapo station.

Well and that's where the strange angel's prophecy started to come true. They led me with Arno and our grandparents into an office where there sat a man in Gestapo attire who bore a certain resemblance to my father. He observed us sternly and without pity, and yet it seemed to me that there was something slightly human in his gaze.

He asked us our names, and Grandpa and Grandma replied in German. The expression on his face was of someone confronted with vermin. Grandpa added that my name was Hana Brehme and my brother's was Arnošt Brehme. The man stared at Arno and me for a long time and then asked how we had come by that surname.

Grandpa immediately pointed out emphatically that our father Josef Brehme who had married their daughter – a Jewess admittedly – was not himself a Jew and they should show mercy to us. The Gestapo officer wanted to know more details about Josef Brehme so Grandpa explained to him that Josef had been the illegitimate son of a German musician called Joachim Brehme.

The interrogator behind the desk again scrutinised us for a long time. He was evidently agitated and possibly in a state of shock because his hands were shaking and he nervously shuffled the papers. Grandpa took advantage of it and started to tell him that in his view Arno and I had been wrongly issued with yellow stars because according to the laws of the Protectorate we weren't actually Jews. Yes it was true that we had started attending the synagogue with them in 1935 but we were minors and what counted was that we had been properly christened and had only two Jewish grandparents. Poor old Grandpa couldn't suspect that during the time we had spent in the potato cellar the Nazis had already wiped out so many Volljuden, that in their quest to eliminate everything Jewish from the face of the earth they had also pounced on many *Mischlingen des ersten Grades*.

The officer was curious to know whether we had any documentation about our origin. Grandpa seemed to have realised that this moment might arise and replied that the soldiers who had arrested us had taken his wallet, which contained papers to prove everything he had said. The agitated interrogator ordered the soldier at the door to bring them.

When he had examined them he declared that he had to investigate the whole matter and had us taken away. In that unfortunate situation we were nonetheless fortunate that they put us all in one cell. It must have been against some regulation or other because the guard looked rather baffled when they brought us all there. Grandpa was sure that the interrogator had been influenced by his explanation but I had a feeling that it was something else. In any event we scarcely slept at all that night because we could not rule out the possibility that in the morning they would simply take us out into the yard and shoot us.

Next morning the interrogator had us brought before him once more and he nodded at us to sit down. Then he ordered the guard to leave us alone with him. He gazed about the room anxiously as if unsure whether anyone was eavesdropping.

Then he told Arno and me that his name was Brehme. Karl Brehme. And that his father was Joachim Brehme, the very same person who was our father's father according to the papers Grandpa had given him. He said our name had saved us because it was the first thing that had drawn his attention when he was given our case to deal with. Or rather he initially read that our grandparents were named Klein and was about to sign the usual order but then noticed that Arno and I had the surname Brehme. He didn't explain what he meant by "the usual order."

He said he had always known that he had a half-brother in Bohemia by the name of Josef Brehme and had even started to search for him when he received information that there was a young gifted violinist living in Prague. But when he eventually managed to visit Prague after World War I, he discovered that his half-brother had deserted to the Russians from the Austro-Hungarian army. Until yesterday, he had assumed that Josef had perished somewhere in Russia because his name had never surfaced after the war.

I must admit that we sat there utterly dumbfounded. Karl Brehme leaned across the desk and in a manner oddly out of character with his fearsome appearance whispered almost conspiratorially that he might be able to do something for Arno and me. When all was said and done it was possible to re-examine our racial origin and come to some kind of arrangement. However the only thing he could do for Grandpa and Grandma is not to have them shot straight away for disobeying the order to join the transport but to send them to the transport now. Even so he said he was taking quite a risk because it might occur to somebody that he was treating them with kid gloves so to speak. Perhaps I'll manage to get you to Terezín he told our Klein grandparents.

So all of a sudden I had a new relative – and a Gestapo officer to boot!

Grandpa and Grandma were also aware of the absurdity of the situation, but as Grandpa managed to tell us: let us be grateful for the fact that this incredible coincidence might save the lives of Arno and me.

That was the last time in my life that I saw my grandparents. Karl Brehme declared almost apologetically but resolutely that he had to separate us but maybe we'd see each other again one day.

Arno flung himself on Grandma and put his arms round her refusing to let her go until he realised that it would make no difference. I went over to Grandpa and kissed him on the forehead. Somewhere inside I knew we wouldn't see each other again.

"It's our only hope" Grandpa said to me when I hugged him goodbye "so let's not be sad. It could have turned out worse – we might have all been dead already."

But the tears were pouring down my cheeks.

The only one who was already dead was Alois. When I asked Karl Brehme about him he told me that they had executed him the previous evening according to the law. He also stressed with a degree of irony that Czechs had denounced us.

I sat for a little longer in Brehme's office with Arno who was sobbing while Brehme started writing something quickly and my mind was in a whirl at the realization that in the space of twenty-four hours I had lost my grandparents who had become my substitute parents and also my lover. Not a very successful first love I thought to myself, more a substitute for one. And I fell into a state of black despair.

But there was to be no end to the twists of fate. The next day Karl Brehme informed Arno and me that he had found a solution that would save our lives. There was an odd, almost sheepish expression on his face as he broke the news to us. He couldn't let the two of us stay together because it would arouse too much suspicion. He said he had some friends – relatives in fact – who would take care of us but it meant that we would have to be apart at least until the war was over.

It was a dreadful scene. I was almost an adult but Arno was still a young boy and he didn't have anyone but me in the whole world. He didn't want to be torn from me and between sobs I begged Karl Brehme to change things. I had no success. He asked us to be sensible, saying he'd already broken so many regulations on account of us and they could send him to prison too. Or more likely he would be shot. He promised at least that Arno and I would remain in contact with one another.

To this day I have no idea how Karl Brehme sorted out our papers. It was already 1944 so he ought to have sent us as part Jewish to the transport just like Grandpa and Grandma. I think he quite simply made use of his status. What is certain is that I was sent off to Krnov in Silesia, which was in the Reich beyond the Protectorate's borders while Arno had to go all the way to Hamburg to Karl Brehme's family. Before our departure, that successful half-brother of my father's commanded us never under any circumstances to divulge that the Kleins were Jews. In fact we were not to speak about the family on my mother's side. If anyone asked us, we were to reply that our parents had died eight years ago and thereafter we were cared for by relatives that had also subsequently died.

It went against my nature to renounce Grandpa and Grandma – and therefore my mother as well – in that way but I was young and didn't want to die. I told myself that I'd possibly be able to make it all up to Grandpa and Grandma if they survived. And I determined that like many Jews who were obliged to conceal their origin in order to survive, I too would acknowledge my origin when the conditions would be more favourable – if only for the fact that the price I paid for my life was so high.

To this day I am terrified of enclosed spaces and I am pursued by nightmares. I am constantly finding myself back again in that cellar with Grandma, Grandpa and Arno and in every dream I know in advance that it will come to no good and that we are hiding in vain. Previously Alois would appear in those dreams too but rarely in the role of my lover. It kept coming back to me how he took advantage of me before he first possessed me. It made no difference at all that in real life I had forgiven him and that I had actually started to like him in a strange way.

I haven't managed to rid myself of most of those dreams. I expect that spending over a year in that potato cellar left more mental scars than I was willing to admit at that time. It also occurs to me that I would never have been so marked by all of that had everything come right for us in the end. But when they separated us in 1944 and they sent Grandpa and Grandma to a concentration camp, our stay in that hole seemed to have lost any sense and in addition – it had become a weird threat.

And then there was Ariel. If my father hadn't written about him he would have undoubtedly ended up in some rear compartment of my memory as a phantasm – as something that may not have happened – because after all I had every right to hallucinate. Maybe I'd have managed to cast doubt on Ariel in spite of the fact that my father had written about him, had it not been for the fact that everything he predicted came true. It seemed to me that I was being carried along by some sinister premonition over which I had no influence.

When I disclosed it to the doctor after the war, he explained to me that Ariel was an *idée fixe*. After all, my father had been unsure whether he had only imagined it and the doctor knew for certain that my father had only imagined it. It's no wonder, he told me, that some spirit or angel should have appeared to me after reading my father's letter over and over again in that hole. The doctor told me to recall the situation I was in when Ariel honoured me with his visit. I was desperate at that moment I wasn't sure that Alois would return from the hospital and I was fully aware that if he had died, it would have been a disaster for all of us. I apparently needed to grasp at some straw, which is why my symptoms at that time had also included a split personality.

I don't know. What is certain is that if Ariel is merely the result of my alleged schizophrenia then the part of my mind that created it has prophetic powers. Because when he said "you'll become the exact opposite of what you are and then you'll become the opposite of that opposite", he couldn't have been more accurate.

When I arrived in Krnov I became an Aryan. My uncle Karl sent me to the Kohler family. They were Germans. They were distantly related to Karl Brehme, so they didn't ask many questions even though they must have wondered where I came by my German accent and all those grammatical mistakes I made at first. It's true, as Brehme instructed me, that I told them that after my parents' death I had been in the care of a Czech family but they must have been curious all the same.

What was new was that I was now known as Hana Brehme and not Hana Brehmeová. My uncle had seen to it that in the papers that travelled with me, the Czech ending -ová had been removed.

The doctor who treated me after the war had a theory that the beginnings of my split personality had something to do with the fact that I had to adopt a new identity and that I hadn't identified with it emotionally. He also told me that I had undergone my first change of identity when I changed from being a Czech girl and became a Jewess who had to wear a yellow star and was then expelled from school. Then he added that when I was in that cellar I changed overnight from being an adolescent girl into the concubine of a much older man. I had justified it on the grounds of having to protect my family. So, in fact, my identity was changing all the time.

Apart from being obliged to remain silent or lie about my past, life at the Kohlers' wasn't bad. And in fact that presented me with a problem because I went there convinced that I must hate them as representatives of the nation that had caused all those atrocities. So my intended hatred conflicted with my realisation that the Kohlers weren't bad people.

They were farmers and they had a homestead not far from Krnov that had been in their family for centuries. The house was roomy and cosily furnished. I was given a room of my own and although I had to help on the farm which, in the absence of men of a productive age, meant a lot of work, I was quite well off, particularly when I consider that it was wartime and things were beginning to go downhill for Germany.

Two sisters, Gerta and Berta, ruled the house because their husbands and sons were in the army. The only man living there was their uncle Fritz who was almost seventy. Also living there were Gerta's daughters, Anke and Rita, who were both about twenty. None of them spoke much about the war, as if it was of no interest to them. I found that odd because the four absent men whose pictures hung on the walls and whom they frequently recalled were risking their lives for Germany elsewhere.

At the beginning I couldn't help thinking of my Klein grandparents and Arno all the time. I was always secretly weeping over them somewhere where the Kohlers couldn't see me. I feared more and more for their safety, particularly Arno's. I had no news of him even though Karl Brehme had promised to arrange for some form of communication.

About two months after I arrived he suddenly turned up in person at the Kohlers' farm in his black leather jacket and asked me in a friendly fashion how I was getting on. Later when he found a moment to be alone with me he assured me that Arno was all right. He was actually attending some school in Hamburg. I naturally asked him about Grandpa and Grandma but he told me curtly that he had no news of them.

That visit by Karl Brehme was an eye-opener for me. I came to realise that the Kohlers were afraid of him. Although they treated him courteously they did so with reserve. When he left the farm a few hours later I could sense that they were all relieved. I didn't ask any questions and went out to clean the stable. Passing through the barn I happened to overhear Gerta saying to her sister that she hoped that man from the Gestapo wouldn't start paying regular visits on account of me. She was worried that people would start to cold-shoulder them.

At supper I deliberately raised the matter of Brehme's visit. I emphasised that I scarcely knew him. He investigated me by chance, when he was trying to find out what had happened to his half-brother, my father. He had only discovered he had relatives in the Czech lands just before the war. Besides, my father hadn't been aware of his existence.

I think that the Kohlers rightly grasped that I was trying to distance myself from Karl. There was a moment's silence while they all concentrated on their food. It was broken by Fritz. He declared that they, the Kohlers, were a decent German family. That's all he said on that occasion, most likely because they didn't know me well enough but it looked as if they had no love for people like Karl Brehme.

My suspicions were confirmed sooner than I expected. About a week after Brehme's visit Gerta received notification that her husband had fallen on the eastern front. And as if that misfortune were not enough, a few days later a further notification arrived this time about the death of Berta's son, Hans. Despair reigned in that household and my determination to despise these people as representatives of the German nation soon left me. It suddenly struck me that we had all found ourselves part of some incomprehensible drama.

One evening Gerta and I were sitting alone in the kitchen and she started of her own accord to relate to me how at first they had put their hopes in Hitler because they believed he'd enable them to live in their own German state but then they had become disillusioned with him.

"We were never in favour of this war" she told me. "I don't know why my husband had to die somewhere in the East and I don't know why Berta's son had to die either."

And then she added something that made me love her forever.

"I also don't know" she said, "where those transports are bound. They say it's to camps. What's for certain is that no one comes back. It doesn't make any sense to me. Some of those people were our friends before the war.

"I know you could report me for this" she continued "and these days it wouldn't even help me that I'm a German or that my son is fighting for the Reich somewhere in France. But I'm at rock bottom and can't sink lower." She was holding her head in her hands as if it was too heavy to carry, and then she burst into tears.

I took her hand. I was sorely tempted to tell her the truth about myself, because I felt that we were united by a similar despair. But in the end I simply reassured her that she had nothing at all to fear from me, and that I also thought the war was senseless. Maybe one day I'll be able to confide in her what I went through.

For a moment she gazed at me pensively, but she asked me no further questions. But from the time of our conversation she and Berta were much friendlier to me though it must be said that even before they always treated me with courtesy.

Although the atmosphere in the house had changed, most of the time I was still quite solitary. I simply didn't belong to that family. They would sooner have been on their own. I would usually withdraw to my bedroom and either try to get to sleep or ponder on Arno, and Grandpa and Grandma, and my parents as well of course. It wasn't clear to me why all this was happening. In his letter Father wrote how he once came to believe in God but belief in God was becoming more and more of a problem for me. I don't mean the existence of God as some kind of prime mover or cause of everything – without that I wouldn't be able to explain the existence of anything at all. I mean God as a judge to whom we are all answerable. I couldn't understand why I should revere a God who had allowed all this to happen. For instance, if it was some kind of punishment then let him kindly inform me why I was being punished. After all, I was sixteen at the time! Maybe I deserved some punishment for having enjoyed sex with Alois but one after another, disasters had started to rain down on me long before. My parents died when I was seven. Then they expelled me from school and then came that cellar. Or maybe God punished preventively in advance because he knew that one day we wouldn't satisfy his requirements?

And what had my father been punished for? After all, it was clear from what he wrote that he was an honourable man. Maybe, he too, as a young man had offended some moral code by his relationship with Johana but most likely that had been his only lapse. Otherwise it seemed to me that he had always tried to live decently.

The priest at the church where I attended Mass every Sunday with the Kohlers would no doubt have explained to me that we have no right to question God's motives but I didn't seek his advice. I knew that I wouldn't rid myself of my doubts regardless of what he told me. Why should I have respect for God's plans when all around me there were people dying who had done nothing wrong? I thought to myself that if it was just some game then it was a strange kind of game. A God like that didn't seem to have any concern for our suffering or our feelings. And even if people went to some much better world right after they died or even straight to heaven, what was the sense of all that suffering beforehand? That doesn't count? If my parents were watching me from somewhere at that moment, could they possibly be happy about my suffering? Are they only supposed to be happy at the thought that they already know that I will be better off after I die, and that it all has some kind of higher purpose?

There was definitely nothing sophisticated about those reflections of mine but they came from my heart. After all, what else could I rely on but my heart, seeing that fate had denied me an education? I had only completed six grades when someone decided that I wasn't allowed to go to school because of my origin. And now at the Kohlerhof, as I privately dubbed the Kohlers' farm? I couldn't even study in the evening. At first I thought that the miserable light in that cellar had damaged my eyes but the doctors later discovered that I had contracted diabetes because of the bad food and stress and that was the reason they said I developed glaucoma though fortunately only partial.

Now that I'm writing about my life, my memories somehow order themselves chronologically of their own accord. I had almost stopped thinking about them in those terms because my life in the hospital is virtually without time. Every day here is the same, even though Sasha says history is being made once more outside. But my history came to a halt some time ago like some broken machine. And so I find it quite surprising that what I've written so far is evidence of some personal history.

I thought quite a lot about Ariel at that time in the Kohlerhof because I had yet to meet any doctor who would explain to me that Ariel was simply my *idée fixe*. What interested me most of all was whether his role was solely to foretell what would happen without being able to influence it some way himself or whether, on the contrary, he had some power to determine our fate somehow. In any event he didn't seem to be a bearer of good news. And what I found particularly annoying was that everything seemed to be planned in advance. Because otherwise how could Ariel know for instance that I would become the opposite of what I'd been? And how could he have known that Father would live to find happiness after all those disasters? And if everything was predestined, why were we given emotions? Why did we have to suffer?

And something else that didn't make sense to me was that the fates of other people must be predestined too – and definitely the fates of the people who played some role in my life. But that would mean that Uncle Karl, for instance, had no choice. It wouldn't be up to him whether he wanted to be a Gestapo officer or not. And if we didn't have any choice there was no difference between a good deed and a bad deed. And whether we tried or not, we would only become what we were destined to be anyway.

As I write this down now, I can see how dreadfully confused and lonely I was at that time. That was the reason – or so I believe – why I started seeing Stefan.

Gerta's son Stefan arrived on leave in the spring of 1944. He had come all the way from France where, so far, he had served fairly uneventfully on the Normandy coast. In fact, he had been granted leave in recognition of a heroic deed in a skirmish with an English landing force. It was fairly unusual that he had been allowed to travel home at that period because by then the German forces were being depleted and they were starting to conscript the very young and the very old.

Stefan didn't talk much about the army – at least not with me. In fact he didn't say much for several hours after he arrived as if he was finding it hard to accustom himself to his home surroundings. I also put it down to my presence. After all, I was an outsider at the Kohlerhof and so I tried to keep out of the way. I went to feed the animals and then did some household chores. It wasn't until the evening that I plucked up courage to go to the shared kitchen in search of something to eat. Meanwhile Stefan started to talk a bit, mostly reminiscing about the time before the war. The atmosphere became tense when his dead father was mentioned. I couldn't leave the room straight away because Stefan started asking me about my past. Nevertheless after a few curt replies I managed to make my exit.

I realise now that there were three reasons why I wanted to make myself scarce. First, I couldn't bear the flood of grief that overwhelmed the family when the death of Stefan's father came up. Second, I was afraid that he might detect some inconsistencies in my replies. Third, he aroused me. The moment I realised it, I mentally scolded myself, of course. I was convinced that I had no right to feel anything for him. After all he was a German soldier even if I'd found him attractive at first sight. I told myself that Grandpa and Grandma would be horrified if they knew the kind of interest Stefan aroused in me the moment I set eyes on him.

I couldn't bear sitting in my room, so that evening I went for a short walk in the woods that lay not far from the Kohlerhof. As I was walking there through the fields I suddenly heard the sound of footsteps on the path behind me. It was Stefan as I expected. He pretended he had met me by chance and asked me where I was going even though it was obvious. He asked if he could join me.

I didn't protest. I eyed him furtively. He was tall and slim and had his mother's sharply defined features and penetrating gaze. And above all – and this was what immediately attracted me – he had a sensual mouth. The uniform really suited him despite belonging to the Wehrmacht.

He told me how when he was a boy he used to take this path with his father who was now buried somewhere on the eastern front. They would always go together to the forest for fire wood. They also used to observe the game and he showed me the hideout where they would often sit the whole night.

"Oh, well" he said, "it can't be helped. There's a war and Dad has fallen for the homeland. He's a hero." And then he burst into tears like a little boy. "Sorry. I had to control myself in front of Mummy and my sisters, but I was really overcome," he explained between sobs. "Maybe you'll understand how I feel. Mummy told me that your parents died when you were still small."

I replied that I did understand what he was talking about, and I just briefly stroked his arm through the uniform. We walked wordlessly to the last of the hides and the tears started to flow from his eyes once more. "It needn't have turned out like this", he said illogically and when he noticed my gaze he blurted out angrily that no one in his family had wanted this war. "What's all this Lebensraum?" he ranted. "There's plenty of room in Europe for everyone, both the Germans and the Jews." And this won me over totally.

I can't remember any more about anything we talked about. All I know is that I didn't tell him who I really was. He did most of the talking anyway. He said it was a long time since he had talked to a girl and certainly not with one as beautiful as me. So I shouldn't be surprised that I made him feel self-conscious. His words gave me pleasure – why shouldn't I admit it? Alois hadn't courted me as romantically as this.

I boasted to Stefan that the only thing that I was really good at was chess and he suggested we play together. He said he also played when he had the opportunity. So as soon as we got home we set out the chess pieces and started a game. He played with concentration and bit his nails but didn't stand a chance against me and lost three times in a row. I was a bit worried that his manly pride might be shattered but it looked as though those three defeats only increased his admiration. Where had I learnt to play like that he wanted to know? I said something vague in reply even though I could see in my mind's eye the potato cellar with Grandpa Klein sitting in it.

At breakfast the next day while Stefan was still asleep Gerta took me to one side. "He's totally crazy about you," she said. "I'm his mother, I can tell. Be kind to him if you can. Goodness knows what will happen to him after he goes back to the front. At least he'd have something nice to remember."

I'm sure that God-fearing woman didn't mean that I should go to bed with Stefan – that would be against her principles – but that's what Stefan wanted most of all. When he and I were left alone the next evening it was obvious he wanted to kiss me but didn't know how to go about it. It wasn't until that moment that I realised that he had never been with a girl because he had been scarcely an adult when he was conscripted. Admittedly I was a few years younger but I had more experience than him and knew that I ought to help him somehow.

We went for a walk together once more and Stefan started to tell me about his childhood again and how previously his family had lived together with Czechs and Poles without hatred and he couldn't understand what had happened. I took his hand and he went on holding it tightly in silence until we reached the hideout. We climbed up to it and I allowed him to kiss me. I don't know whether it was out of compassion or from some form of budding love. All I know is that I was terribly lonely and all of a sudden here was someone who wanted to put his arms round me and tell me he had fallen in love with me. On top of that I found Stefan incredibly handsome.

It was definitely stupid after a two-day acquaintance and in different circumstances things would have certainly turned out differently. But we were in a hurry – each of us for our own private reasons. Looming over him was the prospect of an allied attack after he returned to his unit, sooner or later; whereas I was oppressed by the awareness that it could be several years before I'd see a decent-looking young man because they were all in the trenches somewhere.

I soon realised that Stefan didn't know how to proceed. So I whispered to him that we'd find a better place than that chilly hideout. So we went back, hand in hand to the Kohlerhof stopping now and then to kiss.

In front of the house I told him I'd wait for him in my room if he liked. It was obvious to me that he'd still have to have a chat with his mother and sisters in the kitchen. About an hour later he knocked on my window. When I opened the window he was pale and terrified.

We made love the whole night. We just couldn't stop. Since the moment I lost Alois I had had a strange sexual longing and I really wanted Stefan. And he kept repeating that he had fallen in love with me and he tried to prove it.

When I think about it now, that week with Stefan meant for me an escape into a world where time didn't exist. As if suddenly there was no war. As if my grandparents hadn't perhaps just died in some concentration camp. Like my parents had never died. Everything was drowned out by a longing that bordered on madness. Maybe because we were so close to death. Stefan would come every night and we would spend every night making love. I was completely exhausted the whole day and several times I fell asleep in the cowshed. But I didn't mind. As if I knew almost certainly that I'd never see him again and that I was giving him strength for a long and endless journey.

After he left I spent several days in a weird trance. My body was terribly sensitive on account of that intense lovemaking. I was capable of being aroused by merely touching something that reminded me of him. I had vivid dreams at night in which I was either with him or back in my parents' home or meeting with Grandpa and Grandma.

Gerta knew perfectly well what had happened of course. She started to treat me in almost a motherly way as if I was supposed to become her daughter-in-law. To tell the truth I had no idea what I'd have done if Stefan had returned. Even though I knew it had meant much more to him; for me, that week of sensual pleasure had been, above all, a way of forgetting. At the same time, some sixth sense told me that I wouldn't have to deal with the issue, as Stefan would never be returning.

Nor did he return. A few weeks after the Allies landed in Normandy notification arrived that Stefan had been killed. Gerta cracked up and had the times been different, they would have had to put her in a mental hospital. She didn't speak or eat and spent days lying in bed. She looked like she wanted to die. I used to go see her from time to time but there was no way I could console her.

I was also upset by Stefan's death. During his stay at the Kohlerhof fate had permitted me to build an emotional tie with someone. For me, that was like throwing a life belt to someone drowning. Now I was alone again and had only myself to rely on even though – as I hoped – my grandparents were still alive somewhere like my brother far away in the Reich. But I had nothing to rely on because my identity – as doctors like saying – had been so affected by the shifts of fate that it wasn't clear to me what I should form an attachment to.

I think that was the moment when I started to experience states of overwhelming anxiety and disintegration. Somewhere there was the start of what subsequently caused me to spend so much time in institutions. The world seemed to be totally meaningless to me and in a world without meaning there is no reason to exist. Maybe the only reason I didn't kill myself was Ariel's prophesy. After all, he had predicted that I would become the opposite of what I had been and then would become the opposite of that opposite. What had he meant, in fact?

It's odd that someone should stay alive just because of a few words from a phantom, seeing that it was just an *idée fixe* or a figment of my imagination as my doctor later explained to me. And if, by some chance it wasn't, then he was even subtler than one could ever imagine because if he hadn't appeared to me I would never have found the strength to live and fulfil his prophesy.

In every direction the Germans were beginning to be defeated and there were mixed feelings at the Kohlers. On the one hand they wanted the war that none of them had believed in, to finish but on the other, they were slightly afraid about what would become of them when the Russians reached their home. And, of course, they were sorry for all the soldiers who had died for no reason at the front because Hitler was determined to fight on to the very last.

Gerta slowly pulled herself together but she didn't have much to say for herself. As she put it, she was scorched inside. A strange friendship existed between the two of us, because she knew how deeply Stefan had been in love with me. One evening when we were sitting alone in the kitchen I was unable to contain my secret any longer and so I told her the true story of my life. I only kept my sinful relationship with Alois from her.

Gerta had guessed that there was something in my past that didn't tally with what I had told them when I arrived but even so, I think she was shocked. She wasn't fazed in the least by my origin. Most likely she was actually pleased to have been able to help someone like me. I expect Karl Brehme was what puzzled her most of all.

"We all thought that he had no conscience at all when he joined the Gestapo" she said. "But some decency must have remained in him after all."

She promised not to tell anyone about our conversation. Not that her daughter Berta or Fritz would have any problem with my true story but because we knew that if more people knew it there would be a greater risk that someone would blurt it out. And clearly there was no knowing how long that war would continue.

The second half of 1944 was a period of relative calm for us but then suddenly history started to progress at full speed. More and more Germans were fleeing west from Eastern Prussia and Poland and a few of them called in at the Kohlerhof. Gerta and Berta treated them with the same courtesy they did the emaciated escapees from a transport that we found sleeping in the barn. The sight of those walking skeletons whose eyes alone remained alive dumbfounded me. I kept on saying to myself that that was probably how my grandparents ended up while I had survived quite comfortably in a German homestead and I'd even had a great time with a German soldier. I suffered dreadful pangs of conscience.

That spring when everything had collapsed Karl Brehme turned up in his black limousine. In enormous haste he tried to persuade his distant relatives to leave with him because any moment the Russians would be there and from reports he had received they were committing unimaginable atrocities against Germans. He placated them with the assurance that they would be able to return home after the war when everything was sorted out.

Gerta and Berta would hear nothing of it. "We've done no one any harm" they objected. "Besides we can't leave the farm – who would take care of the animals?"

Karl realised he was wasting his time. He declared resignedly that he had expected as much when all was said and done. But in all events he was taking me with him for his own safety if nothing else. At the time I had no idea what his safety had to do with me so I resisted. I tried to persuade him that I was at home there but in my case Karl was not going to take no for an answer and simply allowed me to take my leave of the Kohlers. Then, after more than a year and tearful farewells I was heading back to the Protectorate.

We drove all the way to Prague. Karl told me he had spent the previous months there. But as it turned out Prague was not our final destination. When we pulled up in front of the house where he had his office and residence he didn't even allow me to get out of the car. While his driver kept an eye on me, he must have been frantically packing his suitcases because about an hour later he emerged with several pieces of baggage and we immediately set off again westward.

We stopped at checkpoints several times but Karl's Gestapo attire worked wonders. He didn't have to show anyone his papers. It was enough for him to thrust his pass under their noses, and most of the time even that wasn't necessary.

I said nothing during the journey until eventually I plucked up courage and asked him about Joachim Brehme my other grandfather whom I'd never known.

He had been a musician who travelled a great deal Karl informed me. He had spent little time at home. He had been nothing exceptional as a musician but used to tour as a member of an orchestra. It earned him enough to live on and in addition he had inherited quite a lot of money from his father who was a Hamburg merchant. The family was fairly well to do. He had had one other passion apart from music and that was women. He supposed that my grandmother hadn't been the only one whose heart he had broken on his travels. He thought it was even possible that I had more aunts and uncles in Europe but so far he had only unearthed my father.

Then he fell silent and gazed at the countryside. It wasn't until we were somewhere near Cham in Bavaria that he added that his father had died before the end of World War I which was probably just as well as he was a patriot. And after another period of silence he said he had a gift for me and he pulled a thick envelope out of a big black hold all. I immediately recognised my father's letter. "It was among things that were confiscated" he said curtly "but it belongs to you."

It was impossible to tell from what he said whether he had had Father's letter translated to German to find out what was in it.

Eventually I fell asleep and when I awoke I realised we had reached the end of our journey. We were somewhere in Germany, that was obvious but at first I couldn't guess where. Our final destination as I later discovered was a farmstead just outside Munich. I don't know whether the owners were also relatives of Karl's but it's unlikely because there were several families crammed into the house and the barn. Everyone who arrived in SS uniform or Gestapo attire immediately burned it after changing into civilian clothes.

It was part of a plan that I didn't understand at first. Only later did Karl explain to me that we were waiting there for the Americans who were supposed to arrive within two days. He wasn't wrong. It looked as if he and all those who had come there were well informed. And I have to say that even in the chaos that overwhelmed Europe in those last days of the war they had everything organised with proverbial German thoroughness. While Hitler was drafting old men and school-aged boys up to the last moment, these men had already done with fighting.

It was here that I finally realised why Karl had been so adamant that I should accompany him. I was to serve as an alibi if the Americans figured out who he really was. Except that the Americans didn't figure out very much at the beginning because they had other worries. Although it was obvious to them when they reached our homestead that this odd assembly of middle-aged men was not there by chance, they had no time to investigate and left only two soldiers to guard the place.

It was two weeks later when the war was over that they started interrogating the members of that curious gathering. Most of them trotted out a similar story to the Americans. Yes, they had served in the German army in the East but they had been only ordinary officers who had started to have doubts about Hitler's judgment long ago. And because they hadn't wanted to fall into Bolshevik hands they had fled west.

Naturally the Americans were interested to know why they had all met up here. Was it really by chance? And Karl and Co. had an answer ready for that too. They said there was a sort of secret information network among the officers who were unhappy with Hitler. So they knew where to make for when the Russians were approaching.

The Americans weren't stupid of course. They didn't believe that some network could exist among ordinary German officers without the Allies knowing. And so the interrogations dragged on. Eventually the Americans discovered that some of the gentlemen assembled there were Gestapo or SS officers. Finally it was Karl Brehme's turn. It was his somewhat unusual name that gave him away. How many Gestapo officers of that name could there have been in the Protectorate?

Since Karl had brought me here solely in order to have something to boast about if the Americans unmasked him he didn't feel any great need to deny his guilt at the interrogation. Yes he had done dirty work but he had also done good deeds. The proof was his half-niece Hana Brehme – originally Brehmeová – a Jewess whom he had saved from certain death. So the Americans started to interrogate me more thoroughly too.

I didn't want to do Karl any harm. After all he really had saved me and Arno and maybe Grandpa and Grandma too if they were sent to Terezín and not straight to Auschwitz. On the other hand, he had had Alois shot without mercy and no doubt many others before and after him. I asked myself, what do I know? Maybe he, too, was just a cog in the machinery of the Nazi regime. Now it's obvious to me that a Gestapo officer couldn't have been a passive cog but on that occasion I assisted him.

How? Simply by telling the American interrogator how and why I had hidden in the potato cellar with the Kleins and Arno and how Brehme had saved us. It is true that he did it because we were related, but even so he placed himself at enormous risk when he obtained the papers that turned me into a citizen of the Reich. And he had even changed my name.

I don't know what the Americans would have done with Karl if I hadn't told them that but what I do know is that although they eventually took him away somewhere and I never saw him again he did survive as I only discovered several years later. They didn't know what to do with me. As I had German papers and was in Germany they took me to a reception camp for war orphans in Munich. It was logical because apart from my Gestapo officer half-uncle, I truly had no one and I wasn't yet eighteen. The American who drove me to Munich told me that he or someone else would return for me as soon as they had sorted out their relations with the Russians who were occupying Czechoslovakia. After all, I had been abducted to Germany, so I ought to have the right to be repatriated. Except that nobody returned for me.

I remember well, the house where I would spend over a year. It stood mostly undamaged in the middle of ruins in the Schwabing district of Munich. Although we were supervised, everybody was so fed up with discipline after the Nazi period, the supervision tended to be symbolic. Not that we were able to make much use of our relative freedom. We had ration coupons for food and anyway we were totally worn out every evening after spending hours clearing away the ruins.

The debris from Schwabing was all taken to some level ground near Dachau Street and it started to turn into small hills. At the time it wasn't obvious to me what the Germans would do with all those piles of debris. It was only just recently when I was watching a TV report here in the hospital about preparations for the Olympic Games in Munich that I suddenly grasped that those nice grass-covered mounds surrounded by the foundations of the future stadiums were actually the piles of debris which continue to conceal within themselves the sweat of all of us who helped clear it away. As well as the blood of all of those who died in them and maybe even corpses because some of the debris wasn't raked over but simply loaded onto trucks by bulldozer and carted off.

There's one thing I mustn't leave out regarding my moral profile. Under the influence of the wartime events I became quite a full-blown nymphomaniac. No doubt doctors would explain it expertly to me – and some have even tried to – but I think I know the reason. When I was making love to Alois and Stefan I didn't have the time to link sex with big emotions. I knew that it was very risky to get too strongly attached to someone and that it would probably cost me dearly.

Sex was an escape. The only escape possible for me in fact in that wretched situation. I expect that's why I soon started a relationship at that orphanage with a German from Munich who was a year younger than me. His father had been killed at the front and a bomb had wiped out the rest of his family. Their house – the one the bomb fell on – wasn't far from our orphanage.

My latest lover, Kurt, was totally devoted to me and that gave me particular pleasure. I even admit that I was slightly malicious at that time. As I flirted with him he was still in a state of shock after the loss of his family. He took the affair much more seriously than I did and even dreamed we would stay together. I still don't know how much I helped him or how much I wounded him. When I broke off with him, he made a scene and wanted to commit suicide but then, about a month later, he started going out with a girl of his own age.

I had several relationships like that afterward and it didn't bother me. I had the feeling that my existence then was totally divorced from any reality and went about in a strange state of mental weightlessness. I had nowhere to go and no idea what would happen. I was content when I received my food tickets and had somewhere to sleep at night. Also, I spent that whole year waiting for the reappearance of those Americans who had promised to help repatriate me if I wanted to return to Czechoslovakia but as time passed it became clear to me that they had forgotten about me.

I don't know how long I'd have been stranded in that camp if fate hadn't come to my aid because I myself could see no way out. After all I couldn't just pick myself up and head off to Czechoslovakia with my German documents could I? How could I prove who I was? And wouldn't I need some special permit to travel from the American zone to a territory that had been liberated by the Russians? I had no one to advise me. It occurred to me to set out for Hamburg in search of Arno but I had never asked Karl Brehme the name of the family where Arno was. I had always assumed they were called Brehme but later realised this needn't be the case at all.

And then something unexpected happened. One day after work, I take a walk in the park and suddenly hear someone speaking perfect Czech! I look around me and see two older men talking about some camp in Bavaria, where thousands of refugees from Czechoslovakia are arriving. I only realise they are Germans when they switch to speaking German. Nevertheless I go over and speak to them.

First they observe me with a certain amazement. They only start to take notice when I explain where I'm from. One excused himself saying he had to rush off somewhere but the other, a tall guy about forty with a blonde shock of hair, introduces himself as Herman. He sits down on an old bench and invites me to tell him more. And I feel I just haven't the strength to hide anything any more, though it's obvious to me that every German can be a potential Nazi sympathiser even though the war is over. But I don't care. I tell him that I lived in Úvaly near Prague when I was a little girl, that my parents died and how my Jewish mother and her parents then became a big problem, how we hid in the cellar and how Arno and me were eventually saved by a relative who I'd previously no idea existed. And I tell Herman straight out that

I'd like most of all to return to Czech territory, because it's the only way to find out if Grandpa and Grandma have happened to survive. Herman is from Nový Jičín a town not far from Krnov and it's something we have in common. He tells me how already last year thousands of Germans were forced to leave their homes and that organised resettlement is now under way. He too was expelled immediately after the end of the war although he was no Nazi. Yes he fought for a while in Russia because he had to but then he was wounded and was allowed to go home. Only now do I notice a wooden stub poking out of the end of one of his trouser legs. "They seized every last thing from me" he complains. He says that the entire resettlement is simply robbery on a massive scale and worse still his wife didn't survive the period in the reception camp where they had been held before their expulsion – her health was already broken by the war.

As a refugee, he doesn't have many contacts on the Czech side, as I'll no doubt appreciate. He's glad to have survived. But maybe someone from one of the reception camps for refugees from Czechoslovakia might be able to advise me. Luckily some relatives have taken him in so he is not obliged to sleep in some temporary mass accommodation. He can take me to Fürth im Wald where the deportees are obliged to wait until the American occupying authorities decide where to send them.

This was a glimmer of hope in my situation at that time. The simple fact of being able to choose whether to speak Czech or German was an enormous boost. All I wanted was to leave with Herman even though he warned me that he wasn't sure whether I'd be allowed to stay in the reception camp seeing that no one actually regarded me as a displaced Sudeten German.

But my mind was made up. I had recently turned eighteen at last and so in theory no one could prevent me leaving a refuge for war orphans. I asked him to wait for me and went to pack a few clothes I had mostly found in the ruins of houses. I put my father's writing in my bag, wrapped in waxed paper and then set off with Herman northward from Munich in the direction of the Czechoslovak frontier.

Herman's relatives lived on the outskirts of Deggendorf in countryside that reminded me of Bohemia. Although I'd originally agreed with Herman that he'd take me to Fürth im Wald I asked him whether I too might stay a while with that family of his saying I wouldn't mind sleeping on straw in the barn. When we reached Deggendorf Herman explained to his relatives that I was an orphan – a bit of an odd case with nowhere to go. The Behns as they were called were not over-enthusiastic as they already had one Sudeten family living with them. But in the end they agreed.

I stayed several weeks at the Behns' and moved into Herman's room the day after I arrived, out of gratitude and also because of my nymphomaniac tendencies. I knew he wouldn't refuse because during the journey he had already told me that I was exceptionally beautiful and wanted to know whether it wasn't a problem for such a young girl all on her own with so many soldiers milling around.

He wasn't capable of anything the first days even though he wanted me and I even suggested it myself. He was still in shock from his wife's death; besides which, he was afraid that she was watching him from somewhere. I left him alone particularly as he didn't mind me sleeping in his room.

I have to say that there was nothing devious about moving into his room. After all there wasn't any great difference between his cold attic and my barn. In a way I'd found him attractive from the outset despite his disability. I was attracted by a sort of dependability that radiated from him. After a few days I even started to consider staying with him because I had the feeling he was someone I could rely on. But at the same time I banished such thoughts. After all my intention was to return to the Czech lands and apart from that I wasn't entirely sure whether I wasn't simply clinging onto Herman because I was completely out of my mind and ready to cling to anyone who expressed the slightest concern for me in my desperate plight.

Eventually I did sleep with Herman. At first he simply watched me each evening as I washed. It clearly aroused him as did my presence in his bed. But in the end he would always roll over onto his side wish me good night and fall asleep. Or he didn't sleep and sighed grievously.

I could have also spent the whole night sighing – I had enough worries of my own – but I felt sorry for him. And so one night when I'd actually stopped thinking about sex with him I started to stroke his hair.

I told him that it was terrible what had happened but the main thing was that he'd survived and he'd be sure to find a way to live normally once more. All of a sudden he burst into tears. His weeping was somehow awkward as if he was ashamed of it but I could see that it relieved him.

It was an odd situation... An eighteen-year-old girl cradling in her hands the head of a former soldier twice her age and soothing him. And he really did calm down and I felt his hands stroking me and then drawing me to him. Previously I had been even slightly brutal with men – greedily drawing everything out of them with my entire body and the lovemaking tended to be over quite quickly too. I would then lay there each time in a huge vacuum because when my body calmed down there was nothing to catch hold of.

But for Herman I felt tenderness. I kissed him and slowly prepared him until I was sure I wouldn't alarm him. I was in no hurry and in fact I was maybe a bit too detached in the way I observed how he let himself be absorbed by the movements of my body. And yet it affected me more than the wildest sex I had known with the youngsters at the orphanage.

I became very close to Herman that night. The very next day it was obvious to me that unless I left him soon I'd never abandon him. At first I decided to stay with him. I said to myself that I had no one in Czechoslovakia and there was only the slimmest chance that the Kleins had survived. Whereas in Germany, I had a brother. I promised myself I would set out to find Arno as soon as I had settled a bit.

Except that after about two weeks I decided to leave. Maybe it was also because I realised that I wasn't yet ready for a permanent relationship and that my idea of a safe haven with Herman was an illusion.

The following day I really did leave. It wasn't easy for me and I cried for quite a long time as I went because I felt perverse.

I won't tell the doctor, but I still think that my departure that time was predestined and that Ariel actually played a certain role in it. The reason is that when I reached Fürth im Wald where the displaced Germans were alighting the following thing happened.

After wandering around for about two hours I was already so exhausted and appalled by what I saw all around me that I started to wonder whether I oughtn't return to Deggendorf and report to the American occupation authorities and then wait until my case was sorted out somehow. After all I couldn't stay where I was. The Americans were taking away thousands of destitute people who had arrived here on the transports from Czechoslovakia as well as pulling out the corpses of those who hadn't survived. It was obvious no one would have any time for me.

I sat down on a low wall and while I was summoning up strength for the return journey, I suddenly caught sight of a familiar face in the crowd. Recognising anyone in that horde of people astounds me so much that it takes me several seconds to realise who it is. Then I remember. It's Gerta!

It seems such an unbelievable coincidence to me. After all thousands of people have been passing through here and if I'd arrived a day earlier or later or even an hour earlier I'd never have happened upon her. But it is her. And Rita and Anke are following just behind her.

From a distance I can already see what a pitiful state they are in. They hang their heads and can scarcely walk, but then Rita raises her head... She catches sight of me. She stops and gazes in silent amazement and I see her shake Gerta by the elbow. She too raises her eyes from the ground and stares at me in disbelief. And all of a sudden although she is visibly exhausted she runs toward me with arms outstretched and we are locked in an embrace tearfully hugging each other in the midst of that human maelstrom while American soldiers shout orders over our heads.

In fact, we have little time for talk because their group is being herded by the soldiers toward a marshalling yard from where a train is to take them to somewhere called Heidelberg. I realise that the soldiers are bound to check my identity and discover that I don't belong to this crowd. Nevertheless I continue to move forward with them in that mad confusion while we feverishly relate to each other what we have been through since the moment that Karl Brehme took me away from the Kohlerhof.

Through her sobs Gerta tells me the appalling story. First the Russian soldiers came and raped them, and in fact they raped them repeatedly over several days. They shot Fritz when he tried to protect them. Then the Czechs arrived and took her, her daughters and Berta to a reception camp. "They took absolutely everything we had apart from what we're carrying and it was useless begging them and explaining that we'd not done anything bad to anybody. While we were at that camp Berta heard that her husband died a while ago. It was too much for her to bear. She just decided there was no point in living any more."

Rita and Anke stand alongside Gerta saying nothing. They both look as though they've been through hell. And in fact they have.

I also hurriedly tell her my adventures. When she asks about Karl, I tell her truthfully that I have no news of him. But I add that I've heard the Germans found guilty of working for the Gestapo or the SS are sent to work camps. Gerta simply nods passively.

I tell her that I'm there in order to get back to Czechoslovakia and she is lost for words. I expect she is wondering what sort of lunatic would want to go back to the hell they have just escaped from. Then she looks at me. "I won't try to dissuade you" she says at last. "You're probably more Czech than German. Let's just hope it's the right decision."

It crosses my mind that I might try to leave with them. After all in a moment they'll disappear from my sight for goodness how long. But then I banish the thought. No I must go back even if I don't see anyone from my family because there at the very least I might find the grave of my parents. And also I suddenly have a dreadful urge to speak Czech.

To be on the safe side I write down the number of the train that is waiting for them. We wave at each other and I keep my eyes on their faces until the crowd swallows them up.

Interestingly enough, after that meeting I knew quite precisely what I had to do. While I was still in the town I spoke to an American officer who was speaking to the refugees in German. I explained to him that I was Jewish and had been abducted to Germany and that I needed help. He suggested I accompany him to the American high command in Cham.

That same evening I was sitting in the office of an American interrogator relating my story to him in detail. On that occasion also I was careful not to say anything that might harm Karl Brehme should he still be alive. So I didn't lay any stress on the fact that he had taken me to Germany as his hostage but simply told him that he had ordered me to accompany him.

The interrogator wrote everything down and asked me a few more questions about my parent's dates of birth, our precise addresses and the exact location of Alois's house. He also wanted to hear details about the Kohlerhof and when I described with tears in my eyes how I had bumped into Gerta and her daughters by sheer chance and what had happened to the others he simply shook his head sadly. "Damn war" he said in English. I still remember it today. Some time afterward I looked up the words in a dictionary.

The Americans gave me temporary accommodation until it was decided what would become of me. They treated me with enormous consideration. I expect they knew something about my past. I also appreciated a supply of normal food after the dreadful scarcity that had reigned in Munich and at Deggendorf.

It was already mid-1946 when I was summoned one morning to the high command and informed that an agreement had finally been reached with the Czechoslovak authorities and I would be driven to the frontier that same day.

And that's what happened. We drove in a military jeep for about an hour through wooded countryside until I once more set eyes on the station at Fürth im Wald where I had bumped into Gerta, Rita and Anke a few weeks earlier. And about twenty minutes later I caught sight of a building at the side of the road bearing the Czechoslovak national emblem. There the Americans handed me over to men in Czechoslovak uniforms.

I can't say that that first meeting with my compatriots after such a long time was particularly pleasant. They all had morose or severe expressions on their faces as if they were determined to repay in kind all those years of German occupation. I had no cause to rejoice yet they said – everything had to be checked. Absolutely everything. They looked disgustedly at my German papers which indicated that I was a German citizen with the German-sounding name of Brehme. They loaded me into a car and drove with me into the interior. In about an hour we reached Plzeň, our destination.

There they brought me before the repatriation commission whose members made it clear to me at the outset that I seemed fairly suspect. I once more repeated my story to them straightforwardly leaving out nothing apart from my sexual escapades. I also mentioned that the Kohlers were decent people. I probably shouldn't have because it annoyed some of the members.

What interested the commission most of all was why someone like Karl Brehme had spared us. Wasn't there perhaps another reason apart from his discovery that we were his relatives? I answered in all honesty that I didn't think so. After all I remembered precisely how shocked he was to discover he was our half-uncle. He simply didn't want to let his relatives be executed. As far as I knew he grew up as an only child so it probably made a powerful impression on him to discover that he had a brother. And it didn't seem right to him to allow his children to be executed.

Someone from that commission started zealously to draw his colleagues' attention to the fact that my father was half-German. An argument broke out. Someone excused my father on the grounds that he was by all accounts a legionary, a patriot who had fought for Czechoslovakia in Russia. That fact in turn was ill received by a youngish Communist member of the commission as I later realised. He emphasised that the legions had fought against the Soviet Union, which had now so gloriously liberated us. But the others castigated him for bringing up such matters there.

It was actually a bit comical to observe that little cross-section of Czech society which was a reflection of how divided the nation was. I think it already crossed my mind at the time that trouble was brewing in the country I was returning to of my own free will. And it also occurred to me that Germany probably had the worst of its troubles behind it. But there was no turning back. I was determined to become a Czech once more.

That honourable commission concerned itself with me for several weeks. They managed to trace some papers in the registry of births and the Jewish community and eventually – with my help – they even came up with a witness: my former math teacher Piták who confirmed who I was and that I was also telling the truth about my grandparents. So I was given Czech identity documents once more in which my name had been changed back to Brehmeová.

What I didn't get back though was my grandparent's house. They had not yet returned from the concentration camp and it was more or less obvious that they never would. This filled me with terrible grief because that was half of the purpose of my return to the Czech lands. There was a young family living in their house who had moved in as soon as the war was over. When I visited them their attitude to me was rather unfriendly as if I was planning to take their house away.

I was secretly hoping that they might feel sorry for me and offer to rent me a room but they made it quite clear that they didn't even want to see me there. The fat guy who opened the door to me didn't even invite me in when I introduced myself.

He told me in an over-familiar way that if I had any designs on the house I should take it up with the Czechoslovak authorities. They had given them the house because I had been given up for dead.

I was in a dreadful situation. I knew that even if I claimed our house back from the authorities it would take some time for them to decide and in the meantime I needed somewhere to live. Perhaps I could have applied to the authorities in Kolín for temporary accommodation but at the time I was at a loss and confused. In the end it was Piták who helped me once more. He put me up for a few days and then sent me to some relatives of his in Prague who were willing to rent me a room.

I immediately started to look for work but it wasn't particularly easy because I had only completed six grades. The logical thing was to go back to school but I had no one who would support me. Eventually I was lucky enough to find a job in a workshop making clothes. Although I urgently needed to earn some money I realised after a few days that I wouldn't last long there. The job involved sewing on buttons and it wasn't good for my damaged sight.

I survived there several months. I spent my days at work and in the evening went back to my rented room. I had no friends. In fact I wasn't better off than in Munich. I was so lonely that in the end I even started to say my prayers a bit. I begged God and Ariel too for help or at least a sign.

At first no sign was forthcoming. And then one day while I was praying I remembered my resolution that if I survived it all I would convert to the Jewish faith. I decided to visit the Jewish community. And something odd happened.

As I was walking through the Old Town in the direction of the Jewish cemetery I saw a man on the opposite sidewalk that seemed familiar to me. I couldn't recall how I knew his face and then I realised that it was the face of Ariel that I'd seen in that strange room on the other side of the mirror in Alois's house!

It suddenly struck me that on that occasion Ariel had resembled Hugo – at least as he was portrayed on the picture in my father's room. But the thought that Hugo might have returned to life was just as terrifying as the possibility of encountering that strange angel once more.

I knew it would be extremely presumptuous to go up to that man and ask him who he was but I had nothing to lose. The fact that I had happened upon him seemed to me like the sign I had prayed for. So

I overcame my fear and crossed the street. I caught up with him and tapped him on the elbow. He turned round and I was no longer in any doubt that I knew him. He could have been about thirty. A tall athletic type, his forehead partly covered by a thick shock of black hair.

"Excuse me" I said. "I have a feeling I know you but I don't know from where." He stared at me intently for a moment.

"I also know you from somewhere and don't know from where," he admitted hesitantly. "My name is Daniel Kaminski if that helps".

I can still recall my emotion when he said his name. I stood there with my knees buckling beneath me and tears welled up in my eyes. After all that wandering and everything I'd lost when everyone I'd loved had disappeared from my life one by one like vapour I had come upon someone who linked me with the past. After all I'd known Daniel when he was boy! He was ten years older than me but he'd occasionally visit us with his mother Ester. Some mysterious bond linked my father and Ester and I was a bit jealous of her for Mummy's sake. She also came to my parents' funeral and afterward I had seen her a few times at the Klein's. She would always call on them when she was passing through Kolín but I had not seen Daniel again after my parent's death.

"I'm Hana Brehmeová" I said. He stared at me dumbfounded.

"But you're... or at least we all thought that you're all dead. This is incredible."

And so I met the love of my life and the father of my son. We stood on that sidewalk and conversed for about ten minutes and then Daniel invited me to a café. I told him my story and he told me his. I discovered that thanks to her contacts Ester had managed to escape to London before the Germans invaded the Czech lands and that she was still living there. Daniel who was twenty-two at the time had stayed in Prague on account of his girlfriend. However in the end she was afraid to remain with him because of his Jewish origin and he fled from the Protectorate at the very last moment in fairly dramatic circumstances. He managed to get to Warsaw before the Germans invaded Poland and from there he escaped to London via Sweden.

What did he do there I wanted to know and he said as if it was a matter of course that he had fought in the British army. No he hadn't been an airman but a simple infantryman who had fought in North Africa and later took part in the Normandy landings. I suddenly remembered Stefan. How odd I thought to myself. The two of them could have met. Perhaps Daniel killed Stefan.

It was obvious that Daniel found me attractive and he certainly attracted me. In fact since my brief relationship with Stefan I hadn't met a man who attracted me so much at first sight. In the end we spent several hours in that café and I even confided to Daniel my intention to become a member of the Jewish community and also explained why. It didn't surprise him in the least. He said he'd always considered me and Arno Jewish children. Our mother was Jewish after all. He thought it was an odd coincidence that we were meeting here of all places. He too had recently decided to return to Judaism in the light of the wartime events even though he hadn't had much to do with the Jewish community before the war.

I observed him closely. He was good looking so I was almost convinced that he had a regular girlfriend although he'd made no mention of any girl in the course of our conversation. In the end I couldn't contain myself any longer and asked him indirectly. "I suppose you'll have to be going soon – I expect you're married or you have a girlfriend."

He grinned. "I'll have to go soon because I have another appointment, but I'm not attached." He noticed me blush and he explained that he had had a girlfriend in London but she had given up waiting for him. "Maybe it was just as well" he said "because I spent the war hoping I'd return here. Luckily I managed to get back my mother's apartment which the Germans had requisitioned."

When we were taking leave of each other he wanted to know when he'd see me again. I reflected for a moment on when I'd be free in the coming days. I expect he took my hesitation to mean that I didn't want to meet him because he quickly added with a touch of nervousness that we were like points of reference for one another. He almost had nobody here. Most of his friends had been Jews and almost all of them had perished.

I discovered that his grandparents the Benáčeks had also died in a concentration camp. He had urged them in vain to flee with him but they said they were too old for that. The main reason he said was that Sára couldn't believe that mass extermination of the Jews could ever happen. A lump came to his throat when he told me that...

I'd be happy to see him I assured him – as soon as possible. I was also on my own and wasn't very happy. But of course that wasn't the main reason, I stammered in embarrassment. I was enjoying his company very much.

On our next date I didn't need persuading to take a look at Daniel's apartment and once there I stayed, only going back to the room I rented from Piták's relatives for my things.

Daniel's apartment had temporary furnishings because all of Ester's things including her collection of musical instruments and pictures had been ransacked. But even surrounded by those bare walls we were incredibly happy. Only then did I realise that all my previous ties, particularly my relationship with Stefan, that for a while I thought might develop into love, had nothing to do with love.

I truly loved Daniel. He was everything to me. I was full of him. I let him spend hours telling me about his previous life. I wanted to know every detail about him and what he did when he wasn't with me. In fact I'm amazed that he managed to put up with my almost crazy infatuation so well.

And we were fortunate in other ways too. As a British army officer Daniel was given a post in the Ministry of Defence so I was able to give up my job in that clothing workshop. But my sight was so bad that I was unable to spend the hours I spent at home waiting for Daniel for study or reading. In spite of that, 1947 was the happiest year of my life apart from those few years at home with my parents and Arno.

In fact the only thing that spoiled that enormous happiness was my uncertainty about what had happened to Arno. Although I had started to make inquiries about him as soon as I returned to Czechoslovakia,

I hadn't got very far. The authorities curtly informed me that their attempts to trace him had been unsuccessful because Arno probably now went under the surname of the people he lived with. We tried to make use of Daniel's connections at the ministry but even he had no success.

We were soon planning to get married. Daniel very much wanted Ester to come to his wedding but at that time she was again fully engaged with concert performances and had no time to make a trip to Prague. In the end Daniel and I travelled to London for our engagement, which was a great adventure for me. Not just because of our engagement but because I think London is a fantastic city. I felt a freedom there I'd never felt before and I was also able to visit places where my father had once performed in concert. But the most important thing was my meeting with Ester.

Ester was the last link with my parents and grandparents and for me it was like returning to old times. She related to me frankly how my father had once fallen in love with her and she had fallen in love with his best friend Hugo. Of course I too spoke to her openly about the letter that my father had written to his mother in which he described how he fell in love with Ester. She said she'd like to read what he had written one day if it wasn't too intimate, because she was truly fond of Josef and would most likely have yielded to his courtship in the end if Hugo hadn't come on the scene.

I talked about everything possible with Ester during the ten days that Daniel and I spent in London, and so the matter of Ariel was also mentioned. I thought that Ester would keep her counsel but she already knew about it. It had completely gone out of my head that Father said in the letter that he had talked about Ariel to Ester's father in her presence.

She gave me a strange look. "My father, Rabbi Kaminski was a well-known mystic. I recall how on that occasion he stood up and kissed your father on the forehead. I'll never forget his words. He said: Being one of the chosen can bring great happiness or great suffering. But usually both."

"That's exactly how it is described in my father's letter" I nodded. And it suddenly occurred to me that I was one of the angel's so-called chosen ones! But what did he want of me? Why did he choose me?

I related to Ester the circumstances of my own encounter with Ariel and she listened attentively. I altered the story slightly in order to conceal my liaison with Alois. I simply said I went looking for him after he failed to appear for several days. I went on to say that the strangest thing of all was that Ariel had the appearance of Daniel. That was why I'd recognised Daniel on the street. If that experience hadn't made such a profound impression that it remained fixed in my mind after the encounter with Ariel I would have probably passed him by.

Ester told me that she had talked to her father about Josef's encounter with Ariel. She said she was interested particularly because Josef had had the vision immediately after Hugo's death. Her father had explained that nobody knew what were the intentions of the angel Ariel. God had both a right and a left hand. With His right hand He did good things with His left hand He sometimes did bad things that made no sense to people. Ariel was the angel at God's left hand. Sometimes he was called the Angel of Death.

She fell silent and contemplated me at length.

Finally she said: "If that's true then Ariel has reaped a rich harvest in this century. And if you are his chosen one then it might not necessarily be a blessing."

She wasn't wrong on that score. The mood in the country started to worsen immediately after we arrived back from London. Ester had promised to come to our wedding at the beginning of 1948 but it looks as if Ariel has not only chosen people but also chosen countries. And the Czech lands are undoubtedly among them.

It started when the Communists at the ministry whose influence was getting stronger all the time started to make things difficult for Daniel. The sore point for them was above all his involvement in the British army.

In those days Daniel and I used to play chess in the evenings. He was a good player and he even beat me occasionally. While we were playing the conversation would usually turn to the political situation. Daniel used to maintain that Communism wasn't a political current in the true sense. It was a religion and the strangest thing about it was that it had grown out of the rationalism and humanism that is the rejection of previous religions. It was a secular faith based on the conviction that because of his reason man was the culmination of history. The Communists said that human reason had not yet had much success with setting social conditions to rights because of social inequality and the exploitation of man by man. They believed that inequality could be done away with and a new social order established.

The trouble was, Daniel went on to say – and at this point he'd usually give me a knowing look – the idea that the culmination of history will be the establishment of absolute justice and equality – that is: a man-made paradise – was a dangerous rationalist construct with strong elements of religious faith. He said it was the most nonsensical thing he'd ever heard.

I wanted him to tell me why it was nonsense. The truth was that I was actually quite taken with the idea. I had my doubts about divine justice because I couldn't really see why God had sent Grandma and Grandpa to a concentration camp, along with lots of other people. Daniel did not deny that his grandfather had been a celebrated rabbi. Basically he borrowed his words to reply to me. He said that God had a left hand and a right hand and we didn't have the foggiest idea about His intentions.

I have to admit that upset me. My reaction was to say that I couldn't give a damn about God's intentions because God was unfair. That used to make Daniel laugh but I meant it seriously. If there was some kind of link between God and our world or if God actually oversaw morality in the human world then He couldn't permit something like Auschwitz. So it seemed to me more appealing to ignore his morality and accept the arguments of Marx and Engels that we shall arrange justly our own way.

"How do you know that Auschwitz wasn't the result of a purely human morality?" Daniel asked. "Maybe God simply left us to our own fate for a while, to all those ravings about human reason having a patent on everything and having no need for God – and that is the outcome. First of all, the Germans tried to create an ideal world by annihilating the races that supposedly got in the way of that objective and now we're likely to be governed by Communists who believe that the ideal world will be achieved by annihilating the bourgeoisie."

I told him that it didn't seem to me that God had left us to our fate. After all, Daniel was aware that an angel had appeared to my father and to me.

Unlike the doctors who would later have care of me in the mental hospitals Daniel made no attempt to refute the angels. He said that the Torah mentioned them in many places. They were God's messengers he explained and were known in Hebrew as *Malakhim*. Sometimes they were referred to as the Sons of God – *B'nei Elohim* or simply *Elohim*. Sometimes they were invisible but sometimes they assumed human form in which case they appeared only to certain people. The Book of Genesis spoke about two angels who visited Lot and told him that they would destroy Sodom. And those angels looked like ordinary people.

He taught me that there was a whole hierarchy of angels. The supreme ones were known as *Seraphim* who also included the archangels. There were also fallen angels such as Shemhazai and Azazel or Satan. People usually depicted angels as winged beings but in reality they had many forms. Only the *Ophanim* had wings. Ariel, who was often depicted with the head of a lion was the archangel of the earth and was in charge of our planet's well-being. In other interpretations Ariel was actually the Demiurge because he created the material world on God's orders. That was also the reason why he was able to smite humans when he saw that they threatened his creation.

Sometimes he was depicted as the angel who controlled and punished demons. No one knew if that was good or bad. But what was certain was that whoever controlled demons had enormous power and could hide behind them. For that reason, it was sometimes argued that God had turned away from Ariel. And sometimes he was even regarded as a fallen angel.

I have quite a sharp recollection of Daniel's explanation. This is because I was confused about it first of all and I begged him to write his exposition down on a sheet of paper. He wrote it for me in large block capitals so it wouldn't be too hard for me to decipher and I carried it around in my pocket for a long time. Whenever I had to wait somewhere I would take it out into the light and study it. Probably, because I enjoyed being in contact with Daniel.

I can also remember how Daniel once told me that angels were a reminder for us that there existed another higher world above the world of humans. He said it was something we should never forget. When people became too proud or became convinced of the unlimited scope of human reason they came into conflict with angels. Angels were the friends of the meek.

"I'm not so sure," was my response in those days. "My impression is that God and his angels simply play with us. It almost seems to me like some kind of experiment. And how can we be sure that divine wisdom is better than the human variety? After all if God created man then he transplanted his faults into him too."

We had discussions like that quite often. Daniel attended the synagogue and believed in God. I had my doubts in spite of my visions. I used to frequent the Jewish community but from the moment I met Daniel I couldn't find the strength to pray. Maybe I ought to have prayed though because the clouds soon started to gather over the happiness we enjoyed in 1947. Maybe that angel would have heard me and if he had some plan for me he could have changed it. Who knows? Maybe it's possible to overturn God's plans through prayer.

The dark clouds turned into a bleak storm when the Communists achieved their ends in February 1948. Daniel and those like him were in the firing line because they were allegedly infected with the virus of Western imperialism. It was no help to them that they had also fought for the freedom that the Communists were now misusing to establish their regime.

Daniel was arrested several days after their glorious revolution in his office at the ministry and accused of spying for the Western powers. It suited their purposes that Ester was living in London because it wasn't hard for them to prove contact with the West. So suddenly I was left alone in our apartment. I was alarmed and dreadfully afraid. I tried to make contact with Daniel but it was impossible.

And on top of that I discovered I was pregnant. I didn't know what to do. Without any education it was hard to find a decent job and it was out of the question to find one that didn't require good sight. I tried applying for jobs but the Communists who were everywhere by then only ever offered me something so strenuous that I would most likely very soon have miscarried. And I was absolutely determined to bear Daniel a healthy child as if I sensed that things would turn out badly for him.

For a while I was rescued by Ester who I'd sent a message to in London via a friend. Two weeks later I received a visit from an unknown man who handed me an envelope with some money. He passed on Ester's greetings and said he'd come again soon. I wasn't sure whether he wasn't a provocateur because he behaved rather oddly. But I didn't have much choice. The money saved me because there was enough to give me a decent standard of living for a couple of months.

But worse things happened in between times. For instance there was an interrogation at which the interrogator tried to drag out of me whether I'd previously noticed any signs of Daniel's espionage activity. It was such a stupid question that I couldn't help smiling which got the interrogator fairly riled up.

He roared at me to watch my step because my own past was not particularly clear. "If you're not going to cooperate we might have to start looking into how you actually found your way to Germany." He told me that all the decent Jews had ended up in concentration camps.

That struck a sensitive nerve in me of course because that is what I used to tell myself in those days – and still do. I have an awful sense of guilt that Grandpa and Grandma didn't survive whereas I did. And mostly that I have survived only because I had willingly grasped the hand held out by my Gestapo uncle and had let myself be persuaded that it would be better if I became a German.

I almost collapsed in front of that interrogator. When he saw how drained I was he let me be. To be on the safe side I told him emphatically that in my opinion Daniel was no spy because something like that would certainly not have escaped my attention. I explained that he had returned here because this is where he grew up. He had also fought for our country's liberation. I naturally said nothing about Daniel's contempt for Communist ideology or his belief in God.

They released me and I returned to our apartment and for weeks on end I scarcely left it. I was afraid I'd miss Daniel as well as the man who brought me money. In fact neither of them came. It was only some time later that I learnt from Ester that her acquaintance had tried to contact me a second time but they had arrested him right in front of our house.

It was a strange set-up in hindsight. From the very outset it was quite wasteful – there was no need at all for them to stake out our house. All they needed to do was cook up some evidence against Daniel, which they probably did in the end anyway. They didn't really believe he was a spy did they? Or did they? Could Daniel have really kept something like that secret from me?

My situation got rapidly worse and so in the end I took an assembly-line job at a factory in Vysočany. I assembled the same components over and over again in a poorly lit assembly shop and at the end of every shift I had spots in front of my eyes. The only positive thing was that I could sit on a stool at the side of the belt so my swelling belly was less of a burden.

Sasha was born on September 11. I was originally intending to name him after Daniel, but then I remembered Daniel once telling me that if he ever had a son he'd like to name him after his friend Alexander who had died in his arms from shrapnel wounds somewhere in Normandy. Of course I sent a letter to Daniel about Sasha's birth but as with the previous ones I received no reply. I informed the authorities at the remand prison that, although I wasn't Daniel's wife, I was the mother of his son and I received notification a few weeks later that Daniel had been sentenced to ten years in prison.

Later I received a few letters from him sent from a labour camp somewhere near Jáchymov. He hinted that he was mining uranium. I expect he couldn't say so openly. He also wrote that he was all right and in good health and told me to take every possible care of myself and little Sasha. He'd marry me when he got back and regretted he hadn't managed to while it was still possible.

I used to send him long letters several times a week describing every sound our son made and every new thing he learned. I don't know how many of those letters reached him because many of them remained unanswered. I consoled myself throughout that period with the thought that they might release him for good behaviour although it was obvious that it wouldn't be soon.

So I prepared myself for a long wait. Sasha kept me very busy. His presence and his progress filled me with happiness but at the same time my anxiety grew stronger. I don't know exactly when it started, but I began to be dreadfully afraid that I was back in that hole in the cellar. At night I used to dream I could hear footsteps and that someone was searching Alois's house. And then when I groped around me, trying to touch Arno's hand in the dark, my confused movements usually woke Sasha.

I also had absolutely lifelike dreams in which I could see Grandpa and Grandma leaving Karl Brehme's office and waving to us from the doorway with dreadful anxiety in their gaze. And only now in those dreams did I realise that the anxiety was not so much connected with their fate but their fear for us. They were going to their deaths and yet they were terrified about what would happen to Arno and me.

I would wake up bathed in sweat and it would take me a long time to get back to sleep. And no sooner was I once more asleep than I would be dreaming about the ruins of Munich and how from time to time I'd find a corpse. And I'd wake up again.

I would try to recall pleasant moments such as making love with Stefan but it didn't help me much because it would leave me with guilty feelings. And whenever I tried to think about Daniel and all the beautiful moments we had spent together I would sink into total despair.

And so I started recalling most of all those few years before the death of our parents. I conjured up again and again the picture of my mother leaning over and stroking me before I went to sleep or going out walking with me, Dad and Arno somewhere. And I'd also replay in my head my parent's private recitals together at home when Arno and I would be sitting under the piano cuddling each other.

Why did all that have to happen? What had I done to deserve it? In 1949 I was twenty-one and yet I felt I had everything behind me. And what's more it all amounted to nothing. I tried at least to give Sasha as much love as I could, but all the time I was horrified that he was growing up into a world that made no sense at all. I was terrified that something would happen to him. And most of all I was overcome with panic that some officials would suddenly appear and take him from me in the name of the state I lived in.

It was simply too much for me. One day I went to the store with Sasha in his pushchair and I was suddenly seized with such enormous anxiety that I was rooted to the spot. I sat down on a bench and clutched my face in my hands. I started to cry and couldn't stop. Sasha started to cry too, which attracted the attention of passers-by. When some sympathetic lady asked me what the matter was I tried to pull myself together because I no longer trusted anyone and was afraid that in that country of informers that sympathetic lady might rush off to denounce me. But I just didn't have the strength to get up. It was as if that dreadful mental weakness had turned into physical weakness. So eventually someone called an ambulance.

That was the first time Sasha was placed in an infants' home after they took me off to hospital. Although I quickly regained my physical strength, the doctors decided that I needed to be placed under observation because of my mental state and they shoved me into the madhouse. Naturally my condition did not improve there – I was beside myself with anxiety about what was happening with Sasha. It became a vicious circle.

I calmed down a little a few days later when Dr. Lichtag who was in charge of my case assured me that Sasha was being properly taken care of and he explained to me that I would return to him all the sooner if I'd co-operate toward my recovery. I was inclined to trust the doctor because when we first met he had happened to roll up his sleeve and I had noticed the tattooed number from a concentration camp.

So I told him my story and concealed nothing. Not even Ariel. It was Lichtag who assured me that Ariel was definitely an *idée fixe* that I had fastened onto possibly under the influence of my father's letter. "He predicted your future" he said. "Maybe you simply needed to be assured that you still had some kind of future."

Okay I retorted but how could I have known that I would become the opposite of what I had been i.e. a German instead of a Czech. And then back again?

But Lichtag was implacably logical. "But you didn't know that was the opposite of the opposite did you? So if something else had happened to you, maybe that would have served just as well."

He sensed that after everything that had happened it wasn't at all easy for me to believe in supernatural power, which is why he harped on that aspect.

"If you'd believed that Ariel really was an angel then God would have had to be a special kind of sadist who only plays with us and even though he gave us the profoundest emotions such as despair he couldn't give a damn about our emotions. Don't you agree?"

I'm sure the way that Lichtag said it was more sophisticated than the way I report it here in my contorted story, but to all intents and purposes, he said exactly that. And astonishingly enough it helped me because suddenly I had the feeling that if we are not simply puppets in the hands of a higher power then I might be able to sort things out by my own devices. The doctor was happy with my response and a few weeks later they discharged me. I was given tranquillisers that I was supposed to take at the first sign of any nervous breakdown and I went off to pick up Sasha from the home.

Seeing him again was one of the most beautiful moments at that time. He had grown slightly and had longer hair but he immediately recognised me – that was the main thing. We were both overjoyed. For the whole of the following week I couldn't get enough of him.

The days now passed relatively calmly. Whenever I was too despondent I took one of those tablets and I felt relief. I wasn't breastfeeding any more because my milk had dried up in the madhouse, but anyway Sasha had grown used to bottle-feeding in the home. Although we lived entirely from welfare payments and were very poor I made ends meet and I even managed to pay my rent.

But then there came a fresh series of calamities. It started with the apartment. Because I wasn't Daniel's wife some pushy official started to assert that I must move out of the apartment. I argued that Sasha was Daniel's son and we were therefore all three related. So the authorities changed their tactics and insisted that I prove Daniel's paternity. I had to write to Daniel and then wait weeks until I received his officially confirmed declaration that he was the father. But the pressure on me to move out wasn't relaxed.

I still reproach myself for having requested that declaration from Daniel. Astonishingly enough he most likely received my letter even though it was their practice to censor any complaints about our splendid people's democracy and most likely Daniel cracked up. Or that's the feeling I have. In any event, at the beginning of 1950 I received notification of his death.

My world fell to pieces once more. But before I ended up in the madhouse again I went to ask the authorities what precisely had happened to Daniel. I was fairly hysterical as I was hauled over the coals by some interrogator. Although I was holding Sasha in my arms he yelled at me that my husband was a traitor to his country and to socialism and clearly even his period in the correctional institution had not helped. Which was why he had been shot trying to escape.

So that was it! They had shot him. Like a dog. I expect the interrogator was scared that he'd said more than he should so he went on yelling at me that unless I fitted myself into the socialist system I could end up in a correctional institution too. He knew all about me. If I'd not been shattered by the news of Daniel's death I might easily have suspected Lichtag of having given them some report on me. But at that moment it was hard not to faint. I staggered home where I realised that this time they would move me out for good.

I sat there and the same thoughts kept going round and round in my head – that this was the end of everything. That I'd never see Daniel again. That I was most likely destitute too. "I don't know what to do" I kept repeating – and I really didn't know what to do. It even occurred to me that the best thing for Sasha and me would be to put an end to it all. All of a sudden my head was full once more of hundreds of images that I couldn't deal with. I could see my parents, my Grandma and Grandpa, and Arno looking to me for safety in that cellar. And at the same time a strange sensual quiver shook me as I remembered Alois.

And as if to indicate that there was some point to it all – to prove that nothing was fortuitous and that Lichtag was therefore mistaken in trying to persuade me that we have everything under control – because there was nothing superior to man – the doorbell rang. There were two men at the door and it was immediately obvious to me who they were. I wondered what they could want since I'd just been talking to their colleague. But it soon turned out that these two were from a different department.

When I let them in, they ask if I have any relatives in the West. I reply truthfully that Ester who is a sort of relative as she's Sasha's grandmother, is living in London. No, they retort impatiently. Don't I have someone in West Germany?

"My brother remained there. He was abducted there the same way that I was later. But I explained that to the authorities ages ago. I have been searching for him in vain. Perhaps he's dead." As I say the words I shudder. They gaze at me for a moment and then hand me an opened letter.

Meine liebe Schwester it begins and at that moment my knees buckled beneath me. My hands tremble unbearably and I can scarcely read on. I realise it's Arno's handwriting but changed slightly – it's more grown-up. And these are Arno's words. He writes how he spent a long time searching for me before eventually receiving help from the Red Cross. He knows where I was living after we were separated from each other because Uncle Karl came looking for him as soon as he returned to Hamburg. So Arno knows that I got to Germany but cannot understand why I returned. He attended school the whole time and has just started law studies. And the best news comes at the end. He is no longer called Arnošt Brehme but Ernest Fink after his foster parents. Then there was a short PS. He'll be sure to visit me as soon as the situation improves somewhat in Czechoslovakia. I won't get permission to visit him will I?

My God I say to myself. Thank you for that at least. But the very next moment it occurs to me what a bizarre joke it is. Shortly after I learn about the death of Daniel whose appearance was adopted by Ariel, I discover that my brother is alive. Whereas I have become a Czech Jew he is now a full-blooded German – according to his papers at least. This is all a bit too much for me to take in and I probably look so flummoxed that the two guys from counter-intelligence – or wherever they are from – take their leave.

I spent several days trying to come to terms with all this new information. I was so totally disoriented that nothing could send me off the rails not even the authorities' decision that I had to move out. The socialist state was generous however. In exchange for the big apartment that they confiscated for the benefit of some bigwig, they assigned me a studio apartment in Vršovice. So at least I had somewhere to live.

In fact it didn't bother me because I'd probably have gone crazy in the apartment that I had lived in with Daniel. But I wondered whether a letter from Arno would reach me there should he write to me again. It was a silly thought of course. I knew very well that all letters from the West were first scrutinised by the secret police and they would find me wherever I happened to be. But I was afraid all the same. So to be on the safe side I immediately sent Arno a letter in which I described everything that had happened to me since my return to Czechoslovakia and I made sure to include my new address.

It was only much later that I discovered that Arno really had received my letter. But since he didn't reply I was convinced for a long time that the authorities had confiscated the letter.

That all happened some time at the beginning of the 1950s. I didn't keep a diary so I can't recall the exact dates, but I know Sasha was about two years old when I went insane. It was shortly after I received the news about Daniel's death. Although Arno's letter had raised my spirits slightly, a few weeks after I moved into the Vršovice apartment I started to be afraid, particularly at night. I felt totally alone and once more I was overcome with the feeling that Sasha was in some awful danger that I was unable to prevent.

That was also the first time I had such a strange dream that I didn't know whether it had been a dream or reality when I woke up. In the dream I was sitting at the table in our studio apartment playing chess against myself, which is something I sometimes do for real. All of a sudden there came a knock at the door. I opened the door even though I was afraid because it was the dead of night in that dream. Daniel was standing facing me – or to be precise someone who looked like Daniel but behaved slightly differently from him.

I spoke his name nevertheless. "So you've moved" he smiled and I was overjoyed to see him. But at the same time I was frightened because it was obvious from each of his gestures that he was not exactly the same as my Daniel. It occurred to me in the dream that it might be Ariel once more but I was too scared to ask. Daniel hugged me and kissed me. For a moment he held me by both hands and then asked where Sasha was. I led him to the corner, which I had screened off with a sheet so that Sasha wouldn't be disturbed by the light while he slept. He was asleep and his breathing was regular but as soon as Daniel approached the cot he opened his eyes and gazed without making a noise at us both.

It was such a strange unchildlike gaze that I was dreadfully scared. My visitor stood there silently observing Sasha and then turned away without a word. He went over to the table and sat down at the chessboard. I sat down opposite him. I should have been pleased to see Daniel, but I was totally on my guard. "Don't ask me anything" he said. "I can't tell you anything. I just wanted to see you". He moved one of the black pawns into the middle of the board – a move that would never have occurred to me because it made no obvious sense.

In doing so he opened the way for my queen and I immediately moved it to a square from which it endangered his king. But it was a trap. After about seven moves I was checkmated. And that convinced me that my visitor was not entirely Daniel because in the past Daniel only ever beat me if I made some serious mistake whereas this Daniel knew from the moment he moved that pawn that he would checkmate me in seven moves.

Nevertheless I told him between tears what had happened since the moment of his arrest. He placed his hand on mine and calmed me, telling me to think of it as meaning that there is a purpose to everything. I wanted to ask him what he meant by that but I knew he wouldn't tell me.

I was overwhelmed by dreadful self-pity. I felt I ought to tell him that I didn't deserve this and ask him to leave me alone. Wasn't he Ariel rather than Daniel? What had I done to anyone? After all I had been a little girl when it all started with that pistol shot that I heard from the garden of our house in Úvaly. Why should anyone – even some supreme power – want to punish a small child?

I sensed that he knew exactly what I was thinking. He gazed at me intently just like Sasha had a little while before. I panicked and dashed to the cot. Sasha was sleeping peacefully. His eyes were closed once more and his breathing was regular.

"I must go" Daniel said and he hugged me in an odd way.

He kissed my face that was bathed with tears. He went and stood for a moment by Sasha's cot. He observed him once more with that strange gaze and then he left. The door shut and I was left alone. I suddenly felt a dreadful exhaustion. I climbed into bed with my clothes on and fell asleep.

When I woke up next morning the entire dream came back to me. I could remember absolutely everything. This was odd because I generally recall only fragments of real dreams. However the nightdress that I had put on the previous night before I went to bed confirmed it had been a dream. I was still wearing it whereas in the dream I had fallen into bed fully dressed.

I got out of bed listlessly and went to take a look at Sasha. The first thing that struck me was his gaze. Usually when he wakes up he gurgles or calls me but that morning he was totally silent. When I pulled aside the makeshift screen he gazed at me with that unchildlike expression as in my dream. It was only when I took him in my arms that he came round as if from a trance. "So what?" I thought to myself. Perhaps he just sensed that I was behaving differently than usual. Children are sensitive. They can react like that.

While Sasha ran around the room I cooked breakfast and I happened to glance toward the table. I wasn't particularly surprised to see a chessboard there. I supposed I hadn't put it away before bedtime. But when I looked at the position of the chessmen I was filled with consternation. The white king was surrounded by black pieces and stood there checkmated! Was it possible that I had gotten up in the middle of the night and completed the game without being aware of it? That it had been a kind of half-and-half dream? Or that it wasn't a dream at all? I refused to go along with that, because I sensed subconsciously that if I started to think that I would go mad.

Nevertheless I couldn't rid myself of the feeling that I was moving partly outside of reality. I was shaking all over and even pills didn't help. I realised that I was heading for a breakdown like the one that had landed me up in the madhouse last time. My head was reeling and I started to cry. But before I fainted my maternal instinct forced me to leave the apartment and go bang on the neighbour's door.

So I ended up in the madhouse for the second time. This time it was for almost two years. And Sasha was shunted off to the children's home once more. Once again I was placed in the care of Dr. Lichtag.

We would often have long conversations. I told him about that dream that didn't have any of the appearances of a dream and once more he had a perfectly logical explanation. Because I was suffering from some kind of schizophrenia the news of Daniel's death had naturally provoked a reaction. He said it was quite possible that I had no memory of getting up and finishing the chess game in the middle of the night. And it was also possible that I'd had a credible vision of Daniel visiting me. After all the essence of schizophrenia was that one's personality split into two and the one need not remember the actions of the other.

To tell the truth that explanation came as quite a relief because the possibility that it had actually happened was even more insane. Thanks to the medication that they gave me my condition improved fairly quickly. I wanted to go home and I begged them several times to discharge me but each time Dr. Lichtag told me not to hurry. He said I had terrible traumas within me that I hadn't properly coped with yet and I risked harming Sasha and myself.

Lichtag eventually gave permission for the nurses to bring him to me from the home twice a week so that I shouldn't feel so bad about Sasha ending up in an institution. Even those few hours we were together helped me a lot.

During those nearly two years in the madhouse I formed quite a close relationship with Lichtag. I realise that it was his so-called professional duty to listen to me but sometimes I had the feeling that he was prolonging our conversations artificially. He would ask me over and over again about the ins and outs of my life story in such detail that I sometimes I wondered whether he wasn't working with the secret police. After a time I persuaded myself that he wasn't the type. He never told me anything about himself. But then things changed.

One evening Lichtag called me into his office and invited me to take a seat. He wanted to know how I was feeling and whether I had experienced any anxiety attacks in recent days. When I told him I hadn't, he nodded approvingly. He was looking at me a bit differently than usual – less doctorly – and I asked him what he was doing in the hospital so late in the evening because he didn't tend to do night shifts. He shrugged and said that his wife had left him. That was why he'd found refuge here. He had work to do and it kept him from thinking about it so much.

It surprises me slightly that he had confessed it to me. After all I am the patient here and he the doctor but I am pleased that he considers me someone he can talk to about his problems.

He tells me that his wife had already found someone else when he was in the concentration camp but they got together again after he returned. Now he realises that she did so mostly because of her guilty conscience, which was why their marriage has never worked. "It's strange how I, a psychiatrist, was incapable of seeing what my friends could see" he sighs.

I tell him truthfully that I haven't much experience because I've never been in a situation like that except slightly with Stefan. I used to tell myself that if he returned to the Kohlerhof after the war I wouldn't know how to behave toward him because I had only had fun with him whereas he had been in love with me. And it was a bit like that with Herman even though my memories are possibly closer to what Lichtag's wife felt toward him. So it is hard for me to empathise totally with him in this situation.

"Naturally" he nods. "I shouldn't even have told you it. I didn't intend to involve you in my problems. I hope it doesn't overburden you unnecessarily."

He suddenly looks terribly disconcerted and I realise that in the space of those few moments my attitude to him has changed. I am overwhelmed with a mixture of tenderness and desire which is radically different from the maternal love that has been the only emotion I have felt in recent years. I have felt nothing like this since they arrested Daniel.

I scrutinise him. He looks about forty-five. He has a long slightly clownish face and his eyes are concealed as usual behind silver-rimmed spectacles. How come I never registered what he looks like during the entire time he has been treating me? His authority must have prevented me observing him more closely. Only now do I notice that he has quite a good body.

As I've already written I discovered my nymphomaniac tendencies when I was in Germany. It took my love for Daniel to suppress them because he satisfied me in every possible way. But now Lichtag has slipped out of the role of doctor and I am aware of him as a man.

He is sitting opposite me at his desk. As soon as he finishes saying "I shouldn't even have told you it. I didn't intend to involve you in my problems. I hope it doesn't overburden you unnecessarily" I place my hand on his and with my fingers I start to caress his skin which was covered in tiny hairs. He flinches but doesn't withdraw his hand. I have seen through the man and can tell that he won't resist me.

"You shouldn't have done that" he says. "I definitely had no intention of provoking anything of the sort." But he leaves his hand on the desktop. "You're very beautiful. You oughtn't to take unfair advantage of it."

I smile at him. I tell him truthfully that I feel like a human being after such a long time. I feel like a woman after being imprisoned inside myself. Perhaps he can look on it as part of my therapy I add temptingly.

I have learnt to speak openly with him so it won't be any problem for me to discuss personal matters with him.

He makes a further attempt at resistance. While he is somewhat nervously pointing out to me that he is my doctor and that any kind of intimacy between doctor and patient is out of the question I walk round to his side of the desk.

I suddenly feel incredibly powerful. I've not felt so self-assured in years. I sense that Lichtag has neither the will nor the strength to resist me and I can do what I like with him. I'm not sure what brought on this desire to provoke him. I don't want to place him in an embarrassing quandary – he hasn't done me any harm. Maybe it simply does me good. So in fact it really is therapeutic.

I am now standing right by him, aware of his quickened breathing and his slightly terrified expression. I know I was forcing him to act contrary to some sort of principles of his profession, but I also know that if he is determined to uphold those principles at all costs he will resist. Instead I see his arm raise itself from the desktop and settle on my hip.

He suddenly starts to speak to me familiarly and that strengthens my determination to seduce him. While he whispers in some confusion "Hana you oughtn't – we might regret it" my fingers slide into his hair and I pull his head toward me. I can feel his other hand slipping up under my hospital-issue dressing gown.

I tell him I want it, I need it and he extricates himself from his chair. He stands up and puts his arms round me. He is about half a head taller than me and as I press myself to him I can feel his sex. We stumble to the couch in the corner of the room in each other's arms and he manages to turn the key in the lock on the way.

After that lovemaking I feel better than I have in a long time but he's clearly racked by pangs of conscience. "It shouldn't have happened," he whimpers, but he doesn't push me away as I lay naked by his side on that narrow couch.

"I shouldn't have told you about my wife. That's what started it all off" he continued in self-flagellation. "The trouble is you really are beautiful. I've never seen such a beautiful body. And you have an interesting face".

As he continued his conscience-smitten monologue his remark about my body and my face turn me on again and I started to fondle him once more. And even though he is still telling me about the mistake he has made he is once more prepared for lovemaking.

It was only after we've made love for the second time that I realise that I don't even know his first name. All the time he has been treating me he has been Doctor Lichtag for me. I now ask him and he smiles sheepishly.

"My name is Egon" he says. "But don't you go addressing me by it in front of the other patients or during my rounds". "Never fear" I assure him. He'll only be Egon for me if he ever happens to feel like it again.

I have to confess that I slept much better that night than before. I had no qualms of conscience at all. The only thing that troubled me was the thought that Egon was clearly conscience stricken and this might make him resolve not to yield to me. And he did indeed try to regain control of himself over the next few days. He would adopt a cold and severe expression on his rounds. And when I encountered him one day in the corridor he just swept by me mumbling some sort of greeting.

I was pretty sure he wouldn't keep it up. I knew he enjoyed lovemaking with me. It was clear to me that he was in a moral quandary and so I just bided my time. About a week afterward he summoned me to his office early one evening. As he later confessed to me he had been intending to tell me that what had happened the other time must never happen again. For one thing he could even go to jail for it. But the moment I closed the door behind me he flung himself on me greedily. This time I turned the key in the lock myself. I was raring to go too.

We did it everywhere possible. On the couch, on his desk and on the floor. He told me he couldn't have enough of me and he had been thinking about it the whole week.

"You're my compensation for the camp – for all that self-denial and suffering. That's something I couldn't even dream of there."

About two days later he called me in – during office hours this time and we had a serious talk together.

"I think we can discharge you," he announced. "It's been at least six months that we only had you under observation. In retrospect I think we might have kept you here slightly longer than was necessary. I hope you'll forgive me for that. If you've no objection I want you to come in as an outpatient for occasional check ups with one of my colleagues. You'll no longer be my patient and so it'll be entirely up to you if you want it to continue."

I told Egon that as far as I was concerned I hadn't slept with him because he directed me to. I did it of my own free will. He needed have no doubts on that score.

I was awash with happiness. I was going home at last. At last I'd be with Sasha again!

So I returned once more to the studio apartment in Vršovice but I didn't stay there long. Egon invited us to move to his place when our nocturnal chats started waking up Sasha. If anyone asked us about our relationship – such as one of his colleagues for instance – we would claim to have met by chance after I was discharged and fallen for each other only afterward.

My years with Egon were a fairly happy time. Not only did we enjoy sex together but it also meant a lot to me that he became a father substitute for Sasha. I didn't love Egon as I had Daniel that's for sure. But I did love him. I think it was also important that I was his common-law wife while slightly remaining his patient still. Whenever I was heading for a mental crackup Egon would help me in time. He had a sixth sense for it and would recognise the symptoms of the illness before I did.

Daniel paid me two more visits. On both occasions it could be put down to my schizophrenia – with a slight stretch of the imagination. But another explanation was also possible. Our second encounter happened when I was already living at Egon's. If it really was a dream then I must have been so deeply asleep in that dream that it took several taps on my shoulder to awake me. I opened my eyes and saw Daniel. He put his finger on his lips so that I wouldn't waken Egon and Sasha. Then he gestured to me to follow him into the kitchen.

I was terrified and in that dream I also had qualms of conscience because I didn't know what Daniel's attitude was to my cohabitation with Egon. But he made no mention of it at all.

"I want to take you on an excursion" he said. "It's quite a long journey but don't worry you'll be back in time."

I got dressed and left even though something inside me opposed him. There was a fairly luxurious automobile standing outside and Daniel indicated to me to get in. We drove for quite some time in silence and I trembled inside with suspense until we arrived at the airport. It was no abstract airport. It was Prague Airport all right. As we crossed the departure hall in the direction of a private aircraft nobody asked for my passport, which seemed odd to me in Communist Czechoslovakia.

Inside the airplane I asked Daniel where he was taking me and most of all I wanted to know if I really would be back before Sasha and Egon woke up. Daniel answered me that for one it was a surprise and for another I mustn't panic. Eventually I fell asleep on his shoulder so if it really was a dream I was actually sleeping twice over – in Egon's apartment and also in the dream that I was dreaming in that apartment.

After we landed I was on tenterhooks. From the aeroplane window

I couldn't tell where we were until I discovered from the Hebrew signs in the arrivals hall that we were in Israel. Daniel laughed. "This is where I live now" he said.

His statement dumbfounded me because on his last visit I had assumed that he had come from beyond the grave and that I was either seeing his ghost or Ariel who had borrowed Daniel's appearance.

Everything around seemed absolutely real except for the fact that Daniel and I passed through the arrivals hall without a single check and that once more some luxury sedan with a chauffeur was waiting for us. The driver was evidently well acquainted with Daniel. After about three hours drive we reached some little town around dawn and Daniel told me this was the place. It must have stood on a hill because the road zigzagged up to it from the Sea of Galilee. It was called Safed. I remembered that. There were lots of synagogues there and the streets wound uphill and down like somewhere in the Malá Strana district of Prague. The strange thing about it was that I had the impression all the time that I had already been there once.

When I told this to Daniel who was silently leading me through the streets he smiled. And again it was a peculiar kind of smile that was and wasn't his.

"Your ancestors once lived here" he said. "One of them who was a Sephardic rabbi in Spain many centuries ago decided to return to the land of his ancestors along with many other scholars. Safed was a peaceful spot and so his family remained here for two or three generations until conflict with the Muslims drove them back to Europe. They moved to Prague where his relatives were living."

If it really was a dream as Egon later assured me the information was amazingly detailed. And what's more I remember absolutely everything. After Daniel had taken me back to Prague and I woke up from the dream I knew precisely what the house he now lived in looked like.

It took Egon some time to convince me that it was yet again simply my *idée fixe* or my alter ego. And to be on the safe side I didn't tell him what I discovered a few days later when I made a trip with Sasha to take a look at the airport. I'd never been there before so I was curious to find out how close I was to the reality in that dream in which Daniel and I flew to Israel. And I was shocked to discover that absolutely everything – and I mean absolutely everything – was just as I recalled it.

The next day I went to the library and borrowed a book about Safed. And I experienced a second shock. In some of the photographs I recognised immediately the houses and synagogues I'd seen!

I have to admit that it threw me off balance. My confidence that I had things under control was shaken. I thought to myself that someone or something is playing games with me. I told myself again and again that this couldn't all be just a coincidence or a dream. But as a result of Egon's conversations I persuaded myself that there was a rational explanation for everything. Such as that some time in the past I had seen pictures of the airport or pictures of Safed and that I had forgotten about them. I couldn't rule it out entirely.

But then Daniel visited me once more. Once again it was at night and once again we took an airplane – to New York this time. And again everything was completely normal apart from minor details. In that dream our flight was really long. I could calculate exactly how many hours it took. In New York Daniel walked around Manhattan with me a whole day. We walked slowly from the South Side along Broadway to Central Park and from there we continued northwards. I remember that I was physically exhausted and suffering from lack of sleep. I can even recall what the various parts of the city smelt like because in each of them a different nationality was predominant. Then Daniel showed me a house on Riverside not far from Columbia University. He told me he lived there.

"How can you be living here, if you're living in Safed?" I objected and he replied curtly that he lived there and here.

He said it was actually a bit more complicated but I wouldn't understand. He gazed at me exactly as he had the first time he visited me and he said it in the same way too.

"Who are you, really?" I finally dared ask him but he simply shrugged. "You can see who I am" he said a moment later. "I'm Daniel.

But I've changed a bit. Everything in this world has many forms and everything takes place in many different variations. Some of those variations intermingle with one another, others don't. In some of them your parents died in others they went on living. In some of them the Kleins could have died in the gas chambers and in others they returned home after the war."

That was the final straw for me. I started to yell at him on that New York street to leave me in peace. It was obvious he wasn't entirely my Daniel I told him and in fact I was scared of him.

What did he want from me? If he really was Ariel I couldn't understand why he'd chosen me of all people. And what did I care about variations of our world that intermingle at certain points? I only had one life to live and it had some kind of logic of its own. It was a fairly dreadful life although I was fairly contented now with Egon. And Daniel – my Daniel – was dead. He was buried, God knows where – the Communists hadn't bothered to tell me. I also told him that if he really was Ariel and was somehow in charge of everything then his experiment was horrible.

I must have exceeded my authority in some way or possibly crossed the boundary of my spiritual power because in that dream I fainted right there at Riverside. And when I woke up I was lying in bed alongside Egon.

Once more I related everything to him and once more he was sympathetic and explained to me that in reality I wasn't in New York and hadn't met any Daniel or an angel who had assumed Daniel's appearance. Nevertheless I did borrow some books about New York just as I had about Safed. In one of them was a photograph of the building that Daniel had shown me. I know one shouldn't but I tore out the page with the photograph and hid it.

Oh, well. I erased it from my memory for a time so the only thing that remained was the picture as a memento of a strange dream. Another reason I managed to forget it was that Daniel didn't appear again.

Perhaps he'd taken offence or something. In any event he left me alone and so I was able to concentrate fully on that single variation of my life as Daniel might have put it.

And things went fairly well for Egon and me in that particular variation. He was much better educated than me of course and he tried to improve my education too. But because of my sight problems he couldn't teach me much. I was simply incapable of reading for any length of time. The letters would become blurred. And when I eventually went to the ophthalmologist he discovered that I had glaucoma and told me that spectacles wouldn't be much help to me. Fortunately the glaucoma was progressing fairly slowly so there was hope that I wouldn't lose my sight entirely.

I wished above all that I wouldn't go blind until Sasha grew up. I recall us celebrating his tenth birthday together and how happy I was. Egon and I were both very pleased with him. He had a natural gift for everything and he excelled at school. He'd sometimes go with his pals to the nearby Stromovka Park and no doubt got up to some mischief there with them but he spent most of his free time reading. He loved Jules Verne above all and was capable of reading the same book ten times. His memory was so fantastic – and still is in fact – that he could recite entire passages from those books. He was very surprised to discover that I could quote from Verne's novels but I never let on to him that Grandpa had narrated them to us in the cellar. I wanted to spare him that knowledge.

We had few friends. Egon never said as much about it but I guessed that his colleagues looked at him askance because he was cohabiting with one of his ex-patients – a girl who was nearly twenty years his junior. And then there were friends of his who were put out because I had had only six grades of schooling whereas he Egon was considered an intellectual. In certain circles things like that are not excused. Occasionally some writer, artist or filmmaker of Egon's acquaintance would pay a visit but there was nothing I could talk to them about. Unless I recited them something from the Verne stories or what I still remember of Grandpa's spiels about Masaryk. Except it wasn't advisable to talk about Masaryk much in those days.

Egon had loads of personas. If I have two personalities then he had six or seven. When I told him this once he burst out laughing. Perhaps I was the one who should be treating him, eh? But whereas medical science was just about capable of coping with schizophrenics there wasn't anybody who'd know what to do with someone with six personalities.

He was severely marked by his past experience. None of his family had survived the war apart from one aunt. When he managed to forget about it he could be incredibly entertaining. When he was in that mood he never gave me the impression that there was any difference between us. But as soon as he went into depression he was aggressive and spiteful. And he also had his professional persona when he would be unbelievably conscientious. It grieved him that he had started an affair with me when I was his patient. He had clearly gone beyond the limits of what was acceptable for him. "But we had such fantastic sex" he'd repeat and say how happy he was that he'd not sent me packing that time.

The only thing that didn't work at all between Egon and me was chess. He simply had no aptitude at all for math or powers of deduction so all my attempts to teach him the game ended in a fiasco. It required almost no effort on my part to checkmate him. Sometimes I'd do it in ten moves.

On a couple occasions he spoke about his experiences in the concentration camp. Particularly when he'd had a bit too much to drink. Maybe he'd have confided in me more had he not noticed on the very first occasion the effect it had on me. I was always absolutely distraught. What upset me most of all was thinking of Grandpa and Grandma – I didn't even want to contemplate what they must have gone through. I didn't want to hear anything at all about the camps. Even without Egon's stories I knew that things there had been utterly frightful and compared to that our time in the cellar had been absolute luxury. And what always troubled me above all was that I had survived thanks to Grandma and Grandpa's sacrifice. After all there had been no reason at all why I shouldn't have shared their fate.

It was always Sasha who helped me overcome such states of mind. By the age of ten he was already better than I was at chess. He had a particular gift for the game so I signed him up for the chess club. He soon started playing in junior tournaments that he won most of the time. He could easily have been a grandmaster one day if he'd really devoted himself to chess and had not been fickle in a certain way since he was a baby. He would devote himself to everything that grabbed his attention one hundred percent, and then he'd throw himself into something else. Apparently he wanted to try everything for which he had a talent. And that was a lot. Books kept Sasha's interest. He would devour them in enormous quantities. So much so that I started to wonder whether it was good for him.

Egon was truly fond of Sasha. I'm sure he wanted to have a child with me but none was born to our relationship. Only once at the very beginning after we made love in his office did it seem that I might be pregnant. I didn't menstruate for two months at that time but before I could do a test I started to bleed dreadfully and something appeared in that blood that looked like a small fetus. It happened the day after my trip to Safed. I never told Egon about it.

He formed a great attachment to Sasha. They would often talk together about various things into the night and they'd also play tennis and go skating in the winter. "He'll be a famous man one day" Egon used to say but I still don't know what he'll be famous as.

Egon joined the Communist Party immediately after the war. At first as he admitted he was an enthusiastic Communist. Like lots of people who'd survived the concentration camps he wanted a completely new world – one in which those horrors would never be repeated again. It probably helped his career in some way in the hospital but that definitely wasn't the reason he did it. And he didn't even need it – it must have been obvious to everyone how good he was. My fairly critical opinions of Communism irritated Egon. He begged me to voice my opinions elsewhere if I didn't want to have further problems. I used to ask him whether being afraid to talk openly wasn't proof that there was something wrong with the system.

His usual reaction was just to shrug his shoulders. Or he'd say something along the lines that it was a historical experiment that the outside world would like to destroy. That's why the system was defensive, and it was a fact that sometimes it went over the top.

But the system went more than over the top and when it started eliminating noticeably large numbers of Jews particularly those at the top of the Communist Party even Egon realised that something was amiss. And then in 1956 when Nikita Khrushchev was condemning Stalin on the one hand while the Soviet Union was brutally suppressing the Hungarian revolution on the other it completely cured Egon.

He often repeated that he'd most rather resign from the party but at the same time he was afraid. "I shouldn't think they'd jail me" he said. "But if they did I don't think I'd survive another camp or prison."

Egon simply needed to believe in something and so bit by bit he replaced his belief in the Communist redemption of mankind with a belief in Zionism. More and more frequently he spoke admiringly about what was happening in Israel and say he'd like to take a look at it although it could only be a pipe dream.

At that time I wasn't working because I was de facto disabled. Not so much on account of the schizophrenia because that was under control thanks to the medication but because of my eyes. I had to protect them and even wore dark glasses when we went for a walk. My life went on in a fairly orderly fashion – one might even say happily – but then everything went topsy-turvy once more.

It all started when the doorbell rang one day. When I opened the door I almost collapsed. There stood a tall young man with an embarrassed smile. He'd changed a bit but there could be no doubt. It was Arno!

We fall into each other's arms and just stand there for around two minutes while we both weep.

"So you've come, Arno" I keep repeating over and over again because I just can't believe it. "You've come Arno" I say as I stroke his hair.

Arno explains that he is on some delegation of lawyers settling property matters with the Czechoslovak authorities, which was why he was able to come. He tried on his own behalf several times but they never gave him a visa. He's glad he can see me for a short while at least. Unfortunately he doesn't have much time because he must take part in the negotiations. Yes he's just completed his studies and now he is working for the German government. And he's getting married soon. There is so much he wants to tell me! And he brings greetings from Gerta and both her daughters. They live just outside Hamburg. Anke is married and has two daughters. Rita stayed single. As soon as things loosen up in Czechoslovakia they'll be sure to come too.

Our conversation is a bit chaotic. I relate to Arno how I almost got married how they jailed Daniel and how he died. I don't conceal the fact that I went insane at one point and spent several years in an institution. And how I have a son Alexander who is extremely gifted.

We speak together in German, because Arno has forgotten his Czech. He tries a couple times but he stammers and can't find the right word. I'm pleased to find that my German is still good.

He also tells me that he's had no luck searching the German archives for information about what happened to Grandpa and Grandma. He has yet to discover their fate. Karl Brehme, who established a fairly successful advertising agency after he returned to Hamburg, maintains that he sent them to Terezín as he promised but he doesn't know anything about what happened to them afterward. The two of us burst into tears once more.

Then he reveals to me that the cellar left its marks on him too. Not to the same extent as me. So far he's managed to stay out of the madhouse, he smiles timidly, but he still has a horror of enclosed spaces and he'd never take an elevator for instance. When he was looking for something recently in a small storeroom and the door banged shut behind him in the draft he almost went crazy until they let him out. He had to spend a few days at home afterward.

"Arno" I say to him "I tried so hard to protect you. It's dreadful that you still suffer on account of it too."

And while we are sitting there in tears there is the rattle of a key in the lock and Sasha appears. He is twelve by now and no longer a little child. He immediately realises that something odd is happening and he stands uncertain in the middle of the room. "This is my brother," I explain to him. "Do you remember how I told you that we were separated during the war? He ended up in Germany with a German family. His name is Arno or rather he's actually called Ernest Fink. They changed his surname."

After hearing this news Sasha shakes Arno sheepishly by the hand.

Arno wants to chat to him without my translation so the discussion proceeds in a rather comical fashion. He tries to ask him about school and suchlike in his peculiar Czech and Sasha answers him in monosyllables. After a while he relaxes when he can see that my gaze is fixed on Arno and how happy I am that I have actually survived to see this moment.

Arno spends a couple hours with us and then he has to leave. He promises to come again. He has received information that things will be easier in Czechoslovakia now in 1960. But I am terrified at the thought that I am seeing him for the last time and when we are hugging each other goodbye I can sense that I am on the brink of a nervous breakdown. Scarcely has the door closed behind him than I collapse into an armchair and sob uncontrollably. I realise that Sasha is terrified by this so I eventually pull myself together even though fear remained lodged in me like a rock.

After Arno's visit something went wrong in my head. It could be best described as *confused time coordinates* because I suddenly found it hard to think chronologically. As I write this recapitulation of my life, I manage without any problem to proceed from the past to the present but at that time it was not at all apparent. I had mental states when my memory of events in my past life would alter arbitrarily. For instance I started to think for some reason that we were the ones – the Klein grandparents, Arno and I – who had hidden Alois in the cellar of our house. Or I'd tell Egon that my parents hadn't died but had emigrated to Germany and were living with Arno. I also maintained that Daniel had never existed, that I had dreamed him up entirely. And when Egon asked who was Sasha's father in that case I replied that it was Ariel. There were other stories in which I lived in Safed and was only visiting Czechoslovakia to see relatives. I was convinced that the police had arrested me and were refusing to let me return.

It was as if all those events went round in a circle. Because the chronological axis had broken down, there was suddenly nothing to hold them together and relate to each other. And since I had spent most of my life so far in the shadow of monstrous regimes, everything was intertwined and one monstrosity recalled another. It was like being in a tunnel with no light at the end of it. At that moment it can easily feel as if you're going round in a circle even though you're going straight ahead.

Yes, this famed twentieth century was like a circle. On the one hand there was all that talk about historical progress and the creation of eternal empires. About perfect justice and equality. And at the same time it was going round in a circle. Like a mule attached to a primitive pump walking round and round a deep well so that its circular motion pumps water to the top. That water is the point of its pointless existence but what's that to the mule?

I was quite simply born into the century of utopias that negated dignity, honour and self-esteem. I too seemed to be walking endlessly in a circle around a well and so every point on that circle was the beginning and end of some story, of some other history. So in the end it was impossible to tell the stories apart.

When I explained all that to Egon he looked worried and rightly so – because however hard he tried, the home therapy wasn't working and I ended up back in the hospital for several months. That unimaginable anxiety caused me to lose all notion not only of time but also of space. There were moments when I didn't know exactly who I was and I found myself totally outside of reality. I used to demand for instance that the doctors immediately summon Arno because I urgently needed to talk to him and I'd be beside myself with rage because he wasn't coming. I had the feeling that the doctors were hiding something from me and playing some kind of game with me.

My condition improved only gradually and I definitely should have stayed longer in the madhouse. But in the end they discharged me on the grounds that I had a psychiatrist at home anyway. And that was an enormous mistake because I was disoriented.

I'm sure that was also the reason why I started an affair with a high school student who lived in our apartment house two floors below us. Before I seduced Kamil, we didn't know each other very well. He'd always greet me politely on the corridor before blushing to the roots of his hair but that was all. I noticed that he would undress me with his eyes particularly in summer when I wore a light floral frock.

I met him on the staircase a few weeks after my discharge from the madhouse. He was just about to slip past me as usual when I spoke to him. I went straight to the point.

I told him that he reminded me a lot of a young German I met in Munich just after the war and how we'd had quite a fun time among those ruins in Schwabing.

After all, my husband who was killed by the Communists, was possibly someone else altogether. An angel in fact.

Kamil stood there dumbfounded and when I think of what I told him I'm amazed he didn't run off straight away. I think I also told him some other nonsense too because I invited him home and I must have talked for at least another hour before I managed to seduce him. He admitted to me later that he thought I was making fun of him a bit and that the non-stop spiel was my tactic for how to bamboozle him just like my assertion that he was possibly just an incarnation of someone from my past.

In the end I told him outright that I used to sense that every time he saw me he was sorely tempted. I was tempted too because I had really enjoyed it with that young German who was his spitting image. Poor Kamil sat patiently in the armchair stammering something to the effect that he found me very attractive too but he knew Doctor Lichtag and Sasha didn't he, and besides that he'd never been with a woman yet.

I sat down beside him and started to caress him. He obviously didn't know what to do but he was clearly enjoying it. I drew him to me and while he timidly kissed me I touched him down below. He started to groan and then suddenly went tense like a steel spring before crumpling into my arms like a little boy.

I tenderly undressed him and led him into the bedroom. He was a little clumsy but he learned quickly. That first day he stayed only two hours because Sasha was due home around five. After that he visited me regularly for several weeks always in the morning when I was home alone. The unfortunate thing was that he missed school on account of it.

Why did I do it? When I told my doctor about it a few years later he explained me that sex meant for me a kind of path to finding myself. He said it was a way of controlling a man and hence the world around me too because the world we live in is a man's world after all. Men had mostly devised all the horrors I had lived through. Everything: Nazism, war, concentration camps, bombs and interrogations.

If that doctor was right about me wanting to gain control over my past and the masculine world then I don't understand why I chose Kamil of all people. Someone who had never done me any wrong. Nevertheless my condition definitely improved although I was dogged by remorse on account of Egon. Fortunately he didn't notice anything and I was convinced that I would enjoy myself with Kamil a couple of times and then end it.

And the truth is also that it didn't at all live up to my expectations. And the doctor hit the nail on the head when he said that what I enjoyed most was instructing Kamil and observing how he was transformed by my touch and how he'd beg me for another exploit. I'm writing this cynically because that's how I felt it. It's not that I didn't enjoy it – I always found it fun with men – but sexual gratification wasn't the main thing.

Although I thought Kamil and I were being very careful we were eventually discovered. The story had gotten to Kamil's parents that in the recent period he had been absent from school during the morning and when they asked him about it he gave an evasive answer. So one morning they kept a discreet eye on him and discovered that he left our building two hours later. The following morning his father pretended to leave for work but was actually lurking in the corridor below our apartment. He heard the door close and a little while later sounds that betrayed our lovemaking.

Tactfully he did not humiliate Kamil by banging at the door. He waited for him at the street door, where he forced a confession out of him. Not only did it lead to Kamil being confined to the home, but his father also informed Egon about our affair.

Egon behaved like a true psychiatrist. Although "his honour" was at stake he made no scene. He spoke to me calmly, repeating several times that he realised that I wasn't entirely competent due to my illness but nonetheless there were certain limits to all human behaviour particularly when others can be hurt when they are transgressed.

"What would you do if I threw you out now? Where would you go? And what about Sasha?"

Naturally all I did at first was cry. Only when I was capable of speaking did I admit that I didn't know why I'd done it. It was escapism or something. I was disoriented. I'd thought that Kamil was identical to a German I'd had an affair with in Munich. And I also told Egon sincerely that it hadn't meant much to me in physical terms, and in that respect it was definitely better with him.

He nodded pensively but I could see he was quite put out. "I shouldn't have taken you so soon from the hospital" he reproached himself. I knew at that moment that he would forgive me. But he hardened himself against me. When I wanted to make love to him a few days afterward he drew away.

He started to alienate himself from me in other ways too although he didn't throw me out. Whenever he was at home in the evening he looked at me without desire. On the odd occasion that I caught a glimpse in his eye of the same passion as in his office that time and tried to take advantage of it he would start to adopt an austere attitude. Like a doctor toward his patient.

Only the relationship between Egon and Sasha was able to overcome the tension that reigned in the apartment. It had already been apparent for some time that Sasha was also musically gifted. To my great joy he took a liking to the violin like my father once had. He made incredible progress and Egon was ecstatic. He himself was quite an accomplished pianist. So he was overjoyed that they were able to play together during the evening not long after Sasha first started to learn the violin.

Maybe everything would have gotten back on some kind of normal footing had two important things not occurred. Some time in 1962 a man who had a foreign appearance rang our doorbell. I simply realised straight away that he wasn't from here.

My suspicion was confirmed by his strong accent when he spoke.

"Are you Hana Brehmeová?" he asked in an oddly official tone as if conducting an interrogation. When I said yes he came into the apartment unbidden. Only now was I able to get a good look at him. He was around forty and was going slightly grey at the temples. He was quite tall with clear-cut features and slightly watery blue eyes.

"I believe I'm your brother" he said after a moment's hesitation. "Or rather, your half-brother."

While he was speaking my brain was working overtime but even so it wasn't immediately apparent to me who it was.

"My name is Alexey Brehme" he said. "Your father married my mother Tanya Fedotovna when he was in Russia. In a small town called Kormilovka to be precise".

And then it dawned on me. Goodness knows how many times I had read about him in my father's letter! The reason it had not struck me straight away was simple. From my father's story I knew that Yefim the revolutionary had abducted him and so I'd assumed that he had most likely died.

Only now did I notice that there was something of my father's looks in his features.

I invited him to take a seat. He was a real Russian because when I asked him what I might offer him he asked for vodka. He said he was nervous and didn't know what to tell me about first. And there was indeed lots to tell.

He described how he'd spent his childhood with relatives of Yefim's, how he'd not been allowed to mention his mother and how afterward he had attended school in Leningrad where they had moved because Yefim became a big wig in the Communist Party. He explained he had attended the so-called "better schools" and from his early years he had been groomed for work in international relations.

The expression "international relations" intrigued me, because Alexey's command of Czech was certainly good enough for him to have said "diplomatic service". It immediately occurred even to me that he was working for the KGB and goodness knows I'm not particularly perceptive.

"I've been in a number of countries" he said "and now I've spent about three years in Czechoslovakia. I'd probably have never learnt about my real father but for the fact that just before Yefim Karaganov died, he must have had a twinge of conscience and he divulged to me that I was actually the son of a Czech legionary. When I was back in the Soviet Union a few months ago, I was able to consult the archives thanks to my rank and connections and I discovered that my father was Josef Brehme.

I wanted to know how he'd tracked me down and he replied nonchalantly that it had not presented any problem. The comrades in Czechoslovakia had rendered him every assistance when he had told them that his father had come from here. They had even allowed him to study my file. I was so perturbed when he spoke of a file that he started to explain that it was of no great importance but I must have expected there'd be a file on me seeing that I was repatriated from Germany. And my common-law husband had ended up in prison, hadn't he?

Before I could answer he brushed it aside and poured himself another glass of vodka. No he hadn't come to interrogate me – after all it was obvious from that file that I had been abducted to Germany.

And also that I was actually Jewish because my mother had been Jewish hadn't she? It must have been evident how surprised I was at the amount he knew so as if by way of explanation he added that he had spent several years in Israel.

I told him I could see he knew everything about me and I started to adopt a familiar tone. He was my brother after all.

"Not everything" he said. "I know you've been ill. How are things now?"

I answered truthfully that for several years now I had been "normal" but I suffered from some form of schizophrenia that could be triggered by conflict.

He asked about his father. I told him how he had travelled across Siberia to Vladivostok and returned to Europe by ship. How he'd not been able to continue his performing career because of the accident and become a policeman. And how he'd fallen in love with my mother, how happy he had been and how that happiness had come to an end when my mother died in childbirth and he had shot himself.

He was also interested in the earlier period of our father's life and so I related to him what I'd learnt from father's letter. But I didn't show him the letter itself because I felt a certain distrust toward that newly-found brother.

He suggested that we should see each other again from time to time. It had never occurred to him that he would discover relatives so late in life.

I told him that I would gladly meet him and that it was a pleasant surprise for me to find I had a new relative because apart from Arno who had ended up in Germany I had no one left. Only my son. I showed him a photo of Sasha and he was suddenly visibly moved.

"So I have a nephew" he rejoiced. "And he has the same name as me. I'd love to meet him".

And I proposed that he should call me some time to agree on a meeting.

So on his next visit Alexey got to know not only Sasha but also Egon.

The meeting with Egon was important above all because the two of them started chatting about Israel.

"I'd really like to visit it some time but I wouldn't get permission to travel" Egon complained. "I've already applied once but without success".

I told Alexey about how Egon had taken charge of me and in a way had saved my life because after Daniel's death I'd been a mental wreck. When I consider that Alexey was definitely some bigwig in Soviet intelligence and therefore must have been ideologically entrenched he took quite coolly the news about how my Daniel had died in a forced labour camp as a traitor to the socialist system. He must have known about it anyway.

He heard Sasha play the violin and asked him with interest about his other hobbies. Then he launched into a lengthy conversation with Egon. And on his way out he said the fatal words.

"If you like, Egon" he said "apply again to travel to Israel. Make the application and let me know! You never know, it might be successful this time. You're a Communist, after all. And I'm also capable of showing my appreciation for the fact that you took care of my sister."

When the door closed behind him Egon sat for a long time gazing at me with amazement. "If I understand rightly Alexey is offering to arrange a travel permit for me. That's quite an incredible coincidence" he shook his head in amusement. "Does Alexey resemble that Ariel of yours by any chance?"

No, Alexey didn't look like Ariel but after my previous experience I couldn't rule out that he was somehow part of Ariel's game of course. And I certainly couldn't rule it out in the light of the things that happened after. Egon received his travel permit and set off for Israel in 1963.

When we were saying goodbye I already had an odd premonition that almost grew into a panic when I saw tears well up in Egon's eyes as he said goodbye to Sasha. Sasha had asked him to bring him a nice chess set from the market in Old Jerusalem and Egon simply mumbled "Sure, sure I'll bring you one" but he didn't look into the boy's eyes as he said it.

But what could I do? I couldn't spoil the trip he had dreamt of by making a scene on the basis of some premonition could I?

Egon really didn't return. In a letter that I received a few months later he asked me not to be angry with him. He explained that he had long ago decided to die in the land of his ancestors and that was all he had wanted ever since the Nazis wiped out his whole family. He told me I could go on living in his apartment as we officially had permanent residence there. And if I needed any help with Sasha I was to turn to his aunt Dita who was his only relative to have survived the war. He had also sent her a letter. She was fond of Sasha. In fact she often visited us and Sasha lived with her for a while during my last period in hospital.

Egon's emigration didn't immediately affect me. It was the next visit from my brother Alexey that finally unsettled me. He made an unpleasant scene and complained that he had some big problems on account of Egon. He wanted to know whether Egon had told me of his intention to stay in Israel. "Of course not," I shouted at him. "After all he knew how unstable I am and realised that I could have gone to pieces and ruined his plans."

I don't know whether Alexey believed me but the fact is that he was quite dejected and left without any further questions. About a month later he came to say a brief farewell. They were sending him back to Moscow. It would be a new experience for him because since the war he had worked abroad. He said it with an uneasy expression on his face. And that was the last time I saw my new-found brother.

Egon might even be said to have fulfilled his role in Ariel's scenario – should such a thing exist – because some time later I received a second letter. He wrote to me that he had settled in of all places – guess where! – Safed! And he enclosed a photo of his house – the very one that Ariel had indicated to me as his home in that weird dream! That was just too much for me and I started to go to pieces once more.

Quite regularly I would fall into that cellar – the potato cellar we had spent over a year in. Only now did I start to realise that the hole under the barn had the effect on me of a sort of gravitational field that attracted everything to it. My life before that experience and my life after it started to appear to me as something that always ended in that hole.

I didn't know how to fight it. At night I'd have frightening, anxious dreams, and eventually the anxiety did not leave me even during the day. I didn't wait to have another collapse somewhere and so I got myself admitted as a voluntary patient to the hospital. Before I did so, I arranged for Sasha to move to Egon's aunt Dita. She was over seventy but she was in good health in spite of her wartime experiences. Sasha had just started to attend high school and was fairly independent and capable of helping her with lots of things.

I had assumed that I'd only spend a few weeks in the hospital until they had "stabilised me" as the doctors like to put it but it is now 1968 and I'm still here. Nevertheless things aren't too bad with me sometimes, although I haven't ridden myself of fits of anxiety during which I totally lose any notion of time and space. Yes, I suppose you could say that at those moments some other hidden personality takes over in me – one that is hidden under normal circumstances.

In fact it's a small miracle that I have managed to summarise my previous life in chronological order because quite often I find myself incapable of telling apart different time frames and specific events. As a result, time, in my recollections, runs backward as if what has just happened is the cause of what occurred previously.

For instance, I can suddenly have the feeling that I'm not in the madhouse as a result of Egon's departure but that I was already insane before then and that was why Egon left me even though I know it's not very logical. And so sometimes I have the impression that if I hadn't gone mad my lost half-brother wouldn't have appeared and he wouldn't have worked for the KGB. That too, is the result of my persecution mania, which escalates when I'm in the throes of a full-blown mental disorder.

But first and foremost I'm always in that cellar. Everything is connected with it somehow. My past, from the period before it, and my past from the period since, both flow into it. But my more recent past seems to flow into it backward because I never really left that cellar even though everything I experienced really happened and I was the main protagonist. Or at least I believe so. I'm still sitting there chatting quietly with Grandma, Grandpa and Arno and we all know we are condemned to death and unlikely to escape it. And no one knows what forces have been unleashed in Europe and who will pronounce that sentence on us.

I can remember how my grandfather once told me that according to Alois some battle must have taken place somewhere in the area of his house because several human skeletons and the remains of armour had been found when they dug the cellar we were now hiding in.

Those people died some time in the 15th century. Maybe during the Hussite wars Grandpa had explained. Their death was certainly no more pleasant than ours might be but at least it was part of a comprehensible scheme of things when there was still a distinction between good and bad. That no longer applies in our times. Rationalism and the Enlightenment had actually abolished those categories so that not even we Jews are being systematically killed off on account of some higher ideal but instead on account of some alleged scientific discovery that our race was detrimental to the evolution of mankind.

Communism made itself out to be slightly more moral Grandpa used to say. They said they wanted to establish some kind of absolute justice but that too was based on scientific discoveries. "You have to understand, Hana" Grandpa used to say "so long as religion is based on faith, you also have to accept a value system in which there exists some hierarchy of good and evil.

"But as soon as you make a science of religion and a religion of science, values have about the same significance as elements in Mendeleyev's Table. Therefore, when everything can supposedly be verified by human reason, there is no room for human choice or for doubts. Everything has a scientific basis and if you don't believe it you are ripe for the madhouse".

That's more or less how Grandpa explained it to me – he was a very well read man. I didn't understand too much of it then and still don't. All I know is that I was born into a fairly insane epoch because it turns out that even that conqueror of supposed truths, i.e. human reason, can make big mistakes so that there can be several social systems at the same time which are the product of supposedly objective scientific knowledge. Although, one might imagine that there is only one objective knowledge and only one truth. And the more the various systems lay claim to the truth, the more they hate each other because when you can't prove the truth you impose it on others by force.

I tried talking about that recently with my doctor but he was afraid. He evaded my questions and said that these are complicated things and that history is sometimes insidious. Even scholars have problems. He just talked the usual nonsense in other words!

I realised that I'd rather put him on the spot by talking so freely. After all he too is part of our system. If he started discussing various systems he'd become a heretic. Maybe he is one but can't admit it. Why should he admit it to some crazy woman when he couldn't be certain that she wouldn't blab about it somewhere?

The fact was that thanks to my imprisonment in that hole all those years ago I was liberated for good. By being consigned there with people I loved and being almost sure that one day they would pull us out of that hole and kill us, I had lost all inhibitions. My soul was lacking something that other people had – something that warned them. When I told that to the doctor he just smiled timidly.

"I'm sure you're right" he agreed, "but don't forget that they regard you as a 'head case' so nothing at all can happen to you. They can't even send you to jail".

It struck me that there was a slight difference between Communism and Nazism, after all. Communism – or at least the kind we have now – respects head cases. That doesn't mean that the madhouse that one ends up in is much better than jail but at least mental illness is a sort of attenuating factor. The Nazis would most likely have sent me straight to the gas chamber as a cripple.

That thought brought to mind Günter with whom I'd had a brief affair in Munich. He was amiable but a bit mad. His mother had died in the bombing and my job was to be her substitute in a way. After we made love he'd always fall asleep on my breast. He told me that he had an awful trauma because of his mother's death and that bombing. He was terrified of the sound of gunfire or explosions and when he was conscripted to the Wehrmacht, some time in 1942, he had tried to explain to them that he was terribly afraid and that he'd gone slightly mad. They had told him to think it over carefully because damaged human material was useless for the purposes of the Third Reich. So he stayed in the Wehrmacht but after every battle and bombing he became a bit more crazy.

I met him in autumn 1945 when I was looking for something to eat not far from the Hauptbahnhof. He was sitting on a heap of trash sobbing with his head in his hands. I sat down by him and waited for him to stop. Then he told me his story, which was fairly typical for the period. How he'd gradually gotten over his admiration for Hitler and how in the end the horrors that the Germans had sown so generously all over Europe were meted out on Germany.

I was actually sorry for him. He was roughly my age and he had been caught up like me in the insane events that had been unleashed by the arrogance of people like Hitler or Stalin. And despite that regime of his – and Günter too at one period had wanted to kill me because I was Jewish – we did have something in common as we sat there at the end of our tethers on that pile of ruins.

I took him into my care for a while and maybe even helped him because he found a refuge in me. Even he didn't know at that time whether any of his family had survived. He used to go everywhere with me. I liked it at first but in time it started to get on my nerves. I wasn't adult enough yet to mother him. I don't know how I'd have gotten rid of him. He didn't react to my emphatic appeals for him to leave me alone once and for all. In the end it was his mental state that came to the rescue because some patrol decided that Günter was mad and they took him away somewhere.

There were more incidents like that but if I wanted to describe them I'd have to start telling the story right from the beginning and I don't think I'd manage. It has been very hard because my own story doesn't normally flow from the past to the present – which is my life here in the hospital – but it cascades with a roar like a waterfall into that cellar beneath the barn, where I continue to shudder with dread.

Quite often I can hear the sounds of boots stamping over my head. It's sure to be the Germans looking for us. And in that terror everything that happened afterward also falls into that cellar. And because I am unable to arrange all those events my head is in a muddle. Gerta is here with her daughters along with Stefan in his Wehrmacht uniform and Uncle Karl Brehme. And that strange night drive to Munich often comes back to mind, too. I can still see the various guards at checkpoints saluting as we drove on as if someone was saying "Open Sesame" as we arrived at those red-and-white poles.

And then out of that waterfall there emerge all those boys and ex-soldiers that I slept with in Munich. Particularly Herman, who took me away from there.

And shining over all of it is Daniel – my Daniel who escaped from the Nazis but didn't get the better of the Communists. And Egon, of course, who now lives at Safed in the house of the angel Ariel.

And in this cellar I once more live through the time when my parents were no longer alive but there was still some hope. Grandpa and Grandma are here and I think of their cozy home. My school pals are here too and the teachers. Some of whom are convinced that I am gifted and smart and that I'll make good. And Arno's here – my kid brother Arno, the centre of whose world I became after our parents died.

Where is Arno now? Why didn't he visit me a second time? Sasha says that this year is the year of freedom now that people can travel abroad freely. Even I could travel somewhere if I got out of this hospital. But Arno could come here. I'm sure no one would prevent him coming now but he has most likely forgotten about me by now.

I haven't forgotten about him or our parents. I haven't forgotten about the enormous happiness in our home or the moments when Arno and I used to sit under the piano and listen devotedly to Daddy and Mummy performing together. Or how at bedtime our parents would tell us stories in which everyone in the end lived happily ever after. I can still feel that security – that infinite security and love.

Where has it all gone? What's happened to it all? Can it be experienced again? That love, that security. Or is it just an illusion that fizzles out in a single instant? Is everything in the world just an illusion?

I'm standing right now at the beginning of that circle. Once more I can hear through the door and windows Mummy's cries growing louder and I want to cry. And I would cry if I didn't know that Arno would start to scream uncontrollably if I show any weakness. Instead I push Arno on the swing and listen with bated breath to the fragments of Mummy's voice distorted by some awful pain. It went on for ages. I don't recall exactly how long – after all I was only seven at the time. All I know is that at the end of it all Grandma comes out and tells us that twins have been born – two little girls – but we mustn't go inside yet because Mummy's not feeling too good and they have to help Mummy first of all.

Grandma is all shaken up and suddenly she calls to Grandpa to telephone the hospital to come quickly because things looked bad with Mummy. And then that terrible thing happened that changed the lives of Arno and me forever. A few minutes later our father staggers out of the house dreadfully pale, and his trousers are all covered in blood. He looks at us in a way I've never seen before. As if he was somewhere else entirely – in some other world. "Your mother has died" he says in a strange voice that terrifies me almost more than what he has just said. Then he turns round and goes back inside. Arno and I stand there. The swing that Arno has just gotten off of sways back and forth on its own in the breeze.

All of a sudden there is a dreadful silence. A dreadful silence. A dreadful unending silence... I strain in vain to catch the sound of

Mummy's voice – that voice I adored. But at that very moment I already know. I know everything. And I fall. At that moment I'm already falling into that dark hole that I'll never climb out of.

III

FALL FROM
A TOWER

Friday, September 7, 2001

Yesterday evening. Sitting for ages over a blank sheet of paper making up my mind to start keeping a diary. Then all of a sudden it seems a waste of time. I say to myself: you'll be 53 in four days' time. A diary is the sort of thing young people keep, and most of them give up sooner or later. What are you hoping from it?

Instead of writing, I start to analyse my motives.

I think to myself: I need to clarify some things and find where to go from here. I've been wandering for the past nine months. If I manage to capture my feelings and thoughts on paper, from which they can't escape, perhaps I'll understand what's happening to me.

I'm convinced that writing is a way of finding the key to one's past. Like my Czech, which is buried under the alluvium of the thirty years I've spent outside the country of my birth since 1968. So I have to write in Czech.

In the end I write nothing, having exhausted myself by reflecting on whether it makes any sense at all.

Today I will reject those considerations. It's good that I've written these first few lines, even though they mostly express my doubts. Now I must take a further step.

I sense it's not going to be easy. But I have to persevere and discover certain answers. And I have to look for them in the period when I was still living in Prague.

I already have one answer. In a way it was my meeting with Leira that motivated me to keep a record. At that moment, just over six months ago, my psyche was uncorked, and somehow all sorts of doubts and memories that I need to categorise cascaded out.

Leira. That meeting is stored quite clearly in my memory.

It's February. I've just arrived at an international conference at Bellagio on Lake Como, north of Milan. I already notice her in the reception of the Rockefeller Foundation, which towers over Bellagio, surrounded by the Dolomite peaks.

She's precisely my type: tall, slim and with a mane of blonde hair. Something clown like about her face. It's difficult to say whether she is actually beautiful: in any event, she's interesting. There's a hidden promise of eccentricity of some kind. Something predatory, perhaps.

A bit later I meet her in the little town that I head to in the evening. I'm trying to avoid Collins, who attaches himself to me at every conference and talks non-stop about trivialities. As I pass a café, I catch sight of Leira inside. I go in and look around, pretending not to see her, and then I put on a big act of being surprised.

"Good evening! We have already met once today, haven't we? I saw you at the Foundation in reception. Have you come to the conference? Are we acquainted?"

She tells me with a slight air of amusement that she's sure I don't know her. But she knows me, of course. I'm Alex Brehme, aren't I? The *famous* Alex Brehme.

I nod. I am about to take exception – with a studied expression of modesty – to being described as 'famous', but she gives me no opportunity. She invites me to take a seat at her table and introduces herself. Her name is Leira and she's a PhD student in political science at Berkeley, although she graduated from Harvard. This is her first major conference.

I raise my eyebrows. I try to keep my eyes from the cleavage between her magnificent breasts.

So it's her first major conference. What is she writing her dissertation about?

She smiles. It just so happens that she's writing it more or less about the topic of my most recent book: *The Globalization of Postmodernity*.

"How splendid," I say with sincere pleasure. So we have a subject in common! An odd coincidence indeed.

Expertly, I immediately switch the topic of conversation to her. How did she come by such an exotic name?

She raises her eyebrows and delicately purses her lips. Her features suddenly assume a playful expression, a slight coquettishness combined with an attempt at gravity. It's that expression of Leira's that I recall most frequently.

"My mother's Portuguese," she explains. "She comes from the town of Leira. The proper spelling is Leiria, but most often, particularly back home in America, it's just Leira. When I was born, my mother named me after the town where she was born. I expect she was homesick."

"A beautiful name," I say. "There's something mysterious about it".

Leira, eh, I repeat to myself. She's extremely attractive and my gaze once more drops to her cleavage. Regrettably she's half my age. I expect I'm an old codger in her eyes.

"You look slightly different on TV," she comments. "I last saw you the day before yesterday on CNN".

I nod. I'm too vain not to ask her what she means by "look slightly different". Worse? Better?

No, there's no need for me to worry, she says, with a throaty chuckle that sounds a bit like a cat purring. What she meant, of course, is that I look much better in real life.

I feel gratified.

So that's the way I recall the first moments of our encounter, and some sentences have actually stuck in my memory fairly precisely. We sat together a little longer before going for dinner in the restaurant next door.

I desire her. It's ages since I desired a woman. It's possible that I've never desired a woman as much as this. Over the years chasing women has become almost a sport for me. I sometimes get the impression I do it out of boredom. And here's a woman that I really want.

I listen to her telling me about her dissertation in her velvety voice. I try to give her well-informed advice. Whenever she chuckles in that throaty way I get a tingle of pleasure. I'd like to reach for her hand.

When she goes off to the wash-room, I watch the way she walks, the movement of her hips, and I am almost unable to breathe with excitement.

For goodness' sake, I say to myself, what's happening to me? Should I tell her right away that I'm crazy about her or go on playing the professor?

I sip my wine and all of a sudden I feel her hand on my shoulder. She just runs her hand lightly along it as she returns to her seat. I almost go to pieces.

"A penny for your thoughts," she comments when she is once more seated opposite.

She gazes at me fixedly. Her female instinct has long since informed her that she has me in her thrall.

"Nothing to tell," I lie. "I was just pondering on the topic for an article that the *New York Review of Books* has asked me to write".

I don't know what possesses me to try this particular trick on her. After all, one of the things I find attractive about her is that this kind of swagger won't cut any ice with her.

But a look of unfeigned interest appears in her eyes, and so I recount to her how a friend of mine, who is an editor for the *New York Review of Books*, was recently chatting to me casually about globalization and how it doesn't encircle the globe like a homogeneous layer through which communications, capital and cultural symbols flow, but instead there's a global "noosphere", as Teilhard de Chardin would have called it, which can be likened to an onion. Quite simply, there are lots of mutually overlapping layers which, in the final analysis create an almost perfect ball, in which communication flows not only through the individual layers but occasionally penetrates other layers too.

And it's precisely when information passes between those layers that they can be distorted, which can have baneful consequences. I want to figure out what happens at those points.

What exactly did I have in mind, she wants to know. The "clash of civilizations"? Hadn't that theory been debunked by now?

I explain that I have something far subtler in mind. I want to fathom out how it is that information that makes sense in one of the layers is transformed into something that means something quite different when it passes into another layer of the imaginary onion. And yet everything seems to holds together, onion-like...

I take advantage of the ensuing moment of silence to switch the subject of the conversation back to her. I ask her about her studies, her parents and her friends.

She replies that she grew up on the sea shore in Maine.

Her pronunciation of "sea shore" is so soft that it once more gives me a pleasant tingle.

She explains that there's a Portuguese community in Maine. Her father met her mother there when he was on a study trip as an oceanographer. His job meant he wasn't at home much, and spent most of his time at sea. And one day he and her mother failed to return from a joint trip. Luckily, Leira was already old enough to fend for herself. She inherited the house and quite a bit of money, so she might be considered a woman of means.

She laughs at the expression.

I start to express my sympathy over her parents' death, but with an odd show of impatience she brushes it aside and teasingly assumes the role of interrogator. What about me? I'm bound to have some personal history, or did I just write books and appear as a pundit on TV?

Although it miffs me slightly, I ignore her "pundit" description with its pejorative overtones, and tell her truthfully that I don't really know where to start. My life has been fairly colourful, although it might not seem so from my appearance.

So I tell her about my childhood in Communist Czechoslovakia and how my mother spent time in mental hospitals. How I emigrated after her death and studied at Oxford and then Harvard. And how I then married a girl I met at university when I was about Leira's age and divorced shortly afterward. And that after twenty years of marriage I recently separated from my second wife Katrina, with whom I have a daughter, Rebecca who is studying in Chicago.

Naturally I don't tell her that I systematically two-timed Katrina for almost the entire period of our marriage, until she finally lost patience when she caught me in bed with an ex-student of mine at our summer home on Long Island.

I don't say so, yet I have an odd feeling that Leira knows it all. She observes me with a serious expression, but inwardly she seems to be smiling ironically.

"So you're on your own now," she says sympathetically.

I nod. I don't want her to pity me. I explain that I have plenty of work: I'm writing another book, teaching at Columbia University, and appearing on TV. I don't betray the fact that I recently started an affair with a TV reporter and it's not working out.

As we walk back to the Rockefeller Foundation later we are mostly silent. I don't have the nerve to invite her to my room. I'm afraid she'd turn me down. Instead I invite her to the lakeside bar for a drink.

With a slight exaggeration and chiefly to keep the conversation going, I remark that this place is endowed with such beauty that one is forced to ask oneself whether it isn't the reflection of a reality more perfect than the human world.

There is disagreement in her eyes.

"You're an agnostic then? Like every proper postmodern intellectual".

I shrug.

What am I to tell her? I'm capable of dreaming up almost anything and engaging in any intellectual game in order to lure a beautiful woman into my bed, but as soon as faith and belief is mentioned I'm at a loss. She's right. I'm an agnostic. When it comes to so-called eternal questions, any deviation from "I don't know" rankles with me.

My great-grandparents died in a concentration camp and my grandmother would have ended up there too if she hadn't died beforehand. And my mother avoided it only by a whisker. So at the very least I can't believe in any higher moral authority. What sort of God permits a holocaust?

I think to myself that the subject matter of our conversation has needlessly shifted in an over-serious direction – it could do with lightening up. But it evidently suits Leira.

"I have my own theory about what people call God," she says with a tinge of playfulness. "Maybe our whole world is something like a computer program. At the beginning someone programmed the basic parameters and endowed the program with the capacity for continuous self-refinement. Everything evolves from lower to higher forms, from the less complex to the more complex. But it's only like virtual reality in a super computer, which refines itself thanks to the program. Maybe the programmer knows the final purpose. Maybe not. Sometimes the program goes down a blind alley and the programmer has to assist it. This might result in the sudden extinction of an entire animal species or an unexpected reversal in human history. Just a minor corrective."

And again it sounds so soft when she says "a minor corrective..."

"Quite an interesting theory," I say.

I emphasise, to be on the safe side, that I've nothing against the idea of a prime mover, or that that prime mover should occasionally intervene in his creation in order to make a minor corrective.

After all I have no time for the opinion that everything evolves by itself, that what was originally dead matter organises itself from lower to higher forms thanks to a series of accidents.

When I speak about God – even though I have doubts about him – what I have in mind is a moral authority and the guarantee of life after death. Apart from that there's no reason why God shouldn't play the role of a super-computer. Anyway I don't see why I should be over the moon about being done the honour of taking part in some computer game. After all it doesn't alter the fact that I myself will expire at the end.

A glint appears in her eyes.

"It calls for imagination," she says. "Maybe those who acquit themselves well in this game will be awarded a further role. After all, in computer programs one can play everything over as many times as one likes. And when the author of the program really likes something, he can copy it, remove and then store it somewhere else in that virtual reality."

Her pronunciation of "virtual" is like someone sucking candy.

Leira is playing with me. She's extremely playful.

I gaze at her across the table top and once more I get a pleasurable tingle. She has depths into which every man is bound to fall, particularly in bed.

"OK," I say pursuing the topic, though a little mechanically by now, "but in the final analysis you have to take into account big and little history. The programmer, who I assume is God or some angel, has a major objective, and as you say, if events don't take their proper course, it's always possible to erase part of them, for instance, or cause a world war because it's necessary in terms of the program, even though in that microcosm, that supposedly virtual reality, billions of particles – in our case, people – have already started to live their little lives and have real destinies with their hopes, sorrows and loves. How are they to come to terms with the fact that from the point of view of the programmer their particular segment of big history is in a blind alley and needs to be corrected? Or erased? What role is there for the individual in that?"

To be on the safe side I ask Leira if she doesn't belong to some sect. Why otherwise would she speculate on such matters?

"No way!" she laughs, and explains that it's just a game. She has plenty of other theories too. It all depends on her state of mind when she comes up with an idea. She recently saw *The Matrix*... Surely I knew the film. That was probably why she came up with the computer idea.

However, she admits that she does have one peculiar attribute. Her mother was a bit of a clairvoyant and was able to foretell the future, and she, Leira, has inherited her gift. Would I like her to tell my fortune? She could read my palm...

I won't deny that if she were less attractive and less interesting, I'd probably refuse. I don't believe in fate, but just the thought that this beautiful woman will touch my hand, arouses me.

So I tell her that it could well be that I need to know what I have ahead – I'm kind of at a crossroads...

A blissful feeling washes over me when Leira takes my hand, turns it palm upward and then gazes at it intently. Meanwhile I feast my eyes on her shapely hands: long slim fingers, the nails well trimmed, but unvarnished. A breeze from outside ruffles her hair and as she leans toward me I detect a heady perfume.

She tells me that I will receive some news, something very important that I should have known long ago. It's somehow connected with my mother.

I try to pretend that I take her clairvoyance seriously, but I tell her in reply that I truly have no idea what there is new for me to learn about my mother.

I'll receive a letter, Leira informs me. A letter that will lead me into the past. It will open doors for me.

I remember the box that I once hid at a friend's, but I immediately forget it because Leira suddenly declares something unbelievable: she says that she can see that we will have an intimate relationship.

Is she really that devious, or did she actually read it in my palm?

"That's great news," I tell her rather hesitantly. "You knock me out. I'm sure you've noticed."

A sort of wild look comes into her eyes. "I find you rather attractive too," she purrs.

But when we reach the Foundation, she allows me only to give her cheek a peck before saying goodnight

Disappointed, I go to my room. I know I won't get to sleep.

I open the window. Cool air wafts in from the lake. I'm dozing in my armchair, almost asleep, when there is a soft knock at the door. When I open the door, Leira is standing on the threshold. I want to say something but she places a finger on my lips. The door clicks shut behind her.

"It was foretold, wasn't it?" she reminds me in her playful way.

Again I try to say something but don't manage even a syllable. I'm so aroused that I'm incapable of speech. Leira takes me by the hand and leads me to the window. We stand there, below us the lake, and I am shaking all over as if about to make love for the first time.

She kisses me. It's exactly the way I imagined it in the restaurant. I fall into a vertiginous chasm, filled to the brim with that intoxicating scent of her hair, which I'd inhaled as she read my palm. It is such an intense sensation that if we did nothing more than kiss it would mean more for me than I have ever felt even in the wildest moments of lovemaking. I hurtle into that abyss – utterly in her power.

As we make love I sense my own body and hers as never before. She winds herself around me like a climbing plant. Her hands, breasts, hips and legs draw me to her centre as if to some intoxicating flower. She never takes her eyes off me. There is that wildness in her gaze that I noticed earlier in the evening, but at the same time enormous tenderness.

I've no idea how long it lasts. I am as if in a delirium and utterly lose any sense of time.

When I come to, Leira is standing over me getting dressed. Where is she going? I want to know, desolate that she is leaving.

She tells me not to worry, she just needs to see to something. She has forgotten to answer an important email and will be right back. Before she goes, she says as if in passing: "We're joined now. Nothing will be the same anymore."

I lie inert as if she has sucked all the energy from me. A blissful languor engulfs me and although I strive to stay awake, I fall asleep.

It's already morning when I wake. Leira isn't in the room. Suddenly I've no idea whether it wasn't all a dream or whether it really happened. I dash down to the restaurant where the conference participants are breakfasting. Leira isn't there.

She doesn't even come to the conference.

Until the break I suffer in torment the tedious papers of my colleagues, whom I regularly encounter at all manner of seminars, where essentially the same things are spoken about every time, and then I quickly make my way to the reception.

I ask after Leira.

I repeat her name nervously to the receptionist, explaining she arrived from Berkeley, and yes, I forgot to ask her surname, but there's nobody of the same name at the conference.

The receptionist shrugs. He looks at me with commiseration. There is no Leira staying here. Could it be a nickname? He's never heard such a name before.

I interrupt him impatiently. I dash to the conference registration desk and frenziedly rummage among the name tags of the participants who have not yet arrived. No Leira.

The gorgeous Italian organiser, with whom I'd have flirted in other circumstances, confirms that no one by the name of Leira has registered for the conference.

I'm unwilling to accept. I can't. Where can I find a computer with internet connection? When she points to a corner of the room I almost run to the screen.

I feverishly search the Berkeley University website and then Harvard. No mention of Leira. Nothing. Not even googling helps.

I'm on tenterhooks the whole day and by evening I'm at my wits' end. I look for Collins, who is due to chair my panel the next day and tell him I'm not well and that I'll have to excuse myself. There's no reason why he couldn't read my paper on my behalf. I suspect I look quite distraught, because my otherwise garrulous colleague stares at me in silence, with a quizzical expression on his face.

I spend the evening walking all over Bellagio, peeking into restaurants and bars. But no sign of Leira. Then I lie down in my room, completely drained, without energy. I don't know why, but the following image returns insistently to my mind:

It's September 1968, the day of my twentieth birthday, I'm sitting at home in the apartment that we once shared with Egon, waiting for friends to arrive for my party. At about 7.30 in the evening, the phone rings. I imagine the caller is someone wanting to share their experiences of recent days. The streets are full of Russian tanks and people are trying to come to terms with the shock of the invasion. Several friends have already called to say they're leaving the country, and would I like to emigrate with them?

Each time I give the same reply: I would – what's there to stay for – except that my mother's ill.

But this time it's the doctor from the mental hospital. I'm to come straight away. He'll tell me everything when I arrive.

Clearly something awful has happened. I could tell from his voice. On the way, my only hope is that mother's condition has simply worsened and that he just needs to consult me.

But when I enter the doctor's consulting room everything is immediately clear to me...

"Your mother is dead," he announces. "Yesterday she was absolutely fine. She seemed to be in excellent spirits and joked when the doctors made their rounds. It was almost grotesque, because everyone is in a state of deep depression on account of the occupation. She was the only person on the ward in a good mood.

"We allowed her to take a walk in the park. Mind you, she spent most of the time sitting on a bench. She didn't talk to anyone, but there were no problems. She even had a peaceful night's sleep.

"When I saw her in morning on my rounds, she told me she had received a visit from an angel. She said they had been acquainted for some time already, but this time he had finally told her what she was to do."

He falls silent. Perhaps he is waiting to hear whether my mother had ever spoken to me about the angel.

Suddenly there is an unbearable constriction in my throat.

"The hallucination didn't seem to have upset her particularly," he continues. "She was quite cheerful like on the previous evening. Nevertheless I thought it best to invite her to see me in my consulting room at ten o'clock. I wanted to talk to her about her angel. She had mentioned it previously and that *idée fixe* had something to do with her problems.

"She was in good spirits, even when she arrived at my consulting room," the doctor mutters nervously.

"She told me that once, in this very room, she first met a man whom she later deceived. After that he hardened toward her and abandoned her. I don't know whether she meant Egon – we're all familiar with that story here, of course – but she didn't mention any name.

"She asked me if I'd open the window.

"I was happy to oblige. The windows in the consulting rooms aren't fitted with bars, but I didn't think there was any particular danger. Perhaps she just needs some fresh air, I thought to myself. I asked her again about the angel, but she suddenly turned serious.

" 'It's complicated,' she sighed. 'The way out, the path to freedom, must be through that cellar, via that hole – downward, in other words.'

"Those are the very words she used.

"I knew she had spent about a year in a cellar when she was a child during the war, but I didn't understand what she was getting at.

"Her conviction that she had been speaking with an angel might have signalled another crisis, so I thought I'd give her some tranquillisers, even though she looked quite calm.

"Before I'd managed to take them out of the cupboard, she was standing by the window.

" 'I'll have to go,' she said. 'I've got to go down there if I'm to find freedom. And to free Sasha.' Then she jumped."

The doctor grasps his head in his hands. He looks distraught.

"It's my fault," he says a moment later. "It was a professional error of judgment. I'll never forgive myself.

He asks me what my mother meant when she said her action would "free Sasha". I shrug, although I know full well. But I just can't fathom out how she could understand what was happening outside the walls of the mental hospital, and what were her grounds for thinking I should leave the country, which itself had turned into a madhouse.

The doctor offers to let me go see her, but first he gives me a warning: my beautiful mother has been disfigured by the fall.

No, I don't want to see her. Definitely not.

Moreover – although I don't tell him this – I hope in time to forget what she looked like when I visited her in hospital. I want to remember her the way she was when she was happy in the company of Egon, particularly at the moments when Egon and I played our instruments in one corner of the room, while she sat in another. Every time her expression showed that we had her attention, but at the same time she was recalling something beautiful from her past.

For some unknown reason my eyes suddenly fill with tears in that room above Bellagio, and I start to sob, a peculiar sort of lamentation, as if something was surfacing that I had held in for a very long time. I think of my mother. How could I have suppressed my memories of her for so long? I go over to the window. A cold wind is blowing from the lake. I can hear the sound of the bells on the mooring buoys and there are lights twinkling at the summits of the alpine hills.

She was trying to tell me something – I repeat to myself in agitation. Leira was trying to tell me something about my mother and possibly other things as well. What was she trying to say?

Early next morning, after a dreamless night, I arrange to be taken by boat to Menaggio before dawn, and then I take a taxi to Milan Airport.

I wrestle with my impatience. The road winds round the lake – the journey seems endless. The beautiful scenery is reduced to a backdrop. I am rushing off without knowing where. Do I want to fly back to the States? To travel to Berkeley? What am I to do, in fact?

Even before the taxi reaches the airport I realise what I must do: I have to fly to Prague – some sign awaits me there.

A sign – I can hear Leira pronouncing the words in her soft way. Maybe she'll be there too. Why, otherwise, would she have spoken about my mother?

I don't meet Leira in Prague, but something odd does happen there. It is connected with the box that I remembered when Leira was reading my palm and spoke about my mother's letter.

As is my wont when I fly into Prague, I call a friend who works in TV to announce my arrival. Usually he invites me to take part in a TV debate, which is when an event of global significance happens to be of interest to the local viewers. On this occasion I learn that the station "desperately" needs me on account of Saddam.

The day after my TV appearance, I get a call from the station asking me whether it can disclose my telephone number to someone who claims he is an old friend of mine from student days. Apparently he has something important to give me. So I meet Viktor again for the first time in over thirty years.

He explains to me that not only did he want to see me but he has also been looking for me in order to hand over some boxes with my mother's effects. He was doing a bit of tidying up recently and happened to come across them. He felt he couldn't just throw them away. He notices my look of surprise.

Surely I remember how we took several boxes to his parents' place before I emigrated... When the police subsequently interrogated him about me, he denied the boxes' existence and forgot about them.

The same day we take a trip to Český Brod, a short distance from Prague. On the way back, Viktor tells me that he has left the university department where we both started our studies and has found refuge working in business. When I started visiting Prague again after 1989, he didn't contact me because in recent years he has been working mostly abroad as a commercial attaché at various Czech embassies.

Shortly afterward I am sitting alone in the apartment I have rented in Prague for the past few years, surrounded by the boxes. In one of them I find a few photos, including some of Egon and my father, Daniel. Then I pull out another snapshot. It shows me holding hands with my mother and she is smiling tenderly. I must have been six at the time. I also discover a photograph of a building in New York on a page torn out of a book. Finally, at the very bottom, I come upon a notebook with squared paper and a sheaf of papers in waxed parchment. Inside I discover a letter, yellowed with age. The writing is very neat and must have been the work of someone with an orderly mind. When I open the notebook I find it contains my mother's handwriting.

How odd! I haven't found Leira in Prague, and yet here is something that has a connection with her, I think to myself. I can't imagine how even the most accomplished mystic could know I'd find something written by my mother, but at that moment it doesn't bother me.

First of all, I open that lengthy letter. My gaze falls on the following sentence:

The principal message of this letter, I hope, is that it is possible to achieve happiness in life if we believe that everything that fate has in store for us has a hidden purpose, and we submit to that purpose.

That's a fact, I say to myself. Even my journey here had a hidden purpose. Maybe my entire life has some hidden purpose, but I've not looked for it so far. And if I've happened to have glimpsed it, I haven't submitted to it.

I read through my grandfather's letter and Mother's memoirs in the course of a single evening. It is past midnight when I finish. I sit for a long time in the bedroom without moving, paralysed by the sense that there is some axis pointing at me from the past ready to spear me like a lance. I am obviously part of a story that started with my grandfather's childhood, but so far I don't know where I fit in. I ought to write something too, I say to myself, but compared with the lives of Josef Brehme and my mother, my own seems quite unremarkable.

Maybe that marks the beginning of the protracted process of mental breakdown that now leads me to start keeping a diary. I'm not sure yet whether I should re-assess everything I've done over the past decades, but I've a strange, nagging sense of disquiet.

It strikes me that Josef Brehme lived in an epoch when time still proceeded in a straight line from the past to the future. The life of the individual went in a straight line too and at its end one could assess if that person had passed muster. Big history and small history were in harmony to a degree. Big history, as we know, dates from the time when the Jews invented it. For them too, it was a straight line with a beginning and an end. And at the end, if we behaved in accordance with God's rules, we would find salvation.

The Enlightenment altered that concept. It believed that we could sort out our own salvation ourselves. Not only did reason suffice, we didn't even need God. But the "death of God" caused history to become cyclical in a strange fashion. In the absence of God it was necessary to accept the idea that the material world exists in infinite time and space. But as soon as we accept infinity, we accept history as a circle, because everything can be repeated over and over again.

People invented utopias and then discovered that all images of an ideal final condition resembled one another. Moreover, the path to their achievement was lined with rivers of blood and concentration camps. The individual was of no value in rational constructs of that kind. And in the final analysis, on whose behalf should we be striving? For those who will come after us and about whom we know nothing?

History has tied itself into a knot. It's gone crazy and become cynical. Mum's memoirs are a sad example of that. Her path from one "ideal" regime to another simply ends in a hole anyway. A collapse.

And what about me? What about my epoch? With a touch of scorn, Leira labeled me as a postmodern intellectual. Perhaps she was driving at something more fundamental. Maybe I'd touched on it myself when I was talking about the present globalised world in terms of an onion. Nothing has a firm axis anymore, nothing moves naturally from one point to another anymore. The beginning and the end have ceased to exist. Things overlay one another and all the layers have the same value, and it is impossible to find one's way around inside it all – although from the outside it looks like a perfectly formed onion. Is there any sense to it all?

And history no longer evolves either in a straight line or in endless circles of rational delirium. History looks more like a Lego set that can be used to build parts of the whole, which can then either be arranged into bigger entities or left to their own devices.

Leira was quite near the mark when she compared the world to a computer game. A virtual world has its own virtual time, above which another, "real" time unfolds. Moreover, that time – the history inside the program – can snap at any moment. One period of history can be grafted onto another, and some parts can even be erased.

Was Leira aware that I would have to reflect on this too?

As I sit like this in my Prague apartment, which isn't my real home,

I feel the same intense hopelessness that overcame me in Bellagio. Tears well up in my eyes once more and I start to sob. I try in vain to control myself.

I'm at some turning point, I tell myself. Something of enormous importance is going to happen. I've no idea what it might be. Perhaps it will shed some meaningful light on my life so far and point me in some direction.

I pace up and down the apartment wondering what to do. Perhaps I should go out into the streets of Prague and clear my head. Or call one of my casual lovers. But in the end I just collapse into an armchair and try to recall the past.

I'm so agitated that recollections start surfacing from God knows where, recollections that I've banished over the years to the very fringes of my memory. All of sudden, for instance, I remember how terribly afraid I always was as a child that my mother would have to return to the mental hospital. How I'd observe her anxiously whenever she started to be hysterical or agitated. That threat hung over me all the time.

My mother stopped working after we moved to Egon's. I was too small to fully understand the nature of her illness, but from their conversations and allusions I somehow gathered that Egon was the psychiatrist in charge of my mother at the mental hospital. Sometimes it was hard not to overhear those conversations, particularly when my mother was upset over something and Egon administered a kind of first aid. At such moments her speech would be rambling and she would cry and laugh at the same time, and I was afraid for her. I was dreadfully afraid.

Eventually I developed an odd form of defence. I used to say to myself: I can't afford to feel any emotion; I must be prepared for the worst. I knew that they had killed my father and things needn't turn out well for my mother either.

It's true that Egon was around and he meant a great deal to me, but his relationship with my mother seemed to me unreal, as if he wanted to sacrifice himself somehow. I understood with my childish reasoning that her beauty might captivate him, but at the same time it was obvious to me that there was an enormous gulf between them. He was an educated and cultivated man, while she was unsophisticated and impulsive, though intelligent. It came as no surprise to me when he ran out on us. It was only when I read Mum's memoirs that I discovered that she had been partly the cause. Poor Mum!

I was fifteen when she ended up once more in mental hospital for many years – for the last time, in fact. In theory I could have rejoiced at the freedom it offered me, because Egon's aunt Dita, in whose home I was living, was already an old lady and couldn't cope with me. She didn't even bother to impose a routine on me. I didn't relish the situation, though. What I wanted was some authority to tell me what to do, someone I might respect, or whose eventual anger I might fear slightly.

I visited my mother in the mental hospital and every time it took something out of me. Either she was apathetic because of the pills or she tended to spend the time blaming herself hysterically. Some sixth sense told me that she wouldn't manage to extricate herself from the mental hospital this time.

Until I reached the age of nineteen I was virtually abandoned. I was afraid of girls. I kept my feelings so much in check that any sort of relationship filled me with dread. The girls in my class found me attractive – I'm tall and dark-haired after my father. One of them even told me I had an exotic look – like a Greek or an Italian.

But I resisted. I developed a whole range of defensive reactions: mostly using the aunt as an excuse. I'd claim that I was only a guest at her place, and that I had to obey her rules. If she threw me out, I'd have nowhere to go. In reality, the aunt didn't really care what I did.

It wasn't until I was at the Arts Faculty that I had my first love affair. Her name was Klára and she was studying interpreting. There was something in her pale features that I found attractive. Perhaps it was her expressive eyes, or her sensual mouth. It's hard to say. But I was certainly transfixed whenever we met. I didn't know how to approach her. I imagined taking a seat at her table in the student canteen, but she usually sat with her girlfriends and I didn't know any of them. Or I thought of accosting her in the corridor under some pretext. What would I say to her? That I'm crazy about her? What if she'd never noticed me? And what if she laughed at me?

Lacking the courage to approach her in person, I decided to send her a letter. I described my feelings, or more accurately, my emotions, and the reasons why I lacked the courage to approach her. And I added that I would fully understand, of course, if she didn't reply; after all, she might already be going out with someone. And even if she happened to know who I was, it could well be that she didn't find me at all attractive.

I wrote that letter without censoring myself because I had no intention of sending it. I even lacked the courage for that. I wrote it because it helped me sort my ideas out, and it gave me a certain illusion of having made an attempt, at least.

I put the letter in an envelope and wrote on the outside: Klára Mensdorfová, student interpreter.

I carried it around in my briefcase for weeks on end as a memento of my cowardice, and eventually I forgot about it, even though I was still interested in Klára. The envelope ended up being fairly crumpled and grubby. Indeed it's possible that I'd used it to note down in haste a telephone number or some other important information.

One day I catch sight of Klára as I'm coming out of a lecture room. She's leaning on a balustrade above the staircase and looking in my direction. Although I'm sure she is waiting for someone else, she's giving me a little wave. I can't tell whether it is intended as a greeting, or whether she's signalling to me that she wants to talk to me.

I am seized by an indescribable consternation. I want to take to my heels, but there's nowhere for me to run to, unless I return to the lecture room.

I am almost unconscious of the fact that she is talking to me.

"Are you Sasha? Sasha Brehme?"

When I nod, she reaches into her pocket and pulls out a crumpled envelope. My letter.

"Would you like to talk about it?"

The truth is that I don't feel like talking about it at all. My urge to flee grows stronger. But I get the better of myself and nod once more. She has the advantage over me from the very outset. She smiles affably.

"I hope you have the power of speech. It would be as shame if someone who wrote letters like this was unable to speak."

I take this to be encouragement. We set off down the corridor together.

"I'm sorry," I reply. "Everything I wrote in that letter is true but I wasn't intending to send it to you. I'm in a bit of shock. How did you come by it?"

A fellow student brought it to me. She found it in one of the classrooms. You didn't leave it there on purpose, then?"

I shake my head. And then it strikes me that I've nothing to lose.

It's as if a dam has burst and everything I feel suddenly starts to gush out of me: how I'd been attracted to her but didn't know how to approach her. In fact I partly repeat what I'd written in the letter and explain that I didn't send the letter because I feared she'd reject me.

"I wasn't even sure that you'd know who I was," my monologue concluded.

"Of course I know you," she says. "Even my girlfriends noticed you staring at me in the canteen. I was expecting you to approach me."

Her words came as a release. But suddenly I'm seized with anxiety. I can't delude myself that I'm not in love with Klára. But what is to be done, now that she knows about it. What if it turns out badly? Will I be able to bear it? And how am I to tell her that my mother is in a lunatic asylum?

In the end it turns out to be easier than I had imagined. One evening when we are sitting together in the student canteen, I tell her everything, the whole caboodle.

About my anxieties, about the sort of childhood I've had. How I've had to look after myself since I was fifteen. How I've avoided relationships with girls for fear of further misfortunes. And how I have been unable to stop myself falling in love with her.

As I assess now, with a touch of cynicism, what I said on that occasion in all sincerity, I realise she was unable to resist the power of my words. I had said precisely what women want to hear. I had portrayed myself as a poor wretch, full of insecurity, whom she alone could save through her love: a youngster in need of her help. And also a virgin, although that wasn't the only reason Klára fell in love with me, or why we first went to bed together just two days after our first conversation.

In my immaturity, I was a bit put out by the fact I wasn't her first, but I soon got over my disappointment. In the end, it was an advantage to me that she had some experience. Only later did I start to criticise her, fairly stupidly. It irked me that she had lost her virginity with her literature teacher at high school, as she informed me. It seemed to me immoral and indecent, particularly since she knew at the outset that he was married.

And so I loved her. Until the end of the first year I was racked by three conflicting emotions: I was almost recklessly in love, extremely jealous and fearful of losing her.

I never introduced Klára to Mum. I was afraid that if Klára got to know her, she'd start to wonder whether I might turn out the same way one day. Madness is often hereditary, after all.

But in the end it was I who walked out on Klára. When my mother died, I was alarmed by the thought that Klára was now the only person to whom I had a close emotional tie. I was convinced that she would abandon me one day.

That was also one of the reasons I emigrated. Yes, I fled Czechoslovakia not only out of despair at what had happened here after the occupation, and not only because my parents had suffered in this country, but also for reasons of cowardice. I ran away cowardly from my relationship with Klára. For fear of being unable to bear the disappointment of an eventual break-up.

For several weeks after Mum's death I systematically stifled my love for Klára, and in the end I was successful. And I was such a coward that I didn't even write her a letter. Before I left I simply told her that I was intending to visit my grandmother Ester in London, because it might be my last opportunity to see my only remaining relative. I think that Klára had no idea at all what my intentions were. I simply send her a postcard from London a few weeks later. With no return address. "Things have changed," I wrote. "I have to stay here now for various reasons. I hope we'll meet again."

But I didn't hope anything of the kind.

I think that by the time I wrote that postcard I was deliberately planning a brilliant future for myself in the West.

It was my first major lapse – a betrayal, in fact. I think that marked the start of my fall, which some, including myself, might have considered my rise. I had cold-bloodedly sacrificed Klára for the sake of my own ends; just as later I sacrificed other women for the sake of my insatiable lust.

It didn't meet Klára again until the mid-nineties, during one of my trips to Prague. I was taking part in an international conference where there was simultaneous interpretation of the speeches. She tapped me on the shoulder when I was pouring myself a coffee in the lobby, after the first panel had ended.

I turned round. Something in her stance recalled the moment when she had been waiting for me outside the lecture room. She was smiling the same affable smile as on that occasion.

She had not changed much during the past twenty-five plus years. She is one of those women who remain slim throughout their lives. Her pale features have been marked by the years, of course, but much less than in the case of other friends, many of whom I no longer recognised after more than quarter of a century.

"How are things, Sasha?" she asked and then added in English: "Or should I say, how are you, Professor Brehme?"

I replied sheepishly that things were fine.

"And what about you?"

She shrugged and then said: "OK."

We stood facing each other for a moment.

"Are you interpreting for the next panel?"

"No, not till this afternoon."

I invited her to a nearby café. At first we conversed neutrally about our marriages, our children and our careers. She knew much more about me than I did about her.

It wasn't until we were about to leave that I felt the need to say something by way of an excuse.

"I regretted for a long time how things turned out that time," I lied. "I wanted to return, but my grandmother, who was the last family member I had left, wasn't well at the time. I felt a responsibility toward her..."

It sounded pathetic.

Klára said nothing.

Then she said, "There's no need to apologise, Sasha. After all, the very first time we talked together in that restaurant I knew I was taking a risk. It was obvious to me that you weren't – how shall I put it – entirely stable."

That hurt. I had a fairly high opinion of myself and at that moment I wondered whether I should take it lying down.

"I was really in love with you," she continued. "I more or less kept waiting for you until the end of my studies, even though I realised that it would have been hard for you to return after 1970, because the regime would have penalised you. But it occurred to me that you might write and tell me how to join you there."

"I had something similar in mind, too," I lied brazenly once more.

I could see she didn't believe me.

"No matter," she said with a dismissive wave of the hand. "It's no longer of any importance." She even smiled.

We got up and returned to the conference.

I bumped into her again several times at subsequent conferences.

I often repeat to myself those words of hers: It's no longer of any importance.

I repeat them to assuage my own conscience, even though in the depth of my soul I know it's not true, because, Alex, it is of importance. Even now. Everything is important!

It is impossible to escape one's past. An account is kept of everything in some strange way. Even my betrayal of Klára is recorded somewhere, along with my infidelity toward other women. I am afraid of ending like Don Juan. That the ghost of one of the dead will take my arm in its steely grip and drag me off to hell. And maybe I'm already there, because all the fame that has enabled me to suppress the occasional pangs of bad conscience suddenly seems to me like ash.

Now, seated here once more in my Prague apartment many years later, disconcerted by my meeting with Leira and by reading my grandfather's letter and my mother's memoirs, I suddenly realise that I have virtually lived without a past ever since I left university. There was no one to provide any contact with it, no one to link me with the history of my family. Ester avoided any excursions into the past, so that my knowledge of what had once happened was very sketchy.

I knew that my father had fought in the Czechoslovak legions, that he later became a policeman, and that he committed suicide after my grandmother Karina died in childbirth. I also knew that my grandfather Hugo had fallen at the Battle of Zborov and that my father had died in a Communist labour camp. And I was also vaguely aware that my great-grandparents had saved my mother and her brother from being transported to a concentration camp by hiding with them in a cellar for over a year.

But there was much more that I didn't know, which is also why I'm sitting here in my Prague apartment all shaken up. My own fortunes seem like a frivolous trip, like a state of weightlessness. What have I been doing, for God's sake, over the past two decades? How could I have attributed such importance to things that are of no consequence at all? What was the origin of my narcissistic intoxication with myself, with so-called fame? How can I relate it to what my forebears went through?

I know I ought to do something, something that would put me back on my feet, but what, for heaven's sake? Should I go to the synagogue and pray? Or simply get down on my knees in the nearest church and ask God for some sign? Can I atone for something?

Then it occurs to me that I ought to apologise to my second wife Katrina. I ought to arrange to meet her and tell her that I was unfaithful to her the whole time, while also loving her. That if I could take everything back again I'd behave differently.

But I'm immediately seized by skepticism. Of course I could tell her all that, but what good would it be? There's no way of repairing our relationship by now. And would I really behave differently if I was given the opportunity? Would I be capable of it?

It crosses my mind to visit my daughter Rebecca in Chicago, but what would I tell her? After all, we became alienated from each other when she was in early puberty. It was obvious even to her at that time that there were just too many occasions when I was unable to stay home on account of some pressing engagement. She once told me that from the age of at least twelve, she knew I was two-timing Katrina her mother. And she added that she might have been able to come to terms with it better if I'd at least found some time for her occasionally.

No, I wasn't an entirely bad father. Rebecca definitely didn't suffer in any way. She had everything she needed, she attended the best schools, and we regularly vacationed together until my divorce from Katrina. But she never felt that I had any real interest in her. Alex Brehme always came first – Alex and his insatiable libido.

The last time I saw Rebecca, at the end of last year, we talked together openly. She didn't bear any grudge, and in fact she emphasised that I was always an inspiration for her. She was proud of having a famous father, a thinker whose intellectual authority was referred to throughout the world, and not some show-business entertainer. Nevertheless, from the tone of that conversation it was obvious that there was a wall between us, that we would never be truly close.

So what now? Was I to return to New York or stay in Prague and hope that Leira would put in an appearance? I'd probably fulfilled my task by finding those two yellowing bundles. Although I was on a sabbatical from university this year, I had to be in America the next week for a Congressional hearing, besides which, it was impossible to know where Leira was.

Then for some unknown reason it suddenly occurred to me that I might find a clue to Leira's whereabouts in the town she is named after. Now I became totally obsessed with the idea.

The very next morning I packed my suitcase, including the things I found in those boxes my mother left behind, and I set out for the airport. I bought myself a ticket to Lisbon. In the plane I was overcome by on odd tremor inside me. Impatience.

I'm in Lisbon and at the end of my tether. I could call up acquaintances that I meet at conferences, but I know I have to make the trip to Leira alone. I also know it won't come cheap, but I don't care. I take a taxi from the airport. The driver is astonished to hear where he is to take me. During the journey he becomes talkative. He knows a bit of English and manages to tell me about his family and even something about the political situation here. Portugal is still a poor country; no local would take a cab to Leira, he explains. But on the odd occasion he has been asked by tourists to take them to Fátima, which is just a short distance from Leira.

The name Fátima arouses me. Does he mean the place where the Virgin Mary once started to appear?

Of course, he nods. I shouldn't miss the opportunity to see it. And he immediately treats me to a digression about its history.

Our Lady first appeared there on May 13, 1917 to three shepherds. At that time they were still children: ten-year-old Lucia dos Santos, her cousin Francisco Marto, who was a year younger, and her seven-year-old cousin Jacinta. They described what they saw as an angel, who looked more like a young boy.

But then they had another vision and this gave rise to the Marian cult. Millions of people make the journey there every year from all over the world

I suddenly have a powerful feeling that the very moment I made up my mind to go to Leira I was heading for Fátima. It's bound to have some connection with the angel that I've read about in my mother and grandfather's memoirs. Suddenly I'm utterly convinced of it, and I ask the taxi driver to turn off and drop me in Fátima.

But then when I'm standing there with my suitcase surrounded by a throng of people I've no idea what I'm doing here. It is as if I can see myself amidst this odd tumult as if from above: a small abandoned figure with a suitcase containing Mum's effects. What is he seeking, this confused man?

In the end I come down to earth. I notice a hotel a short way from the chapel that stands on the spot where the vision first appeared. It's called Fátima. What else?

I check in quickly and return straight away to the street. I'm desperately searching for something, some answer. I want to learn as much as possible about that apparition. I walk to all the important sites and buy several tourist guidebooks and publications. The history of the miracle gradually reveals itself to me and I eagerly leaf through one book after another. Meanwhile I am witness to the incredible spectacle of thousands of people advancing on their knees to the site of the miracle in order to pray for healing or forgiveness.

The Angel of Peace. That was another name for the apparition. The Virgin Mary apparently promised the children that if they prayed fervently she would bring peace to a world torn apart by the First World War and would save Russia. She is also said to have predicted that another war would follow World War I, and that Russia would spread its delusions around the world and unleash wars. Some nations would be destroyed. The world would suffer war, famine and terror. Russia would persecute the churches and become an instrument of godlessness.

In 1917, the Virgin Mary appeared five more times in Fátima, each time on the thirteenth day of the month – the last time on October 13. A third prophesy is also said to have existed, but the Church had kept it secret until last year, when it announced that the Virgin Mary at Fátima had foreseen the attempt on the Pope's life. In one of the guides, however, I discovered that there were doubts about whether the Church had truly revealed what she had forecast. The third prophecy was allegedly so dreadful that nothing was said about it for decades on end. Was that dreadful event really the attempted murder of the Pope? I read there that the Turk Mehmet Ali Ağca shot the pope on

May 13, 1981. I try in vain to recall what I was doing that day.

There is something about in all of this that deeply intrigues me. It seems to me that there is some mysterious connection between the discovery of my grandfather and mother's memoirs and my impulse to make the journey here. And everything is connected with Leira somehow. And also with the angel that both my grandfather and my mother wrote about.

My agnosticism is slightly shaken, but habitual reactions are not easily suppressed. So I cynically dismiss the fact that Ariel appeared to Josef Brehme just five weeks after the Virgin Mary appeared in Fátima. I reason that the end of World War I evidently provoked a great deal of supernatural activity. Or the capacity of more sensitive individuals to see something that seems supernatural. Moreover, it would seem that these supernatural forces were quite diverse – in Fátima it was a vision of the Virgin Mary, while at Zborov it was Ariel, who is supposed to be God's angel of destruction, the bearer of bad tidings.

Toward evening I'm sitting in a small café trying to sort my ideas out. The pile of books on my table, which I am eagerly leafing through, attracts the attention of a priest at the next table.

"You seem to have a lot of questions," he says in perfect English.

I nod, and he smiles.

"Even celebrities can be prey to doubts, then?"

He turns out to be a professor of theology at Trinity College, Dublin. He is evidently highly educated in matters of faith, because when I ask him about Ariel, he inundates me with information.

Ariel is possibly the most mysterious of the archangels, he tells me. Various characteristics are attributed to him. Quite often he is portrayed as the angel of wrath or the spirit of vengeance. He and the archangel Uriel have similar attributes. He is ruler of the Earth and hence also ruler of all the elements – earth, water, air and fire.

Was I aware, the priest asks me, that the poet Percy Bysshe Shelley had a guardian angel by the name of Ariel? Or so he maintained. But not even that Ariel was altogether a good fellow it seems. Shelley gave the name to the schooner on which he sailed the Mediterranean. That fact even caused him to quarrel with Lord Byron, who insisted on calling the ship Don Juan, the name chosen by his poetry circle.

Apparently, just before his last voyage on that schooner – or so his wife claimed – Shelley met his doppelgänger, the presage of death. He was drowned just before his thirtieth birthday in a storm not far from Livorno.

In Paradise Lost, John Milton writes that Ariel was a rebel, who was defeated by the Seraph Abdiel on the very first day of fighting in Heaven. He certainly did not turn into Lucifer, but in a way he is a fallen angel. He is associated by some with the demon Arioch.

I nod, although I'm none the wiser. I go on to tell the priest about my mother's memoirs and my grandfather's letter. I tell him that although I have no belief in such things, it's odd that both of them refer to their encounters with an apparition they call Ariel. Didn't he agree?

He now regards me with unfeigned interest.

After a moment's reflection he says, "I sense that you doubt it. I have no intention of persuading you otherwise. Anyway, scientists have been trying for a long time to offer a rational explanation for everything that we believers consider miracles.

"In the early fifties, a Canadian neurologist by the name of Wilder Penfield was operating on the brains of epilepsy sufferers and discovered that when he stimulated certain parts of the brain's temporal lobe with electrodes, the patients heard voices and saw ghost-like apparitions. Epileptics often maintain that demons or angels control the events that affect them. Moreover, neurologists have confirmed that an injury to the left hemisphere of the brain can cause disorientation, and the brain then interprets stimuli originating in the right hemisphere as something coming from outside, from another 'self.'"

The priest gives me a few moments to think about what he has said, before adding, "The scientists' explanation sounds very logical, but a believer could argue that in the brains of epileptics and people with injuries to the left hemisphere, some sort of window is opened enabling them to see and sense phenomena that are indiscernible to so-called normal people. What if the things we regard as illness or injury enable them to receive signals that elude the healthy ones amongst us?"

Then he says with a slight smile, "God's ways are His own. Nothing He does or wants is necessarily clear to us. Our Lady here in Fátima wasn't always particularly friendly either. She tended to be urging human beings to repent, and in no uncertain terms. Incidentally, she told two children to whom she appeared that they would soon die. And they did – during the Spanish flu epidemic. Telling little children they were going to die wasn't very humane, was it? Why couldn't they have been saved? What role did they play in God's plan?"

I'm seized by a kind of torpor when I return to my hotel. Fátima is so permeated by belief in the supernatural that my convictions are undermined. I came here to look for Leira, but here, even more than in Prague, perhaps, new scope has opened up to me. Something I fear, but am drawn to by its enormous gravitational pull.

Typically for me, however, the cynical thought crosses my mind before I fall asleep that Ariel is possibly something like a computer virus.

To think something of that sort in Fátima definitely qualifies as blasphemy.

Saturday September 8, 2001

My New York apartment. I observe from the window the silhouettes of the buildings on the opposite shore, in New Jersey. The majestic stream of the Hudson glistens through the trees, affording a comforting view, unlike my apartment.

This apartment is almost bare. It is totally devoid of the coziness that Katrina was capable of creating at home. I got rid of lots of books after our divorce. I don't miss them. Those I need I borrow from the library. Or I buy them and when I've read them I donate them to the local second-hand bookstore.

I prefer to do my writing in my office at the university which is just round the corner. I've brought only absolute necessities here.

There's a chess set on the table. I now play against myself, just like my mother used to do. One or two moves each day.

I've also kept my violin and the collection of scores that Ester once gave me. They mean a great deal to me and since her death I have played from them almost every day.

Ester.

It is October 1968 when I arrive in London and knock on the door of the apartment where Ester was supposed to be living. I'm not sure whether she's still alive. My mother last exchanged letters with her in 1963. If she's still alive she must be over seventy by now.

I'm carrying just one piece of luggage, which is all I took with me from Czechoslovakia. I don't know what I'll do if I don't find Ester. Fortunately the door opens. Standing there is an old lady whose beautiful, soulful face is framed by a thick wreath of grey hair.

There is a question in her gaze.

Later she tells me that she immediately thought it was me, but she wasn't sure. After all, she had received her most recent photograph of me before my mother ended up in the psychiatric hospital for the last time. She leans against the door frame as if unable to bear some load.

"So you're Sasha – my Sasha. Daniel's flesh and blood," she repeats in tears.

Several moments pass before it occurs to her to invite me in. We sit down facing each other at the kitchen table, and in between sips of tea I relate to her in a rambling fashion my mother's death and my decision to leave my occupied homeland. I tell her about my time at university, about my childhood, and about how I have often wondered what my father was really like.

"Daniel was the fruit of a great love," Ester says. "Your grandfather Hugo was a hero, who fell at Zborov. I won't talk about him if you don't mind. His death fills me with sorrow. He was the best friend of your other grandfather, Josef. His fate was tragic too. It looks as if our family is prone to disasters," she smiles bitterly.

I feel an immediate attachment to her. I loved my mother, but never with my whole heart. I had to be careful and protect myself. I was constantly afraid of some calamity. I was terrified that my mother would end up in the madhouse again. She radiated a self-destructive instinct that eventually won out.

With Ester I have a sense of security. I'm glad when she offers to let me stay with her. She lives alone, her husband died long ago. She says she is fairly well off and she won't go broke because of me. She'll be pleased to take care of me.

She gave up her concert career five years ago, she tells me. She could have come to Prague, and had decided to on several occasions because she very much wanted to see me, but each time fear got the better of her. She wasn't sure she could bear to return to the country where they had killed her son.

Ester is my first port of call in the West. She tells me about her concerts, about her marriage and about the sadness that she has borne throughout her life. And also about the guilt she feels about having survived when all her nearest and dearest perished.

But scarcely a word is said about Daniel, my grandfather Josef, or my mother.

We go to concerts and the theatre together. Ester pays for my English courses and each evening, after dinner she gives me some extra coaching. I've given her life fresh meaning, she says: I'm her last great project.

And we also play music together. "It's an incredible shame," she frequently repeats, "that you never went in for music professionally. You have great talent."

In the spring of 1969 we address the issue of my future. I apply to Oxford and, to my surprise, I am offered a place. My choice is political philosophy. I live in college but I make trips to London to see Ester whenever I can.

I cope well with my studies, as with everything else for that matter, but my relationships fall below my expectations. It's not that I have any difficulty dating girls, on the contrary; but the relationships never last long. I haven't the desire – or more likely, the courage – to get too involved.

My relationship with my first date, Gail, the daughter of a doctor's family from Bristol, was short lived. Although we had lots of fun together, I stopped finding her interesting after three months. Worse still, she started to scare me, because she kept on talking about love and our future together.

But I didn't need more than sex with her.

It was the same with my other girlfriends. I found one or two of them a bit more interesting, but now I wouldn't even recognise them. During my time at Oxford I already realised I had a long path ahead of me. I knew I'd be a professor and there would be more universities to come. I didn't want to be tied down.

I didn't reminisce much about Czechoslovakia in those days. From time to time I'd miss a few of my friends from high school and university but I quickly forgot them. And I systematically pushed Klára out of my memory, because every time I recalled her I felt heartache.

In fact I wanted to forget everything that had any kind of close tie with that ill-fated country. I wanted nothing more to do with it if possible. I noted that some guy called Husák, who was a colourless, cynical opportunist, to judge by the photos in the newspapers, had replaced Alexander Dubček at the head of the Communist Party. Under his leadership, so-called "normalization" got under way in Czechoslovakia.

Occasionally I read Czech books, particularly Kundera, Klíma or Škvorecký, and then I discussed them with Ester, but even that was something like a story from another world for me by then. An epoch had come to an end in the country where I grew up, and I had no key to understanding the new status quo, because I didn't have anyone in Czechoslovakia any more. I simply exchanged letters from time to time with former friends.

I wanted to be famous. And so even then I knew I'd end up in America. Britain was too small for me. Everything that was of any real importance in the world at that time was taking place in America. But I wasn't rushing anywhere for the time being.

In the end I might have stayed a few more years in Britain, but at the beginning of 1972 Ester announced to me that she was gravely ill with lung cancer. She never smoked, but her husband was a heavy smoker. Their apartment was always full of his pipe smoke... She knew she had only a few months left, and she wanted to leave things behind her in good order, as she said. I was not to worry. She was glad to have discovered me, her grandson, at the end of her life, because I reminded her of the people she loved.

She decided to transfer ownership of her apartment and her life savings to me. "It'll be better this way," she said, fending off my objections. "If you had to sort everything out in probate it would waste your time. And you haven't any time to waste. Use the money wisely, and chiefly for your studies. That's the best investment. It'll pay many times over."

She died in April 1972. I was by her bed in the hospital, holding her hand. I felt much greater sadness than when I had learnt about my mother's death. Maybe because I really didn't have anyone left now. It's true that somewhere in Germany, there was Uncle Arno and possibly Uncle Alexey in Russia, but I knew nothing about them. In fact, I had no wish to know.

Now when I look back, I see Ester partly through my grandfather's eyes: as a beautiful young girl from a Jewish village in Ukraine. Josef Brehme first noticed her when he was introduced to the members of the quartet. Ester was standing in the background and yet even at that moment she was possibly the most important person in the whole of his story. That's what she was like her whole life: beautiful, talented and wise. She connected my grandfather's and my mother's destinies with my own. My grandmother, the only grandparent I got to know.

After her death I was free. I had no commitments, and no one for me to take care of. And nobody cared about me. How was I to handle all of that freedom?

That same spring I applied to Harvard. None of my professors was in any doubt that I'd be accepted. Who else should get in, if not their best student?

I'd planned everything in detail. I'd keep my London apartment for the time being and let it out to provide me with funds to cover the rent of a small apartment in Boston and other expenses. And the money I'd received from Ester would be ample to pay my tuition fees, in case they did not waive most of them at Harvard. And I still had no inkling that I'd soon be making a decent salary, because I'd also start to work as a teaching assistant while studying there.

I find it hard to recall these things. For too long I have been absorbed with myself – with my career and advancement. I have put out of my mind a lot of unpleasant things that could have gnawed at my conscience, such as my betrayal of Klára. That's another reason why I have difficulty in establishing a clear chronological axis for my past life. It's all a vague jumble of experiences. But I have to go on.

The beginning of my American career was marked by my failed marriage to Debra. I married her, or at least it seems to me now, because I was cut off from a lot of things. I didn't know how to cope sensibly with the freedom I had gained after Ester's death.

It was a desirable match. I had no money worries and was regarded by everyone as an up and coming star.

It was exhilarating. During my first year of studies, I, a refugee from Eastern Europe on whom fortune had smiled, lived it up with girls, whose very admission to Harvard meant they belonged to the cream of American society. Perhaps I was driven to a certain extent by a perverse delight at sleeping with future members of the elite, who would one day control the destiny of the most powerful country on earth.

Debra was slightly different. She liked to talk about spirituality and how she didn't regard a career as the be all and end all. But when it came to sex, she was utterly depraved and drove me wild. Indeed, the idea of our getting married emerged after one deeply satisfying night of sex. It was total stupidity, of course, as is now obvious to me.

And there was yet another aspect to our relationship that I really don't enjoy recalling. Just as previously in the case of Klára, cool reason prevailed over my emotions, or at least over my compassion.

I calculatedly took advantage of Debra in order to obtain American citizenship. I needed it quite simply because only in America could I have a great career and I didn't feel like going through the complicated application process, with its various temporary visas and work permits. The very moment I gave the nod to her idea of marriage I suspected how it would turn out. I knew that I'd be able to play the role of husband for half a year at most and then I'd be having an affair with some female student again.

I was wrong only on one count: the affair was with a newly fledged professor of anthropology. She was studying the cultural aspects of something in eastern Moravia and urgently needed to improve her Czech. And since she was very good looking I was unable to refuse when she approached me. Unfortunately, her husband found out about our "language lessons", and without thinking twice he went to complain to my new wife.

Debra came from a well-established New York Jewish family. Her forebears had already arrived in America in the 19th century. They were sort of Jewish aristocrats and Debra was what was known then as a "Jewish-American princess". They didn't have much faith in a refugee from Eastern Europe, however brilliant.

I don't know what happened in the family circle when Debra announced to them that she wanted to marry me. But from various hints it was plain to me that she had gotten her own way only after a major battle.

Her well-heeled relatives were proved right, of course, because I two-timed her as they predicted I would. What could one expect, anyway, from an individual who had neither had a family to speak of, nor a family history? They were also mystified by that fact that I had no real inkling how my Jewish relatives had survived the war. My mother had hidden somewhere and my father had fought in the British army, I used to reply. It's a miracle I'm alive, really, but then the existence of each of us is actually a miracle, isn't it?

They definitely had no wish to hear such talk. They were pious people who kept the Sabbath and observed other customs. They didn't even eat pork, which I like. They firmly believed that everything was controlled by the will of God. How was I to admit to them that I regarded my acquaintanceship with Debra as fated perhaps only in the sense that I'd acquire American citizenship after the wedding?

My recollections of my first marriage are not pleasant. I was calculating and cynical and on top of that, my affair with the delightful anthropologist was outed. Her husband and Debra's family decided to wage a vendetta and worked to get me thrown out of the University. However, an ethics committee that dealt with the matter eventually decided that I had the right to sleep with the professor as I pleased because she had never taught me and after all we were both adults.

I occasionally recall how, in spite of my exoneration – or maybe precisely because of it – the jilted husband sought me out in a bar near the university, where I happened to be discussing the whole matter with his wife. She was just telling me that we could now live together – an idea I wasn't too keen on – when the lunatic rushed into the bar and without any preamble started a fight with me. He probably didn't expect Alex Brehme, the rising star of American political science, to be an accomplished athlete. I repelled his attack with little difficulty and inflicted a nosebleed on him in the process.

But the professor of anthropology considered my self-defence disproportionate and interpreted her husband's attempt to thrash me as an expression of his desperation and love. I expect they already made it up on the way from the bar, or some time later. In all events, she disappeared from my life. It was good riddance for me, in fact.

For a long time, my life with Debra and my affair with the anthropologist seemed to me like incidental amusement in the course of my early career. Professionally I was doing exceptionally well and I regarded my failed marriage simply as a price I'd paid for success; a minor hiccup on the path to the highest goals.

So I didn't suffer any excessive pangs of conscience even when the court dissolved our marriage. And I wasn't lonely in the least because I was never short of women.

At that time I was preparing for my doctorate and my thesis was a reflection on the relationship between Enlightenment humanism and Marxist-Leninist theories. The basic argument was simple:

Marxism-Leninism was simply a blind alley of Western rationalism and humanism, although the original idea was entirely humanistic – building a paradise of equality, justice and material abundance, which would allow us to forget about God, that pathetic "opium of the people".

The era of modernity had essentially split into two currents: on the one hand, there were those who wanted to achieve a paradise created by human reason with the help of revolution; on the other, there were those in the other camp who relied on evolution in the form of continuous progress.

The protagonists of both currents believed that man was lord of the Earth; and, moreover, that, in a way, they were bringing salvation. And they did have another thing in common: a belief in the rational organization of society and unstoppable progress. That was why modern states, both democratic and totalitarian, laid great stress on the rational potential of bureaucracy. That idea had first been formulated by Hegel, and indeed the entire basis of Marxism was Hegelian. Except that when western Marxism was blended with Russian despotism, an explosive mixture was created in the form of Marxism-Leninism.

I can no longer recall everything in that dissertation. I am aware now that it wasn't even very original. It was enthusiastically received, nonetheless, and immediately published as my first book.

That marked the start of my meteoric academic career. I was dubbed an expert on the ideology with which America was engaged in a reputedly historical battle. Those on the right liked my arguments because I described Marxism-Leninism as an irreparable caricature of the original humanist project, while those on the left were taken with the way I had interpreted democracy and Communist totalitarianism as non-identical twins that had the same potential at the outset.

The book's success helped me obtain my first permanent post at the prestigious Georgetown University, which brought with it several advantages. Thanks to the fact that the university is located in Washington D.C., in other words, at the centre of political power in America, I was soon able to act as an advisor to several members of Congress and to some key people in President Carter's administration. I was hitched up to the media bandwagon. There was almost nothing related to Eastern Europe that did not require a media comment by Alex Brehme.

And yet the language of the Sovietology era was incredibly simple. Thousands of books and doctoral theses were written about trivialities. The world was neatly divided into two competing parts, and almost no one in America was in any doubt that one part was a world of Good while the other was a world of Evil. The experts on the Soviet bloc therefore had an easy task. They either confirmed that the Soviet empire was truly evil, or they tried to identify hopeful signs for the future in developments in the Eastern bloc, a future in which the people dominated by the Evil Empire would return to us, to the Empire of Good.

Every supposed "reform" proclaimed by the Kremlin was dissected far more thoroughly than it merited. While citizens of the Soviet Union and its satellites retold cynical jokes about attempts at so-called reform; in America, conferences were held and books were written about every single shift in the thinking of Brezhnev and his colleagues in the Politburo.

It was good business. All you required was knowledge of the language of Sovietology and you were immediately accepted as one of the initiated. The talk was all about a bipolar world, containment, nuclear deterrence, mutually assured destruction... Occasionally a new term cropped up that had been introduced in Europe, such as Realpolitik or détente.

I took part in dozens of conferences that were all very similar. Even in those days, I realised that many of my colleagues from the university milieu eventually personally identified with the subject of their research to such an extent that they were capable of making enemies for life over of a clash of opinions about issues that I regarded more or less as mere means of raising my profile still further. They would often put forward their arguments with a passion and tenacity that seemed disproportionate to me, if one took into account that the actual policies toward the Soviet Union were ultimately determined by entirely pragmatic considerations.

At one of my very first conferences, a bitter argument broke out between two stars of Sovietology of that time. Professor Yevgeny Rumin, of Russian origin, defended the thesis that Leonid Brezhnev was a crypto-reformist, who was being kept in check by the generals and the KGB. Rumin had come to the USA at the end of World War II and maintained that he had his contacts in Moscow, and hence his own sources of information; but, as he would hint enigmatically, he couldn't reveal their identity, because they were people in the highest echelons.

Rumin came under attack from Professor Leo Kohn, who used to pride himself on using strictly scientific methods. This celebrated prognosticator was famed for having forecast that around the year 2000 the Soviet Union's economy would outstrip that of the West, so not only would the military threat increase but the Soviet model would become increasingly attractive to young people in the USA and Western Europe. But in Kohn's view, Brezhnev had no role to play in that bright future. Members of the new middle class that the Soviet universities were churning out would soon take his place as the country's leader.

After one of Kohn's slightly acerbic comments about his paper, Rumin declared: "I thought we were here to analyse the status quo. After all, the State Department is looking forward to our recommendations. But if your wish is for this conference to indulge in futurological speculations, crystal ball gazing in other words, which, as everyone knows is not a serious discipline, then we might as well try forecasting who's going to win the next Super Bowl. My money is on the New York Giants."

Kohn didn't take that lying down, of course.

"If we are not allowed to engage in serious assessments of possible future developments, based on the study of trends and facts, then our discipline is pointless," he fulminated. He went on to qualify reliance on anonymous sources as irresponsible, and Rumin's rejection of futurology as "a mental collapse into the realm of triviality". I can still remember that expression well.

He had a deep, gruff voice, whereas Rumin tended to mutter softly, so the contrast between them couldn't have been more perfect.

The two of them nearly came to blows. The atmosphere at the conference was as tense as the US-Soviet relations it was supposed to be discussing.

The conference therefore divided into two camps, with Rumin and Kohn jealously keeping an eye on which camp this or that up-and-coming star in the field would join. In the end I made a pragmatic choice. By then Rumin was an old man and his influence in academic circles was on the wane, while Kohn was at his peak. The fact that I sided with Kohn and that later, at coffee, I praised his approach to the study of Kremlin policies, paid off handsomely for me when I made up my mind to leave Georgetown for another prestigious university.

It was an advantage to me that I regarded that discipline as an intellectual game. It was never any problem to me to think up several alternative theories, and because they were all equally probable there was little point in getting too emotionally worked up over them. From the outset, I thought of conferences chiefly as a useful opportunity to acquire the necessary contacts – and subsequently, women as well. If I needed to make a really important point, I would write a book or an article.

Likewise, any interest I had in the country I originated from remained for many years at the level of abstract speculations. For me, names such as Husák, Biľak, Jakeš or Štrougal were simply pieces on the chessboard upon which I played my academic career. I was more or less indifferent to the fate of people in Czechoslovakia. I'd written that country off. It had been stolen from me. I was definitely disinclined to indulge in lamentation over the tragedy of central Europe as Milan Kundera, for instance, occasionally used to do from his Parisian exile.

Deep down, I was convinced that the Communist regimes couldn't survive, whereas many of the East European intellectuals who ended up in the West thought they were more or less eternal. It had already struck me when I was writing my doctoral thesis that western democracy's totalitarian twin would die of consumption because it wasn't fit for adulthood with its infantile philosophy of achieving the common good by means of revolution. The reason being that almost immediately after the so-called revolution the absolute ends must necessarily come into conflict with reality. A system like that can be kept alive only by means of a brutal regime and every brutal regime eventually becomes exhausted of its own accord. And when it relaxes its repression, particularly if the system isn't bolstered up by genuine faith, the regime has no chance of surviving long.

I don't deny that my successes gratified me in those days. I by no means had my present cynical attitude to everything. My work seemed important to me, even though I realised how shallow it was. But I was no fighter striving for the end of the Soviet empire. There was little I could do to bring about its fall anyway. What mattered to me first and foremost was to play my part faultlessly and without faltering, and to have a good career. And by and large I undoubtedly succeeded.

Nevertheless, I did stumble at one point, and the cause came from an entirely unexpected quarter.

The anti-regime trade union movement Solidarnosc was just coming into existence in Poland and the Communist rulers in the Kremlin were in a quandary over the Polish Pope in the Vatican. At a conference held in a hotel on the very theme of the complicated situation in the Soviet bloc, I discovered at reception that a certain Alexey Brehme was listed among the members of the Soviet delegation.

There could be no doubt as to his identity. I could remember quite well, even after so many years, how this successful half-brother of my mother's – my uncle – had once visited us. Nor had I forgotten that he had been recalled to Moscow because he had arranged for Egon to obtain a visa to Israel, where Egon had remained. The very sight of Alexey's name sent shivers up my spine. It was immediately obvious to me that I could expect unpleasant questions not only from my colleagues, but also possibly from the FBI or CIA, which I had occasionally assisted in the preparation of analytical reports. But in the end Alexey was to play an even more bizarre role in the conference.

On the very first day he came and sat by me at lunch. He reflected quite loudly on the results of the morning's panel, and while casting nervous glances at the neighbouring table, where several of his colleagues from Moscow were seated, he feverishly scribbled something on a napkin. He pushed it toward me without interrupting the flow of his comments for a single moment.

He had written: *Help me. I want to emigrate. Please contact the relevant authorities. They must guarantee my safety. At the next table there are two agents who have me under surveillance.*

A crafty system, I thought to myself. After all, Alexey himself is a KGB agent, unless they threw him out because of the business with Egon. They keep one another under surveillance. Who is *he* supposed to be keeping an eye on? I wondered.

But I grasped the seriousness of the situation and after lunch I went straight to see some people from the CIA. They suppressed their surprise at the fact I had an uncle in the KGB, and one, moreover, who had the same name as me, and they immediately set to work. Alexey was potentially a big catch.

Toward evening they contacted me. They told me that a "small army" of FBI agents had been assembled in the hotel. They instructed me to sit next to my uncle at dinner and let him know by some means that at a given moment he was to make his way to a small lounge beyond the main hotel vestibule, where he would be safe. A few FBI agents posing as waiters would find some ploy to block the path of the KGB agents, if they decided to follow Alexey.

But it turned out to be more complicated, because his Soviet colleagues constantly surrounded Alexey. They must have already suspected him, and perhaps the fact he had talked to me at some length at lunch was motive enough. So I had no choice but to seat myself opposite him and the two KGB agents and during the conversation try to think of a way to pass Alexey his instructions. In the end I opted for a frontal assault.

Were they aware, I asked the two of them, that Alexey was actually my uncle? They looked surprised, although they knew it very well of course. Wasn't it odd that, purely on account of circumstances and lots of chance happenings that we now found ourselves on opposite sides of the barricades, so to speak? My uncle Alexey was fully committed to the ideas of Communism, I continued. I was very disappointed at lunch not to have managed to convince him about our American stance on the question.

The two agents regarded me with suspicion. They weren't sure what my intentions were. Nor, obviously, was Alexey.

There wasn't any real point in engaging Alexey in further conversation, I continued, because there was a yawning gulf between us, even if we do share a lot of genes, thanks to my grandfather, who was Alexey's father. But perhaps I could give him a copy of my paper, nonetheless.

I handed it across the table to Alexey, hoping that his colleagues wouldn't immediately confiscate it in full view of everyone present.

Alexey started to leaf through it, while I engaged the agents in conversation. I'm sure they were in no doubts that there was some message for Alexey hidden in the text of my talk, but for the time being they maintained decorum. I desperately went on thinking up more and more questions and forcing them to set out Moscow's position on the Polish events until Alexey found my instructions.

He acted professionally.

"I'll read it later," he said, and yawned in a fairly bored sort of way. Then he cut into the conversation. "I think Wałęsa is an agent of the USA and so is the Pope, of course," he said to our amazement.

Although his colleagues were most likely of the same opinion, they acted as if he had spoken out of turn. Unabashed, Alexey continued to expound his conspiracy theory. I noticed how the waiter, an FBI agent, who was pouring him some wine, raised an eyebrow in unfeigned surprise.

"It's obvious," Alexey insisted, "that such an enormous and well-organised movement didn't come into existence without preparation. They must have been planning it for at least two or three years. But we're not going to allow the planned dismantling of the socialist system."

Alexey's colleagues were so transfixed by his words that when he suddenly stood up, literally mid-sentence, and announced that he needed to go to the bathroom, they didn't react straight away. They couldn't run after him anyway, even if they'd wanted to, because the waiter suddenly faked a very convincing accident. The tray with glasses of wine in his right hand just happened to collide with the first of the agents to stand up, and the wine spilled all over his suit. Two or three waiters immediately rushed up to wipe the Russian down and block the way until Alexey disappeared out of the restaurant. When the two Soviet agents, now openly engaged in their police duties, finally dashed out of the restaurant, my uncle was already in the hands of the FBI behind the locked doors of the private lounge.

The news of the Soviet agent's defection appeared the very next day in all the main media, and his story would keep the professional Sovietologists busy for a long while afterward. But I was in a quandary. My failure to disclose the existence of my uncle in the KGB was regarded by the CIA and the FBI as an act of disloyalty toward the USA, and was even possibly fishy.

At the same time, the FBI provided me with a bodyguard for a few months, just to be on the safe side. They feared, probably with good cause that the outraged Soviets might have in mind to settle accounts with me, or possibly try to squeeze out of me my uncle's whereabouts. It cramped my style for a while, because with an agent breathing down my neck it wasn't easy to convince some woman that there was anything romantic about a dinner date with me.

I never set eyes on Alexey again, in fact. The FBI had spirited him away to some top-secret location to interrogate him and also to protect him from very likely attempts by the KGB to assassinate him. Some two years later news emerged about his death, but a year afterward I found a postcard in my mailbox with the following text:

Alex Brehme No. 2 no longer exists, but your old uncle is fine. Thanks for the help. The card was sent from Arizona.

I realised that the FBI had changed my uncle's identity and shifted him some place else. No doubt he had been handsomely remunerated for his betrayal of Soviet state secrets and was in no way destitute. The fact he had sent me a postcard struck me as rather risky, but maybe he wanted to assure any unauthorised readers that I no longer played any role in his life and would therefore be incapable of betraying his address even if they tried to squeeze it out of me.

My mother hadn't told me much about Alexey, apart from the fact that my grandfather had fathered him when he was travelling through Russia as a Czech legionary. I know about him chiefly from my grandpa's letter. In the light of that, my attitude to Alexey has changed slightly and I see him as someone with a tragic fate who was kidnapped as a child, so it was easier for the Soviet system to turn him into an agent. And in spite of all that drilling he had retained some humanity. He had a conscience of some kind, when all is said and done.

Whatever Alexey's motives had been, that affair forced me to change my employer, because my colleagues at Georgetown started to treat me with caution. So in 1981, partly with Kohn's assistance, I transferred to Columbia University in New York. A fantastic school and a great place. I'd moved up in the world, in fact.

As I write now about my uncle Alexey, I start to wonder whether Leira isn't an agent too. That encounter with her was so odd, after all... What woman would sleep straight off with an older man the very first night? And how come she'd disappeared without trace? It's true she didn't ask me about anything of any consequence, but perhaps she was searching for something. Am I missing any documents?

No, that's nonsense, I tell myself, immediately dispelling dark thoughts. She took nothing from me. On the contrary, she gave me something. She guided me to my inheritance, and that has changed my life. But how could she have known about all that for God's sake?

Needless to say I have already asked myself the same questions many, many times. Over six months have elapsed since I met Leira and I'm still none the wiser.

If I were to speak about my situation at the end of the 1970s, when my career got under way, I'd describe it as a state of weightlessness. My career had soared sharply, but it was more like the ascent of a helium-filled balloon.

Yes, even then the danger was that the balloon would end up in the stratosphere and burst when the internal pressure grew too great, I was rescued by meeting Katrina.

I know it will be painful, but I can't omit the story. Moreover, I remember precisely everything concerning her. She brought into my life a certain gravity, so that most of my memories of our relationship have remained, which is not true of my other liaisons. She exerted a powerful gravitational pull, and part of me still adheres to her. Why conceal the fact?

I enjoy recalling how we first met. Shortly after the business with Alexey, I was invited to a family party by Jason Taylor, a colleague on the faculty and my future brother-in-law.

I noticed Katrina immediately. She was seated at a table to the right of the door and listening attentively to an elderly lady.

What was it about her that I found so deeply alluring? The sincere interest she showed in what was being said? The seriousness in her features? Her deep gaze? I don't know. It's impossible to provide a rational explanation for the feelings that lead to love, or for love itself. It's possible that I already sensed in her that extraordinary inner firmness that I, who lacked it, was attracted to.

I started to contrive a way to make her acquaintance, but no effort was required, as Jason led me straight to her.

"Katrina," he said. "My sister."

She contemplated me with total calm and also with unfeigned interest.

It was intended to be just a brief, formal conversation, because Jason wanted to introduce me to some other guests, but he didn't get his way. I longed to know something about her. The formalities over, I immediately asked her what her profession was, even though the question might have appeared importunate.

She graciously disregarded this. She replied that she was completing her medical studies and starting to look for a position. Eyes were her specialty and she was hoping to have her own practice one day.

Before I managed to come up with some witty and encouraging

response, Jason was back again. I thought to myself that I would have to find some pretext to return to Katrina as soon as possible. I tried to hide my annoyance when he started to introduce me to his uncle, whom he had fetched from the other side of the room. Uncle Taylor from California, I used to call him later. Jason told me with a wink that his uncle had once been a member of the administration. The wink was to alert me discreetly to his uncle's career in the CIA, as Jason explained later.

Uncle Taylor already knew something about the business with my uncle Alexey, so he took me to one side, and for about ten minutes he quizzed me about my insights and opinions, while nibbling bits of meat from a paper plate. He got only one-word answers out of me because I was afraid Katrina would elude me. Meanwhile we were under scrutiny from an FBI agent. The guests cast uncertain glances in his direction.

Katrina was the only woman I ever loved deeply and over a long period. Already by then, at that party, she attracted me differently than most women. I didn't immediately think about sex, and in fact it didn't even cross my mind even though she was very pretty. I wanted to be with her always and imbibe the aura she emitted and gave me an extraordinary sense of security.

I sensed something immensely firm within her, an unshakable scale of values. This was evident whenever the conversation turned to something of real significance.

I must admit that I found it quite unnerving during those first meetings. I wanted to shatter her certainty. In fact I wanted her to be like me – a total relativist when it came to values. But in time I came to admire her solidity. Every Sunday she would attend her Congregational Church and I respected her for it.

When we started to live together, everyday projects brought us the greatest joy, such as reorganizing our apartment and arranging the different rooms. Before I got to know Katrina, I assumed that bourgeois joys were simply a nuisance to someone like me that they were beneath me. But with her, I derived great pleasure from such things. I wanted to share them with Katrina, because in her world they seemed to be part of an order that aroused my respect. Home and family were of profound significance to her, although I never fully understood that, in spite of my admiration for her at the time.

She brought her friends into my life. Neither Pam and Jack nor Julie and Ted had anything in common with my field of study. Katrina had known them since they were all undergraduates together. For the first time in many years I wasn't mixing with people whom I described as friends chiefly because they could come in useful in the future, but simply because I enjoyed their company. And because it was important to Katrina. We used to get together regularly, almost every week, in fact.

I was happy at that time. Why? Because I enjoyed being with Katrina. The answer may sound banal, but it's the only one I can give. I held her in high esteem. I was interested in everything she did, just as she was in my activities. In those days I had the impression that the things I did were not solely for me.

We both loved trips to the seaside. On Sunday we'd buy *The New York Times*, load the deckchairs into our old car and head out of the city to Jones Beach. We'd find some sheltered spot and spend the whole morning reading that voluminous newspaper. And above all we delighted in being together, not having to say anything because words were superfluous.

On one of our trips, Katrina told me she was pregnant. I can still recall the happiness I felt. Here was I, someone without a family, about to have a real family of my own! I knelt in the sand and kissed Katrina's belly in the place where the seed that would be Rebecca had germinated.

Our shared fondness for long trips to the seaside, particularly in low season when we could take long walks on deserted beaches, led us to decide to take out a mortgage on a summer cottage that we had discovered not far from Islip. During those first years we would drive there almost every weekend. The inlet was right beneath our windows, and when we wanted to go to the ocean shore, we simply had to cross the bridge to Fire Island. Pam, Jack, Julie and Ted were our regular guests. I wrote my first books there.

What made me start to cheat on Katrina? I think the trigger was an event that revived, with unexpected intensity, my insecurity and cowardice.

This is my memory. In early February 1984, I set out with Katrina and Rebecca on one of our regular visits to Taylor's family in Washington. They live at Bethesda on the city outskirts in a spacious house surrounded by a park. He and his wife are doctors at the local hospital, but whenever we are due to visit them, they take time off.

Sometimes Katrina's brother Jason and his sister Jane are visiting with their families at the same time. And occasionally the parents of Katrina's father arrive from Virginia.

I enjoy these reunions. I knew nothing of the kind when I was a child. I had no father, no siblings and my only grandmother lived in London. After my marriage to Katrina I'm suddenly part of an extensive family whose members maintain close contact. The family prides itself on its long tradition that dates back to the Pilgrim Fathers in the 17th century. They are all church members and I had to agree to be married in the local church.

After staying in Bethesda for two days with the Taylors and Jason's family, we set off for West Palm Beach in Florida, where Katrina's parents have a summer residence. We are due to stay there a whole week, but on February 9 that year Yuri Andropov, the Soviet Communist Party General Secretary dies and the TV stations manage to discover where I am spending my vacation.

Everybody understands that it would not be good for my career if I were to be missing from among the commentators responding to this event, so I head back to Washington. I have the Taylors' entire home to myself, but I don't spend much time in it over the next two or three days, because Andropov's death unleashes a wave of media speculation.

On the evening of February 12, I am invited to a TV station, where, as is now the custom in modern media, they promise a serious discussion. In the end, however, as almost always, it descends into a show.

Whenever you are lured to some TV show everyone talks about the need to discuss that particular topical issue in depth, to place it in context. In reality what they want from you are either witticisms and a laid-back approach, because the viewers mustn't be "bored", or you are confronted with someone with an opposite opinion. Apparently viewers enjoy most of all watching politicians or so-called experts arguing on TV. Discussion shows have long ago been transformed into entertainment and nothing more.

It has happened to me on several occasions that presenters, particularly younger ones, were so unnerved by the pressure to make interviews entertaining that they didn't listen to a thing I said. They had their questions written on pieces of paper and some of them, for safety's sake, even had questions in response to my presumed answers. But whenever I diverged at all from their script, the interview was suddenly in danger of collapsing altogether. A couple of times I even rescued presenters by asking myself a question, when they were too nervous to frame it themselves.

That evening, before the start of the show, the director handed the young female presenter a script that focused on Andropov's past as head of the KGB, and she stuck tooth and nail to what she had on the paper.

Instead of the promised discussion about what Andropov's death might mean for the Communist world and relations with the US, she pressed myself and my colleague from George Washington University to depict the situation in the Kremlin as a contest between various groups in the secret services. When I call that approach into question a couple of times she is clearly displeased and in the end she decides to pull a large-caliber weapon on me: I, of all people, she says, should know something about it, seeing that the KGB agent Alexey Brehme is an uncle of mine.

Yes, that it true, I nod, and I try to control myself. But as she may be aware, I first set eyes on my half-uncle at the conference at which he defected (I naturally make no mention of his visits to our apartment in Prague). And two years later, I continue, my uncle died. (And this time I conceal the fact that my uncle is probably alive and well, because he recently sent me a postcard from Arizona.)

"In all events I fail to see," – at this point I raise my voice somewhat – "what a KGB agent who deserted to the Americans some time at the beginning of 1981 and whom I saw only at an official lunch and dinner before he was spirited away by the FBI, could have told me about the present conflicts in the Kremlin, even if he were still alive."

"I'm a political scientist, not an interpreter of alleged conspiracies in third-rate TV shows," I say to conclude my speech. "Should this TV station decide to return to serious journalism, I shall be available, but for now I must take my leave." Then I get up and leave the studio.

Out in the street, I breathe in the cool air. At this moment I'm pleased that I've not let myself be manoeuvred into the usual media game. That's something you don't need, Alex, I say to myself. After all, you now have a sufficient reputation not to allow journalists to treat you as they please. This small, but in my view, victorious skirmish, considerably improves my mood on the way back to Bethesda.

But then it happens. When I reach the Taylors' the phone rings.

"We've been searching for you several hours, Alex," my father-in-law gabbles agitatedly. "There's been a tragedy. This afternoon Rebecca fell in the pool and almost drowned. Katrina didn't wait for the ambulance but drove her to the hospital on her own. She was probably so upset that she lost control of the wheel and had a serious accident. They're both in the hospital – Katrina is in intensive care..."

He poured out the news to me before I had a chance to say anything. At his very first words, particularly the word "tragedy," I start to feel sick, physically sick. An unbearable anxiety grows in me.

Worst of all, it's a feeling that is all too familiar. After many years, I experience once more the same dread and the same weakness that I felt as a child at moments when my mother was having one of her fits and I lived in fear of her being taken off to the madhouse and never coming back. Just as in those days, I now start to shiver uncontrollably.

I spend the journey to Florida in a sort of semi-swoon. I still don't know whether Katrina would survive, I don't know what news I'll hear about Rebecca when I reach the hospital. All I know is that I wouldn't endure Katrina's death. And if Rebecca were to die too, that would be the end. Everything would fall to pieces. Everything.

The rather cowardly thought flashes through my brain that I should have taken greater care. I shouldn't have indulged that happiness. I became too vulnerable when my love for Katrina made me give up an existence in which I couldn't afford to love anyone.

I expect most people don't think this way. They haven't had my experience. They haven't had to live through various disasters and haven't been trained in preventive self-protection. They solve crises as they arise and they either endure or they don't. But I lived on my guard from earliest childhood.

It turns out that Katrina has suffered a few fractures and a fairly serious injury to her spine. Apart from a few grazes and slight concussion Rebecca is all right, fortunately. Even Katrina will make a complete recovery after a few months.

But I continue to suffer a kind of internal injury. I suddenly become wary. I tell myself that I have to build myself a defensive wall so that I needn't have such a fear of total collapse were our marriage to end for some reason.

If I have another woman from time to time I won't be so dependent on Katrina, I delude myself. Perhaps I even believe it's my right – to have both: to have Katrina as an anchor while being a balloon constantly rising. And when it tires it returns to base. I even delude myself that I'd actually be doing a service to Katrina, or rather, to our marriage.

The first time I am unfaithful to her I feel such a sense a guilt that I fail in bed, something that has never happened to me before. It's a sign, but I ignore it. And it's the beginning of the downhill slope. Well, as far as my marriage is concerned, at least. Moreover, Katrina is so trusting that during the first few years, as she later admits, she truly believed all my cock-and-bull stories about unexpected lecturing or consultancy assignments in Washington and elsewhere.

Katrina wasn't just a splendid wife, she was a splendid mother too. Almost everything Rebecca knows, including her skills, she learnt from Katrina. My contribution consisted of occasional story-telling. I managed that OK. I'm good at making up stories.

But maybe I'm too critical of myself. In fact I know I am. Katrina herself took issue with me when, after our divorce, I told her that I considered my greatest failing to have been the fact that I had given so little to Rebecca.

"Come, come Alex, you're being too hard on yourself. You weren't a bad father. I expect you've forgotten, but you'd often take Rebecca on walks to Central Park, and you used to go to movies together. When you were home you'd read her entire books and tell her stories that you made up. You taught her to play chess and tennis. You used to play various pieces of music together. You don't recall it because you're so good at displacing everything."

Those were her very words. It was a very precise diagnosis.

The fact is that I've been running away since I was a kid. I'm in a state of constant fear, like on that flight to Florida when I started to be afraid my world was collapsing, as it had in Prague. Or that I'll carefully build up a relationship with someone, such as with Egon, and it'll suddenly end. It's hard to remember the nice things when there's a yawning gulf at the end.

A psychologist would tell me I lacked paternal authority. I'm afraid to confront life head on and assume responsibility. All I wanted from women was to be spoilt. Like a little boy. And at the same time I was callous toward them because I wanted to take revenge on them for my mother.

In the end I didn't escape loneliness anyway. I was always alone. And now I'm totally alone.

Maybe I ought to find some important conference to attend. Maybe Leira would seek me out there. Or at least I'd regain my appetite for picking the most attractive woman. The more famous I became, the easier it was to seduce them.

I used to meet some of my female colleagues repeatedly, and in fact I'd sometimes choose conferences at the last minute according to whether one of my favourites was attending. Before I bumped into Leira at Bellagio, it was Jovana Miller. I first met her about eleven years ago at one of the symposiums about the fall of Communism.

She had just completed her doctorate and had taken a post in the international relations department of some college in the back and beyond of Pennsylvania. She wanted to get out of that place at all costs, and I modestly offered her my assistance. She had beautiful wavy hair, a nice figure, and expressive, rather carnal features.

When she had finished presenting her far from uninteresting paper on the probable break-up of federations created under Communism, I had a good excuse to pay her a compliment and invite her to a coffee. During her speech I had already observed with enjoyment her long, slim legs beneath the desk. At one point, when she had nervously crossed her legs, the hem of her skirt had ridden up a bit, so that when she uncrossed them, her skirt remained halfway up her thigh or thereabouts. It set me fantasizing, and it was only because I found her contribution thought provoking that I did not allow my imagination free reign.

She was patently delighted that Alex Brehme had invited her for a coffee, which was a good start. She confided to me that she was writing a book on the topic she had just been speaking about. I was fulsome in my admiration.

"Structural Problems in Communist Federations" was a theme that nobody had paid much attention to so far, I told her, but there were already indications that all the former Communist federations would collapse. Even Czechoslovakia, where I was born.

Jovana was either masterful in feigning surprise, or she was genuinely unaware of it. But it definitely drew us together, because she disclosed that she was from Yugoslavia, or more precisely, from Serbia. She had left for America with her parents when she was fifteen, so she scarcely had an accent. Miller was her husband's name. She was formerly Jovanovič, and but for the fact it was hard for Americans to pronounce, she would have reverted to her old name now that she was single again...

Things were working out excellently. I was sure she had spoken about her status so I'd note she was divorced. She was well aware that I hadn't invited her solely on account of her lecture. I remained impassive but immediately went on the attack. Should she need someone to write a foreword to her book, I'd be quite interested. I'd given quite a lot of thought to the topic.

I was right on target. Jovana's eyes lit up.

That would be absolutely fantastic, she assured me. With a foreword by Alex Brehme, she could try getting it published by some prestigious publishing house. Would I really do that for her?

I nodded. Of course I would, otherwise I wouldn't have offered. But we ought to discuss the whole thing properly. Naturally I'd read the entire manuscript of the book later, but she ought to give me a few more details about how she had conducted her research, for instance... We immediately made a dinner date. After dinner we continued our discussion of the manuscript in the hotel bar, and finally in my room.

Unlike my other short-term relationships, the one with Jovana lasted several years. We'd meet regularly, usually in Washington, which was near for her in Pennsylvania and me in New York. Her book was a success, which meant, of course, that she got a better job – in San Francisco, unfortunately. We endeavoured to keep seeing each other even afterward, but it was rather impractical. So we'd meet up only at conferences.

Actually our relationship was unusually firm. Jovana married again meantime, then divorced and married a third time. But as soon as we met at a conference she would seem to forget she had another life. I didn't know much about her husbands, and I didn't talk to her about Katrina anyway. But our physical relationship wasn't the only thing that linked us. After all, sex loses its appeal even between lovers who knew each other as long as we did. The fact is that I enjoyed talking to Jovana. Indeed she was the only one I discussed my projects with, and I found her interesting enough to listen to her plans.

Jovana was not my only lover over these past eleven years, but she was definitely the most interesting of them. Although she knew there were others, she didn't hold it against me. And I, for a change, suspected that she occasionally had flings with other men at conferences I didn't attend. I didn't mind. I didn't want to own her.

Now it's all over. After meeting Leira, I'm not interested in other women. And that's not all. For the first time in my life I truly reproach myself for all the women I've used and abused. After all, many of them slept with me only because I offered them the sort of help I gave to

Jovana that time.

OK, I could tell myself that it was their affair, when all is said and done. Why agonise over this form of prostitution on the part of budding lady professors and authors? I didn't force them to do anything. And yet I do agonise over it.

I have a persistent feeling that I have squandered something fundamental.

I can remember my mother telling me I was gifted. I'm sure she thought I'd be famous one day. She was right, but my fame is oddly empty, somehow. Is all fame empty? And are most men only motivated to acquire fame by the desire to attract interesting women and seduce them more easily?

A photo of my mother hangs above my desk. She is holding me in her arms and smiling. She has a happy expression that I very seldom saw her wear. She was outstandingly beautiful.

Now I know her story, it breaks my heart to look at her. I'm full of emotions. I can see her in my mind's eye standing as a seven-year-old outside a house from which a shot is heard. I can see her in that potato cellar. I can see her in the automobile in which her Nazi uncle is abducting her to Germany through a nighttime landscape.

I also have here a photo of the house in Safed where Egon lived. It was too late when I went to see him. All I found was his grave in the local cemetery with a sign in Hebrew on the headstone.

I wanted to thank Egon. For taking the place of my father, who was killed by the Communists, for playing duets with me and for having had patience with my crazy mother. I wanted to apologise to him for holding against him for years the fact that he emigrated. I now know he had the right to. I can't reproach him for wanting to die outside Europe, where they murdered almost all his kin.

And I have a photograph of my father too. Ester gave it to me. In it, he's standing somewhere in London dressed in his army uniform, and he is smiling. I can't recall whose face his reminds me of. It's definitely someone I know intimately. I'm not thinking of myself or Ester. There's a reflection of someone else in that face -someone who fills me with a strange unease.

Now I'm speaking of photographs, I should not to ignore an event that shook me up not so long ago. Maybe it was the reason why I started writing this diary.

One day, for the umpteenth time, I was sifting through those things of my mother's that I'd brought from Prague and I came across a letter that I'd not yet read. It had been tucked into a bundle of correspondence.

I carefully withdrew it from the unsealed envelope. The letter had been sent in 1963 and addressed to Hana Brehme. My attention was drawn to the rubber stamp of the institution in which my mother had spent her last few years. Alongside the stamp someone had written the laconic instruction: "Not to be given to patient. Risk of adverse reaction."

The letter was in German. I started to laboriously decipher the text. After the first few lines I realised it was a letter from Gerta, the Gerta whose house she had lived in during the war.

She informed my mother that her brother Arno had died. Since his visit to Prague, Gerta wrote, Arno had behaved strangely. Very strangely, in fact. He had kept repeating that he had received a further blow. That his sister had gone mad. He had started to be seized by an odd obsession: that if he managed to clarify the fate of his grandparents, the Kleins, perhaps something would change for the better.

Although he had been trying to trace them for several years, it was just after his visit to Prague and perhaps thanks to his work for the German government, that he eventually gained access to the documents that proved that Albert and Helena Klein had not been sent to Terezín or to a concentration camp, but had been shot at the execution ground in Prague on the direct orders of Karl Brehme, the very same day they had taken leave of him and Hana.

As Hana had already heard from her brother, Gerta wrote, Karl Brehme had become a successful businessman after the war. His advertising agency had grown so big that he had transferred its headquarters to New York. "None of us understands how he managed to convince the Americans to let him, a former Gestapo officer, into the country,"

Gerta wrote. "Maybe he sold himself to them."

What was certain was that after making his discovery, Arno seemed to lose his wits. He had set off for New York in search of Karl. He had been terribly upset before he left, incensed that Karl had deceived him and Hana. After all, Karl had always claimed that he knew nothing about the fate of their grandparents. He, the self-styled humanitarian, had even hinted that he had intervened so that they should be sent to Terezín.1

In reality he had been a foul murderer, a criminal.

Arno's meeting with Karl had led to a fight. Nobody knew precisely what had happened. All that had emerged from later enquiries was that Arno strangled Karl.

He had not even mentioned the actual fight in the letter he wrote to Gerta immediately after he had been placed in detention by the US authorities. He had mostly described his conversation with Karl. Karl had apparently admitted that the Kleins indeed had been executed on his direct orders. He had maintained that he had had no alternative: it had been the price he had to pay to save Arno and Hana, because otherwise his colleagues in the Gestapo would have started to ask questions.

That had enraged Arno even more.

What happened next? Gerta didn't know for sure. Arno had confided to her his terrible fear of prison, the dread aroused in him by the sound of policemen's boots. He was being held in a windowless cell. He had a horror of confined spaces, as Gerta knew very well. He was constantly gasping for breath because he felt there wasn't enough air in the cell.

His German family, the Finks, had received an official letter a few days later; informing them that Arno had committed suicide.

When I finished reading the letter, I sat transfixed. Then came regret. I wasn't sorry for Arno – I'd scarcely known him. I felt sorry for my mother who had spent the last years of her life thinking that Arno had forgotten about her.

But it was something else that had transfixed me. I had realised that but for Leira I would never have discovered how Arno met his death. She was the one who had told me I'd find the key to my mother's past in Prague – and hence to my own past as well. Otherwise the box would have never found its way to me and I wouldn't have found that letter at the bottom of it.

I immediately made my way to the public library and searched out every newspaper from December 1963. It wasn't hard to find news items about Karl's murder and Arno's subsequent suicide. But apart from the information that a German citizen Ernest Fink had murdered another German citizen, Karl Brehme, for reasons unknown, I discovered nothing new. I had learnt more from Gerta's letter than the reporters had been able to ascertain.

But then came the shock. In one newspaper there was a photograph of the house in which Karl Brehme had been murdered. At first I couldn't work out where I'd seen it before. It was only when I got home and was putting Gerta's letter back in the box that my gaze fell on that photograph that my mother had once torn out of a book, as she mentions in her memoirs. It was the house that Daniel had taken her to in her dream.

Sunday, September 9, 2001

After the Communist regime fell in Czechoslovakia I set off for Prague in the spring of 1990. I don't know why I was suddenly convinced that I'd find my real home there.

But the moment I landed in Prague I was in for a shock. I went from the plane into a grey airport building where I waited for ages to go through passport control. The officials and the police were unpleasant, not to mention the airport personnel. The regime might have fallen but it still lived on in the heads of the natives.

Prague, which I had unwittingly idealised in my memory, seemed like an embalmed corpse compared with 1968, when I had left it. Then, it had been colourful and bursting with energy. Now, it had cracked facades, stench and smog, Communist-style shops, and sullen, bad-tempered people everywhere. Whenever I wanted to eat in a restaurant I had to pretend I spoke only English. Czechs weren't welcome in some of the eating places in the city centre.

I soon realised that the home I'd dreamed about had long since ceased to exist. Something dreadful had happened to this city and the people living in it. It seemed to me like the moment in the story of Sleeping Beauty when she wakes up after her long sleep. She opens her eyes and sees a handsome prince promising freedom and love, but everything around her is overgrown with brambles and the beautiful castle she once lived in is a crumbling ruin...

When I met my former student colleagues, I realised we didn't speak the same language any more. Most of them regarded the western world with a mixture of admiration, envy and incomprehension, while they had a very high opinion of themselves. It was as if the only way to survive during the Communist era was to succumb to the illusion that some kind of uniqueness remained preserved beneath the shell of the regime.

At that time, I was sufficiently cynical not be put off by all that. I didn't attempt to force my views on people. During my trips to Prague I concentrated on exploiting the only valuable resource that my former homeland had to offer, which was women. Unlike their American counterparts, most of them didn't have too many hang-ups about moral dilemmas, particularly when it came to a well-heeled lover from the West.

Most of my amours during that period have gone from my memory, even the names. In fact I was cheating on the women with whom I was cheating on my own wife. They only interested me as a means to sexual gratification, as an adventure. Naturally I told them I was interested in their minds.

There was only one it didn't apply to. During my very first trip to Prague, I became attached, for a while, to Andrea.

I remember her name precisely, of course, and also the beginning of our affair, because we met under very unusual circumstances.

I had scarcely booked into my hotel when I set off for the cemetery to lay a wreath on my mother's grave at last, after my twenty-two years' absence. When eventually I located it with some difficulty I stood a long while by the unkempt grave trying to recall the few happy moments I'd enjoyed with Mum during my childhood. Then I noticed a woman, about thirty years old, standing by the next grave. Clearly she took regular care of it. When I turned in her direction I discovered she was staring straight at me.

Had I come from abroad? Was I an émigré?

I nodded and told her I left in 1968, straight after my mother's death. I didn't have anyone else. And my mother didn't have anyone else apart from me, which was why the grave was so neglected.

Perhaps she'd lend me her trowel and fork.

She came over to me. She had an interesting face, narrow shoulders. Straight black hair. As she hands me the tools, I notice her long, aristocratic fingers.

When I start to rake the sand around the grave, she stops me.

"We ought to pull out all those weeds first," she says.

Strange. Without saying anything more, the unknown woman with the sad expression starts to help me tidy the neglected grave.

"My parents died at the beginning of the seventies," she then says. "My father was a theatre director, my mother a literary manager. In 1971 they were sacked by the theatre. Mum fell ill as a result. Don't they say that stress can cause cancer? After she died, my father just wasted away and he died too, a few years later. I was only fifteen."

Then she smiles.

"There was no way to flee the country at that time, otherwise I would have tried. It wasn't so difficult in 1968, was it?"

I agree with her, but at that moment I don't feel like talking about myself. I want to know how it has been for her. What happened to her after her parents had died?

"I lived at my aunt's," she replies, while continuing to pull up weeds. She's a musician – a pianist. Paradoxically, her parents' death meant that she was now able to apply for the conservatory. If they had lived she would probably have had great difficulties for political reasons.

All of a sudden another history is unfolding in front of me. A different picture – much more enticing than the shabby city.

"I'm also a bit of a musician," I say, "but only for my own enjoyment. I used to be quite good, but unfortunately I didn't apply myself. In America I became a political expert."

"Are you Alex Brehme, by any chance?" she asks. "They said on the radio that Alex Brehme, who is a regular guest on Voice of America, was visiting Prague. He's supposed to be meeting the President tomorrow."

I nod. It hadn't occurred to me that my visit would be mentioned on the news.

The job is almost finished. I take the tools and smooth the soil, where the weeding had disturbed it. It is early spring, and the ground is still slightly frozen. As I stand up I notice the bare branches of the trees. All around me, for as far as the eye can see, there are just tombstones.

Then I say, "My mother committed suicide, in a mental hospital. She was an unhappy woman. I don't know much about her, unfortunately. My father was murdered by the Communists in a concentration camp. He'd escaped from Czechoslovakia after the Nazis invaded and fought in the British Army."

She looks at me with sympathy.

Would she like to go for a coffee?

I recall precisely blurting this out spontaneously, because I've no intention of seducing her. There is something weighty about her, a sort of candidness, something fateful. Something I might all too easily injure, or fall for. I'm always very careful not to have anything to do with a woman I might fall in love with. That is my concept of fidelity toward Katrina.

"I can't at this moment. But if you have the time I'm playing a recital in a church early tomorrow evening. You could come and meet me there."

And so after my meeting with the President, I wander through Prague until I reach Dušní Street. Before I enter the church I can hear that the concert has already started.

Andrea and a somewhat older violinist are playing Dvořák's

Romance for Violin and Piano in F minor. I'm very familiar with the piece, as I used to play it with Egon. I'm suddenly overcome by a strange nostalgia.

Andrea is excellent, in fact, she is brilliant. She's wearing a black dress. It's the first time I've seen her legs. Only at that moment does it occur to me that I might make a play for her. But at the same time I resist it. I sense that behind that beautiful and refined exterior there lurks some kind of danger.

I also remember very well our dinners together. During those fourteen days I spent in Prague, we dined together at least five times. And nothing happened the whole time.

On almost every occasion we chatted late into the night. There was something in her that overcame the inhibitions that prevented me talking about myself. Or rather I was capable of talking about myself without feeling the need to dazzle her with tales of my successes (related with excessive humility, of course) or with my intellect.

When I first spoke to Andrea about my childhood, the first time I had returned to that subject in many years, memories long repressed came back to mind. I was unusually frank with her in respect of my private life. I didn't conceal my marriage to Katrina, as I would generally do, nor did I claim that my marriage was at breaking point. And for the first time in the presence of an attractive woman I also said that I loved Katrina. And that I had been unfaithful to her several times, for which I reproached myself.

I now think that my frankness was a kind of self-defence, because the better I got to know her, the more she attracted me. It was obvious to me that if I were to start anything with her it would place my marriage at risk. I knew that I might really fall in love.

Andrea repaid my frankness in kind.

She had been married for several years but it hadn't worked out. She used to play concerts outside Prague as well, which gave her and her husband plenty of opportunities to strike up other relationships. She didn't go into detail. I didn't feel like asking her how many of those opportunities she had made use of.

"I didn't marry again," she added. "I don't manage to meet Mr. Right somehow. Or if I meet him, he's married."

She was looking me straight in the eye and I had an almost unbearable desire to take her by the hand. But I didn't. In fact, I got a fright when I realised that that single touch would mean far more to me than entire nights spent with other women.

This was a completely new discovery for me. I saw that I was vulnerable, I, for whom mistresses had been the proof of my stature.

The day before my flight home, Andrea suggested we play something together. After all, I'd spoken so many times about how I play the violin in my spare time and I described to her how Egon and I used to play together. She could invite me home, she said. She had a piano and even an old violin.

So I found myself in the apartment in Dejvice that she had inherited from her parents. The furnishings were old and there were books everywhere. Heaps of sheet music lay on the piano and around it.

We started with Dvořák, the same piece I'd heard her first play at that concert. Then we tried some Janáček and Mozart.

There was a natural teamwork between us. She drew me to her when we were playing. She was playful and sometimes mildly flirtatious. I knew that if I were to embrace her and make love to her now, I'd be happy. Our relationship would be like that music.

I said goodbye to her before midnight. I promised to look her up the next time I came to Prague. "We have lots to tell each other and lots that we can play together," I joked.

But I was not in a joking mood when I left. It was as if my suppressed desire had spread a heavy blanket over me. I couldn't stop thinking of her even in the plane.

That remarkable depth in her was a link with something I'd already forgotten – what I could have been if I hadn't turned into Alex Brehme.

That was when I first realised that I had gone astray. There existed another, more authentic life than the one I had led. And if an authentic life is possible, then it indicates another possible reality. Or at least belief in such a reality. It was depth like that had once attracted me to Katrina, whom I'd betrayed...

Originally I wasn't planning to return to Prague until the fall, but couldn't get Andrea out of my mind. I'd grown weary of brief affairs. I took advantage of a conference in Paris that took place a few weeks after my first trip to Prague. I managed to cancel my meetings at the French Foreign Ministry and to pull out of the conference. It wasn't difficult. My paper was scheduled for the first day.

I called Andrea from Paris.

"I happen to have a few free days," I lied. "Would you have time to go out to dinner, or to play something with me? I really enjoy recalling it."

"We could do both," Andrea suggested. "I'll cook something, you'll bring some nice wine from Paris, and we can play after dinner."

I was so impatient to get to Prague, I felt like a little child. And yet I hoped that I'd manage to maintain the same detachment as during my last visit, and in the plane I even thought of how best to extricate myself should the situation become too intimate.

But things didn't turn out that way.

When Andrea opened the door and I handed her a bouquet of flowers and a bottle of wine, she offered her cheek for a greeting peck. I don't know how it happened, but I kissed her on the lips instead of the cheek. That brief touch was unbelievably intense. I was aware not just of her lips, but also of her scent and the warmth that radiated from her.

I have no clear recollection of what happened next. Maybe I was used to being in control of things, including foreplay.

Now here I was suddenly kissing Andrea while she impatiently helped me out of my coat. We didn't say a word until it was all over.

Only then did I start to explain to her how much I had longed for her. I apologised for my weakness in fact. Although I was intoxicated with love, I already knew at that moment that I was hurtling headlong toward something. Usually after making love to another I would immediately send a mental apology to Katrina and I'd actually look forward to being back with her. Now I was dismayed that I would have to leave Andrea.

She sort of apologised to me too.

She told me not to be angry with her. On principle she didn't make a play for happily married men, but she hadn't been able to stop thinking of me. She had had no inkling it would end like this when she invited me.

I stroked her hair. She turned toward me and there were tears in her eyes.

Yes, we were hurtling together somewhere although we both knew it couldn't end happily.

It was obvious we would have to discuss things in the morning and it wasn't going to be pleasant. But for the time being we were together. And we were completely overcome with desire.

The next day, caution got the better of me, exactly as I'd anticipated. I knew for certain that if I didn't end the affair, I could no longer go on living with Katrina and Rebecca. And Andrea definitely could not be merely a mistress to spend a night with on my occasional trips to Prague, even though she said she respected my marriage. But there could be no doubt that our relationship would not survive in the long term alongside any other.

I stayed one more day with Andrea. Although I spoke about having to think it all over and about how hard it was for me to be without her, I already knew what my priority was.

Maybe I was deluding myself that Katrina and Rebecca were my main consideration. In fact there was far more at stake. If I'd given Andrea precedence, I would be torn away from the order of things to which I was accustomed. I'd have to change everything. And that could have unforeseeable consequences.

Sitting here in this bare apartment I tell myself that I made a mistake. I ought to have had the courage. At that time I was offered a rare opportunity to rid myself of Alex Brehme, and find a path inward from outside. A path to myself.

I met Andrea on only two further occasions. Both times we went for coffee and a friendly chat, but we both felt that there was now some kind of wall between us. Nothing was said about our two nights together. Not a word.

Then, a few months ago, a letter arrived for me at the university.

Prague, June 20, 2001

Dear Alex,

Like me, I'm sure you've not forgotten our two nights together in Prague. For a long time I was desperately in love with you.

I know you try to tell yourself that you don't deserve love. I've grasped a few of the things that you told me. You're famous but in your mind you despise yourself. But I believe that deep down there is hidden that little Sasha who trembled in dread that his mother might end up in the madhouse again. You're terribly afraid of that Sasha. You're terrified that if you lost the shell that now protects you, that fear might return once more.

I fell in love with you on account of what remained of Sasha when we were playing together and when you were telling me about your childhood. I wasn't attracted by what you've become but what you once were and could still be. You decided to return to what you became and the whole time my wish has been that you would be happy. I hope you are.

But that's not the reason for this letter. I'm ill and I don't have much time left. For that reason you ought to know that you have a son in Prague. He'll soon be eleven. His name is Sasha.

I expect you remember that my parents died a long time ago and even the aunt I lived with after their death has passed away. So Sasha has only you now. Should you happen to be in Prague I'd like to introduce you to him while I'm still able to.

Forgive me for not telling you about him before. You went away and you had your own life and I didn't want to interfere in it. Perhaps I now can. I read on the internet that you divorced some time ago.

Your Andrea

There was a photo with the letter. On it Andrea has her arm round the shoulders of a little boy. He's wearing a striped sailor's T-shirt, short pants and sneakers. He looks like a sporty child. Brown or dark eyes and wavy black hair. His expression reminds me of someone. I try to recall what my father looked like from the photos I have of him, but then I realise that this is my mother looking at me. It's her face. The kid will turn out to be as good-looking as she was, it occurs to me. And at that moment I start to feel anxious in case he inherits her illness as well. On the photo he looks carefree and easygoing. There isn't the slightest hint of that intense unease that radiated from my mother, even in photographs of her.

The letter left me disconcerted. I thought to myself that this was a further reminder of my cynicism.

Then it flashed through my mind that it might be a proffered hand. What if fate is offering me a last chance to face up to life responsibly? I can hardly allow Sasha to end up like me. To be left alone and in the care of some distant relatives, or even end up in an institution. No one deserves the sort of empty life like that led by the famous Alex Brehme. No one should spend his entire life running from himself.

It didn't take me long to decide on my course of action. I dialled the number of my travel agency and asked them to book me a flight to Prague for the very next day.

At the airport I bought a few toys for Sasha and pondered a long time over what to take the dying Andrea. In the end I bought an interesting-looking book about Stravinsky, comforting myself with the thought that she might still have the time and energy to read it.

I prepare myself for the worst as I wait those few seconds for Andrea to open the door of her apartment. My memory of her is that of a beautiful woman, and now I'm apprehensive about what a grave illness might have wrought with her. But Andrea has scarcely changed, surprisingly. She looks like she did on the photograph she sent me.

In shock I say to myself: death could already be close by. It's within range and those around us needn't even notice.

Sasha is still at school when I arrive. The previous evening I'd agreed with Andrea that I'd come in the morning to give the two of us a chance to talk.

At first our conversation is stilted. Andrea tells me how the doctors figured out she had the illness and the various things they had tried, almost as if it had nothing to do with her.

"There's nothing to hope for any more," she then said. "That's also why I decided to write to you."

I have a strong urge to tell her everything about myself. How I'd deceived myself and everyone round me. But she knows anyway. After all, she summed me up quite accurately in that letter.

I start by saying that the news of my son's existence has filled me with resolve to do something meaningful at last. I also confide to her how an event in February knocked me sideways so that my doubts about myself have been growing ever since. I don't mention Leira, but simply tell her how I found the box with my mother's effects and how I'd found in it her memoirs and my grandfather's letter.

Andrea is very keen for me to tell her briefly the contents of those two documents. I don't know whether I'd agree to do so in other circumstances, but it occurs to me that we're a family now.

"You know all sorts of things about my mother," I say. "I told you quite a bit about her, although at that time I myself didn't know a great deal."

And then I tell her what I learned from my mother's account: how she lost her parents, how she hid in the potato cellar, how an angel appeared who looked like my father, how she became a German and then a Czech once more. And how they shot my father somewhere near Jáchymov while he was trying to escape.

I also share my grandfather's story with her: his journey to Siberia and back to Prague, how an angel appeared to him too and prophesied that he would find happiness with my grandmother. And how that happiness came to an end when she died giving birth to twins.

At the end of my narrative Andrea sighs and tells me she too inventoried her past recently. She gets up and goes to a cupboard of dark wood, from which she takes a sheaf of photos.

She slowly sits down again and says that among them there is a picture of me. She can't recall now whether she took my photo during one of our encounters eleven years ago or whether I gave it to her. But the odd thing is, she adds, that when Sasha discovered the photo some time ago, he told her of a strange dream that had recently perturbed him. He had dreamt that some man had come and talked with him. And when he saw the photo of me he said it was the man from his dream.

Andrea falls silent for a moment before continuing, "Because I don't believe in the supernatural, I told myself he had invented the dream. It's possible isn't it?"

I have to suppress an urge to laugh. So Sasha is another member of our family to have seen an angel. How come the angel has the gall to borrow my likeness?

I'm unwilling to accept that possibility. I'm looking for a more rational explanation.

"Perhaps Sasha rummaged in those photos earlier. You know what kids are like. Maybe my image got stuck in his memory."

"Maybe," Andrea shrugs her shoulders. "After all, you're his father. Perhaps an image of the father's appearance is written into the genetic code somehow, who knows? I'm not sure of anything anymore. But that's not all, there's something else, and it's something that really defies explanation.

"Sasha said the man told him I ought to have a medical examination. I went the very next day. That's how I discovered I have cancer.

"I don't want to think of all the implications. I'm just unable to at this moment. Yes, they all could be coincidences, but they needn't be either. How should I know?"

It occurs to me that there could be a rational explanation. Maybe Sasha had noticed that Andrea was having problems with her health, or that she'd changed. And having invented that dream, he used it as a means to make her go to the doctor.

Andrea and I say nothing more about it. We change the subject. Sasha is due to come at 2 p.m.

He looks exactly the way he did on the photo Andrea sent me, but maybe a little more vulnerable.

He knows from Andrea who I am. She told him before I arrived. Our first meeting is different from the way I imagined it, however. No hugs, no tears.

Sasha contemplates me with calm interest and gives one-word answers to my questions. It lasts like that for about an hour. I try to lighten the conversation with the occasional joke. It doesn't help much.

Eventually Andrea gives him permission to visit a friend. We sit facing each other in silence. Andrea eases the tension.

"Perhaps he's a bit scared of you, Alex," she suggests. "I expect he can still see that dream. When I told him who you are, he burst into tears. And there was something in that dream that terrified him. It's bound to be connected with you."

I spent a few days in Prague and every day I met with Sasha. I told him about my life. How I'd once fallen in love with his mother although I was married in America. Such things can happen, I try to explain to him.

I took him to see my apartment and I invited him to dinner with Andrea. All three of us went to the cinema twice. And when I discovered he liked travel books, I bought him a pile of them

Maybe we became a bit closer

"Next time I'll take you to New York," I promised him, but instead of showing enthusiasm he just nodded sheepishly.

But when we were saying goodbye, he suddenly hugged me and he had tears in his eyes.

"Take care, Dad," he said. "Don't go back there."

Dad, he said. For the first time.

I was so shaken that I failed to catch what he'd said.

"Don't go back there."

And then he asked, "Will you come before Mum..."

He didn't finish the sentence, but it was obvious what he was asking. My knees almost buckled under me. I looked at Andrea with a question in my eyes.

And she conveyed to me with an alarmed expression in her face that she hadn't talked to him about it.

I didn't fly directly to New York. The next leg of my trip was Hong Kong. It was my last conference. I'd cancelled all the rest.

That evening I meet up with Murphy in the hotel bar. He's now teaching at Harvard, as he never fails to point out. He is just finishing his fourth beer and for the next hour or so he expounds to me non-stop the content of some article he has just sent to *Foreign Policy*. It's about Russia, or rather about the Russians' traditional sticky-fingered attitude to countries that once belonged to their sphere of influence.

He spouts for my benefit names of Russian politicians and arranges them into various power groupings. The one that fascinates him most is the Kremlin coalition around Putin. He informs me with the air of one of the initiated how these various cliques in Russian politics are regarded by some of the people in the Bush administration. They are novices. Bush moved into the White House only a few months before, so Murphy has plenty of scope for speculation and "reliable" information from the circle of people close to the President.

I find it hard to listen to him. I've already endured hundreds of similar conversations, and besides, I have a heartfelt aversion to all of these neo-conservatives of Bush's – many of them former Trotskyites – and even more so to the Russian political elite. When Murphy tries to convince me that Putin would democratise Russia by authoritarian means, I find it hard to keep a straight face.

However, I contain myself and say on the spur of the moment:

"I was twenty when the Russians invaded Czechoslovakia and I still remember it quite well. And even though Communism has gone from Russia, whenever I see a Russian politician, I get the feeling from his gestures and manner of speaking that nothing has changed there."

Murphy lectures me that such pseudo-psychological attitudes to Russia are fit only for bar-room chit-chat. Whereas he had been sharing with me the results of his extensive and informed analysis!

I don't even let him finish speaking.

"I don't need to analyse anything," I tell him defiantly. "Whenever I see Putin on the TV he makes me want to throw up. It's obvious to me that there'll be no democracy in Russia."

I add that I'm tired after my flight and go off to bed.

In my hotel room I feel queasy at the thought that I have to attend the conference the next day. I'd sooner stay away. For one thing the speakers there will be people I meet over and over again, and for another, I'll be obliged to listen to lots of abstract bullshit, given the subject of the conference: Global Governance.

Everyone is talking about global governance these days. But it's no more than political science fiction, because the fact is that global governance doesn't exist. The United Nations is proof enough.

Freeloading bureaucrats run all the big international organisations, the member states are incapable of agreeing on anything sensible, and the world is heading for disaster. We plunder natural resources, destroy the environment, sit on entire mountains of weapons of mass destruction that are available not only to Bush and his neo-con camarilla, or to the former KGB agent President in the Kremlin but even some to a totally unpredictable general somewhere in Pakistan.

I fall asleep in a very bad mood. I can't help thinking about Andrea and Sasha. And on top of that I keep on waking up in the night because of jet lag. And in my state of semi-slumber, more and more doubts about the sense of everything start to spawn in my brain.

My paper is supposed to deal with the role of global civil society. Sometimes it's referred to as global networks.

What I am preparing to say is essentially positive. My main argument is that the globalization of financial markets and economies is being matched by a globalization of civil society, and this helps bridge the deficit still resulting from the slow pace of globalization of political institutions.

A superficial assessment might conclude that the widening gap between escalating economic and technological globalization on the one hand and sluggish globalization of politics on the other could potentially engender enormous problems, but in politics one must not take into account solely official organizations such as governments or transnational intergovernmental organizations but also the rapidly expanding network of non-governmental organizations and other forms of transnational civil society.

I was intending to use that idea as a springboard for reflections on potential new forms of global governance, but all of sudden I have no further desire to continue drivelling on like this. I fall silent and then declare to the surprise of my listeners that I was planning to talk about new forms of global governance represented by transnational networks, but as I now reflect on it, I am by no means sure of anything.

"To tell you the truth," I continue, "I'm beginning to favour the view recently voiced by a lady acquaintance in the course of an informal conversation. She saw the world as a computer program in which a fault has developed. The programmer has fallen asleep or something, and we are rapidly heading toward a new global calamity.

"Since the fall of Communism an odd kind of optimism has prevailed. One of my respected colleagues is even talking about the end of history in the form of the final victory of liberal democracy. I can't help feeling, however," I say, sharing my anxiety with the audience, "that this idyll is about to end. While we sit here telling political science fairy stories, someone out there is hatching a new catastrophe. After all, mankind has evolved from catastrophe to catastrophe. There is a lot of talk about progress, and how, thanks to this so-called progress, life gets better and better, but alongside those things that improve our lives, or seem to, we are also developing the capacity to wipe one another out."

That all seem to have spilled out of me almost unintentionally. I gaze at my listeners, some of whom are actually writing down what I am telling them!

For heaven's sake, I think to myself, surely they can't think this is some academic reflection, can they? Or maybe it's because it came from the lips of Alex Brehme. In this muddle-headed world, a celebrity can spout any old nonsense simply because he's a celebrity. And yet I am telling them something fairly fundamental. There is an accumulation of angst inside me and it had to come out. No doubt Murphy would have babbled something about a pseudo-psychological approach, but there's no way I'll abide by what that clown calls analytical reflection.

I don't feel like uttering nonsense that others take seriously simply because I'm the one uttering it, and using the jargon, moreover, of these would-be intellectual gatherings. I can't continue with it. It's not possible.

"My mother," I say, "spent over a year in a cellar during World War II in order to avoid being taken in one of the 'transports'. What were these 'transports'? They were the highly organised first phase of mass murder. They were devised by a nation considered by many to be the most civilised nation in Europe – the nation of Goethe, Beethoven, Schiller and Hegel. Who at the end of the 19th century could have conceived that such a thing would be possible? And yet World War I arrived and the only lesson that mankind learned from it was that methods of mass murder could be refined even more. So World War II followed. Everything has being 'mass-based' since then, for that matter. We now have mass culture, mass consumption, and mass taste. It's said that we have drawn lessons from mass murder organised using the methods of industrial civilization, or at least we are sufficiently afraid of weapons of mass destruction. Except that after World War I it also seemed that mankind had reason enough to fear another war.

"My mother, who survived the Holocaust before the glorious onset of Communism, went mad on account of it all. She committed suicide in a mental hospital. It strikes me that her existence and its conclusion are very much in tune with what the Germans call the *Zeitgeist*, 'the spirit of the times'. The only normal place that remained for someone like my mother was the madhouse.

"Talking of *Zeitgeist*, what is the spirit of the present times? Total emptiness! The Western world has lost its way and turned God into a mere hypothesis. Moreover, it has developed technologies whose destructive potential is a definite temptation to those beyond the bounds of our civilization who have a fanatical belief in God – their God...

"We comfort ourselves with the thought that no one would use such weapons because of fear. That is our logic. We are pampered and soft after a mere half-century of affluence. We think that life is something that can be pleasurably consumed – just like almost everything else.

"Except that there are cultures that believe that human life is simply an insignificant instrument of something superior. Our logic is anathema to them. And it's going to be easier and easier for them to obtain the weapons and technologies that we are developing in the belief that, in spite of their destructive potential, we will use them solely to make life more pleasant because, after all, we are civilised…"

Surprisingly enough the audience has listened to my pessimistic outburst with unusual suspense. But all of a sudden I'm tired of talking about that too.

It's the end, Alex, I say to myself. You need a rest. You need to find a new meaning for your existence. You're not going to convince anyone here anyway, because our culture doesn't experience anything in depth any more. Even warnings about possible mortal dangers have become mere media commodities should some journalist happen to be sitting here. Tomorrow they'll quote you in the newspapers and you'll get invited to CNN, where the presenter will question you eagerly about your latest great theory.

And so I close my speech by saying, "Everything I wanted to say about the subject is contained in the printed version of my paper, and I have to ask you to excuse my departure as I need to deal with some pressing matters."

I didn't know what matters, in fact, or rather I didn't realise until later. In my hotel room I gathered together my things, tossed them into my suitcase and set off home to New York, even though Sasha had begged me not to go there. I wanted to be alone. I needed to get something clear in my mind.

When I got home I found a message from Rebecca on the answering machine

"Hi Dad. I'm spending a couple days in New York. Where are you?"

I think to myself ironically that she has no inkling that she has a brother. And nor did I until just recently.

Then there's a message from Katrina. She would like us to make an appointment with a lawyer at the beginning of July. There are still some little things that need clearing up regarding the division of our property.

The next day I go for lunch with Katrina. In the end we don't spend much time discussing the matters we need to settle with the lawyer. My thoughts are full of Sasha and so I tell Katrina all about it. I leave nothing out. I tell her that although I often cheated on her it meant nothing in the great majority of cases. I tell her that I once fell in love with Andrea and then quickly ended the relationship. On account of her, Katrina.

My ex-wife has taken a deep breath and is about to reply, but I don't feel like discussing my infidelities with her at this moment. Instead I tell her how I found out that Andrea is dying and that I have a son. And how I made the trip to Prague to see them.

When I repeat what Sasha said to me when we were saying goodbye, tears well up in my eyes. I am overcome by the same helplessness, sadness and despair that I felt in that room in Bellagio after my meeting with Leira.

Katrina takes my hand. She says nothing but waits for me to calm down. I still have to tell her about my grandfather's letter, my mother's memoirs, as well as about Arno and the angel Ariel if it is all to make any sense.

It takes me a long time to tell. When I finish, I realise that I've been talking continuously for over an hour. Katrina always was a good listener.

"I'll have to digest it all," she then says. "There are some odd things happening in your life."

She's right, of course. And she still knows nothing about Leira, whom I prefer not to mention.

"What are you going to do about your son?" she asks.

"I'll have to consider it all carefully," I say with a shrug. "I suppose I ought to return to Prague as soon as possible in order to adopt him formally... But I don't know what then. How am I going to bring him up? Will I manage it? Should I bring him here? Or move to Prague?

I really don't know yet..."

Katrina gazes at me for a long time.

At the end of that long silence, she says something that brings the tears back to my eyes:

"If you decided to bring Sasha back here, Alex, I'd give you any help you needed."

That's her all over, I think to myself – generous and true to her principles. My emotion almost immediately gives way to shame. All of a sudden I recall quite vividly what I was doing that time, eleven years ago when I returned from Prague after the two days with Andrea during which Sasha was conceived. I was home just long enough to reassure myself that Katrina suspected nothing before I was heading for another conference. Shortly afterward I first met Jovana. Maybe that love affair was deeper than usual because in some ways she was a substitute for Andrea. And maybe that was the moment when I should have stopped deluding myself that my marriage still meant something to me and that I was rendering Katrina some kind of service by returning to her again and again.

It took six more years for Katrina to lose patience once and for all; for my brazenness to become so unbounded that I invited one of my female doctoral students to our summer cottage at the seaside on Long Island. I'd told Katrina that I was going to Washington for a consultation, even though it must have been obvious to her that probably not even the President consults experts on the weekend.

I didn't occur to me that she might be intending to make the trip to Long Island without me. In fact she wasn't. It was all a coincidence.

My companion and I had just arrived at the cottage when the telephone rang. I didn't want it to appear as if I were hiding from anyone – after all, I'd told the girl that my marriage was on the rocks and I'd soon be seeking a divorce.

So I answered the telephone, said "Hello" and immediately replaced the receiver.

"Probably a wrong number," I lied, but to be on the safe side I unplugged the telephone.

The woman's voice hadn't been Katrina's so I assumed the coast was clear.

It was Pam who called. She'd mistaken our Long Island number for our home number in Manhattan. She'd immediately corrected her mistake and in passing mentioned to Katrina that she hadn't realised we had visitors.

Katrina immediately got the picture.

As she told me later, she had long been aware that I was cheating on her, and she herself wasn't even sure why she decided to bring matters to a head at that particular moment, maybe because I had taken my lover to our joint cottage. I'm sure she didn't come to Long Island in order to have proof of my infidelity, even though she did photograph us "in flagrante" with cool professionalism.

I didn't want a divorce. When Katrina mentioned it, I panicked. But when she handed me her photographic spoils in a restaurant where we were discussing our future, I realised I had no choice. I would have fallen through the floor in shame if I'd been present while some judge viewed photographs displaying my pale backside, the doctoral student's head twisted away, the horrified expressions of the two of us, and our hysterical groping for the sheet. Not to mention the possibility of a photo like that being leaked to the media. The *National Enquirer* would relish it.

Perhaps it's not surprising that my sexual craving dried up for a while after Katrina and I had separated. I was in a state of depression and, moreover, I had no one to cheat on. Quite simply all the magic had gone out of womanizing for me.

The mechanism I'd created over the years was so powerful that when I eventually did sleep with a lady journalist, I suddenly remembered that there was no betrayed wife waiting for me and I was overcome with a sense of failure. I left the hotel room feeling that it had been absolutely pointless.

I aged rapidly in the period between my divorce and my encounter with Leira. Not in the sense of physical decay, but of mental fatigue. I was devastated by the loss of Katrina, whom I had once feared for so much that I started to cheat on her. The thought of how I'd wounded her made me sick of myself. Moreover, since the divorce, I had started to ask myself whether the fear of losing her hadn't been merely a convenient excuse for me to give free rein to my insatiable appetite for women.

While it's true that after my divorce I wrote *The Globalization of Postmodernity*, which triggered the usual media merry-go-round I was, in fact, burned out. My brain is trained to produce "ideas" non-stop, so writing the book wasn't a problem. My mental erosion manifested itself chiefly as skepticism.

That time I derived no enjoyment from writing. Although I suspected from the outset that *The Globalization of Postmodernity* would be a bestseller, I did not relish at all the glitz I'd experienced with every previous book launch. Every possible sort of prise, book readings, discussions at universities...

I was simply beset by the feeling that the world had gone nuts. You can toss the media the gloomiest possible analysis of the present-day world, and the TV stations, magazines and newspapers will cheerfully dissect it minutely, because for them it is sensational nourishment.

I offer a rather apocalyptic perspective on the world in *The Globalization of Postmodernity*. Rationalism has finally exhausted itself, I argue, and mankind doesn't know where to go from here. What happened in Western Europe is a somewhat nihilistic rejection of hierarchical value systems and reason has now spread to the rest of the world. Although it is often said that Western civilization differs from the rest, the post-modern lifestyle, architecture and overall disorientation of opinion are permeating the entire world. The defiance in the Islamic world is simply an attempt to erect a value barrier against absolute relativism. Post-modernism is in fact the biggest enemy of the classical monotheistic religions. It replaces the idea of a single omnipotent God, which serves as a central axis in the creation of culture, by a supermarket of ideas, all of which have roughly the same validity.

Were post-modernism a powerful system of values, it might not particularly matter, I argue in the book. Instead it is the expression of total powerlessness in the face of the failure of human reason, which, after banishing God from its world, created, at best, the industrial civilization that is destroying nature in a wholesale fashion, and, at worst, monstrous oppressive systems.

Postmodernism is a reaction to the massive spread of stupidity, while also being a product of it. Television pop-culture produces such a quantity of crassness that it is hard to tell which is better and which worse. Apparently we are not even supposed to try to construct any hierarchy of taste, but to be guided solely by what pleases us.

Postmodernism is thus the final, decadent phase of individualism. Not even in the world of ideas or the world of art is anything objectively better or worse. All that matters is the degree to which something is liked. But if scales of values are not formed by upbringing or education within the framework of some structured discourse, but instead under the pressure of the advertising industry, postmodernism is nothing other than the victory of adolescence. Our entire modern pop culture is the absolute tyranny of the young. The taste of the young is the lowest possible denominator.

I don't intend to get carried away with repeating the main arguments of my book. There's no reason to repeat them in these notes. I'm simply horrified that the society of pop culture and consumerism accepts even scathing criticism almost as a joyful event, because it sells well. But this repudiates the critical purpose of the work, because everything gets chewed up into a mush of catchy clichés for ignoramuses to flaunt.

Another reason why I derived little pleasure from the success of *The Globalization of Postmodernity* was that I lost the motivation to exploit it as bait for potential mistresses. I slept with the presenter of one well-known debate show because I just couldn't pass up a catch like that. Not simply on account of her, but also because of her husband, who is a well-known politician. Apart from that, I ignored all the female post-graduates, lady journalists and budding authoresses who wanted to talk to me. I had no wish to talk about anything.

My dejection caused even Katrina concern. When I met up with her about six months after our divorce, she told me several times that she couldn't recognise me at all. She said she thought I'd be radiantly happy now that I finally had the freedom I had evidently striven for in order to indulge in my extramarital escapades. Instead I radiated skepticism. What had happened to me?

She even started to recommend me the services of one of her colleagues, a psychologist. She said that someone ought to take a proper look at me.

But it wasn't psychoanalysis that I needed. I know what my problem is. I sold my soul to superficiality and lust. I had displaced everything of substance that I had possibly ever been or that I might have become.

I even stopped enjoying life at the university, which I'd previously found pleasurable. It occurs to me more and more that the university environment is distorted. It's a meeting place for people with limitless egos, who need constant reassurance about their exceptional qualities. The snag is that competition for top posts or prestige has highly elastic rules. It is very hard to measure objectively the quality of professors, particularly in the humanities.

What is generally used as a criterion are the numbers of citations in specialised publications, but that is often a matter of chance and connections. I know lots of colleagues in top universities who are published in the most prestigious journals even though they have never come up with one original idea in their lives. In the best of cases, they display originality in recycling the ideas of others. That is how most so-called specialised books get written, and that is the basis on which professors are awarded permanent posts.

It could be argued that at least industriousness can be assessed. It's not hard to distinguish a lazy individual from a hardworking one. But what attests to industriousness in the academic world? The number of books written? But these can be churned out like on an assembly line, as I've already said. The number of subjects a professor teaches? But what if he or she simply spouts the same propositions because they have been teaching the same thing for twenty years already? It might be thought that quality of teaching might be a certain yardstick, but even that doesn't apply. After all, the evaluation is done by the students, and we know how that works. All it needs is for a professor to lose favour with some of them and they'll turn the whole class against him. Perhaps I've become a bit over-sensitive. However, what is certain is that at least a year ago I started finding it increasingly difficult to take part in the university's operation because it was teeming with narcissists. I'm irritated by all that excruciating adulation for people who have obtained their titles from an Ivy League university! For heaven's sake, I know from my own experience that almost anyone can study there if he's accepted!

But what is there left for me now that even the university arouses in me such animosity? Should I take early retirement and just write something now and again? And when I do, then only about things that really interest me? I can afford to, that's not the issue. I've enough money even after my divorce from Katrina. Royalties are coming in all the time, often from the sale of books I wrote many years ago. It occurs to me that I could sell my soul to the administration as a permanent consultant. They'd welcome me with open arms.

But would an escape from my previous existence help me find what I'm looking for? After all, I've no idea at all what I'm looking for? Faith? Neither my trip to Fátima nor Leira's clairvoyance have brought me nearer to that.

But without a faith I lack an anchor. I have nothing to hold onto, because I now have an absolute aversion even to the secular humanism that I made do with previously. Mankind made up its mind to solve all the mysteries of the world with its reason. Man was exalted to become the measure of everything. But I believe less and less in human reason. Self-deception is all it's good for.

When Rebecca was little I told her a story about an intelligent maggot living in a tree inside an apple. The maggot had no idea that she had hatched from an egg laid on the surface of the apple by her mother, *Cydia pomonella*, the codling moth.

For a long time she was convinced that the world ended at the apple skin. Then she bored inside and discovered that the apple had a core, and she also found the stalk. When she became stronger she settled down in a crease in the apple tree's bark. That was a big journey for a maggot, almost to the world's end... How was she to know that the apple tree also had a trunk and roots that brought it moisture and nourishment from the soil? Or that it stood on the Earth, which is part of the Universe? Or that she herself, the little maggot, would undergo a miraculous transformation, when she would pupate and turn into a moth?

Maybe our entire universe is an apple hanging from a tree along with many others. How come we're so sure that when we have managed to describe this apple from inside we'll understand everything that's outside it? What if, after what we call death, we will actually undergo metamorphosis, just like that maggot?

I think Rebecca understood the meaning of the story better than I did. For me it was just a story.

Everything was for me simply a story, because I am always making things up. Until recently nothing had any importance. All my theories were just a game for me. From the moment I started to cheat on Katrina my entire career was just a game. I lived inside the apple and enjoyed its flesh, but I forgot that the apple has some meaning and that I should ask about it at least. I was always on the go just to forget that one day the apple would fall to earth; that I didn't have much time.

For a long time I thought that games were the aim of everything inside that apple. Now that's all over but I'm not prepared for it. I'm full of angst and defiance. I'm utterly sick of hauling new cars, television sets, furniture and God knows what else into my apple in the fond hope that I can hoodwink the ineluctable course of things.

I tell myself that to have concluded this means I've made certain progress. After all, for years I was just playing. I enjoyed easily acquired fame, and for a while I actually believed that political science would discover something fundamental about the functioning of society. Or to be more exact, I prided myself on being the one discovering something fundamental, and being able to talk and write books about it.

All of a sudden, I don't even care about human society. I've started to be bored with reflecting on the laws governing the society of maggots imprisoned in the apple. No, it's worse than that: I'm becoming cynical.

What was the point of all that talk about the "clash of titans" between the democracies and authoritarian regimes, which was a standard menu at most conferences at the end of the twentieth century? The struggle for freedom and human rights! Human dignity...

After all, the societies where there is supposed to be freedom are drowning in unbridled consumerism – anything can be bought, including political success. The whole system lives on credit. Everyone is in debt to everyone else and the biggest debtors are governments. One day it will all burst like a soap bubble. Democracy had long since succumbed to the power of money and interest groups. In the final analysis, the average individual uses that freedom that everyone invokes simply to buy better things and enjoy himself more. In the absolute majority of cases, that freedom had nothing to do with inner, spiritual freedom. It is just a flimsy mirage consisting of external impulses.

The whole of Western society has been enslaved by the so-called entertainment mega-industry. The most appalling insanities are spewed at people from their TV and cinema screens, their sole purpose being to make us forget that our lives will be over one day. In the meantime they try, by means of advertising, to get us to buy as many useless things as possible.

I write this in the full awareness that thanks to my ability to work with words and encapsulate complex matters in witticisms, I myself enrolled in that circus and I enjoyed it. Entertainment had long ago absorbed what used to be regarded as serious news and also taken over intellectual topics. In fact even books about serious political events are mostly written these days as potential best-sellers...

The upshot is that my esteemed colleagues go over the top and often present their arguments in apocalyptic terms. When it comes down to it, those various clashes of civilizations or the end of history are no more than sops to pop culture, which now has even scholarly literature under its control.

A year ago I would have refrained from judgments such as this. I was still part of that industry – acting the clown on TV and writing best-sellers according to the same recipes as my colleagues.

Now it all makes me sick. Sick to my stomach.

I can't imagine myself now answering questions from TV presenters who don't give a damn about what we're talking about, because the only thing that interests them – as it did me for so long – is to sparkle and bedazzle. To climb. To become a familiar face.

Ever since I met Leira and found what my grandfather and mother wrote, it sickens me. I need to find something more solid, more mean-ingful. I need to makes sense of this world. At least to the extent that I might be capable, unlike the other maggots, of sticking my head out of the apple, climbing down from the apple tree and enduring this nightmare.

But how am I to do it? I sold my intellect to the world of stupidity long ago, and whenever I try to turn my attention to "eternal ques-tions", even for a moment, my well-trained agnostic instincts thwart my attempt with a cynical counter-attack.

Maybe I'm just burned out. When I read after myself what I've just written, I realise that my criticism of democracy wasn't meant entirely seriously. Maybe a couple of journalists might still be found who are ready to engage in serious journalism.

What if the fault is chiefly in me, I wonder. There is nothing new for me to grasp. I've probably already said it here, but after the divorce with Katrina I even grew tired of women. I would seduce them simply from force of habit, mechanically, without any enjoyment. On top of that, I lost my ability to be detached. As a result, I would get myself into embarrassing situations, because I no longer had any common sense and would choose young women, with whom I could no longer cope.

The point is that an older man must not only play the role of an au-thority but also adapt himself to the younger woman, and demonstrate to her that he is still young – in spirit, at least, if no longer physically. But because of my sudden mental ageing, I started to have an aversion to the world of the young.

I used to tell myself that I wouldn't pretend interest in the supposed uniqueness of my partners, just because I longed for a young body. Why should I bolster the omnipresent hypocritical pretence that young people are genuine individuals, as mass culture encourages them to think, even though it long ago imposed on them identical taste in fashion, music, art and everything else? They all watch the same films, talk about the same arts events, listen to the same, essentially unbearable music, which accompanies the most crass texts. And even those who have so-called intellectual ambitions mostly read the same things and speak about them in the same language. If older people are to accept that culture they have to behave like them. I have occasionally tried to play that game, but it was obvious that it was an effort on my part, and my behaviour revealed only too clearly that my interest was purely physical.

The most embarrassing moment of all was my flirtation with a young Czech journalist called Monika, who did an interview with me last spring for her magazine. As I look back on it, I feel so ashamed that I'd sooner keep quiet about the incident. But when I started these jottings three days ago I promised myself not to leave out anything of significance.

It starts in a Prague restaurant where Monika has invited me to lunch after the interview. I know scarcely anything about her abilities as a journalist but I am totally knocked out by her physical attributes. I am captivated particularly by Monika's magnificent bosom.

I use almost automatically one of the ploys that has already proved successful in the past with young Czech women. Firstly, I mention as if in passing that, for a talented journalist such as herself, I could possibly arrange a visit to the School of Journalism at Columbia University. I have noticed that she has good English, so she might give a talk there about the experiences of the emerging generation of journalists in the post-communist world.

She is delighted, naturally. She would very much like to visit New York, but where would she find the money? I have anticipated that question and have an answer ready: she needn't worry about the money, the school will help pay for the air ticket and she could stay at my place, for instance. I'm a harmless old professor...

I tell myself that I have sufficient influence at the university to get them to make a contribution to her flight. And if they refused, I could pay it myself. It will be worth it.

But this time I've found a really tough nut to crack. Monika really does come to New York. Her "lecture," if it can be called that, consists of a nervous, incoherent babble that a dozen people at most manage to endure to the end. Nevertheless I reassure her repeatedly in the course of dinner that her talk was extremely interesting. The fact that half of the audience left before the end is nothing unusual, I tell her. All sorts of odd things happen in New York. The important thing is that the editor of the local magazine stayed to the end and he has assured me he'll write about her outstanding lecture.

To add weight to my words, I ask her about some of the points she made in her talk. When she starts to speak about them in Czech, I discover they are not so uninteresting after all. We finish two bottles of Spanish red wine, which I ordered after she mentioned how much she had enjoyed Rioja in Madrid. She said she was there two years ago when she was still a student.

The two of us return slightly tipsy to my apartment and I am expecting her to display me some gratitude, at least by having some more wine and continuing our friendly conversation. But instead she bids me good night and disappears into the guest bedroom.

I sense that I haven't yet achieved sufficient familiarity with her to risk creeping into her room and launching my time-tested monologue about how mad I am about her, how I'll survive if she turns me down, but I've never stopped thinking about her since we met in Prague. So I go off to bed too, feeling slightly miffed.

Things continue that way for the next few days. We spend our evenings in restaurants and then we chat back at home. She has had ample time to realise what an important figure I am in America, because she has been present at a couple of autograph sessions and I have taken her with me to a TV station where they recorded an interview with me. And yet she still keeps me at arm's length.

Perhaps she's religious, I tell myself, and to be on the safe side, I ask her. She tells me she isn't.

In the end I do try my monologue, but she politely rejects me. She finds me very likeable, of course, and she is gratified that someone so distinguished should not only find her interesting but also attractive, but she needs time.

During the remainder of her stay I am on tenterhooks to know whether the necessary time will elapse before her departure for Prague. Moreover I really am suffering because she is not at all shy and walks around the apartment in the evening in a short t-shirt beneath which is only the outline of her panties. She doesn't wear a bra.

Although she naturally can see how frustrated I am, she manages to refuse me right to the end. Maybe it is in order to attenuate my bad mood, which I am no longer able to conceal, that she tells me before her departure that she cares for me. If I had the time I could maybe visit her in Prague. Her summer vacation starts at the end of July.

I am so weakened with desire that I'm unable to refuse Monika's offer, although my instincts should caution me against it. In fact I'm even obliged to cancel some conference at the last moment on account of the unplanned trip to Prague. During the weeks that follow I busily fantasise about what we'll enjoy together. As it turns out, my imagination outstripped the reality.

She is waiting for me at the airport and she is nice to me during our first dinner together. But when I invite her back to my Prague apartment, she makes the excuse that she has a family engagement. Then she tells me that she has cancelled part of her vacation. She tells me she has to report on some controversial event – a techno party known as CzechTek, which is due to take place this time somewhere near Český Krumlov, in southern Bohemia.

The media are full of gossip about the noisy music and misdemeanours of the festival participants. It's a big break for her as a journalist, she explains. But she would be only too pleased if I wanted to accompany her.

Her change of plan irritates me but her invitation strikes me as being very promising. I agree to go.

Monika comes to fetch me the next morning in an old red Škoda car, which she drives with a certain bravura in view of the roadworthiness of the vehicle. Maybe in order to blend in with the ravers, she is wearing rather grubby, baggy pants and a shabby t-shirt. Her amazing bosom is concealed beneath a hoodie of uncertain colour. Her head is covered in a baseball cap. In spite of it she looks fine.

She explains to me that she could adopt two different approaches to her reporting assignment. Either to adopt the tone of the social critic and highlight the law breaking and the desperation of the local inhabitants terrorised by the noisy music, as well as the drug and alcohol use. Or, on the contrary, she can adopt the method of psychological submersion, as she calls it, and attempt to identify what induces young people to attend.

I'm convinced that things are headed in the right direction, because on the way she agrees that I should book a hotel room in Český Krumlov. She warns me, however, that she won't get back from the techno party until evening, but that doesn't particularly bother me. The thought that this time she will share not only a room but also a bed, gets me aroused after such lengthy abstinence.

My mood is excellent and I spend the afternoon sightseeing in the town and sitting in cafés. We have agreed that Monika will call me when she returns and then we'll go out to dinner.

Except that she doesn't call. It's already evening and I've received no news from her. Several times I call her. In vain. She doesn't answer her cellphone.

I feel a growing resentment but it is suddenly dispelled by concern. What if something has happened to her? Maybe I'm doing her wrong by beginning to assume she has stood me up once more.

Around ten o'clock that evening I can bear it no longer. I call a cab and ask the driver to take me to the techno party site. He says nothing but spends the whole trip observing me discreetly in the rear-view mirror. He's probably wondering what a well dressed fifty-year-old might be up to at such an event.

I have to admit that prior to that experience I had no inkling that anything like CzechTek existed. I had seen clips on TV from the mega festival of techno music in Berlin, which, because there was the big city in the background and nearly a million people regularly attend, looked on the screen like some kind of colourful commotion. A very different scene, however, offered itself to my gaze at Lipnice, the site of the festival. On a muddy meadow, which I weave my way to between vehicles and tents, tripping over trash as I go, I discover a sort of human herd swaying to the rhythm of mindless mechanical music, emitted at an unbelievable intensity by enormous loudspeakers.

Suddenly something I've been feeling for some time formulates itself in my mind in a clairvoyant abbreviation: here in this isolated spot, as I watch the loneliness of these figures drunkenly swaying in front of thundering black loudspeakers, I am aware of the alienation and emptiness not only of our civilization, but also my own. It is obvious that they too realise I don't belong here either in terms of age or style of clothes. They don't behave aggressively, but I definitely attract attention.

What am I doing here, for God's sake?

In answer, I tell myself that whereas, for certain people, something that was once represented by the search for God has now dwindled into absurdly mind-numbing computer-generated rhythms, I have become enslaved by a different vacuity, which has driven me from one woman's arms into another's.

Perhaps I am being a bit harsh on these narcotized youngsters, because they have come for just a few days and then they'll leave, whereas I stand trembling before my dehumanised idol all the time. Why? Mostly to elude my inner self.

Whatever the case, the entire scene strikes me as so repulsive and the parallels with my own existence so blatant, that I'm in total shock.

Nevertheless, I endeavour to find Monika. Because my search has so far been fruitless I decide, much to my distaste, to head for where the din is loudest of all, beneath the giant loudspeakers, where several dozen solitary individuals continue to gyrate even at this late hour. She is not even there. Fortunately I catch sight of her red Škoda, recognizing it by its archaic shape. So I head for it, occasionally stumbling over recumbent bodies in the dark.

In the end the only option left is to take a look into the surrounding tents. In some of them youngsters are asleep, from two of them ecstatic groans can be heard. Just as I'm about to give up, I catch the sound of Monika's voice coming from a smaller tent. Or rather it is her laughter, because she is trying to stifle a giggle.

I leaned down to peep inside. Monika is sitting naked astride some fairly unkempt-looking young guy and rhythmically rocking back and forth with her hips. The guy's muddy pants are pulled down to his ankles. Another young guy, also naked, is holding to her lips a cigarette, from which there wafts the unmistakable smell of marihuana, while almost impassively stroking her breasts, the breasts that have driven me to distraction over the past few months and got me into all of this.

I feel like saying something, but nothing comes to mind. Although she doesn't register my presence at all, the young guy under her manages a moronic grin in my direction.

There can be no doubt: she has opted for "total psychological submersion". Another cutting remark I might have directed at her doesn't occur to me till later. But there is no cause for me to insult her. I have no further right to her. I am simply a passing acquaintance for her, an older guy who paid her trip to New York. She hasn't behaved politely but I asked for it.

The next day I'm already on my way back to New York. About two days later I receive an email from Monika explaining that her reporting assignment kept her there until the early hours. And then she discovered at the hotel that I'd left. She hopes I'll look her up the next time I come.

I have no intention of doing so, of course.

The next trip I made to Prague was after my encounter with Leira. And by then everything was different.

Monday, September 10, 2001

Noon. A routine meeting with the investment banker who takes care of my shares. As usual we meet in the very south of Manhattan, where he works.

We are lunching in a small restaurant near the World Trade Center. He is telling me something and I'm trying to concentrate on his words. It's quite hot, definitely over seventy-five, and muggy.

I'm glad the restaurant has air conditioning. My eyes stray along the street outside. There's nothing of any particular interest. As everywhere in Manhattan, the sidewalks are teeming with people rushing to lunch. Cars slowly move down the street in an unending stream, in which the predominant colour is the yellow of the cabs. Now and then the wail of a police or ambulance siren can be heard.

I can see clouds reflected in the skyscrapers' windows, with the sun shining through the clouds from time to time. There is no clue that something should happen.

And then I see her! Or, to be precise, her legs first of all. I don't need to look up to know whom they belong to. After all, over the recent months I have replayed in my mind a hundred times every single detail of our meeting in Bellagio.

She is standing on the opposite side of the street, talking to some guy. She is wearing a black suit and her blonde mane is drawn into a bun. She is just as beautiful and out of the ordinary as in Bellagio. The man is telling her something while she indicates her wrist with a touch of impatience. She points at her watch. She is hurrying somewhere. Then she waves her arm in the direction of the north tower of the World Trade Center. The man nods.

Leira is holding a file in her hand. I try to make out what is written on it. I am so intent on deciphering it, that I needlessly waste at least thirty seconds in which I could have got up and run after her.

The penny suddenly drops. What am I waiting for?

To the broker's astonishment, I spring out of my chair and dash outside. The heat and humidity hit me in the face. I look around me desperately. At last I catch sight of her. She has shaken the man by the hand and is departing. I furiously struggle across the street through the cars and shout her name loudly. I'm almost out of my wits. Naturally she can't hear me above the din of a New York street.

She disappears round a corner. I hurry in that direction, ploughing through the crowds, but by the time I reach the corner, almost out of breath, she is gone. She has vanished like a mirage. Was she really here?

I dash here and there for a while, but she is nowhere to be seen.

I stop in the middle of the street and almost get run down by a car. Total hopelessness descends on me.

How could I have let her get away? Why didn't I leap up the moment I set eyes on her?

I make my way back, almost dragging my feet. My feeling of disappointment causes an odd weakness to spread through my calves and thighs. All of a sudden, I catch sight of the man Leira was talking to.

I break into a run once more. I can see him slowly walking away. He is going in the opposite direction from the one Leira took a short while ago. He is in no hurry. It's almost as if he is waiting for me. Then he turns into a side street. I'm suddenly afraid that he'll vanish too.

I run to the intersection and dash into the street where I lost sight of him, and at that moment I almost collapse in amazement.

Leira is standing facing me! Her face wears that playful smile of hers.

I want to ask her how she got here. Did she manage to run round the entire block of buildings in that short time? Is there a passage linking the two streets? I have lots of other questions, but I am so weak and out of breath that I don't manage to utter a single word.

"I owe you some answers, don't I," she says.

I nod. I draw breath to ask the first of my questions but she cuts me short with a gesture of her hand.

"I'll willingly explain all to you, Alex, but I'm in a terrible hurry at this moment."

She points to the famous twin towers of the World Trade Center.

"This is where I work. I've taken a break from my studies for a while. There are some things I need to get clear... I'm working as an insurance agent for Marsh and Co. Surely you know the company? Their offices are on the 93rd floor.

An insurance agent, well, well... I say to myself as her words sink in. My gaze shifts to the file that I'd scrutinised so intently from the restaurant. I read the word "March". Alongside it is some advertising slogan that I don't even bother with.

"We could meet tomorrow if you like," Leira suggests. "I'm very busy the whole day, but I could manage breakfast. Could you call for me at 8.30 up in my office? On the 93rd floor?"

"You're not going to run away again?" I blurt out

I can feel how I'm trembling all over. I feel queasy.

Leira gazes at me. I can see that flash in her eyes.

"Listen, Alex, I really have to go. I have a very important meeting." But she makes no move yet.

And at that moment, in the middle of a sidewalk, with a brightly-coloured New York crowd streaming past us, she takes my hands in hers. "No, this time I won't run away," she assures me.

In spite of my nausea, I feel a blissful tingle in my back like that time in Bellagio.

This time she is not reading my palm. She is gazing straight into my eyes.

"You ought to think over very carefully what you are to do, Alex," she says emphatically. "Pay attention to what I say. You have a very important decision to take. You'll either come to meet me tomorrow or you'll leave for Prague. Only one of those decisions is the correct one."

I feel like yelling: For heaven's sake, here you go soothsaying, once again! Don't you realise at all what chain of events you unleashed, most likely by chance, by reading my palm in Bellagio? What is this game you keep playing?

But there is no time for me to start to talk about it. Leira turns and quickly walks away.

I'm unable to run after her. My legs are leaden from tension and tiredness. I actually have to sit down for a moment on the decorative ledge beneath a shop window.

When I look back in her direction, she is gone. She likes playing hide-and-seek, I think to myself.

I go back to the restaurant and join the broker.

I apologise to him. I explain that the woman was an acquaintance I needed to speak to.

He looks confused.

"I didn't see any woman. I noticed that you were observing something outside, but I didn't see what or whom. But maybe my view was blocked."

"No, no," I try to persuade him. "She was standing over there on the other side of the street. It would be hard to miss her."

"All I could see was you, when you were on your way back," says the broker with a shrug. "You walked, or rather ran past the window of the restaurant and then disappeared round the corner."

"I was running after a man my acquaintance had just previously been talking to. But he'd gone by then. But she was there instead. Do you think she could have run the entire block while I was on my way back? Is there some passage there?"

"Are you OK?" the dealer asks me uneasily. "You don't look yourself..."

I admit to him that the occurrence has upset me somewhat and explain that the woman has played an important role in my life in the recent period. In the end I tell him that we can discuss my investments next time. I have to go sort something out.

In fact I'm not in a hurry to go anywhere. I slowly walk to north Manhattan. I'm in such a state of tension that I just keep going. In spite of my previous tiredness and nausea I walk the whole way home. That's more than 120 blocks! I like New York and sometimes I take long walks, but this time it was more like sleepwalking. I keep on staring into the crowd hoping to catch sight of her again.

Tomorrow, then, I say to myself. Tomorrow morning.

I have so many questions for you, Leira.

For instance, whether everything you told me about yourself and your doctoral work wasn't just an invention. And if it wasn't why did you suddenly vanish? And what were you really doing in Bellagio anyway? After all, your name didn't appear anywhere on the list of conference participants! I must have read that list a hundred times at least. I have a copy of it at home.

What sort of game were you playing with me, damn it?

I don't know why, but I sense that Leira's reappearance signifies something. I'm starting to be superstitious. It seems to me almost impossible that it could have been by chance. Can such chance events really exist? In such an enormous city?

After all, there was no reason why I should have been sitting in that restaurant, why I should have turned my head and caught sight of Leira, when she was talking – extremely briefly as it happens – with that guy.

What was she trying to tell me? She took me by the hands and started soothsaying once again.

She tells me I have to make up my mind. How could she have known that I have to go to Prague as soon as possible? Seeing that she enjoys playing the wise woman, why didn't she tell me straight out which decision was the right one? What is she really after? Does she want me to come for her or to go to Prague? And what business is it of hers whether I go to Prague or not? Who is she to go hinting that tomorrow of all days I have to take one of two possible decisions: the so-called "correct one"? I mumble angrily to myself like that almost all the way. I don't arrive home until late afternoon.

I try to calm down. Early in the evening I pick up the newspapers. *The Daily News* informs me that public health officers have found lethal fungus in some building on Upper East Side. All the papers write about Congressman Gary Condit's affair with 24-year-old Chandra Levy, who has mysteriously disappeared. Something tells me that Gary will have a job extricating himself from that one.

Then my eyes happen to fall on an article about the results of the last Gallup poll. It states that 55% of Americans are unhappy with the way the situation in the USA is developing. With a certain satisfaction, I think to myself that at least I'm not alone.

In one newspaper I read that according to Bush, China is the greatest threat to the United States. Someone has advised him to come up with the designation "strategic competitor" for China.

Who's giving him such stupid advice, for heaven's sake? It gives me an uneasy feeling. Real threats always emerge from somewhere we least suspect. What's needed is forecasting, not dreaming up stupid names for well-known realities.

I put the newspapers down in disgust.

Jargon has been changing all the time in my field of activity over the past decades. We all started with the vocabulary of a bipolar world, two big superpowers. Sovietology was an enormous industry. I should think it provided half of our political scientists with a living.

Then came the post-Communist period. The vocabulary now focused on building democracy, the market economy, the rule of law. We spoke of "third-wave democracies" and civil society. Conferences followed hard on each others' heels. Everywhere the topics were the same: the democratic transformation of authoritarian systems, the transition from a planned economy to a market one, the new political elites, the creation of multi-party systems.

The debate had hardly had a chance to get off the ground before globalisation arrived on the scene. It's hard to say how many conferences I've attended on this topic. Global responsibility, global inequality, the pros and cons of globalisation... We no longer talked about the First and Third Worlds but about the North and the South. There remained only one global superpower. A few colleagues penned bestsellers predicting the imminent fall of this new Rome. They said the end of history had arrived and the clash of civilizations was on its way. You could choose what you liked.

"Revolution" became the term most used. I took part in conferences about the communications revolution, the technological revolution and the revolution in the organization of modern societies. Then came the period of post-modernism, "liquid modernism", or the "risk society". Society was feminised and the patriarchy found itself in retreat. Ideologies disappeared and "third ways" are sought. And these are all revolutions.

Almost everyone in my field is constantly retraining and updating their vocabulary. You see it's not just what you say it's the way that you say it. If you don't know the jargon you don't get taken seriously. If you yourself enrich the jargon of the TV age and the burgeoning conferences then you're a star. That's another reason why *The Globalization of Postmodernity* became a bestseller.

Nobody examines anything in real depth any more, the times are racing ahead too fast.

One thing is for sure: the two world wars and Communist totalitarianism undermined the belief in mankind's ability to establish paradise on earth with the help of human reason. There is a lot of doubt around nowadays, even though science is developing as fast as ever before.

Apocalyptic forecasts are appearing. We are told that we have only a few decades left before all sources of energy are depleted. Just ten years ago everyone believed that new discoveries would arrive at the right time. Scientists would solve all the problems. Now no one is entirely sure. All sorts of religious cults are proliferating, at least in America.

Even in science things are becoming complicated. On the one hand, amazing progress has been made in the fields of genetic and microbiological research, but on the other, there is a lack of certainty about what to do with the results. Aren't we, as a species on the verge of some staggering mutation? Won't genetic modifications and cybernetics end up creating superhumans, who won't need us any longer?

Astrophysics, which, along with other sciences, boasted that we no longer needed God, has come up with theories that virtually necessitate the return of some sort of creator. My colleagues in the departments of physics and math talk about an elegant universe whose basic structure does not consist of particles of matter because particles are only "variously tuned strings", apparently. The universe is like a musical work whose overall harmony is held together on the basis of precise constants and rules. If, at certain moments in the evolution of the universe, there were slightly less or slightly more of certain types of energy or matter, a universe allowing the emergence of life could not exist.

There is a proliferation of mathematical models that offer a theory of everything. They combine Newton's physics, Einstein's Theory of Relativity and quantum physics into a single entity, sometimes, if needs be, at the cost of throwing a few more spatial dimensions into the equation. Except that this harmony of everything possible is more and more uncertain, and less and less understandable and imaginable. If an electron can be in two different places in the form of particles and waves, then one can imagine the existence of two different worlds alongside each other, and that at every moment everything splits in many different universes.

Leira was playing me along a bit, but maybe there was an element of truth in what she said in Bellagio, that our world was like a virtual reality, whose constants were pre-programed. In such a program, everything, including we who perceive reality and reality itself, is written in the same language. The position of an electron is said to depend on the observer. That's also why it is hard to distinguish where the object begins and subject ends. Scientists too maintain that it is impossible to separate the objective from the subjective, the observed from the observer.

Another reason I'm writing all this is that since my first meeting with Leira, more and more often I have the feeling that I don't live in the real world. Or rather, I'm not sure what reality is and if my life so far has been real. If it isn't just a dream, I became a TV image. I'm like a figure from some reality show.

So I'm trying to find some kind of language for my questions, to try to find answers, but all I have at my disposal is the language of the maggot that remains imprisoned in its apple until its metamorphosis occurs. It's all totally crazy. Ever since I started to shut myself off more and more often inside the four bare walls of my apartment, crazy ideas have started to accumulate in my head. They pile up and merge into one another and what was previously a comprehensible world is becoming more and more of a mystery

Even so I have to consider rationally how I am to decide. I don't know whether I have to do it precisely tomorrow as Leira indicated, but it also occurred to me several times recently that I could move back to

Prague for good. Return to the beginning of the circle. And close it. Prague was at the beginning of the circle. In the beginning I was a Czech. Maybe I should stop being so superior. Maybe I should try to grasp what the Czechs have been through. Yes, close that circle. Go back to the moment when I hadn't yet become Alex Brehme. No more being afraid, no more running away...

The thought of continuing to flaunt myself in the American media fills me with repulsion. And the university? I'm sure I could teach in Prague. Or maybe I wouldn't teach. I'll happily take early retirement. I could devote myself fully to my son and give him what I didn't receive.

After all, I've already reconciled myself with my country to a certain extent. In the mid-nineties it finally took the path back into Europe, about which there had only been empty rhetoric at first. Fortunately it matters less and less who is in government there. Prague has become visibly more prosperous and is beginning to resemble a Western city. So long as I don't listen too much to what Czech politicians have to say, my visits to Prague have become more pleasant. I'm sure I'd become used to my surroundings again. And meanwhile I'd look after my son

So shouldn't I really start packing straight away tomorrow and leave for Prague, as Leira hinted?

I called Andrea this afternoon, when I got home. She says she is in a bad way. Really bad. There was urgency in her voice. Sasha is looking forward to my visit.

More than two months have passed since I first saw him at the end of June. I haven't had a thing to do in the meantime. Most of the time I just sit at home trying to sort out my thoughts. What am I waiting for, for God's sake? What if Andrea suddenly dies?

Yes, I ought to take matters into my own hands right away. If I really mean to play the role of a father in Sasha's life I ought to register my paternity with the authorities. Andrea promised me to help me obtain the necessary papers. While she still can.

But what now? Now that I've found Leira again?

I expect I'm simply building up foolish hopes. After all, she could have looked me up at any time during the last six months. She knew where to find me, and she didn't. She is bound to have had her reasons. All I need from her, in fact, are the answers to my questions.

But I'd be a liar if I didn't admit how much I hope to discover what chance it was that brought Leira to the headquarters of that foundation in Bellagio. Did she come there by mistake as a tourist? What if she had someone? And what if she doesn't have him any more?

The fact is that I've no idea what I really want. Wouldn't a meeting with Leira ultimately complicate my plans to behave like a person with a conscience and sense of responsibility for the first time in so many years?

And what will I tell Leira? Am I to act disgruntled and demand an explanation? Or am I to feign "detachment"?

I don't know.

In Bellagio I already sensed that she had seen through me, that there is no point in trying to pull the wool over her eyes. The whole time I was talking to her, and also afterward when we made love, she seemed to be both outside of me and inside me. It doesn't make much sense, but that's precisely the way it was.

Moreover, even after our meeting today I still have a feeling that has stayed with me ever since Bellagio – that Leira doesn't exist. Yes, in reality she doesn't exist! She's simply a materialization of my innermost yearnings. If I told anyone about this, they'd probably think I've flipped.

And yet. I think about her all the time. More and more parts of our conversation, which I'd banished from my mind immediately after she vanished in Bellagio, are now returning to me. It's as if I was afflicted with some kind of amnesia after we had made love. When I started writing this account three days ago, I described how Leira read my palm.

She told me on that occasion that I was to expect some missive with important news, something I ought to have received long ago. And it was connected with my mother. She said the letter would contain a key. "If you don't find it," she said, "you'll leave only a void behind, but if you find it you'll open the right door."

And I asked her what she meant by that. What would be waiting for me? And when? Weren't those things apparent in her clairvoyant prognostication?

She shrugged. She was still holding my hand. A powerful thrill went through me.

"There awaits you everything you yearned for when you were still a little boy."

A kind of wild look suddenly came into her eyes, and she immediately made that incredible statement: "I see that the two of us will have an intimate relationship."

Yes, that's precisely what she said! How could I have forgotten. Was I intoxicated by the thought that we would have an intimate relationship?

And did it really happen? Wasn't it just my imagination? When I ran after her today she suddenly vanished. She couldn't have just evaporated! Admittedly she reappeared but the man she was talking to vanished instead.

Was she there at all?

Tomorrow I'll call my broker and describe Leira to him again. And that man too. Perhaps he'll recall having seen them after all. There were so many people there!

It occurs to me I ought to call the firm where Leira is supposed to be employed. Its offices are in the World Trade Center. I ought to have made sure that it isn't yet another illusion. It's too late tonight. It's night already. Even if I found the firm's phone number, I'd get only a recorded message from its answering machine.

Perhaps I really am going crazy. I have dreadful pangs of conscience, about my mother, for instance. And it's not just because Leira spoke about her.

I can now see how indifferent I was to my mother's suffering when I was growing up. How come I didn't show greater interest in her past? It's true that she used to refuse to speak about it, but did that fail to alert me to the fact that she was hiding a dreadful secret, a trauma that she couldn't cope with? If I'd known more, I might have been able to help her.

And what did I do instead? I let my mother die. Then I left and for many years I basically forgot about her. I was building my career, and seducing women! I was intoxicated with fame.

Why did I not ever reflect on what that psychiatrist had told me that time? Her last words?

"I'll have to go," she apparently said. "I've got to go down there if I'm to find freedom. And to free Sasha."

I was convinced that she wanted to give me the opportunity to emigrate. But maybe she had something completely different in mind.

What use did I make of the freedom she gave me?

I wrote political bestsellers, spoke on TV and cheated on women.

Was I able to make any sense of anything? Am I able to now? Anything fundamental, that is?

My entire supposedly brilliant mind is totally useless, because if one is truly to make sense of something; concentration, integrity and depth are required.

Identification with the thing one is reflecting on: Faith.

Not that pathetic game I was playing, a game in which it's possible to imagine anything you like and juggle with ideas as if they were coloured balls.

Even God was one of those coloured balls for me. Just another theory – I could think up ten others. Except that I haven't ten lives. There are ideas that one doesn't joke about. I won't have another opportunity to tackle them seriously.

One can sense the deepest point, the bottom in what my mother wrote. The fall to the bottom of that cellar from which life appears like a tower whose highest point can never be reached by someone at the bottom. That person feels the whole weight of the world on them. They stick their head out of that hole and everything around them starts to topple like some kind of backdrop.

Someone like that has no power over anything. Anything can wound them, almost everything can kill them.

I climbed that tower. I thought that when I was at the top I understood everything and could treat people however I liked. I was invulnerable. It didn't occur to me at all that those dots moving about in the canyon-like streets below might have thoughts and feelings that were just as valuable as my own, as I sat there at the top of the tower with my splendid view.

I never entertained in the slightest the possibility that there could be another world above the world of human beings. That there could be anything like fate. That there could exist angels, whether real or symbolic, whereby that part of our soul not yet crushed by the purportedly victorious march of reason, reminds us that we don't have everything under our control...

For a long time that didn't come home to me. I was already scaling my tower at the time when my mother's mind was keeping her imprisoned in a cellar from which she didn't manage to climb out. It pleased my mother too. After all, she used to say "Sasha, you'll be famous."

Maybe she wanted her suicide to free me from the burden of her existence, so that I could climb unencumbered. And did I climb! Right to the very top of where, as I suddenly discovered, one is even more alone than in some cellar. And where I also discovered that none of us has things under control. Not even I, the celebrated Alex Brehme.

I ought to find it in me to make some gesture. An apology at least. I can't apologise to my mother any more. But what about Katrina?

I often think these days about how our marriage might have turned out if I'd managed to control myself. At our last meeting she made a generous gesture. She'd help me, she said, if I were to bring Sasha here. And when my eyes filled with tears she took my hand. I could still see that she cared about me. That she was concerned about me.

And I'm concerned about her too. I try to imagine what she is feeling. The sadness that she must have felt, because she knew about my infidelities but didn't want to destroy our marriage on account of Rebecca. The sadness she must have felt when she found herself alone after so many years of marriage. I feel anguished because I know her so well.

In the recent period the moment I first saw her keeps coming back to mind. The gaze with which she examined me. Did she suspect even then what awaited her with me?

Did you suspect it, Katrina?

Do you remember how we'd drive in our old Ford from Manhattan all the way to Jones Beach?

Do you recall those long walks along the seashore, during which we'd often be too in love to say anything. Or how I told you about my plans and you listened to me attentively?

I recall the little things. The tiniest little things. Such as the wind ruffling your hair, the scent of your perfume... The feeling of bliss when I held your hand. Or the shape of your belly, when you were carrying Rebecca in it.

At that time I halted my race to the top for a while. I was filled with happiness, such as by the new table we bought for our new apartment. Or by talking to you about your job. I shared your joy.

I was there when Rebecca was born, when she slid out of you into this world. I held her in my arms and then laid her on your breast. That was happiness. Like our weekend walks with Rebecca in the stroller. It seemed that nothing could mar our happiness.

Do you remember our first Christmas? I managed to get hold of the perfume you used to wear when we first met. I had to ask in at least twenty shops, because they had stopped manufacturing it... I remember how happy it made you. And how happy I was that you were happy.

I don't know what I was thinking of to have thrown all of that away. Maybe I didn't understand that simple things like that make the world go round. That we ought to be humble and rejoice in them.

An idea can be repeated over and over again, and it can be written down. But not feelings, definitely not those that are seemingly most banal of all. Some things are never repeated. They are given to us only once.

I loved you even after I started to cheat on you. I fondly thought I could go on like that for ever. That I would return to you and that you would take me back each time. I was such a megalomaniac that I thought I had the right to. I was convinced that I could be victorious on every front. There was no need to show regard for anyone because good behaviour was something for the weak, not for those of us who had reached the pinnacle.

Those scenes in Fátima keep on coming back to mind. Hundreds of people approaching the scene of a miracle of long ago. They too hope for a miracle. That they'll be cured and capable of living like normal human beings in an ordinary everyday world of people. The ordinary everyday world that I disdained. What did I find in its place, though? Just emptiness, as I now see.

I'd love to tell you, Katrina, that those first steps with you were the happiest of my life.

Last time I talked to you about my infidelities and about my trip to Prague, but I didn't tell you that. Maybe I'll find an opportunity tomorrow. You are so generous, that even since our divorce you have regularly given me birthday presents. And you've even invited me to lunch tomorrow, for my fifty-third birthday. There's so much I'd like to tell you!

But maybe I really ought to go straight to JFK tomorrow morning and fly to Prague. Leira can wait. If she wasn't lying, I'll still find her on the 93rd floor when I get back from Prague. And if she was lying, I won't find her there. Not even tomorrow.

I'm sure Katrina will understand why I have to go Prague. We can celebrate my birthday some other time. I really don't have much time; Andrea could die any day now.

Except that at this moment I still don't know what I'm going to do.

I have to take the decision on my own. That angel dictated my grandfather's fate, after all. Or at least Josef Brehme was convinced of it. He travelled all the way round the globe to find the love of his life. If he had become a famous violinist, maybe he wouldn't have found happiness. There would have been more Johanas and more Sabinas. Maybe his path to the top would have been paved with Sabinas. Maybe there was some meaning in that tragic career, in that fall from the summit to the very depths of Siberia.

My mother was given hope, just for a short while, that she might live a normal life. She met my father, who looked like the angel that previously appeared to her. But they sent that angel to his death and my mother back in the direction of her cellar. To the prison of the sick mind from which there is no escape. And then she jumped. Downward after the angel.

And now I'm here. I look out the window toward the river. It is dark. Lights glimmer on the other side of the shore. Warm air wafts into the room through the half-open window.

Leira says I have to make up my mind. Only one option is the right one. It sounds like a fairy tale. If I knew the whole story I'd know which was the right step to take.

All I know for sure is that I don't want to be Alex Brehme any more. I'd like someone to call me Sasha again with the same affection I felt when my mother said my name

And above all, I too would like to be able to say someone's name with such affection. So that the other person felt it. So that they could be sure I loved them.

So that I could take a long walk with some woman and walk together in silence, because we are so in love there is no need to say anything more.

Is it possible that I love Leira in that way? Or am I confusing lust and love yet again? Could she possibly love me in that way? After all, she said that time in Bellagio that we are now joined. That nothing will be the same. That I have to find the key.

I don't know whether I found the key. But something has stirred inside me. I don't know if it's the right key. But I definitely cannot remain the person I was. I need to find a path to redemption.

Immediately when I woke up this morning my mind was fixed on Leira. Slightly childishly I kept on repeating her name. Like a rhyme.

Leira. Leira. Leira.

Then I said the name backward.

A shock ran through me. Oh, my God, surely not, I keep on saying to myself. Is it possible to encounter an angel in the form of a beautiful woman and experience the most intense love making of one's life? Isn't the very thought blasphemous? And why would the angel do it? I prefer to banish the thought.

But a few hours later I meet Leira again.

If Leira is in fact Ariel, which my skeptical brain rejects with all its might, why would the angel give me a choice, unlike my mother or grandfather? He didn't waste any time on them, did he? Or did they also have a choice too? Did my grandfather have the choice not to shoot himself? Or my mother not jump?

How did Leira put it when I first saw her? Everything is engulfed for me in the heady scent of her hair and the thrill of her touch. Of the feeling that she is entering me and becoming part of me. I am to look for a key, she said. If I don't find it I'll only leave behind a void. But if I find it, I'll open the right door. Something important will be waiting behind it...

And today she added: Only one of those decisions is the correct one.

I can't remember everything from today's conversation. I seem to have fallen into a dream all of a sudden: in it I am standing at the window in an old house looking out at the garden. I see a child on a swing. It's a little boy who greatly resembles my mother... He swings down and then up, and at its highest point the swing halts for a moment, for a single moment of eternity, before the boy begins to swing down again backwards.

There is unbounded delight in his eyes, but also fear. As if he suspected that something dreadful is to happen. I'd like to run to him and reassure him that he needn't be afraid. That is why I'm here, after all, so that he shouldn't be afraid, but I too am afraid. Terribly afraid.

I close my eyes for a moment, and while I gag from nausea and my back tingles from Leira's touch, I can hear her whisper: "It is a choice between heaven and earth, between eternity and the moment, between love and mere longing. If you make the right choice you'll see the end of the story. If not, everything will repeat itself."

Then all of a sudden there is an awful silence. An awful unending silence... I open my eyes, the garden and the little boy are gone. I am standing on a New York street, all alone. Above me tower two glistening skyscrapers. The Twins...

Also available from Jantar Publishing

KYTICE

CZECH & ENGLISH BILINGUAL EDITION
by Karel Jaromír Erben

Translated & introduction *by* Susan Reynolds

Kytice was inspired by Erben's love of Slavonic myth and the folklore surrounding such creatures as the Noonday Witch and the Water Goblin. First published in 1853, these poems, along with Mácha's *Máj* and Němcová's *Babička*, are the best loved and most widely read 19th century Czech classics. Published in the expanded 1861 version, the collection has moved generations of artists and composers, including Dvořák, Smetana and Janáček.

PRAGUE, I SEE A CITY...

by Daniela Hodrová

Translated *by* David Short
Foreword *by* Rajendra Chitnis

Originally commissioned for a French series of alternative guidebooks, Hodrová's novel is a conscious addition to the tradition of Prague literary texts by, for example, Karel Hynek Mácha, Jakub Arbes, Gustav Meyrink and Franz Kafka, who present the city as a hostile living creature or labyrinthine place of magic and mystery in which the individual human being may easily get lost.

www.jantarpublishing.com